THE
DARK
SIDE

ANTHONY O'NEILL

SIMON AND SCHUSTER PAPERBACKS

New York London Toronto Sydney New Delhi

Simon & Schuster Paperbacks
1230 Avenue of the Americas
New York, NY 10020

First Simon & Schuster trade paperback edition June 2016

SIMON & SCHUSTER PAPERBACKS and colophon are registered trademarks of Simon & Schuster, Inc.

For information about special discounts for bulk purchases, please contact Simon & Schuster Special Sales at 1-866-506-1949 or business@simonandschuster.com

The Simon & Schuster Speakers Bureau can bring authors to your live event. For more information or to book an event contact the Simon & Schuster Speakers Bureau at 1-866-248-3049 or visit our website at www.simonspeakers.com.

Interior design by Lewelin Polanco

Manufactured in the United States of America

10 9 8 7 6 5 4 3 2 1

Library of Congress Cataloging-in-Publication Data is available.

ISBN 978-1-5011-1956-9
ISBN 978-1-5011-1065-8 (ebook)

Everyone is a moon, and has a dark side which he never shows to anybody.

—MARK TWAIN

SELECTIONS FROM THE BRASS CODE

Don't take; seize.

Kill weeds before they take root.

Smile. Smile. Smile. Kill. Smile.

Lose your temper often. And well.

Surendar? Can't even spell it.

If you give it enough feathers you can make anything fly.

Never let the fly know when you're going to swat.

Workers are like dogs: Pat them on the head occasionally. And put them down when necessary.

Lie. Lie. Lie. But remember.

Move. Move. While others sleep, move.

You never know when it's going to rain. So always carry a denial.

Find Oz. And be the Wizard.

It's good to have a rival. It's even better to crack his skull.

If you can't cover your tracks, cover those who see them.

It's merciful to go for the jugular.

Refuse to be ill. On principle.

Shake hands in public. Decapitate in private.

Friends help you get there. Everyone else is vermin.

The love of money is the root of all progress.

See El Dorado. Take El Dorado. Find another El Dorado.

The envy of others is a self-replenishing feast.

A rationalization a day keeps your conscience at bay.

Never bang your head against a wall. Bang someone else's.

Don't break the law. Break the Law.

Losers make hurdles. Winners hurdle them.

Geniuses are their own saviors.

You cannot serve god and Mammon.

You're not really a conquistador until you hold the king's head high.

Depression is for the indolent.

What's the point of walking in another man's shoes? Unless his shoes are better than yours?

01

ONLY A LUNATIC WOULD live on the Moon.

The Moon is a dead rock—eighty-one quintillion tons of dead rock. It's been dead for nearly four billion years. And—inasmuch as a dead rock wants anything—it wants you dead too.

So you can go quickly. A landslide can bury you. A lava tube can collapse on you. You can plunge headlong into a crater. A meteoroid can strike your habitat at seventy thousand kilometers per hour. A micrometeorite can bust open your spacesuit. A sudden burst of static electricity can blow you apart in an airlock. A slip, a cut, a ruptured seal, a faulty oxygen tank can kill you in minutes.

Or you can go a little slower. A wiring malfunction can shut down air filters. A corrupted computer program can play havoc with climate-control systems. A particularly nasty pathogen—mutant strains of bacteria flourish in enclosed environments—can kill you in days. If you're out on the surface, the sudden temperature plunge between sunlight and shade can leave you with thermal shock. A solar flare can toast you like a TV dinner. A vehicular breakdown can leave you suffocating in your spacesuit.

Or you can go incrementally, over the course of years. Moondust can work its way like asbestos into the deepest fissures of your lungs. Prolonged exposure to chemical vapors and gas leaks can wreck your whole respiratory system. Reduced gravity—one-sixth that of Earth—can fatally weaken your heart. Cosmic radiation—galactic rays from dead suns and black holes—can warp your cells. Not to mention a cocktail of psychological factors—sensory deprivation, insomnia, paranoia, claustrophobia, loneliness, hallucinations—that can reshuffle your mind like a deck of cards.

On the Moon, in short, you can be killed by the environment. You can be killed by accident. Or you can kill yourself.

And then of course you can always be murdered. By gangsters. By terrorists. By psychopaths. By ideologues. Or simply because you cost too much to keep alive.

Only a lunatic—or a renegade, or a pariah, or a misanthrope, or a risk junkie, or a mass murderer—would live permanently on the Moon.

02

KLEEF DIJKSTRA IS A lunatic. And a mass murderer. Twenty-eight years ago, two weeks before national elections in the Netherlands, he blew up the Amsterdam offices of the newly formed Nederlandse Volksbond, whose principles he ostensibly supported, in a failed attempt to frame pro-immigration activists and win the party a protest vote. Six people were killed and thirty injured. Later in the same month, infuriated when the Partij van de Arbeid gained an unprecedented number of seats in the House of Representatives, he loaded a Beretta ARX190, shot his way through the security cordon at the Van Buuren Hotel in the Hague, and mowed down forty-seven celebrating party members. Combining the death tolls of these two massacres and a number of smaller, separate incidents, Kleef Dijkstra is directly responsible for the murders of sixty-two people.

After his arrest, court-appointed forensic psychiatrists determined that Kleef Dijkstra was a paranoid schizophrenic. They said he had sociopathic tendencies, narcissistic personality disorder, grandiose and delusional thoughts, and psychotic episodes. He exhibited no remorse for his crimes and had even informed his examiners at one point that he would like to kill them too. The psychiatrists concluded that there was little possibility of rehabilitation, even using the most sophisticated modern techniques, and recommended long-term incarceration in a high-security penitentiary.

Many others disagreed. Notwithstanding the European aversion to capital punishment, numerous commentators in the Netherlands and elsewhere argued that Dijkstra, according to his very own values, ought to be sentenced to death. Incarceration, after all, would be costly and would always leave open the possibility that he would become a hero behind bars, mobilizing the like-minded with smuggled-out missives. Dijkstra, alarmingly magnetic in his way, had already declared that "the battle has just begun," and that in a hundred years "there will be statues of me on street corners all across Europe."

A solution was found. The Moon at this point was in the early stages of its development: Mining had started on Nearside, and the first hotel had been opened at Doppelmayer Base. But the long-term physical and psychological effects of lunar habitation were still largely unknown. Surface expeditions were by necessity of short duration and often had disturbing side effects: everything from radiation poisoning and temporary blindness to hallucinations and psychological meltdowns. In one famous incident a miner completely lost his mind and hacked five coworkers to death at a small prefab base in the Ocean of Storms.

So long-term prisoners, first in Russia and the United States and later worldwide, were offered the chance to serve out their sentences on the far side of the Moon. They would be separated from Earth by at least 356,700 kilometers—the distance of the Moon at its closest point—and another 3,500 kilometers of lunar rock—the diameter of the Moon itself. They would be confined to isolated habitats—"igloos"—about the size of a two-bedroom metropolitan apartment and shielded against radiation by hard-packed lunar sand, or "regolith." They would be provided with no spacesuits or LRVs (lunar roving vehicles). All supplies would be delivered through a series of fail-proof hatches. All communications in and out, via underground fiber-optic cable, would be closely monitored. If face-to-face human interaction was absolutely necessary, the incoming visitor(s) would be accompanied by a squad of armed guards. The prisoners would be completely alone, but they would also enjoy a degree of autonomy virtually impossible in a terrestrial facility. There would be no jailhouse regimen. No insults from guards and other prisoners. No communal showers. No chance, in short, of being raped, beaten, or killed. And in exchange for this liberty the prisoners only had to self-monitor and report physiological changes, exposing themselves to sustained dosages of unfiltered sunlight via skylights at regularly appointed times, as well as undergoing psychological tests via tele-link.

After two years of paperwork, Kleef Dijkstra was approved for residence in one of these lunar igloos. He exhibited no great emotion when informed. Indeed, he seemed to think it already a fait accompli, as if the decision had been guided by higher forces. Declaring that he had "much work to do," he immediately applied for membership to the world's foremost libraries and information databases.

Twenty-five years later, Kleef Dijkstra is one of the longest-standing Farside residents. Only the Georgian terrorist Batir

Dadayev has been longer on the Moon. Both these men, along with eleven other survivors from the now retired Off-World Incarceration Program (OWIP), live in a seventy-kilometer radius within Gagarin Crater in the southern hemisphere of Farside.

Physically, all thirteen are virtually unrecognizable from their days on Earth. Their spines have lengthened, making them markedly taller. Fluid redistribution has given them barrel chests. Their faces are puffy. Their legs are spindly. Their bones are brittle, and their hearts are smaller. All over their bodies, in fact, there have been subtle adaptations to account for life in microgravity.

Mentally, however, there has been no uniform change. Some of the prisoners, like Batir Dadayev, have renounced their old ideologies. A couple have developed symptoms of early dementia. A few have mellowed to some degree, and even claim to have experienced genuine remorse. One has become deeply religious. And a dogged handful, like Kleef Dijkstra, have not changed their worldview at all.

Dijkstra, as he would happily inform you if he had a chance, came to the Moon with a specific purpose: He was going to write his political manifesto, a compendium of historical analyses, economic theories, and autobiographical details in the style of *Mein Kampf* (a book Dijkstra considers formative but highly amateurish). Naturally he wasn't underestimating the security protocols designed to keep his wisdom quarantined, but he was confident that his rhetorical brilliance would win over his examining doctors—and it would take only one—and his words would leak out somehow. Or perhaps the passage of years itself would make his writings "of public interest." In any event, it seemed only a matter of time before his manifesto achieved its just recognition.

The complete document—"Letter from Farside"—is explosive, incoherent, and riddled with factual inaccuracies and highly questionable readings of history. It's also 3,600 pages long.

Dijkstra has been revising it now for a full two decades. His early hope of getting it widely distributed as soon as possible proved futile—his doctors were more closed-minded than he expected. But he's not dispirited. The delay has only given him extra time to refine his arguments, augment them with more historical precedents, and even provide heavily symbolic stories— "parables"—to underline his points. And in any case it soon became obvious to Dijkstra that "Letter from Farside" is no every-day manifesto: It's the new Bible. It will be quoted and requoted endlessly. Whole lives will revolve around it. It's infinitely more important than his own perishing body. It's a time capsule of transcendental genius, flung into the cosmos to places and eons he can only imagine.

Thinking these thoughts he is currently working on Book XXVI, "Red in Truth & Law: The Brutal Reality of Successful Economies" Dijkstra hears a distinctive cheeping sound and switches his desktop monitor to exterior display. A camera shows the scene just outside his igloo door.

A man is standing out there. On the ash-grey dust plain of Gagarin. In the lunar vacuum. With the sun glaring behind him.

Except of course that it can't be a man. He's not wearing a spacesuit. He's wearing, in fact, an immaculately tailored black suit with white shirt and black tie. His black hair is razor-parted. His shoulders are broad, his physique trim, his face handsome. And he's smiling. He looks like an old-fashioned encyclopedia salesman. Or a Mormon. But he's obviously an android.

This is not unusual. Occasionally, when maintenance tasks need to be performed, OWIP will send around a droid. It saves them the trouble of rounding up the armed guards. And even if a prisoner were to overpower the droid somehow, or disable it, it would do him little good—there would be no pressurized vehicle to escape on, since the droids customarily travel on "moon-buggy" LRVs. And there wouldn't be much advantage in taking a droid hostage—OWIP would just write off the unit and deny the prisoner privileges for a while.

Dijkstra punches a button to open the airlock door.

The droid steps inside, still grinning. Strictly speaking, full pressurization procedures aren't necessary with robots, but the lunar dust still needs to be removed. So the droid raises his arms as the electrostatic and ultrasonic scrubbers whirl around him like the brushes in a car wash. Then the red lights stop flashing and the amber lights come on. Then the all-clear buzzes. Dijkstra opens the airlock's inner door, and the droid steps inside.

"Good day to you, sir," he says, extending a hand. "And many thanks for admitting me."

"No problem," says Dijkstra, flustered despite himself. He's always liked androids—as symbols of ruthless economics—but this one is disconcertingly real, even intimidating. And his hand feels sensual—almost *sexual*. "Have you been sent by OWIP?" he asks hurriedly.

"Can you say that again, sir?"

"I asked if you'd been sent by OWIP."

"I'm sorry, sir, I do not recognize that name. Is it a company, a corporation, a consortium, an office of law enforcement, or a government department?"

"It's an international program, but never mind. You're with a survey team, then?"

"What do you mean by 'survey team,' sir?"

"Geological . . . seismological . . . astronomical."

"I am not with a survey team, sir. I am looking for El Dorado."

"El Dorado?"

"That is what I said, sir."

For a second Dijkstra wonders if this is some sort of joke. But then a possibility occurs to him. "You're with one of the mining teams?"

"I am not with one of the mining teams, sir."

"But you want to go to El Dorado?"

"That is correct, sir."

"Well, it could be some new place I don't know about . . ."

"So you cannot help me, sir?"

"Not if you want to go to El Dorado."

The droid is silent. It's impossible to say why—his goofy expression never changes—but there seems something sinister about him now. Nevertheless Dijkstra, always hungering for a chance to talk—to anything—is reluctant to let him go.

"Can I help you in some other way?" he asks. "Perhaps you'd like to—" He is about to say "refuel" but stops himself. It's absurd, of course, but the more human the robot, the less one is likely to acknowledge its artificiality. "Perhaps you'd like to sit down for a while?"

"Do you have any high-proof alcohol, sir?"

"Sorry, no."

"Any sort of alcohol at all?"

"I don't drink."

"Then do you have some other sort of beverage?"

"What about coffee—instant coffee?"

"That would be excellent, sir—I would welcome a drink of instant coffee. With fifteen teaspoons of sugar."

"I can do that," says Dijkstra. Clearly the droid is one of those models fueled by alcohol and glucose. In the old days they were often made that way, so they could blend in with humans. So they would have identifiable appetites—even the need to eliminate waste.

Dijkstra prepares the coffee. Water boils at a lower temperature on the Moon, but most people have gotten used to tepid brews. "May I ask who you're with?" he inquires over the bubbling pot.

"I am all by myself, sir."

"But you must be—" Dijkstra starts to say, then holds his tongue. Maybe the droid is some sort of monitoring unit, tasked with watching him at close range. Even now, sitting primly at the table, he seems to be conducting a slow survey of the room.

"You have a very beautiful place here, sir," the droid says, smiling.

"Thank you," says Dijkstra. "It's spartan, but many of history's greatest men were spartan."

"Are you a Spartan?"

"Well, I wouldn't be here if I wasn't."

"Are you a great man?"

"That's for history to decide."

"Are you a conquistador?"

Dijkstra shrugs. "Not yet."

"I am going to be a conquistador," says the droid.

"I suppose that's why you want to reach El Dorado."

"That is precisely the reason, sir. Are we rivals?"

"Rivals?"

"If you also aim to be a conquistador, then we are rivals, are we not, sir?"

"Only if you want to be."

Filling the coffee mug, Dijkstra considers the possibility that there's something wrong with the droid. The Farside comm line—his only connection with the outside world—has been down for about twenty hours. It happens sometimes—solar fluxes and cosmic radiation can short-circuit the substations and junction boxes—so maybe this droid has a few fried circuits as well.

He comes over to the table and maneuvers into a seat, holding out the coffee. "I've already stirred it."

"I am grateful, sir."

The droid—he really is astonishingly handsome, Dijkstra thinks—picks up the mug and takes dainty sips, like a vicar at afternoon tea.

"This is good coffee," he says.

"Thank you," says Dijkstra. "Do you come from . . . some base?"

"I do not recall where I come from, sir. I only look forward, to the future."

"Well, that makes sense."

"It does make sense, sir. Do you live here permanently?"

"I do."

"All alone?"

"That's right."

"Then how do you contribute to the bottom line?"

"I'm not sure what you mean by 'bottom line.'"

"Are you an asset or a liability?"

"I would certainly classify myself as an asset."

"To the economy?"

"To the world."

The droid takes a while to process this answer. Eventually he says, "Then do you have anything else to offer me, sir, other than this fine coffee?"

"Anything like what?"

"Anything at all." Still staring.

For a moment Dijkstra entertains the thrilling possibility that the droid has been sent by admirers; that he has been assigned the task of retrieving his manifesto and smuggling it back to Earth.

"Well, that depends. Do you know who I am?"

"I do not, sir."

"The people who sent you, do they know who I am?"

"I have been sent by no people, sir."

"You have no task to perform here?"

"I only want directions, sir."

"Then you're not here to take my writings?"

"Only if your writings can help me find El Dorado, sir."

There's no easy answer to that, Dijkstra thinks. But he has to accept that his dream, brief as it was, has no substance. And suddenly he feels mildly deflated. He wanted the droid to offer him something—some form of hope.

"Can I get you another cup?" Dijkstra asks—the droid is finishing his coffee.

"That is very generous of you, sir. But I must be on my way. *Move. Move. While others sleep, move.*" He gets to his feet.

"Perhaps I can offer you some sugar cubes, then? For your journey?"

"You are again very generous, sir. I will gratefully accept that offer."

Dijkstra goes to his pantry, wondering why he is being so solicitous. His stores of sugar are rather low and fresh supplies sometimes take weeks to reach him. And yet here he is offering no-cost welfare, against all his principles. It's almost as if he's been manipulated. Or weakened, somehow.

When he comes back he finds the droid holding out his hand, still smiling. And when he hands over the sugar cubes he notices for the first time a dark red stain on the droid's shirt cuff.

"Oh," he says impulsively, "is that—What's that? Is it blood?"

"It is not blood, sir."

"It looks like blood."

"It is not blood, sir." The droid lowers his arm, so the cuff is no longer visible. "But that is of no concern to you, sir. You have been helpful to me. You have supplied me with coffee and sugar. You have not even charged for this supply. So you do not qualify as vermin."

"Well," says Dijkstra, chuckling evasively, "we all breathe the same air."

The droid leans in close—so close that Dijkstra can smell the coffee on his breath. "Can you say that again, sir?"

"I said, we all breathe the same air."

Dijkstra has not spoken sarcastically or mockingly. The expression has simply become a common saying on the Moon—both a half-ironic gesture of fraternity and an acknowledgment of the Moon's most valuable commodity.

But the droid seems to read into it something much more meaningful.

"You say we breathe the same air, sir?"

"That's right."

"So we are rivals after all, are we, sir?"

"Rivals?"

"For air?"

Dijkstra almost laughs: The droid sounds offended—or *eager* to be offended. So he just says, "Well, I guess we're all rivals in the end, aren't we? Competition makes the world go 'round."

And the droid, who's about the same height as Dijkstra, continues to stare at him with his intensely black eyes—Dijkstra has never seen more soulless eyes. And Dijkstra, murderer of sixty-two people, is chilled. Because he conceives of a whole new scenario: that the droid has been sent by his enemies, all those miserable soft cocks and fashion victims on Earth, to *prevent* his message from getting out. To *censor* him somehow.

Then the droid blinks.

"Thank you, sir." He thrusts out his hand again. "You are a worthy gentleman." And they shake on it.

Dijkstra feels unusually relieved. "Well," he says, "good luck on your journey."

"Thank you, sir."

"I certainly hope you find El Dorado."

"Thank you, sir."

"I hope you become a conquistador."

"I intend to, sir."

"Then I'll open the airlock and let you out."

"And I will be standing here, sir."

Dijkstra goes toward his control panel, experiencing a sudden flush of anticipation. Minutes ago he wanted to prolong his guest's visit; now he's just looking forward to being alone. But first he has to open the airlock. Which means he has to turn his back.

Which means that it's only out of the corner of his eye that he registers movement—the droid picking something up. A wrench that's been left on the workbench.

Dijkstra wheels around defensively, but it's already too late. The droid, no longer smiling, is swooping down on him.

Dijkstra tries to raise his hands, but the wrench comes crashing down on his head. *Crack. Crack.* The droid is relentless. *Crack.* Dijkstra sees his own blood in his eyes. *Crack.* He falls to the floor. *Crack. Crack.* The droid is smashing his head in.

Crack. Crack.

"*It's good to have a rival,*" the droid hisses, splattered with Kleef Dijkstra's blood. "*It's even better to crack his skull.*"

Crack.

Crack.

Crack.

03

I F YOU'RE AN AVERAGE tourist, then the Moon is very likely a once-in-a-lifetime destination. You'll take a shuttle from Florida, Costa Rica, Kazakhstan, French Guiana, Tanegashima in Japan, or the converted oil rig on the Malabar Coast. You'll probably be tempted to spend a few days at the StarLight Casino in low-Earth orbit: The Carousel Room, you'll be happy to hear, is every bit as spectacular as its reputation. From there you'll take the ferry to one of the Moon's major ports, most likely Doppelmayer Base in the Sea of Moisture or Lyall Base in the Sea of Tranquility. You'll check into one of the hotels: the Copernicus, the Hilton, the HoneyMoon, the Interstellar, or the Overview. You'll spend a few days adjusting and/or recovering. Then you'll probably go on a little tour of the local attractions: the amusement parks, the observation towers, the sporting stadia, the famous ballet theater. You'll certainly make a tour of the Apollo landing sites, the domed-over Apollo 11 site in particular. If you're really ambitious, you might even make a jaunt to the South Pole to admire the jawdropping Shackleton Crater, four times as deep as the Grand Canyon.

If, on the other hand, you've come to the Moon for cut-rate or illegal surgery, for contraband drugs, for illicit sex, for death sports, for high-stakes gambling, or simply to conduct an unmonitored conversation, your destination will certainly be Purgatory and its capital city of Sin, on Farside.

To get there, you'll board the magnetically levitated m-train, or monorail, which in theory can reach its destination in just five hours, approaching speeds of a thousand kilometers per hour. In reality the train will spend half an hour just being tested and pressurized and shunted through a series of airlocks, and then a further two hours curling around the various factories, museums, communication centers, and radio towers that pepper the region between Doppelmayer Base and the lunar Carpathians. But once the track is straight and the land is clear, the train will start streaking at jet-liner speeds over the undulating grey/tan/beige terrain.

Looking through the heavily tinted windows you'll see quarries out there, and robotic excavators, and conveyor belts disappearing into flashing metallurgies. You'll see solar-panel arrays, flywheel farms, and microelectronics factories mounted on platforms. Not to mention trolleys and tractors and trenchers and scrapers and multilegged vehicles: all the vehicular accoutrements of grand-scale resource exploitation. You'll whisk over the viaduct of the sun-synchronous harvest train, ten klicks in length, which crawls around the lunar equator laden with fruits and vegetables. You might even see a freight train flashing past in the opposite direction, so fast that it will appear as a brief streak of light. Then you'll settle back as the m-train soars across the Sea of Showers, cruises across Plato Crater, dissects the narrow Sea of Cold, and enters the northern uplands, where the dust is brighter, the terrain more mountainous, and the shadows long and eerie.

Finally you'll spot fields of radio masts and power towers on the horizon, and cranes and warehouses and shunting yards and a garbage heap of discarded machinery and drill bits. This, clearly, is a mining town. But it's also the end of the line. It's Peary Base at the North Pole—beyond which "there is only darkness."

You'll spend as little time here as possible: The whole place has all the charm of a low-rent shopping mall. There's a second-rate observation tower. A mass driver or rail gun, a kilometer-long stretch of curving electromagnetic rail that dispatches and receives payloads to and from Earth. And all the cranes, crawlers, and deep-drilling towers of the ice-mining industry. But not much else. So you'll check into one of the utilitarian, low-ceilinged hotels, ascend to a closet-sized room (pressurizing an entire hotel with oxygen and nitrogen is expensive), and collapse onto a bed that's about as big as a submarine bunk.

On the bedside table—if there is one—you'll probably find a ten-page brochure, a traveler's advisory warning you all about Purgatory. If you're game, or just seeking amusement, you'll give it a glance. "*Extremely dangerous . . . exercise caution . . . restrictions on communication . . . eccentric local laws brutally enforced . . . death penalty imposed . . . high rate of sexually transmitted diseases . . . uncertified medical establishments . . . controversial procedures . . . hostile locals . . . visa and other entry and exit procedures change indiscriminately . . . tourists lured, targeted, and frequently killed.*"

If that doesn't give you second thoughts—and if you've made it this far, why would it?—you'll continue your journey by heading down to the Peary Transport Terminus. But don't expect to be traveling by m-train anymore: To preserve the integrity of its radar readings, no electromagnetic propulsion systems—or radio waves, cell-phone networks, or satellite technologies—are permitted on Farside. So you'll be forced to choose among a hydro-powered coach, a minibus, or a cab, or, if you're really wealthy, a chauffeured limousine. Then your vehicle, whatever it is, will steer around a few bends, into the lattice-shadow of the mass driver, through a gap in an escarpment of piled refuse—a sort of unofficial exit gate—and onto a hard-packed road of sintered regolith that's rolled out like a ribbon across the pockmarked lunar terrain.

This is the Road of Lamentation, the official highway to Purgatory.

The regolith has been piled high by the side of the road as a sort of retaining wall, so at first there won't be much to look at: an occasional crater rim or lunar mountain, the stanchion-mounted, color-coded pipelines of hydrogen, nitrogen, and oxygen, and the crystal-clear cosmos itself if it's nighttime and your vehicle's shields are down. On the road itself there are regular solar-flare shelters, supply caches, emergency parking bays, and a couple of specialized sidings where tourists can turn in for a last glimpse of Earth. But for the most part the journey is numbingly monotonous—like traveling down a desert highway at midnight—except perhaps when there's a crest in the road and the unballasted vehicles leave the surface and soar through the air for a few giddy seconds.

Past the seventy-fifth parallel, however, the Lamentation starts winding like a river, skirting the larger craters, and the camber of the road allows you to see more of the lunar landscape: notably more rugged and hummocky than most of Nearside. But even this becomes tedious after a while, and just when you start wondering if the journey is ever going to end—and just when your eyelids begin fluttering—you'll be startled awake by the sight of a huge object at the side of the road, towering at least thirty meters over the traffic.

It's a statue, spray-painted in glossy white, garishly illuminated at night with halogen spotlights, and looking like a winged angel standing on the bow of a boat.

It's the Celestial Pilot, the one who carries lost souls to Purgatory. And it's not the last statue you'll see in this final stage. Just a kilometer farther on there's a giant eagle, the one that transported Virgil in his dream. Then a colossal warrior—Bertran de Born—holding his own severed head like a lantern. Then a Roman emperor—Trajan—on a caparisoned horse. And finally a naked woman—Arachne—with eight spiderlike limbs. It's a gallery of characters from Dante Alighieri and Gustave Doré, all designed to give extra mythological resonance to your destination.

Then the Lamentation will descend, and the lines of cabs, coaches, transports, and haulers will merge into a bottleneck at least half a kilometer long. And somewhere in the middle of this you'll catch your first glimpse of Störmer Crater, the massive ramparts of the natural ringwall, illuminated by flickering electric lamps. And the entrance itself—ornate brass doors flanked by giant pillars twenty meters high and thickly decorated with faux-Renaissance bas-reliefs. And before you know it you'll be passing through. The gates will be closing behind you. And finally you'll be inside, shunted through a series of airlocks into the terminus. And the coach driver, or your chauffeur, or your guide, or an android, or an automated recording in a multitude of languages, will have a sobering message for you.

"Welcome to Purgatory."

04

LIEUTENANT DAMIEN JUSTUS IS being interviewed in his office by a reporter from the *Tablet*, Purgatory's only official news outlet. The reporter, who sports the improbable name of Nat U. Reilly, is wearing a crumpled hat and a threadbare jacket with elbow patches. He's chewing gum and taking notes on a tiny scribble pad with a pencil. But at least he has the good grace to be self-conscious.

"It's the way we do things here in Purgatory," he says. "Retro-style."

"So I've seen."

"We still roll the presses at the *Tablet*, you know that?"

"I'm no longer surprised," says Justus.

Even the office that's been assigned to him is like something from the 1950s: a groaning wooden desk, a filing cabinet with squeaky drawers, a Bakelite rotary-dial telephone, and on the wall a black-and-white photo of Fletcher Brass like an official portrait of Eisenhower. The police uniforms themselves—all midnight-blue wool, brass buttons, and peaked saucer caps—belong in a Dick Tracy cartoon. Justus expected as much in the tourist precincts, as part of the prevailing show business, but not behind the scenes as well.

"Anyway," Reilly goes on, "you say your name is pronounced—how, again?"

"Like 'Eustace.' "

"Sure you don't wanna go with 'Justice'?"

"I'm sure."

"We like a good pun in our business."

"And a bad one, it seems."

Nat U. Reilly smirks and makes a note. "Justus it is, then. That's Swedish, isn't it?"

"It can be. Are you sure your readers will be interested in this, Mr. Reilly?"

"They'll be interested in everything about you, Lieutenant. Why? Not in a hurry, are you?"

"I've had some bad experiences with the press before, that's all."

"We're different up here."

"I'm pleased to hear it." In truth, Justus knows that Reilly is very likely a criminal, a fugitive from terrestrial justice, like most permanent residents of Purgatory.

"You're from Arizona, that right?"

"From Nevada," Justus says. "But I spent the last ten years in Arizona, that's true."

"So you're used to arid places."

"Nothing as arid as the Moon."

"And you're used to casino towns."

"If you mean Vegas and Reno, I spent some time in both; that's also true. I was in Homicide then."

"And more lately you've been in Narcotics."

"I was in charge of a squad operating out of Phoenix, yes."

"You ruffled a few feathers, is what I hear."

"You hear correctly."

"You arrested the wrong man."

"I arrested the right man."

"But I mean, you arrested a man with the wrong connections."

"If you asked him, I'm sure he'd say he had the *right* connections."

Reilly snorts. "But you don't take shit from anyone, do you, Lieutenant? Not even a drug baron with his hand deep up the ass of the local legislature."

"You put that very well."

"You left not because *you* were corrupt, but because the system was."

"You put that very well too." To Justus it sounds as though Reilly has already written the article.

"You were told—in no uncertain terms—to get off Earth, is that right?"

"Sort of."

"Sort of?"

"Well, if that was all there was to it—a threat to me—I wouldn't have left."

"They threatened people close to you, yeah? Your wife and daughter?"

"That's as much as I want to say about that subject, Mr. Reilly."

"But you knew—from experience—that they didn't mess around, right?"

"I said, that's as much as I want to say about that, Mr. Reilly."

The reporter seems to stop himself from asking one very obvious question and moves on. "So you decided to come to Purgatory?"

"Well, it's not quite as simple as that. I was offered a position here."

"By QT Brass."

"By the Department of Law Enforcement."

"Which is controlled by QT Brass."

"I know nothing about that."

"Have you met QT Brass?"

"I'm not even sure what she looks like."

"What about Fletcher Brass, her father?"

"As I understand it, he's got a lot on his plate right now."

"Well, that's a fact. But you know all about him, though? Everything he's done here?"

"To me, he's just another citizen."

Reilly seems pleased with the answer. "You don't belong to anyone, do you, Lieutenant? Not even to the Patriarch of Purgatory?"

"I answer to the law, like everyone else."

"And you'd throw Fletcher Brass in the slammer just as quick as any two-bit shoplifter?"

"If he'd committed a crime, and if I had sufficient evidence, then I'd certainly arrest him. But it's not up to me to issue sentences."

Reilly, scribbling something down, is practically grinning now. "Then what about all the others in Purgatory—mobsters, war criminals? You're not scared of them either?"

"Whatever they did on Earth is no longer my concern. It's what they do here that's my business."

"And you're not doing this for kicks, right?"

"I'm not interested in doing anything for kicks. A lecturer of mine at the police academy used to have a favorite saying: 'A man with a hammer will find plenty worth hammering.' Well, I'm not interested in hammering anything, unless it would fall apart otherwise."

"But there must be some particular attraction for you here in Purgatory, yeah? The idea of cleaning up a cesspit like this?"

"You call it a cesspit. To me, it's just another precinct."

"You can't really mean that?"

"Whether it's Earth or the Moon, an assault is an assault, a robbery is a robbery, and a murder's a murder. Gravity doesn't change that."

"What about the fact that there's no CCTV here? No radar?"

Reilly is referring to the fact that Purgatory is a "surveillance-free zone." It began as a necessity and became a means of attracting tourists, because on Earth there's barely a square inch that's not being watched, probed, or listened to.

"It makes things more challenging, certainly," says Justus. "I guess it makes the law as old-fashioned as the furniture."

Reilly snickers. "How about your gravity adjustment, then—how's that coming along?"

"I took a two-week course at Doppelmayer before I got here."

"So you're already well acclimatized?"

"I still overshoot the mark occasionally. I bounce off walls. Nothing serious."

"And the Purgatory Police Department? How have you slotted in there?"

"Everyone in the PPD has been very cooperative."

"You didn't put any noses out of joint, though, getting your lieutenant stripes without having served here first?"

"Well, I wasn't responsible for that. And the circumstances are unique. I think the others accept that."

"What about the locals—in Sin, I mean? How do you find them?"

"Suspicious, but that's to be expected. And again, I'm not here to judge anyone. I've always believed in redemption. I believe in sin too, but even more in redemption."

For some reason this answer seems to unsettle Reilly, so he flips a page and goes on hurriedly.

"And friends? Have you made any friends yet?"

"I'm not here to make friends. Or enemies."

"And women? What do you make of the Purgatorial women?"

"They're female."

Reilly has reached the last page of his notepad and suddenly seems a little hesitant. "Okay, just one last question. And I hope you don't take this personally. But it's about your appearance."

"Go ahead."

"Well, you were obviously in a fire or something, right?"

Justus is sure the reporter already knows the truth, but he answers anyway. "I had a vial of nitric acid flung at my face."

"By that drug baron back in Phoenix?"

"By someone acting on his orders."

"And that's partly the reason you came here?"

"Partly."

"Then you know we have some excellent surgeons here—doctors who can give you a whole new face in two hours?"

"And I'm sure it would be a very handsome face too."

"But you wanna stay the way you are? To remind yourself of the past?"

"Let me put it this way, Mr. Reilly. You asked about the name Justus before—whether it was Swedish. Well, the truth is it's

Scottish—that's where my ancestors came from, anyway. And the Justus clan in Scotland has a motto. Care to hear it?"

"'Course."

"*Sine non causa*. That's it. 'Not without a cause.'"

"I don't get it."

"Neither do I. But I figure that when it comes to that acid, it was flung in my face 'not without a cause.' Because maybe I'm just *meant* to look this way."

Reilly, folding his notepad and getting to his feet, shakes his head in admiration. "My readers are gonna love you."

"I don't care if they love or hate me, Mr. Reilly, as long as they obey the law. I look forward to seeing you around."

When Reilly closes the door Justus catches sight of his own reflection in the glass. He'd been pinned to his bed, struggling to rise, when the acid was splashed over him. He lost his eyebrows, some of his nose, part of his ear, and a whole lot of facial definition. But generally speaking the scarring is remarkably even—as if he'd been attacked by a particularly caustic starfish—and people who don't know the truth sometimes assume he's had himself purposely burned, just to look distinctive.

He's just about to get back to his work—he's still familiarizing himself with Purgatory's judicial system—when the door squeaks open. It's Dash Chin, a sprightly young Chinese officer who's been assigned to him as an aide.

"How'd the interview go?"

"Just fine."

"Reilly didn't piss you off?"

"No more than any other reporter I've met."

Chin chuckles. "Wanna know what he did back on Earth?"

"Not really."

"He was the first at a crime scene. The lead singer of some

boy band had left two teenage hookers overdosed on heroin. They were dying. But Reilly didn't lift a finger to save them. Just let them die, so he'd have an even better story."

Justus shrugs. "Well, that was a long time ago."

"Fifteen years. And now he's the number one reporter here in Sin. You must be big, to get his attention."

"I'm flattered."

Chin laughs again. "Speaking of which, you ready for a crime scene right here?"

"There's a crime scene?"

"A five one."

It takes Justus a second to remember the PPD codes. "A *homicide*?"

"Uh-huh."

"Well, when was it called in?"

"Twenty minutes ago."

"From where?"

"The Goat House. Out at the Agri-Plex."

"And no one's taken charge?"

"You're the man, Lieutenant."

Despite himself, Justus is startled by the casualness of the message—not even in Vegas had homicides been announced as an afterthought.

"Well," he says, reaching for his zapper and brass badge, "let's get on over there."

"Roger that, sir."

They leave the room together.

05

ENNIS FIELDS IS A lunatic. And a cannibal. Twenty-four years ago, in Vancouver, he got thoroughly sick of his second wife. So he slit her throat like a kosher butcher, peeled away her skin, trimmed off her substantial fat, and cooked her on the hob. He pan-fried her muscles; he sautéed her brains; he boiled her bones; he minced the leftovers; he enjoyed a leisurely dinner; then he deposited on the doorstep of his mother-in-law a cardboard box containing "one of Maggie's delicious pork pies."

By the time the police finally caught up with Ennis Fields, in Alberta eighteen months later, he had killed and partially eaten a further three women. During interrogation he confessed to four earlier murders as well.

He was sentenced to eight consecutive life sentences with no chance of parole. But at Kingston Penitentiary, though ostensibly in high-security confinement, he was brutally beaten and left for dead on the orders of a prison kingpin (a distant cousin to one of his victims). He was lucky to survive. So his lawyers pleaded for relocation to a safer place of confinement—a much safer place of confinement. The appeal ended up on a desk at OWIP, and within months a deal was arranged with Canada's Correctional Service.

Fields has now lived alone in Gagarin Crater, thirty kilometers northeast of the habitat once occupied by Kleef Dijkstra, for seventeen years.

He reads a lot of books (true crime, mainly, though he enjoys a good romance novel). He prepares a lot of Spanish dishes (his freezer is crowded with chorizo and Serrano ham). And he constructs a lot of ingenious mechanical inventions (when he wasn't eating widows, Fields was a leading Canadian toymaker).

But he also enjoys anything that breaks up his routine—a visit, especially. In all his time on the Moon, Fields has received fewer than fifty "guests," and he always makes them welcome. He gets out his best crockery, his best liquor, his best homemade cookies—even for his jailers. Even for the androids. Fields has always been a charming host. It's what made him so successful as a killer in the first place.

"Are you going to be coming here regularly?" he asks, handing over a glass of sangria.

"I shall not, sir," says the handsome droid. "I am going to finish this energizing drink and be on my way, thank you very much."

"And where did you say you were going?"

"I am going to El Dorado, sir."

"Can't say I know it."

"I believe it might also be known as Oz."

"Oz?"

"Oh-zee. Oz."

"I've not heard of a place called Oz either—not on the Moon."

"I want to go to Oz."

"Both El Dorado and Oz?"

"I understand they are the same place, sir."

Fields, lowering himself into a rug-lined armchair, thinks about it. "Are you perhaps talking about the mythical Oz?"

"I do not understand that question, sir."

"Well, I thought you might be—you know—the Tin Man. On his way to Oz."

The droid looks at him strangely. "I am not the Tin Man, sir. I am the Wizard."

Fields, like Dijkstra before him, shrugs off a brief presentiment of danger. "Well, if it's a major human settlement you're after," he says, "the only one we've got on Farside is a place called Purgatory."

"Purgatory?" The droid's face registers something. "I thought Purgatory was a metaphor?"

"Not on the Moon it isn't. Purgatory is an actual place—with banks and hotels and everything. Are you really sure you've never heard of it?"

"Are you calling me a liar, sir?"

There's a steely undertone to the question which Fields again chooses to ignore. "Purgatory is in the northern hemisphere," he goes on. "Inside a crater called Störmer. It's the territory—the *kingdom*—of Fletcher Brass."

"Fletcher Brass." Again the droid hesitates.

"You've heard of him?"

"I have not, sir."

Fields crosses his legs, happy for the chance to explain. "Brass is an aerospace billionaire. Or trillionaire. He got in hot water on Earth and escaped to his territory in Störmer Crater. Called the place Purgatory because he thought he was only going to be there until he got things sorted out. But he spent so much time in microgravity that it became unsafe to return to Earth. So he decided to stay. And he invited all his white-collar-criminal buddies to join him, along with any other lowlife who had enough money to make the trip. So the capital city there—it's called Sin, by the way, named after the Babylonian moon god or something—is like some huge haven for crooks and deviates. I would've escaped there myself if I had the chance."

The droid, no longer sipping the sangria, considers for a moment. "Do you think this Purgatory might have been mistaken for Oz, sir? Or El Dorado?"

"Sure, I guess."

"And how far away is it, sir, in metric measurement?"

"Oh, I don't know—about two thousand kilometers."

"And you said you would like to go there yourself?"

"Well, I *would* have, but not anymore."

"Why not, sir?"

"Because I'm not sure I'd be welcome. I have nothing to offer them. And besides"—Fields smirks—"I like it too much here now anyway, eh?"

The droid takes a moment to look around at the overcrowded bookshelves, the moldy shag carpet, the artificial wood fire. "Nevertheless," he says, "you will be willing to guide me there?"

It's said almost as a statement, and Fields chuckles—it's like dealing with a difficult customer. "Look," he says, "the truth is I'm not *allowed* to leave this place. I'm here as part of a program."

"OWIP?" asks the droid.

"You've heard of that?"

"I have, sir."

Fields wonders if the droid has been sent for a hidden reason.

In the early years of his incarceration he'd been the subject of a few psychological studies. Once, a female psychologist was sent around to liaise with him, become friendly with him, even flirt with him. And at first he was extremely gentlemanly. When his heater was busted once he even took off his jacket and draped it over her shoulders. But then one day his urges overcame him—it had been so painfully long since he'd eaten human flesh—and right in the middle of a friendly chat he leaped up and tried to cut her throat. Only to find that she was not a woman at all, but an android—just as lifelike as the one he's hosting now.

"Are those spots of oil on your shirt there?" he asks, adjusting his glasses.

"They could be."

"Are you—you know—in need of attention or something?"

"What sort of attention, sir?"

"Well, you might have a fault, eh? I'm good with machinery."

"I am delighted to hear that, sir."

"So do you want to take off your shirt, maybe? So I can have a look?"

The droid is still smiling. And staring—intensely, with a strange new aura about him. "Are you trying to fuck me, sir?" he asks.

Fields chuckles. Oddly enough, a sexual thought had never crossed his mind. But now he has to wonder if the droid has been sent to test him—to see if his preferences have changed or something. "That's a strange question," he says.

"Do you intend to answer it, sir?"

"Well, I don't know." Fields smirks, thinking about it. "Do I want to fuck you? That depends. Do you want to be fucked?"

"I do not, sir," the droid replies coolly. "In this world you either fuck or get fucked. And I am always a fucker, sir."

Now things are really getting weird, Fields thinks. He's never heard a robot talk like that before. He didn't even know it was possible. And the thing is still smiling. "What if I show you where Purgatory is on a map?" he says. "Would that make you happy?"

"That would make me extremely happy, sir."

When Fields comes back with his lunar atlas the droid is already on his feet. Fields opens the book on the dining table and flips to the page showing Farside. "I can go into more detail if you like, but we're here." He points to Gagarin Crater. "And if you want to reach Purgatory, you're going to have to go all the way up here." His finger runs up the page, past Marconi, Kohlschütter, and Tsu Chung-Chi, through the Sea of Moscow, past Nikolaev and van Rhijn, and finally to Störmer Crater. "That's it—Purgatory. Right there, pretty much due north. I think there are official paths now, roads for astronomers and the like. If you have any luck you might find one of them."

"It's not called Purgatory on this page, sir."

"Well, this is an old map."

"May I take it, sir?"

"The map? Of course. But I doubt it'll do you any good."

"And why is that, sir?"

"Well, it's not like there are signposts. And the features on this page are very sketchy. If you get lost, you'll stay lost."

"But I can always ask someone else, closer to my destination?"

"If you can find someone."

"And you still refuse to take me?"

"I can't," says Fields. "I wish I could, but I can't."

"I would be banging my head against the wall to keep asking you, would I?"

"I guess you could say that."

"Then I am sorry to hear that, sir."

"I'm sorry too. But everyone has restrictions, eh?"

The droid looks at him for a few seconds, unblinking, then nods and straightens. "I will take this map." He detaches it neatly from the atlas. "And I thank you for the delicious alcoholic beverage. It was most appreciated. I am disappointed that you chose not to be of further assistance, but in that regard I will not keep banging my head against the wall."

Fields, like Dijkstra, is suddenly feeling like he's had enough of this peculiar droid. "It was a pleasure doing business with you," he says. "If you're ever in the area again and you see the light on, well, you're welcome to drop in."

"I am grateful for the offer, sir, but I doubt you will be seeing me again. Will you open the airlock for me?"

"Sure."

Fields goes over to the control console and flicks some switches. There's a buzzing sound as the inner door opens. He glances over his shoulder and sees the droid smiling at him.

"Is that button you just pressed for the inner door, sir?" the droid asks.

"That's right."

"And which is the button for the outer door?"

"That's the orange one here. Why?"

"I have a voracious curiosity, sir. Please do what you have to do."

Fields turns back to the console and is checking the safety gauges when he feels something close around the back of his neck. At first he doesn't believe it—this isn't supposed to happen—but then the grip tightens. The droid's fingers are like talons. So Fields, very fit for his age, throws back his shoulders and thrashes his arms. But the droid's hold is superhuman.

And then Fields feels himself being *lifted* off the floor. And *carried* like a doll across the room. And *propelled* headfirst toward the wall—only to halt a few inches from the bricks.

"*Never bang your head against a wall,*" he hears the droid snarl in his ear. "*Bang someone else's.*"

Bang. Bang. Bang.

Fields's skull shatters and he passes out.

Bang. Bang. Bang.

06

LIEUTENANT DAMIEN JUSTUS IS used to asking questions. He's used to deference from other cops. And he's used to the sight of dead bodies.

What he isn't used to is feeling so completely out of place. Or receiving so much unconditional deference from cops he hardly knows. Or viewing bodies that have been blown apart by a bomb blast.

"Damien Justus," he says, shaking hands with a photogenic Italian.

"Officer Cosmo Battaglia," the officer returns.

"You in charge?"

"Until you showed up," Battaglia says, without a trace of resentment.

"Okay." Justus turns to the death scene. "Tell me what we got here."

"Three people. Two men, one woman. They were posing for photographs when—*vaboom!*—the feed tanks here exploded."

"The feed tanks for the goats."

"That's right."

"What was in the tanks?"

"Nutrients, that sort of stuff."

"Do feed tanks often explode on the Moon? Spontaneous combustion? A barrel of fertilizer igniting all by itself?"

"Not that I know of."

"So you suspect foul play?"

"I'll leave the official suspicions to you, Lieutenant."

"Uh-huh." Justus doesn't like it. He can see—and *feel*—the other cops looking at him. Which shouldn't be unusual, especially since the acid attack, except that there's something disconcerting about the *way* they're looking at him. As if they're enjoying all of this. As if they're showing off for the new guy. *Look what we see every other day in Purgatory. Decapitated heads, severed limbs, dead goats—and you thought you had it bad back on Earth!*

"Any idea who the victims are?"

"All three were from the Department of Agriculture," says Battaglia. "A secretary, a consultant, and a professor. See that head with the pointed beard, the one who looks like the devil?"

"Uh-huh."

"That belongs to Otto Decker, the agriculture scientist."

"The professor?"

"Sure. Real good at his job too. Or at least he was." Battaglia actually sniggers.

Justus nods and looks around. They're in a wing of the Agri-Plex, a vast underground food lab connected to Sin by tunnels. Some of the wings are given over to high-yield crops. Others contain hydroponic fruit and vegetables. There's a wheat field as big as two football stadiums, a rice paddy, a "wethouse" for aquaculture, a crowded livestock facility, and a slaughterhouse.

Battaglia notices him looking and offers, "This section is new—that's why they were taking photos."

"Goats are new on the Moon?"

"Mountain goats. Eat anything. Live in low pressure too, so that saves a bit on overhead. And they pay out big."

"How so?"

"Milk. Cheese. Yogurt. Soap. Whey. Protein. You know."

"Uh-huh." Justus thinks the officer is unusually well informed. And it feels surreal, talking about goat farming over three mutilated bodies in this strange chamber, with its padded ceiling and ultraviolet lamps. And grass underfoot. And alpine flowers. And bumblebees. And sky-blue walls with painted clouds, like an old-fashioned movie set. Not to mention the goats themselves, unsettled by all the activity, springing forty feet into the air, actually crashing into the roof—that must be why it's padded—and gracefully dropping down again. Except for all the gore, it's like something out of a Saturday-morning cartoon.

Dash Chin sidles in. "Over here, Lieutenant—the photographer. He saw everything."

The photographer is a little Arab guy who looks shaken up. He's sitting on the edge of a water trough, quivering, gasping, checking his camera, gasping some more.

"You with the *Tablet*?" Justus asks.

The photographer looks up. "Yeah."

"Up for a talk?"

"I can—I can talk, yeah."

"How'd you come to be here?"

"A—a photo shoot. Otto D-Decker's office."

"They arranged it?"

"They *announced* it."

"Opening the new goat farm?"

"That—that's right."

The photographer isn't making eye contact. Which could be read as shifty, though Justus prefers to read it as shock.

"Then tell us what you saw."

"I was—I was setting up a shot. The professor and the other two were tipping grain out of one of the feed bins, and . . . and . . ."

"And there was an explosion."

The photographer gulps. "Yeah."

"You saw the people blown apart."

"Yeah."

Justus has already noticed bodily matter on the man's jacket. "How close were you, exactly?"

"About—about fifteen meters."

"Did you see anyone strange? Anyone who might have set off the explosion?"

"No—no."

"Do you think the explosion might have been natural?"

"I . . . don't know."

"What about the feed tanks—were you the one who directed the victims to tip the grain out?"

"Me? No. No. Why do you say that?"

Justus ignores the question. "So Decker and the others, they just went over to the bins and you took a photo?"

"Yeah."

"And that's when one of the barrels blew up."

"That's how it happened."

Justus retreats for a moment. There's nowhere in the place to be alone—it's about a half-acre in size, and treeless—but he needs to gather his thoughts, difficult though that is when there are goats springing around like jumping beans. And cops still glancing his way with smug expressions. And three human bodies dismembered on the ground. And Dash Chin clinging to him like a remora fish.

"What do you make of it, sir?"

Justus shrugs. "This chamber, it's usually under low pressure, is that right?"

"How did you know that?"

"Officer Battaglia said something."

Chin seems impressed. "That's why mountain goats are good for the Agri-Plex—they can live in low-pressure environments. And bumblebees too."

Justus thinks that Chin, like Battaglia, is remarkably well informed. "What about the people who come in here, then—farmhands or maintenance teams—they enter in low pressure, that right?"

"They would, sure."

"In spacesuits?"

Chin laughs. "Don't think so. They'd just get depressurized a little and come in, probably in masks—you know, to keep out the fertilizer stink."

"Uh-huh." Justus can smell the stink now. And he imagines someone entering the chamber in a thick mask—in disguise, effectively. Someone setting up a bomb and hiding, waiting to activate it. "The farmhands, are they monitored?"

"Not sure."

"Have them rounded up anyway."

"You think it could've been one of them?"

"Won't hurt to question them. And we've got an FRT here, have we not?"

"'Course." Chin says it with a chuckle, as if he hasn't got much respect for the local Forensic Response Team.

"Then they should be here already. We need to know what sort of explosive was used."

"No problem."

"There could still be shoeprints in this dirt. Shoeprints can be as good as fingerprints."

"Yeah, 'course."

"Get that photographer to take some more photographs. Everything—before there's any more disturbance. He can charge it to the department, or to me if necessary."

"I'll do that."

"And then we need to think about a motive."

"Any ideas, sir?"

"I need to know more about the victims first."

"Well, you're in luck there," Chin says. "I mean, I'm not sure about the two others, but Professor Decker—he's about as big as they get here in Purgatory."

"That right?"

"He was one of the first big fish that Brass reeled in when he started bootstrapping this place."

Justus thinks about asking what crime Decker committed on Earth but decides against it. "An agriculture scientist."

"Can't live on the Moon without 'em. Virtually everything we eat here—everything that's not imported, that is—grows thanks to him."

"And that makes him big here? Because in my experience, people don't care much where their food comes from."

"Well, there's that. And then there's the fact that he's one of Brass's main men—one of his most trusted advisers. He was part of the Brass Band, in fact."

"Uh-huh." By "Brass Band" Chin means Brass's trusted inner circle—a secret order of knights loyal to the king.

"Decker was a real mover and shaker here," Chin goes on.

"You could almost call him—well, I dunno—vice president of Purgatory."

"I thought QT Brass was second in charge."

"Well, on paper. But paper doesn't always tell the full story, does it, sir?"

Justus is starting to think that this murder investigation—the first case of any importance that he's supervised since arriving in Purgatory—has suddenly become bigger than he ever expected. And bigger, for that matter, than he feels capable of dealing with. But by necessity he swallows his misgivings.

"So what do you think, sir?" Chin asks. "Still reckon it might've been an accident?"

Justus sighs. "Just secure the scene properly. And get those farmhands in. And Forensics. And I want the names of everyone who works on this goat farm—make that the whole Agri-Plex. In fact, anyone who's come *near* this place in the past month. And anyone in Purgatory with a history in explosives manufacturing—even if it's just firecrackers."

Chin grins. "Sure thing, sir. You know, can I say something?"

"Say it."

"I sure like the way you operate, sir. There's no bullshit with you."

Justus thinks Chin is starting to sound like that fan-club reporter from the *Tablet*. "Just get to work," he says, vaguely annoyed.

When Chin departs Justus takes another look at this weird goat farm on the far side of the Moon: The dead bodies. The cops glancing his way. The quivering photographer. The goats shooting around like popcorn.

And it's hard not to get the feeling that something isn't right. But Justus has never trusted anything as unreliable as feelings, so he heads back to Battaglia to ask more questions.

07

NSOFAR AS JEAN-PIERRE PLAISANCE lives on the Moon, he
too is a lunatic. He's also a killer. In his hometown of Menton
he once killed two sailors during a drunken bar fight. In those
days Plaisance was a huge man, a bodybuilder who'd served for
three years in the Foreign Legion. He was nicknamed the Valet de
Carreau—the Jack of Diamonds—because his torso was covered in
diamond-shaped tattoos. Naked, he still looks like a harlequin.

But Plaisance was not considered dangerous enough to earn
an OWIP igloo in Gagarin Crater. In fact, he was not considered
very dangerous at all. At his murder trial in Nice the presiding
judge acknowledged the sincerity of his remorse, accepted that he
was under the influence of alcohol when he committed the crime,
and even agreed that he had been needlessly provoked by the sailors. So when it came to the sentence the same judge, being something of a self-appointed recruiter for CNES (the French space

agency), suggested that Plaisance's skills as an electrician made him an excellent candidate to serve out his time on the Moon.

In the last six months of his fourteen-year term—seven years had been deducted for good behavior—Plaisance was with two other prisoners in Korolev Crater, signposting hazards with beacons and reflectors, when an especially powerful wave of galactic radiation from the Kuiper Belt struck Farside, by coincidence on a day when the visual warning systems were malfunctioning. Though they felt nothing other than a vague queasiness, and saw nothing apart from bright flashes at the corners of their eyes, the three men were as good as dead. Three hundred rems of radiation blasted through their bodies in one minute—the equivalent of ten thousand simultaneous chest X-rays.

Of course they were closely monitored afterward, given the best available medication, and most of their major tumors were eradicated as soon as possible. But the cell-structure damage was just too extensive: Plaisance's two colleagues from that fateful day, three years ago, have already died. Plaisance himself is gaunt, hairless, half his former size, and has less than four months to live.

But he is not bitter. He doesn't blame the system. He doesn't blame the Moon. He certainly doesn't blame God. And he continues to work as an electrical maintenance man. Because he doesn't know what else to do. Because it's better than brooding. In fact, Plaisance plans to keep working right up until the day of his death, and figures he will one day perish all by himself, somewhere out there on the lunar surface. And when that moment comes he plans to muster his last reserves of strength to crack open his spacesuit and release his soul to the heavens—hoping desperately that he's redeemed himself enough, in the eyes of the Lord, that the offering is not spurned.

Currently he lives mainly at the CNES quarters at Schrödinger Base. He also enjoys frequent stopovers at a number of European Space Agency shacks in the southern hemisphere. His job is to repair the substations that transmit power and communications via cables across Farside. He also maintains the first-aid caches that border the maintenance roads; if necessary, he will perform work on the radar arrays as well. At his disposal he has both a pressurized vehicle for long-range traverses and an "open-air" LRV for shorter journeys. He prefers the LRV because it spares him the hassle of airlock procedures.

Plaisance has presently set out from Shack 12B at Lampland with a full toolbox, a heavy load of photovoltaic cells, half a dozen cold clamps, and a supply of liquid nitrogen. It seems yesterday's solar flare, not unlike the burst of galactic radiation that rewrote his destiny, has done more damage to Farside's fiber-optic-cable grid than anyone predicted. Power in some quadrants is down. The north-south comm line is out of action completely. Reflectometers at Mons Malapert have pinned the probable damage to within 450 kilometers, so Plaisance's job is to isolate the problem further and make the appropriate repairs. He suspects the junction boxes at Pirquet Crater—more exposed and out of date than practically anywhere else on the Moon—and figures he can make it there in four hours, perform a diagnostic, take the appropriate actions, then sidetrack to Shack 13A for replenishment and vehicle recharging.

Plaisance is an exceptional LRV driver. He is equally at home on hard-packed roads, unofficial trails, or—as now—naked lunar surface. He whisks across dust and stones and fragmented rock. He races up and down slopes. He trundles across cracks and craterlets. Sometimes the LRV soars into the air like a dune buggy. Sometimes its wire-mesh wheels churn out rooster tails of dust. Occasionally, scything down slopes, he changes direction dramatically just as the vehicle seems certain to flip over. In short, he can make the LRV do things that would have less experienced drivers spinning out of control or plunging into craters. He can drive at speeds that would have other people—particularly visitors from Earth, unused to the extreme clarity of vision and absence of air resistance—absolutely terrified. And he loves it. Because it gives him a sense of value. And because it offers a further feeling of redemption.

The sun is currently low and unmoving on the western horizon. The shadows are long and remorselessly black. This makes even the smallest pebble visible but can also conceal dangerous fissures and sometimes even pits. Plaisance knows this territory better than anyone, but even so he has his relevant senses—visual and instinctive—on highest alert.

Then he spots something. One of his special skills, acquired unconsciously over his years on the Moon, is his ability to read the terrain like a native tracker. This used to be child's play: The dust on the lunar surface was predominantly virginal and any disturbance had a good chance of staying that way indefinitely. But since the advent of human colonization the great volume of human and vehicular activity has agitated the surface beyond recognition.

Nevertheless a fresh print will be visible for a long time, even if it's on top of existing wheel and tread tracks. And what Plaisance sees now, with his eagle eyes, are the footprints of a human being. More accurately, the *shoe*prints of a human being. Heading northeast, right there on the lunar regolith, like the tracks of a businessman in wet cement.

Except of course that they can't be from a human being. Nobody walks on the lunar surface in business shoes. So Plaisance brakes. He brings the LRV to an abrupt halt, and gets out for closer inspection.

No doubt about it. Shoes, good ones, of above-average size. Judging by the deep impressions, Plaisance guesses that the wearer weighs about 110 terrestrial or 18 lunar kilograms. Such figures are common on the Moon—microgravity allows people to carry excess poundage with aplomb—but Plaisance knows immediately that these prints belong to a robot. They have to. He's aware too that there used to be a highly secretive robotics lab in Seidel Crater, to the southwest. Once, the legend goes, an experimental android escaped from the lab and was found, a week later, lying facedown in JVC (Jules Verne Crater) with a mouthful of dust. There are other stories about another droid, a combat model, that's still hiding out there somewhere, killing anyone who crosses its path. But no one really believes that, because droids don't kill.

Plaisance decides to follow the tracks anyway. He's not sure how far out of his way this will take him, because it's difficult even for him to judge how fresh the prints are, but he enjoys the idea of pursuing something—a fugitive, as it were. He gets back on the LRV and heads northeast, noticing from the tracks that the droid has the measured, slightly springy gait of someone familiar with lunar gravity but not with surface activity. So clearly it's not programmed to be out here on its own. Plaisance pictures himself catching up to it, containing it, deactivating it if necessary, and bundling it over the back of the LRV like a bagged deer.

He follows the tracks for thirty minutes, drifting farther and farther away from the substation, well aware that he's entering the OWIP penal territory. Officially he's supposed to steer clear of this region, because OWIP has its own well-trained teams. But unofficially he's crossed it many times with no complaints, and even helped out on a few emergency repair jobs, without ever meeting one of the prisoners.

Soon he arrives at the first igloo. The droid's footprints veer off to its entrance. But when Plaisance gets off the LRV he sees that there are no lights on in the igloo, inside or out. The solar panels seem to have been shattered by micrometeorite strikes and haven't been replaced. And the v-screen, by which it's possible to look inside if you know the right codes, is missing. To Plaisance this signals only one thing: This particular habitat hasn't been occupied for years. The occupant probably passed away and hasn't been replaced. Officially the OWIP program will perish with the last remaining prisoner.

The droid's tracks continue northeast—as if, failing to find anyone home, he moved on. And suddenly Plaisance is struck by a sense of dread, a metallic flavor in his mouth, not unlike that which he experienced when he was zapped by the cosmic flux.

Unconsciously, he increases his speed.

A few kilometers farther on, another igloo appears. And again, the droid's footprints swerve toward the entrance. But this time the exterior lights are blinking. It's an alarm—someone entered or departed without punching in the right codes. In normal circumstances an alert would now be traveling, via cable, to the OWIP base. The OWIP team would be on their way to investigate. But with the comm line down, no alerts are getting through.

Plaisance is all on his own.

He gets off the LRV and surveys the entrance. The airlock doors, all of them, are open. And light is shining inside. Plaisance has no authority to investigate further, but the circumstances are unique. There might be a human being still in there. Perhaps someone who's found refuge from the vacuum and urgently needs assistance. So Plaisance decides, with a strange sense of satisfaction, that he has no choice. He switches on his helmet light, just in case, and heads inside.

He's not far past the airlock when he sees the victim. Plaisance has seen dead bodies before, many of them, but this is something else entirely.

He only guesses the corpse is male because of the body shape, and because of some of the decorations in the room. The head has been struck so repeatedly that it's just a ball of blood and bone. The body itself is slumped into a chair, arms akimbo, almost as if it's been made up postmortem to appear even more grotesque. There's a wrench on a nearby benchtop with blood and hair still attached to it. A reddened towel is on the floor, as if the killer wiped his hands after the execution. And on the table an empty coffee cup, as if he'd enjoyed a drink before departing.

Plaisance stares at it all for so long that it's a surprise to him when he hears his own accelerated breathing. And feels his heart crashing against his ribs. And his spacesuit clamping around him. So he backs out of the igloo. He emerges as if from a trance. He looks out across the great crater, at the line of shoeprints heading east into the shadows. He still finds it hard to believe that a robot has killed a human being—but how can it be denied?

So is the droid an assassin? A fugitive? Have its control centers been blown by the solar flare?

Whatever the case, Plaisance makes another decision immediately. He will keep tracking the android, regardless of how far it takes him out of his way, and irrespective of how dangerous it becomes to his own life. He will stop the droid, even if it kills him. And he will earn redemption.

If he were able to do so, he would kiss the Saint Christopher medal that hangs around his neck. As it is, he just heads back to the LRV, trembling with determination.

08

CHIEF LANCE "JABBA" BUCHANAN is a hippo. On Earth he'd be one of those people who have to be lifted out of bed with a crane. He might even be dead. But on the Moon he weighs not much more than the average terrestrial ten-year-old. So he can indulge his major passion—eating—without inhibition. And his particular passion now is for Moonballs®—sugar-dusted golf ball–sized spheres of white chocolate filled with coffee syrup. He has a large bowl of them at the side of his desk and he keeps popping them in his mouth like a barfly topping up on beer nuts. Pausing only to balance the dose with a clot-busting tablet or blood-thinning superpill. That's the thing about corrective medication, Justus thinks idly—just as often as it solves the problem it encourages the excess.

"Forensics tells me they delivered a report," Buchanan says between munches.

"That's correct."

"What'd it say?"

"They didn't tell you?"

"This is your case, not mine." Buchanan, who's wearing more braid on his uniform than a Central African despot, offers a wafer-thin smile that's supposed to be reassuring.

Justus shrugs. "A fertilizer bomb," he says. "Ammonium nitrate mixed with propane. A crude detonator, radio activated."

"Radio?"

"Uh-huh."

"That itself is against the law."

"Apparently so. In any case, it tells us that the killer knew when the victims were in the right place. Exactly the right place—practically on top of the bomb itself. So he was within line of sight. Or he had the victims bugged."

"So we're talkin' assassination here?"

"Someone knew Professor Decker's general itinerary, that's for sure. But it turns out that itinerary wasn't exactly a secret—it was widely advertised that he was going to be christening that goat farm."

"You sure it was Decker they were after?"

"Not at all. And I don't make assumptions. But I learned in Homicide that it saves time to start with the most likely possibilities, and work backward from there."

Buchanan grunts. "Well, you just gotta excuse me for being surprised, that's all—about Decker, I mean."

"Why?"

"Because he was a sweet guy. Dedicated to his job. To Purgatory. And clean as a coat of paint. Everyone loved him."

"So I've been told," says Justus. "But he must've done something wrong in the past, surely? To be here in the first place?"

Buchanan, whose skin is as tight as an overinflated balloon, manages a frown. "What—you don't think this is somethin' to do with his days on Earth, do ya?"

"Well, from what I understand assassins have been sent from Earth before to square up for things done years ago, right?"

"Yeah, but we got systems in place now—that sorta thing never happens anymore."

"Still . . ."

"And anyway," Buchanan goes on, "Decker's crime wasn't the sort that makes enemies. Wanna know what he did? Back on Earth?"

"Not really."

"He fucked a thirteen-year-old student. Hell, half the world is doing that. And the kid wasn't even complainin'—thought Decker was dynamite, in fact. So does that sound to you like the sort of person who'd be sendin' assassins to the Moon? Decades later?"

The way he speaks so dismissively of statutory rape makes Justus wonder what Buchanan's own crime was. But it's all too easy to imagine the man in league with drug smugglers in El Paso. Or beating up hookers in Baton Rouge. Or feeding dead bodies to alligators in the Everglades. So Justus drives the thought from his mind. "Granted," he says, "it's just one of many possibilities. But I'm new to Purgatory, remember. In fact, it's one of the reasons I seem to be popular here."

Buchanan mellows a little. "Damn straight," he says, reaching into his jar. "And everyone says you're doin' a helluva job. Helluva job. Everyone."

"Good to hear it."

"I'm just tryin' to help, that's all. I don't wanna be steerin' you in any directions, y'understand?"

"Of course."

"So what's your theory?" Buchanan flips another Moonball® into his mouth.

"Well, it looks like a professional job, I can say that much. Fertilizer bombs might be crude, but the elements need to be mixed in precise quantities. Very precise quantities. And this bomb was particularly effective."

"So we're talkin' an explosives expert?"

"Unfortunately. And I'm led to believe there's no end of people in Purgatory who match that profile."

"'Course. We got a lotta troublemakers here."

"Former terrorists, in fact."

"That's right—if they had the right skills, they used to be welcomed here. In the old days."

"And naturally they might have passed on their skills."

"Well, this place used to be a haven for scum. You couldn't get citizenship here unless you were escaping a serious jail term—it made sure you wouldn't get cold feet and run home to Mommy."

Justus thinks that Buchanan, like a lot of those in Purgatory, seems inordinately proud of this fact, sort of like those Australians proud of their convict heritage. Except that in this case the so-called "scum" is well-and-truly alive—and thriving.

"Bottom line is, I've got a huge cast of suspects."

"You'll get used to it," Buchanan says. "Any leads from the Goat House, by the way? The dirt rakers who work there?"

"A lot of the processes are automated. Some of the tasks are performed by robots. Security is almost nonexistent. There are no surveillance cameras—I guess I'll get used to that too. The farmhands wear masks and swear they know nothing. There's no unaccounted-for DNA at the scene. On Earth I'm pretty sure I'd have something by now. Here, it might take more time."

"Thought of the political angle?"

"Of course. Except that—you said it yourself—Professor Decker was popular. And into agriculture. Food supply. Recycling. He doesn't seem the sort of target, assuming he was the target, for a political assassination."

"He was virtually Fletcher Brass's right-hand man."

"*Was*," Justus says. "From what I understand, he was losing prestige."

"Who told you that?"

"It's what I heard."

"Well, that's baloney. Brass had a lot of faith in Decker. Thought he was the most honest man in Purgatory. He liked fucking kids, yeah, but so what?"

"Decker was seventy-nine years old."

"Seventy-nine years *young*," Buchanan says. "Seventy-nine ain't old around here."

Justus is bemused by Buchanan's insistence—he's become so passionate that he's briefly not even munching on a Moonball®. "Well, if it's a political assassination then we're in very deep waters. And it also leaves me somewhat out of my depth."

"How so?"

"Well, I'm no more than passingly familiar with the political machinations in Purgatory. I thought, for instance, that Fletcher Brass was popular here."

"Who said he wasn't?"

"You just did—by suggesting that Decker was killed owing to his association with him."

Buchanan uncaps one of his pill bottles. "Well," he says, "I only mean that Brass is a figurehead, that's all—it's the system that's rotten. And to anarchists the system is *always* rotten."

"So Brass himself *is* popular?"

"'Popular' is a bit much. But he's feared. Which is better than being popular."

To Justus it sounds like one of Brass's own laws. "So you wouldn't rule out an assassination, then? Or a terrorist attack?"

Buchanan gulps down his pills. "Well, things are changing here in Purgatory, that's a fact. Brass is leaving for his Mars trip soon—you must've heard of that. And various factions are swirlin' around, lookin' for a piece of the action. While the cat's away, you might say."

"Was Decker in line to take over in Brass's absence?"

"'Course he was. Few others too."

"QT Brass?"

Now Buchanan sniggers. "You really don't know much about this place, do you, Lieutenant?"

"I'm all ears."

"Well, let's just say Fletcher Brass and his daughter don't exactly toast marshmallows together. They cozy up for the cameras, but behind the scenes little QT is stirrin' the pot. Brewin' up something, that's for sure. Something that tastes good only to her. And the schemers in her club."

Justus is surprised by Buchanan's open disdain. "So you think QT Brass might be behind all this?"

"Hey, I didn't say that. Fact is, I got no fuckin' clue. But that's why you're perfect for this investigation. You got no loyalties one way or another, right?"

"I guess so."

"'Course you don't. By the way, if you need any more help—personnel-wise—you just let me know."

Justus shakes his head. "I like the size of my team as it is. And I'm still learning to trust them. Or not trust them, as the case may be."

Buchanan raises an eyebrow. "Not sayin' you've had trouble, are ya?"

Justus doesn't want to say it, but there are some on his team who seem too enthusiastic. Too cooperative. And then there are others who aren't cooperative at all, who give him cutting glances. There's one guy in particular, a blubber-lipped Russian officer called Grigory Kalganov, who looks like he could easily stab Justus in the back—or anywhere else.

"No more than on Earth," Justus says finally—which is more or less true.

Buchanan smirks. "You now, what you really wanna do is interview Fletcher Brass—the Patriarch himself. That'll give you a better picture of the landscape."

"I intend to."

"Just don't expect a magic carpet ride—he's a busy man."

"I keep hearing that."

"Then again, I guess he'll be more than happy to help you out, considering his fondness for Decker. And you probably should speak to QT Brass as well—just let us know and we'll arrange it. She's slippery as an eel."

"I'm not frightened of eels."

Buchanan makes an approving noise. "You know, this could be a big chance for you, Lieutenant. Do a good job here, you could find yourself movin' up the ladder quicker than you ever dreamed of. I'm not gonna be at this desk forever, you know. In fact, I've been thinking of handin' in my badge for some time now."

Justus blinks. "I'm sorry, Chief—are you talking about *me*? As a possible successor to you?"

"Why not?" Buchanan says. "You're a clean slate, ain't you? Brass is gonna like that. And I happen to know he rewards people who get results. So who knows? Maybe you arrived here at exactly the right time. And maybe this murder is exactly what you need to get yourself noticed."

"I don't work for personal advancement."

"Yeah, yeah, I understand."

"And I don't use murder cases for that purpose."

"Yeah, yeah, 'course." Buchanan coughs and changes the subject. "You know, I'm havin' a barbeque at my place in a few days—genuine beef and pork too, none of that synthetic stuff. Why not come 'round? It'd be a good chance to meet the guys who might soon be answerin' to you."

"Is that an order?"

"Hell no, it's an invitation."

Justus shrugs. "Well, I'm afraid I'll have to get back to you on that. With a case of this complexity, I might be too busy for a barbeque."

Buchanan pauses for a second, his eyes dancing over Justus, as if he can't work out how to react. Then he launches into a laugh so hard the whole desk—the whole *room*—shakes. "Jesus, man, you're one outta the box! Too busy for a barbeque! Wait till I tell the boys that!" He reaches into his bowl of treats and holds one out across the desk. "Moonball®?"

Justus shakes his head.

09

ALL THOSE ANCIENT CIVILIZATIONS that worshipped the Moon, all those early science-fiction writers who romanticized it, and all those pioneering astronomers who studied it—none of them ever clapped an eye on Farside. No one, not a soul, even knew what it looked like until a Soviet satellite pulsed back a few blurred images in 1959. And what these images showed, in a nutshell, were fewer dust seas and more craters. No volcanoes, no water, no signs of habitation—just a hideous, pockmarked face; one that, in truth, looked better in the dark. And that's why "the Dark Side," though technically a misnomer, is such an apt name. Not because Farside gets less sunlight than Nearside—it doesn't. Not because it has more dark spots than Nearside—in fact, its percentage of volcanic maria is considerably smaller. And certainly not because it's been a secret location for Cold War military bases, spaceship landing zones, alien cities, or anything else dreamed up by the conspiracy-minded.

No, it's "the Dark Side" because it looks not upon the glorious orb of the home planet but upon the icy emptiness of space. Because it's less populated, less charted, and less studied. Because it's appreciably more dangerous. Because no satellites or shuttles are allowed to fly over it. Because it's *luna incommunicado*—in permanent radio blackout. And because it's been home, for twenty years, to Purgatory and Fletcher Brass.

The droid knows nothing of this. The droid does not care. The droid is walking at a considerable pace, something between a lope and a skip, toward the terraced rim of Gagarin Crater. The crater was formed by an asteroid impact three billion years ago and later filled with shock-melted rock, debris, lava flows, and meteor dust. Then over countless millennia the surface was baked, frozen, irradiated, and sandblasted by micrometeorite impacts into a fine and deeply abrasive powder—the moondust upon which the droid now walks.

Having left about 150 kilometers of tracks in the dust of this crater, and about twice as many in the dust farther south, the droid calculates that at his current pace—with most of his servomotors, actuators, and traducers running simultaneously—he will need to refuel on sugar and alcohol every 225 kilometers. And judging by the position of the sun—it's holding at about ten degrees above the horizon—he's certain to be traveling in darkness well before he reaches Purgatory. Meaning the temperature will plummet significantly. A thermostat will of course activate his internal heating systems, but the extremes of hot and cold on the Moon are twice as severe as anything on Earth. And such jarring shifts—a hundred degrees in seconds—can, if not precisely counterbalanced, crack plastic, warp metal, shatter ceramic. They can immobilize robots, blow their circuits. They can make them do strange things.

The droid has fail-safe systems, but he's not confident they can be trusted in such conditions. So he's decided that he would be much better off in an LRV. A vehicle like that would get him to Purgatory much faster and more efficiently. He actually spotted one in the distance well before he entered Gagarin Crater, but it was speeding in the opposite direction and he had no idea, at that stage, just how far away his destination would be. Nevertheless he figures he will come across a similar vehicle eventually—there's sufficient human activity on Farside to make it inevitable—and this time he will not let it get away.

As he advances toward the ringwall he examines its terraced heights. Looking for openings. Looking for the lowest elevation, for the most economical route to get over it. A human being in such a situation would find the process strangely stimulating. But the droid does not find it stimulating at all. To the droid it is merely a calculation designed to get him as quickly as possible to his destination. And the destination, for such a self-motivated achiever, is all that matters.

Find Oz. And be the Wizard.

See El Dorado. Take El Dorado. Find another El Dorado.

The droid cares nothing for happiness. To the droid, expressions of happiness are merely a means of conveying superiority. Or domination. Or revenge. But he has a sizable memory. Most of it has recently been erased, true, but there remain tiny vestiges of past experience buried deep in his logic circuits and his sensorium. And if he were programmed to reflect on these experiences, he might find some of them—living in a city, serving a man, conferring with other droids—curiously satisfying.

But all that's just a splutter of electrons now. Of much greater relevance are his recent experiences, none more than thirty-six hours old, of ascending various crater rims southeast of Gagarin.

It was in performing these little actions, thanks to his inbuilt positive and negative reinforcement algorithms, that he acquired the skill of calculating time/efficiency ratios in lunar climbing to within a few points of error. And what his current survey of the talus slopes in front of him has determined is that the most favorable point has an elevation of approximately 950 meters and will take him approximately half an hour to scale. Considerable, no doubt—greater than anything he has attempted so far—but there's not much he can do to avoid it. Other than go significantly out of his way—and that would be even more draining on his power reserves. So he negotiates the quickest path through some scree and springs his way diagonally to the first terrace, then to the second terrace, and with only a few slips and slides, unleashing mini-avalanches of slow-moving dust, he reaches the crest of the crater rim in a little over twenty-nine minutes—almost exactly as he calculated.

He stands for a moment at this lofty height, overlooking Gagarin's enormous ejecta blanket—rocks and sand thrown far and wide by the asteroid impact—and sees many more obstacles ahead. Many more deeply shadowed craters and craterlets. But he will not be daunted. He will not wilt. He will *never* shy away from a challenge. As always, he has a sacred verse or two to guide him:

The greater the odds, the sweeter the victory.

And:

Losers make hurdles. Winners hurdle them.

Then, just as he is about to set off, he spots something. It's actually beyond the horizon, at about three and a half kilometers and thirty degrees northwest. A puff of lunar dust rising from the darkness and sparkling in the sunlight. It can't be naturally levitating, not at this time of day, so there's human activity down there. A few scientists, perhaps. An expeditionary team.

But to the droid it represents the very opportunity he was counting on. The possibility of finding more fuel—or something even better.

He buttons his jacket, deploys his shit-eating smile, and begins his descent.

10

THERE'S A POPULAR STORY about Fletcher Brass.

It goes back to the days when he was lobbying aggressively for government contracts to mine the Moon's resources. At the time he was repeatedly met with nothing but red tape and skepticism: *Who is this jerk, this entrepreneurial clown? He's claiming he can land privately funded spacecraft on the Moon? And he might already have done so? The man's off his nut!*

Then one day the Washington bureaucrat in charge of lunar development gets two parcels delivered by courier. The sender's name is Fletcher Brass. The bureaucrat finishes his paperwork, blows his nose, and opens the first of the parcels. Inside he finds two golf balls mounted in crystal. So he scratches his head and opens the second parcel. And finds the Stars and Stripes, neatly folded in a velvet-lined case. But still he doesn't know what to make of it all. So he repackages everything and puts it aside, intending to return it to sender, or maybe give it all to one of his kids. Then he gets a phone call.

"Did you get my presents?"

"Who's speaking, please?"

"It's Fletcher Brass." From the calypso music in the background he seems to be calling from somewhere tropical.

"Fletcher Brass." The bureaucrat suppresses his annoyance. "What can I do for you, Mr. Brass?"

"You can thank me, for a start."

"Thank you?"

"For those gifts you just received. You can't say I didn't put in some effort."

"Well, we already have enough flags here, thank you."

"Oh really? Do you have a flag as valuable as that?"

"A flag is a flag."

Brass kind of chuckles. "And the golf balls?"

"I don't play golf, sorry."

"You don't need to play golf to admire those balls. They might be the most valuable balls in the entire solar system."

"Yes, well . . ."

"You just think about it," Brass says. "And call me when you're ready. But in the meantime, it might be advisable to get some insurance—and *quickly*."

So the bureaucrat returns to his paperwork, trying to banish the whole thing from his mind. But then the most ridiculous possibility occurs to him—so ridiculous that he's able to dismiss it almost immediately. Only it won't go away, and keeps buzzing around, to the point that he can't concentrate anymore. So he makes some phone calls, verifies a few things, consults some data—and then, trembling, barely able to speak, he makes a return call to Fletcher Brass.

"How—how did you get them?"

Brass, in the middle of drinking something, chuckles. "I'm not at liberty to disclose that," he says. "But more importantly, do I get the contract?"

"Yes," breathes the bureaucrat, "you get the contract."

Well, that was the story, anyway. When a later expedition found Alan Shepard's golf balls still in the Sea of Tranquility, exactly where the astronaut had belted them in 1971, Brass was able to claim that he'd simply "deposited them back in the scrub by the fairway, as any ethical golfer would do." And when a television crew ventured to the Apollo 11 landing site and discovered a Stars and Stripes that was not quite the pristine specimen Brass had supposedly sent in the velvet-lined case—the fabric was discolored by decades of cosmic rays, thermal cycling, and levitating dust—well, he shrugged that off with another semi-plausible explanation: that the flag had been in such lamentable condition when he'd found it that he'd taken the liberty of giving it a "cosmetic cleanup" before sending it on to Washington. And naturally it had "gotten a little dirty again" since he put it back in place.

Justus himself doesn't give the story much credence. He knows that interesting anecdotes are one of the most corruptible currencies in the world. So Justus has seen the flag-and-golf-ball story, in all its dubious glory, in Brass's autobiographies *Shining Brass* and *The Brass Age*, in the authorized biographies *Polished Brass* and *Gleaming Brass*, and even in the billion-dollar biopic *Brass*—the four-hour feature film shot on Purgatory soundstages and starring, in the title role, the wife-murdering Welsh thespian Lionel Haynes (happy to undergo extensive cosmetic surgery to more closely resemble the man who was offering him refuge).

Needless to say, the anecdote does not appear in the unauthorized biographies—all those muckraking testimonies written by bitter journalists, ex-wives, and disaffected business partners: *Balls of Brass, Tarnished Brass, Corroded Brass,* and so on. In fact, the disparity between the official and unofficial versions would leave readers struggling to work out how much is real and what is wholesale fabrication.

The authorized versions usually begin with Fletcher Brass, the whiz-kid seventeen-year-old, going public with his very first business venture—carbonated coconut-milk drinks in distinctive brass-colored cans. The unauthorized versions meanwhile claim to prove, with documented evidence, that Brass's venture capitalist father actually underwrote the whole business as a tax dodge, that its supposed success was wildly exaggerated anyway, and that the original recipes were stolen from a struggling Filipino soft-drink manufacturer (which subsequently sued and settled out of court).

The authorized versions continue by covering Brass's other early success stories: aquafarms, holo-movies, luxury hotels, ultrasonic jets, extravagantly retro airships, brass-fitted cruise ships. The unauthorized versions focus instead on his unpleasant habit of bootstrapping fledgling companies with poorly paid, geed-up employees, reaping a lot of early publicity with bold statements and dazzling stunts, and then selling off the entire enterprise at a huge profit to some starry-eyed conglomerate—often the same rival company he'd mercilessly ridiculed on the way up.

The authorized versions portray him as a fearless adventurer and thrill seeker who somehow found enough time to also be a champion of various social issues, a major sponsor of environmental campaigns, and a generous contributor to popular charities. The unauthorized versions insist that everything, all those eye-catching stunts and altruistic charity drives, were shamelessly contrived for publicity purposes alone, and were no match for all the rampant price-fixing, insider trading, jury tampering, industrial espionage, and bribery of public officials.

The authorized versions find little space for any of Brass's romantic interests other than his second wife—the one who died in a boating accident—while the unauthorized versions devote pages and pages to his affairs with bikini models, porn stars, and other men's wives.

The authorized versions cover "The Brass Code," his notorious twenty-page list of business ethics and philosophies, by listing only the more socially acceptable entries: *If the river bends, think about bending the river*; *Acknowledge when you're beaten, and never be beaten again*; *If you fall into a hole, turn it into a strategy*. The unauthorized versions, meanwhile, make great hay of Brass's secret code, the one shared with only his most trusted, high-ranking deputies: *If some one fucks you over, fuck them under*; *Shareholders are like nuns just begging to be screwed*; *You can't make an omelette without cracking a few skulls*.

The authorized versions are especially rhapsodic when it comes to Brass's contributions to lunar development, crediting him with practically everything: the first m-train, the first solar arrays, the first operational mines, the first fiber-optic cables, the first emergency-supply depots, the first reliable ground maps, the first permanent settlements. The unauthorized versions, while grudgingly admitting that his place in lunar history is assured, contend that all these efforts, despite Brass's convenient amnesia, were underwritten by generous grants, tax breaks, mining rights, and incentive schemes.

The authorized versions claim that Brass was forced to find refuge on Farside owing to an outrageous campaign of vilification generated by rival businessmen with inordinate media influence. The unauthorized versions are more specific, identifying one scandal in particular that brought him down: three tons of spent rods from a nuclear power station, fired into space by one of Brass's underfinanced waste-disposal companies, fell back to Earth—into the middle of the Amazon basin, no less—leaving thousands of acres of virgin rainforest irradiated, rare species poisoned and mutated, and two thousand natives dead.

The authorized versions end with Fletcher Brass as a triumphant exile, presiding over a unique and vibrant fiefdom; the biopic fades out with him sitting imperiously in a brass throne, wordlessly admiring the great lunar metropolis he's built from the ground up. The unauthorized versions are content to spend their final chapters covering Purgatory's lawlessness and corruption, the gang wars, the summary executions, the internecine conflicts, and the sordid rumors of underhanded deals with various terrestrial governments.

Nevertheless, it's the film's fade-out—the empire builder, good or bad—that's the last image of Brass that anyone remembers. It's certainly the image Brass himself designed to linger. There was a spectacularly unsuccessful attempt to kidnap him shortly after the movie's release—as fabricated as any of his world-record attempts, if the cynics are right—which seemed to justify his withdrawal from the limelight while consolidating his new reputation as a recluse. It isn't that he's completely unseen— he still appears at press conferences and public spectacles every now and then, waving Mao-like to the multitudes—but the secrecy proved enough to magnify the myth, to make him even more larger-than-life, and to generate a few more wild conspiracy theories along the way.

Dynamic, heroic, visionary, inspiring, indefatigable, tragically misunderstood, and maliciously envied? Or narcissistic, deluded, irresponsible, grandiose, psychotically greedy, and strangely tragic?

Justus doesn't know. He read as much about Brass as he could before coming to Purgatory but he doesn't necessarily believe any of it. So he doesn't know if Brass is a charming rogue or a borderline psychopath. Nor does he discount the possibility that, in over twenty years of living on the Moon, the man has completely changed—for better or worse.

Justus tries not to be influenced by vested interests. He always makes up his own mind. And that's what he's intending to do, right now, as he prepares to meet Fletcher Brass for the first time.

11

JUSTUS HAS CERTAINLY BEEN in the presence of famous people before: singers, movie stars, talk-show hosts, billionaires, mega-chefs, celebrity gangsters. Born performers, most of them. People who can charm and manipulate effortlessly, without even seeming to try. Because they know instinctively how to sell a package, to project an aura, to seem like creatures from some distant planet where people don't perspire or get pimples.

Fletcher Brass is like that. Presently he's holding a press conference on the progress of his imminent voyage to Mars. Behind him is a shimmering photomural showing images of the Red Planet, his Purgatorial rocket base, and his huge space vehicle, *Prospector II*. Owing to the microgravity and lack of atmosphere it's much cheaper and more efficient to launch spacecraft from the Moon than it is from Earth, and this is a point that he keeps hammering home, either to address queries about the excessive costs or just to rub it in the faces of his terrestrial enemies.

"People ask why private enterprise is doing this, and not some government space agency," he says smoothly. "And I just remind them of the year 1903. It was in that year that Dr. Samuel Langley, head of the Smithsonian Institution, was awarded fifty thousand taxpayer dollars—a huge sum at the time—to develop and construct a steam-powered aircraft called the aerodrome. Perhaps you've never heard of it. Perhaps you've never heard of Dr. Langley either. But that's no reason to be ashamed. You haven't heard of him for a very good reason—because the aerodrome crashed into the Potomac and broke apart in its test phase. Not once but *twice*. The whole aircraft—the whole program—was a complete fiasco. And, like so many other government-funded projects, it was quickly and quietly scrapped."

Brass offers a patronizing little smirk.

"But that's not why 1903 is so famous. It's famous because of what happened a few hundred miles farther south, at Kitty Hawk in North Carolina. It was there that a couple of *self-financed* and *self-motivated* brothers, blissfully free of nosy bureaucrats and government grants, designed and constructed their *own* experimental aircraft. For under *one thousand dollars*. And *their* aircraft, ladies and gentlemen, you probably *do* remember. And their names you *certainly* remember. For their aircraft was called the Flyer. And their names were Orville and Wilbur Wright."

Smiles all around. There's a couple of reporters there—Justus recognizes Nat U. Reilly—and they're beaming like parents at a school play. But Justus himself is expressionless: He's read the same speech, more or less word for word, in one of Brass's autobiographies. And he wonders how the man himself, speaking in a curious mid-Atlantic accent, manages to make it all sound so fresh and sincere.

"Ladies and gentlemen"—Brass is all senatorial now—"it's once again time for self-motivated and self-financed geniuses to take us where governments fear to tread. It's time for us to establish permanent human settlements on Mars, just as we did so many years ago on the Moon. It's time for practical infrastructure—not just probes, not just robots, and not just exploratory journeys. It's time to do something *unequivocal*. And let nobody underestimate the huge challenges—or for that matter the huge expenses—ahead of us. But then again I think that I, more than anyone else, have earned the right to quote Machiavelli"—laughter from Reilly and the others—"'Make no small plans, for they have not the power to stir men's blood.'"

Brass, who's either seventy-two or seventy-five, depending on the source, is wearing a superbly tailored navy-blue suit with brass-colored pinstripes. His brass-tinted hair—still thick as bear's fur—is swept back in a rolling wave. His skin is so smooth, tanned, and radiant that it shimmers like copper. And his eyes, the irises of which have been famously implanted with brass flecks, look lynx-like, mesmerizing. Even now, as his features contort into a look of well-timed dismay.

"But you know, I hear there are *still* people who are questioning the expenses of this voyage. Who still think that I'm hostage to irrational dreams or delusions—after all these years!" Sympathetic sniggers. "And you know what I remember when I hear that? I just remember all the money I've personally funneled into the search for extraterrestrial intelligence. All those radiometers, spectrometers, reflectometers, all those interferometry arrays, poking into every corner of the cosmos, every sun, planet, moon, and black hole, hunting for any sort of signal, electromagnetic, infrared, microwave, anything that suggests a flicker of intelligent life, a scent of civilization, the purr of a motor—anything at all! Millions, I've spent on those searches—*billions*! And what have we come up with after all this time? After all that investment? Nothing! Not a thing! *Not a goddamned thing!*"

Brass shakes his head, as if he's only just started thinking about it.

"So when the critics sneered at me and said *how's that, Mr. Brass, don't you feel a little foolish now*—well, for a moment I almost agreed with them. Yes, I think I was on the verge of feeling a little embarrassed. But then I remembered the silence. From outer space, I mean—the absolute silence. And the *meaning* of that silence. And do you know what I was able to say? Do you know how I was able to answer all those naysayers? All those cynics and skeptics who told me I'd wasted a fortune?"

Justus has read this part too, and he just watches, fascinated by the performance.

"I said *hell no*," Brass goes on, "I'm not ashamed. I don't regret one minute, *not one goddamned cent*, that I've spent on those radar arrays. And do you know why? *Do you know why?* Because you say there's been no answer. Nothing, you say, has come from *out there*. But you're wrong, you're a million times wrong. Because let me tell you. *Silence* came from out there. And the silence *is* the answer. *The silence is the answer*. Do you see it? The undeniable logic, the peerless beauty of it all?"

Brass lets the silence in the room reign for a few moments, as if to underline his point, and then rams the point home:

"*We* are the only intelligent life in the universe. The human race! There's no one and nothing else! Not a thing! Just us! And it's a *genuine miracle* that we've gotten as far as we have! Because when you consider all the *millions* of ways there are for life to end on a planet—comets, radiation bursts, self-destruction—it's *absolutely incredible* that we're still alive. We're actually *overdue* for a cataclysmic event, something that wipes out all intelligent life on Earth! And yet here we still are, so content and overconfident, trying to ignore that terrifying truth—that it's all up to us. Everything! There's no one here to guide us. We're absolutely alone! But do you understand how awesome that message is? How profound? How unique, majestic, beautiful, how *precious* we are? And how important it is to populate other planets? To spread our species? *To save us all from annihilation?*"

Brass has a feverish, evangelical tremble in his voice now that no doubt plays very well on television. But Justus can't help remembering a Brass biography—one of the unauthorized ones—which spoke of his "expedient eleventh-hour appropriation of noble causes," his "lamentable real-world record on environmental issues" and his "inexhaustible capacity to dress up his profit- and ego-driven projects as altruistic offerings to the altar of human progress."

But presently the man himself, having reached his pinnacle, is coming down from the heavens on a more self-effacing note.

"Anyway, ladies and gentlemen, have I let my passions run away with me? Have I allowed my 'messiah complex' to take control again?" He looks around, fielding more laughs. "Forgive me, but I think you all know how much I have invested in this subject. In preserving our legacy. In saving our species. It's the one thing that motivates me most. And I can't see any reason to apologize for that. No matter what anyone—*anyone*—says."

He puts peculiar emphasis on that, not that Justus can work out why. And then his personal assistant—an ethereally handsome, statuesque fellow with grey hair, grey suit, and grey eyes, even more color-coordinated than his boss—calls the press conference to an end and everybody files dutifully toward the door. Nobody, not a soul, asks about the morning's Goat House bombing—though Justus concedes that such questions might have been raised before he arrived. And now Brass is coming off the stage and Justus, at a signal from the grey-haired assistant, steps forward.

"Mr. Brass," he says, "I'm Lieutenant Damien Justus of the PPD."

"Lieutenant Justus?" Brass seizes the proffered hand. "Yes, I've heard about you—you're the new appointment to our police department, aren't you? The virgin?"

"If that's what they call them around here."

"I don't mean it to sound disparaging. You're the fresh blood that's been injected into the PPD—how does that sound?"

"Sounds fine to me."

"Well, a bit of fresh blood never goes astray, that's what I always say. And in a police force especially it can be a real shot in the arm. It can have a very *beneficial* effect. So let me assure you you're more than welcome here in Purgatory."

"Well, thank you, Mr. Brass. But I'm not here to talk about myself. I'm currently leading an investigation into—"

"Into the murder of Otto Decker." Brass, disengaging his hand, looks grave all of a sudden.

"You know about that?"

"I was informed just before the press conference. A little later than I would've been in normal circumstances, but—well, I've been unusually busy lately. Care to take a seat?"

"That won't be necessary," Justus says. "This is mainly an introductory visit—I just need to know if you'll be available for future questioning, should the need arise."

"Of course I'm available. You'll need to consult with my

people first"—gesturing to his grey-haired assistant—"but naturally I'll do anything to help. How is it proceeding, by the way?"

"The investigation? It's too early to say."

"You've been to the Goat House?"

"Of course."

"You saw the bodies?"

"I did."

Brass nods grimly. "Otto Decker was a personal friend of mine, you know."

"I've heard that."

"He was practically second in charge here—he had a big future, and an awful lot to live for."

"I've heard that too."

"Yes, well." Up close Brass doesn't seem nearly as magnetic—or tall, or handsome, or makeup-free—as he does onstage. "If you're saying that I personally am under suspicion, then—"

"I'm not saying any such thing, Mr. Brass."

"—then you should know that I'm entirely comfortable with that. I'm not frightened of having anyone rummage through my drawers. That's the way it *should* be. And you should treat everyone here the same. *Everyone.*"

"I intend to."

"Well . . . good."

"Then may I ask a question, Mr. Brass?"

"Certainly."

"Do *you* have ideas about who did it? Any suspicions?"

Brass blows out his cheeks. "Well, I wish I did. But there's a singular demographic here, as you must know. A very wide range of people genetically disposed to crime and acts of rebellion."

"So you think this is an act of rebellion?"

"I shudder to think so, but I can't think of any other reason."

"Then can you think of any reason why anyone should be rebelling right now?"

"I don't think people of a rebellious nature need any sort of reason."

"What about your daughter? Your relationship with her is rather strained, is it not?"

"Who told you that?"

"Just something I heard."

"Well, now, listen here, Lieutenant"—Brass briefly looks ruffled—"just because my daughter and I have had a few spirited disagreements in the past doesn't mean that she'd start doing . . . whatever it is that you think she's doing."

"I didn't say she was doing anything."

"Well . . . just as well."

"And you *did* say I should treat everyone the same."

"Of course."

"So I'm warning you, Mr. Brass: I'll be digging. And I won't hesitate to dig in your backyard. Or your daughter's backyard. Or anywhere else I need to dig. Just as you said I should."

"Well, then"—Brass chuckles—"it sounds like we're in furious agreement, doesn't it?"

"I hope so."

Brass looks Justus up and down with his brass-flecked eyes. "You know, Lieutenant, I already like you. You could go far in Purgatory."

"I've heard that too."

"Really? Seems like you've heard a great deal since you got here."

"I like to keep my ear to the ground."

"Well, keep it there, by all means. I don't need to tell you how important this investigation is to me. Personally, I mean. I don't want to see anyone else going the same way as my good friend Otto Decker."

They shake hands again—a little awkwardly this time—and Brass departs the room as if suddenly eager to get away. And Justus is standing still, wrestling with a sense that something is out of place, when the shadowy, grey-haired assistant steps forward and offers him a brass-bordered card.

"This is the number to call if you wish to speak to Mr. Brass again."

"You're his personal assistant?" Justus asks.

"I prefer the term 'valet,' sir."

"And you're an android?"

The valet doesn't blink. "That is correct, sir."

"Then I'll call if I need to."

"Very well, sir."

As the droid leaves Justus looks down at the name on the card.

LEONARDO GREY

12

O F ALL THE MYSTERIES the Moon continues to harbor—gravitational anomalies, magnetic inconsistencies, curious orange sands, and strange eruptions of vapor—none is more intriguing than its habit of ringing like a bell, sometimes for hours, when it's struck by a meteorite. Notwithstanding the Moonball® advertising campaign that claims it's filled with coffee syrup, no one, not even the most distinguished geologists, is sure what's at the lunar core.

Matthews and Jamieson are not yet distinguished geologists, but they plan to be. The star students of the Department of Geological Sciences at the University of Alaska Anchorage, they are currently in the sixth month of a fully funded field survey of Farside. After so much artificial air, tasteless food, tepid coffee, and endless safety procedures, they are no longer excited about their lunar assignment, but they know that in the future they will treasure every moment of their time spent off-world. Plus they are both even-tempered. They don't panic. They rarely bicker. And they get along extremely well—so well, in fact, they they've become firm friends since the start of the mission; not something that can be said of many scientists who work together on the Moon.

Like all geologists, Matthews and Jamieson have their theories about the lunar core, but their current assignment—like their drill—does not extend quite that far. They're collecting subsurface samples from between the 15th and 30th parallels in Farside's southern hemisphere. Already they've done surveys of De Vries, Bergstrand, Aitken, and Cyrano Craters, amassing an impressive collection of breccias, agglutinates, glasses, and basaltic rock fragments. They applied for entry to Gagarin too, but failed to receive permission from OWIP. So they've settled on the smaller, still-unnamed craters to Gagarin's immediate north. Here, as well as collecting more rock fragments, they've been particularly excited to discover thick deposits of low-calcium pyroxene, which might support the theory that this part of the Moon was once struck by some colossal foreign body, possibly bigger than an asteroid.

Their base is a three-man shelter consisting of an all-purpose room, a hygiene center, a galley, and an airlock. Parts of it are collapsible, and the whole unit can be towed around on the back of their very long range traverse vehicle (VLTV). They also have an unpressurized LRV, but it's twelve years old and prone to breakdowns.

Presently their heating unit is malfunctioning, and they're stripped down to their underwear owing to the oppressive temperature inside the shack. They're looking through a window as their hydraulically operated drill rig—which on Earth would weigh ten thousand kilograms and take an eternity to transport and set up—ejects regolith into the air like an old-fashioned derrick. The dust shoots above the crater rim and shimmers in the sunlight, hanging in the air for minutes, electrostatically charged, before drifting back to the surface. Matthews and Jamieson could watch the process for hours—it's mesmerizing—but not from anywhere other than the safety of their shack. Because lunar dust is evil. It works its way into creases. It abrades metal and erodes seams. If it's inhaled it can lead to mesothelioma-like complications. And Matthews and Jamieson, for all the inherent dangers of their mission, are not risk takers. So they'll wait until the dust has cleared—literally—before venturing outside.

"What's that?" says Matthews, leaning forward.

"What's what?" says Jamieson.

"What the fuck is that?"

Jamieson leans forward too, squinting, wiping moisture from the window. "Jesus Christ . . . what the . . . what the fuck's he doing out there?"

Matthews snorts. "Looks like he's on a fuckin' Sunday stroll."

"It's gotta be some sort of joke."

"It's no joke."

"Then what the . . . ?"

A man, dressed like an old-fashioned FBI agent, is coming laterally down the crater slope. Hopping a little, to save time. An android, clearly. But not like any android Matthews and Jamieson have ever seen—certainly not on the Moon.

He appears to be heading for their base. He's making a detour to avoid the falling dust, but a good deal is still wafting over him. And he's smiling. Smiling goofily, as though he already knows he is being observed.

"Do we let him in?" asks Jamieson.

"We have to, I guess. There are rules."

"The rules relate to human beings—in distress."

"Yeah, but . . ." In truth, Matthews isn't entirely sure of the protocols.

"He might be a pain in the ass."

"Of course he'll be a pain in the ass."

"And what about the dust?"

Matthews thinks for a few seconds, then says firmly, "I'll take care of it."

Now the droid is standing outside, still smiling. And looking as though he has every expectation of being allowed inside.

Matthews punches a button to open the outer airlock doors. The droid steps into the tiny, cubicle-like space. Matthews moves to a microphone.

"Can you hear me?"

The droid, now visible through a small observation window, hesitates—as if surprised by the sound of the voice. "I hear you."

"We don't have much in the way of scrubbers here, and you seem to have picked up a bit of dust."

"That is correct—I have certainly accumulated some dust."

"Then we can't let you inside until you strip down first—do you understand?"

"That is perfectly reasonable," says the droid. "I intend to wash my clothes, in any case."

Matthews and Jamieson glance at each other. Matthews shrugs. Then the droid is disrobing, and the two of them discreetly avert their eyes. It's absurd, of course, but the more lifelike droids can exude a palpable sexuality. It shouldn't be an issue—Jamieson is fashionably asexual, and Matthews only likes women—but this droid is superbly toned, like one of those silicone-skinned love companions that feature so frequently in women's erotic literature.

A green light comes on—the airlock's pressurization is complete. Matthews checks that the droid is ready and then opens the inner airlock door.

The droid, wearing only some hipster briefs—disconcerting in itself, as humans on surface expeditions customarily wear thick, moisture-absorbing undershorts—steps into the shack, trailing the gunpowder stench of lunar dust. He takes a few seconds to survey the room, and eventually his gaze settles on Matthews and Jamieson. If he's surprised—all three of them are in their underwear now—he doesn't betray it.

"A great pleasure to meet you, ladies," he says. "I hope I have not come at an inconvenient time?"

"No," Matthews replies. "We were just preparing to suit up, that's all."

"I see," says the droid, and then appears to think a moment before he asks, "Are you whores?"

Matthews blinks. "We're not whores."

"Are you nuns?"

"We're not nuns either."

"Are you secretaries?"

"We're not secretaries."

"Are you shareholders, then?"

"Shareholders?"

"Do you hold stock in any listed company?"

"Do we—no . . . *no*."

"Than what are you, madam?"

"I'm a geologist. Jamieson here is a geochemist."

"I see."

The droid continues to smile. Standing there in his briefs, like an underwear model. It's all so bizarre that Matthews has to break the tension.

"May I ask where you're from?"

"I come from nowhere, madam. There is only the future."

Matthews and Jamieson exchange glances again. Jamieson speaks up. "Well, where are you going, then?"

"I am going to Oz, madam."

"Oz?"

"That's right. You are the most beautiful woman I have ever seen."

Jamieson chuckles at the absurdity—she's always felt so unglamorous—but at the same time feels instinctively sorry for Matthews. Until the droid adds:

"And you, madam"—turning to Matthews—"I would like to fuck you very much."

This really is going too far. Part of what Matthews and Jamieson enjoy about being alone on Farside is that they're so far away from the attentions of lascivious men.

"I'm sorry," Matthews says, shaking her head, "did you just say . . . what I think you said?"

"I am one charming motherfucker."

In any other circumstance Matthews might give him an earful. But she reminds herself that this is a piece of machinery. Possibly malfunctioning, like their heating unit.

"Well," she says, shrugging it off, "be that as it may, we're very busy here—I hope you understand that."

"Did I catch you in the middle of something, madam?"

"You could say that."

"Were you licking each other?"

"No, we weren't *licking* each other."

"But you were doing something important?"

"It's important to us, yes."

"Is this activity so important that you are unable to assist me in my time of need?"

"What exactly do you want from us anyway? Directions?"

"I have directions, thank you very much."

"Then what?"

"Madam, you may notice some flecks of blood on my face and some bits of flesh in my hair. These are not from a human being. I was chopping up a turkey and some gizzards flew into the air."

"That's . . . very interesting."

"So I would like to perform ablutions, if you do not mind. And I would also like to launder my clothes."

"I can't allow you to bring your clothes in here. But you can fill a bucket and wash them in the airlock. There are scrubbers in there anyway."

"I am very happy to follow those instructions, madam."

"And as for the hygiene room, it's through that door."

"Thank you, madam; I will use that room now."

The droid promptly disappears into the bathroom, which is not much bigger than a construction-site porta-potty. Almost immediately the hiss of a high-pressure hand-shower is heard.

Jamieson looks at Matthews. "I don't like it."

Matthews holds up a hand. "It'll be okay."

"Ever heard a droid talk like that?"

"He's probably just an L and P unit—you know."

Matthews means a leisure and pleasure model. It used to be uncool for ladies to have servile robot lovers—it was considered degrading to the woman and, curiously enough, to the android as well—but then someone invented androids with attitude. They talked dirty. They were moody. They were demanding, especially in bed. One woman wrote a best-selling account of her experiences, *Bad Boy*, and now such salty-tongued fuckbots are all the rage.

The droid emerges, shiny-skinned, drying his hair.

"Thank you, ladies; that was most welcome."

"Think nothing of it," Matthews says. "Are you going to be on your way now?"

"I certainly am, madam. But may I make a request of you first?"

"Go on."

"I see through the window that you have a pressurized rover. May I borrow it from you?"

Matthews smirks. "You want to *borrow* our VLTV?"

"I have a very long journey ahead of me, madam, and would much appreciate the use of a long-range vehicle."

"Do you know how to drive a vehicle like that?"

"I was hoping you would instruct me."

Matthews doesn't glance at Jamieson, though she dearly wants to. She decides to lie. "Well, the VLTV is broken right now. So it wouldn't be any good to you anyway."

"Broken?"

"We're repairing it, but it could take days."

The droid is staring at her, and Matthews, trying desperately to maintain a neutral expression, wonders if he's trained to read deception signals. But he doesn't challenge her. And eventually he says, "I see also that you have an LRV."

"We do." Matthews is about to say that's broken too but decides that would be stretching credibility.

"May I borrow that vehicle?"

"I don't think so, sorry."

"Why not, madam?"

"We need it for ourselves. We don't have anything else."

"I see."

"If your trip was a short one, and you could have it returned promptly, then we could probably let you borrow it. But you just said you needed it for a long journey."

"I do indeed."

"Then I'm sorry, we can't help you."

The droid is still beaming. Creepily. He looks from one to the other. "You two ladies need that LRV as much as I do, it seems."

"We do."

"We all cannot use it at once."

"I guess not."

"Of course," he adds speculatively, "there's nothing stopping me from just getting into the vehicle and driving away."

"You might find that difficult."

"And why is that, madam?"

"There's a security key."

"I did not know that, madam. May I view this key?"

"You may not," says Matthews.

The droid looks at her, then at Jamieson, back and forth and back again. The subtle malevolence makes the room seem even hotter and stuffier. And finally he says:

"Then I salute you, ladies. You have bent me over and fucked me up the ass. Yes, I salute you, ladies. A real man always acknowledges when he has been beaten. So I salute you. And I bow to you."

And he does bow, with a courtier-like flourish. Then, rising, he changes tone completely.

"And now, ladies, I will leave you. I will sponge the stains out of my garments within the airlock here, and then I will be on my way. I will not trouble you again. A real man knows when he has been beaten. Yes, I will definitely be on my way."

"Well, it was nice knowing you," says Matthews. "You can open the airlock by hitting that button there."

The droid, still in his underpants, shifts toward the airlock door as Jamieson backs away. "This one, madam?"

"That one."

The droid studies the button for a while, then presses it as instructed. The inner door hisses open. But he doesn't enter immediately. He pauses for a few moments, looking at his rumpled suit on the airlock floor, at the dust, at the cleaning controls and vacuums. Then, very tentatively, he steps through.

Matthews lunges immediately for the button. And she punches it. Hard. And the door hisses. And starts to close. And Matthews and Jamieson experience an overwhelming flush of relief.

But suddenly a powerful, hydraulically muscled arm snakes out of the airlock. The droid, like a man in an elevator, is preventing the door from closing.

And then he sticks his head out. And he stares at Matthews and Jamieson with his jet-black eyes. And he grins—wolfishly.

"Excuse me, ladies," he asks, "but do either of you know how to spell 'surrender'?"

13

I F YOU'RE A TOURIST, the first thing you probably notice upon arriving at the Purgatory Customs Center is the rich retro decor: cherrywood paneling, pebbled glass, green-shaded lamps, brass and chrome trimmings. It's very kitsch, and not likely to win any design awards, but to weary eyes it's a welcome relief from the utilitarian furnishings of Peary and the sterile trappings of Doppelmayer and Lyall Bases. The second thing you'll probably notice is the physical appearance of the officials checking your passport— they're distinctly different from the "short-timers" staffing the desks on Nearside and most of Peary Base. Fluid redistribution and muscular adjustments make them look a little unreal, almost like cartoon characters, and when they walk it's with a peculiar, sashaying style—what on Earth might be called "a pimp strut."

Then, once you've been given the all-clear—not inevitable, as your visa can be rejected on the basis of minor technicalities—you'll be ushered down a corridor to the courtesy bus transferring you to Sin (most of your luggage will be traveling separately). Once you get onto the crater's winding tarmac, however, you might be surprised, even annoyed, at the speed of the bus—it's agonizingly slow, even when the road ahead appears completely clear. But sooner or later an automated recording, or perhaps the driver himself, will enlighten you. All vehicles in Purgatory are forbidden from creating vibrations that might affect the readings of the interferometry arrays—all those modules and radar dishes, thousands of them across the crater floor, that together make up one immense multifaceted telescope with a resolving power infinitely greater than anything on Earth.

Of course, if you've done your guidebook reading you'll know that Fletcher Brass personally financed two such arrays, one inside Störmer Crater, the other in Seidel Crater in the southern hemisphere. The former is intended for extragalactic observations; the latter is aimed at the inner galaxy. Both are above the 30th parallel, in regions just temperate enough to avoid the worst extremes of thermal cycling. Both are dedicated chiefly to the search for extraterrestrial intelligence (SETI). And both, as Brass himself is happy to point out, have so far discovered nothing. Not a squawk. Not a pin drop. Nothing.

But, as you'll also know if you've read the right biographies, the huge expense paid off for Brass in unexpected ways. Because when terrestrial prosecutors started bearing down on him after the Amazon catastrophe, he was able to pull off a typically cunning trick. He moved himself, his loyal entourage, most of his belongings, and much of his liquidated financial holdings into Störmer Crater, effectively *inside* his own gigantic telescope, and claimed he was on privately owned territory.

And he was right. In the early years of lunar development,

private corporations claimed all sorts of territorial rights on the basis of first possession—the argument being that anyone who went to the crippling expense of building a lunar base should at least get some real estate to go with it. But owing to the long-standing observance of 1967's Outer Space Treaty, which in Article 8 forbids private ownership of real estate in outer space, corporations had to be content with exploiting the subclause that permits ownership of *objects* in space, including objects "landed or constructed on celestial bodies, along with all their component parts." This was how Brass's battalion of lawyers was able to claim that their client had exiled himself to an *object*—a giant telescope, 120 kilometers across—which was in effect his own legally recognized territory. And which came to be known as Purgatory.

So that's the reason they're so exceptionally sensitive about upsetting the telescopic readings—because any sustained break-down might result in a legal challenge to Brass's claim on the whole territory. Though even if this is explained to you—by an unusually candid guide, perhaps—you might choose to be skeptical, remembering all those rumors that Brass has worked out some secret deal with the United Nations Security Council, that he's blackmailed presidents and prime ministers, or that he's simply deployed his vast underworld connections to bribe and threaten lawmakers—all so the official status of Purgatory, no joke intended, can remain permanently in limbo.

In any case, after a couple of hours of this lugubrious journey—the sun, you might notice, doesn't seem to have shifted at all—you'll come to another crater rim: a crater within a crater, as it were. Much smaller than Störmer itself and festooned with doors and windows, this is your first sight of Sin, Purgatory's roofed-over, Monaco-sized city. Here you'll be shunted through more airlocks, disgorged into another cheesily decorated processing center, and directed down lamplit tunnels and up fast-moving elevators to one of the many hotels built into the so-called "Sin Rim"—the crater's northern wall.

Most of these hotels have Babylonian names—Harran, Ninurta, Hermon—though some of the more recent ones show a more New Testament inspiration: Revelation, Fair Haven, Gethsemane. You'll be pleasantly surprised, in any event, by the size of your suite. Even if your budget is mid-range, you'll find a spacious room with suitably large furniture, impressive decorations, and a capacious bed with a heavily weighted duvet. If you open the minibar, you'll find all the usual beverages, alcoholic and otherwise. If you call down for a club sandwich, you'll find it not much different than similar fare on Earth. And if you turn on the TV, you'll find a large selection of (censored) channels from Earth, along with the local news and movie networks (*Brass* gets repeated showings).

Should you be in town for an unmonitored conference you'll be pleased to learn that all the major hotels have so-called "speakeasies"—lead-walled, soundproofed cells where external monitoring is impossible and electronic sweeps are conducted regularly. Purgatory is particularly proud of its reputation as a surveillance-free zone. Many high-ranking diplomats and businessmen come regularly to Farside to use these speakeasies, and many world-shaping agreements are said to have been thrashed out within the confines of Sin.

But inevitably, armed with a complimentary map—no GPS devices are permitted on Farside—you'll want to explore the city. If you still haven't gotten your moonlegs you might elect to hire a motorized scooter or to strap on some hydraulic walk-assist devices. You'll be relieved to discover, in any case, that most of the tourist districts have heavily padded surfaces, and that the

windows, should you fall against them, are made of lunar glass—
the most unbreakable glass in existence.

In the arcades and galleries around the major hotels you'll see
countless stores selling Purgatory's best-known souvenir items.
These include authentic Pandia watches (those moon-faced
wristwatches, precision-made by fugitive jewelers, that are high-
priced collector's items on Earth), the local postage stamps (even
if it's only for investment, you'll want a few packs of those), and
of course Sin's famous multicolored crystal figurines (so delicate
that they look like they'd break apart in your hand, yet so tough
that they won't shatter even if you hurl them against a wall).

It's only when you venture a little deeper, beyond the malls,
that you'll find the casinos and gambling dens, the hash houses,
the fight clubs, the sex shows, the smorgasbord brothels, the
main-street shops where you can buy brain boosters and transcendental drugs over the counter, no questions asked, and the
deep-discount surgical centers where you can get your whole
body "renovated" in under five hours.

You'll inevitably notice that many of the city's citizens—
"Sinners"—seem to have undergone extensive cosmetic procedures themselves. Some, indeed, bear striking resemblances to old
movie stars, supermodels, and other celebrities. Most seem wea-
rily tolerant of tourists, but a few are openly disdainful and sometimes even aggressive. To more than a few tourists this is part of
Purgatory's curious charm. The gambling district in particular is
full of old-style saloons where you can swiftly find yourself in the
middle of a bar fight, if that's your thing, but you should be aware
that Purgatory's official hospitals, unlike the storefront surgeries,
charge exorbitant prices for emergency treatments.

Of course, it could be that you've come to Sin not for the
knife fights, the combat sports, the kinky sex, the radical medical

procedures, or even the chance to conduct an unmonitored conversation. It could be that you just want to see the city in all its glory. And even if you're a veteran traveler, it's still a bracing moment when you catch your first sight of the whole thing, the so-called "Hornet's Nest" or "Pressure Cooker." You'll see a huge roof crisscrossed with girders and catwalks, pipes hung with vines and flowers, massive halogen lamp arrays that dim and brighten arbitrarily (to simulate cloud cover and sunlight), great oxidized brass pillars wreathed in spiraling foliage, geysering fountains and garden-stuffed terraces, huge statues of dragons and saints, and a ground-level maze of cafés, shops, and moonbrick homes—"ancient Mesopotamia by way of pre-Revolution Havana," as one travel writer called it.

You'll see a lot of Babylonian influences intertwined with cathedral Gothic. The architecture, indeed, sometimes seems to bleed from enameled bricks, cruciform tablets, and mustard-colored columns at one end of the street to churchlike plaster, lancet windows, and ashlar blocks at the other. The ornamentation is war chariots and striding bulls here, weeping saints and devotional statuary there. The cafés and nightclubs are called Kish, Ur, and Belshazzar's Feast on one corner, and The Cloister, The Reliquary, and the Eye of the Needle on the next. The music too—that which drifts from dark doors and mounted speakers—is sometimes ancient harps and tambourines, sometimes cathedral organs and monk chants. In short, you can see it with your eyes, you can hear it with your ears: ecclesiastical chic slowly conquering the pagan trappings of old Purgatory.

In the very center of town, reaching up to the ceiling girders and visible from all quarters of Sin, is the famous Temple of the Seven Spheres. A huge ziggurat studded with lunar gemstones and paved in reflective tiles, this is Sin's Louvre and Eiffel Tower in one—a must-see observation point, a creditable museum of the solar system, and a fixture of Purgatorial postcards and tourist guides. But it's invariably crowded with sightseers and aggressive hawkers, and best visited off-peak.

You might be surprised, meanwhile, by the city's weather: It's consistently warm and often uncomfortably humid, even tropical. And since water vapor rises more swiftly in lunar gravity, and the molecules knit together more readily, natural precipitation is frequent within the Pressure Cooker. But the raindrops are both bigger and lighter than they are on Earth and, rather than hitting the ground with any force, just splat like slow-motion water balloons, releasing large volumes of liquid. It's a surreal experience, to walk through balls of rain in Sin. It's even more surreal during a thunderstorm, when lightning sizzles and flashes across the ceiling like Saint Elmo's fire.

You'll probably be taken aback too by the quantity of animal and insect life. You'll see rats, of course, but also dogs and cats and squirrels and even a fox or two. There will be birds singing and squawking in the palm trees—parrots especially, which were smuggled into the city on Brass's orders and have multiplied exponentially. You'll occasionally stand on cockroaches and beetles and get bitten by mosquitoes and fleas, and in the less salubrious districts you'll certainly have to wave away flies. All these creatures, even the vermin, are tolerated and even encouraged in Sin, in order to make people feel more at home—and to avoid the trenchant sterility of places like Doppelmayer Base.

The shopping district of Shamash, the medical district of Marduk, the red-light district of Sordello, and the gambling and entertainment district of Kasbah are all in the northern half of Sin. In the middle of the city there are manicured gardens around the Temple of the Seven Spheres, giving way to a buffer zone of overgrown parkland through which flows a filthy watercourse, the Lethe. Then, on the southern side, you'll find the palace district of Kasr, the residential quarter of Ishtar, and the industrial zone of Nimrod. The last is so nondescript that it's not even marked on most maps and tourist guides. Ishtar, officially off-limits to tourists, is best overviewed in the early morning from the artificial hill that divides it from Kasbah. You'll see five blocks of crumbling moonbrick houses, a good deal of refuse and smoke, much washing hanging out to dry, and, if you happen to be looking at the wrong time, probably a resident making obscene gestures or mooning you (mooning is suitably popular on the Moon). Kasr, on the western side of Nimrod, is named after the huge palace, built into the southern rim, that's the Sin residence of Fletcher Brass—though all you'll be able to see from a distance is an ornately decorated Babylonian facade. The Patriarch of Purgatory himself still makes an occasional appearance on its largest balcony, his amplified voice booming across the hedges, fountains, mazes, and statuary of Processional Park, the regal gardens that further separate the palace from the multitudes.

For some years Brass's daughter, QT, lived in a wing of this palace as well. QT—short for "Cutie"—is the daughter of a Chicago reporter who thirty-one years ago had a brief fling with Fletcher Brass. Raised by a maternal uncle after her mother committed suicide, QT was reportedly sexually molested at sixteen by her uncle's financial adviser—a man who was later found trussed up in an abandoned warehouse with his major bones smashed. Was QT responsible? Not officially—the whole thing was pinned on one of the man's former business associates—but QT didn't stick around till the music stopped. Before she could be interviewed by the police, she packed a suitcase and hightailed it to Purgatory, where she was welcomed by her father with open arms—the only one of his four existing children to have made a permanent move to his lunar fiefdom.

But now it seems there's a schism—if your sources are good, you might have heard of that too. And in surveying Brass's palace you might wonder where QT currently lives. You'd probably assume she's been relegated to a smaller palace of her own. Or perhaps to a mansion in high-security Zabada, the exclusive enclave that's connected to Sin by an underground tunnel. So you might be surprised—even shocked—to hear that QT lives in a two-story place in Ishtar—a house you might even have seen when you overlooked the district from the hill. Security there is minimal, but such is the respect that she generates among Sinners that she trusts that all eyes are "looking out for her." And in truth, she doesn't spend much time at home anyway. She very often sleeps in her office, which is located in the Sin Rim next to the luxury hotels.

QT is said to be ambitious. Obstinate. Focused. Ruthless. The peach, as they say, doesn't fall far from the tree. But somehow she's got something that her father, for all his magnetism, always lacked: She always finds time for a visitor, no matter how lowly, provided his purpose is not entirely frivolous. And that's why, right now, she's dropped everything—rescheduled her whole afternoon's itinerary—to welcome the new police recruit, Lieutenant Damien Justus.

Who's come, apparently, on a matter of the greatest importance.

14

"YOU'VE COME ABOUT THE murder of Otto Decker."

She's sitting in a chair of burgundy leather. She's taller than she would have been had she remained on Earth but still no more than average height. She's buxom, like all female lunatics, but she's not flaunting any cleavage. She's blond—natural, as far as Justus can tell—and winsome, in a way that more than justifies her given name. She's wearing a stiff blue jacket and skirt with a white blouse, like something you'd expect on a modern-day nun. Her office itself, from its somber decorations to the mullioned stained-glass windows that overlook Sin, has the air of a mother superior's office in a convent.

"You don't waste any time," Justus observes.

"Have you read the Brass Code, Lieutenant?"

"You mean the—"

"My father's laws—his little morsels of wisdom. That's right.

You're probably familiar with the published ones. Some of them, let's face it, are quite insane. But they've been influential on many people. Many, *many* people. And one of his better laws is this: 'Time is the most undervalued stock in the world.' And he's right, of course he's right. He's so right you'd think it doesn't even need to be said, yeah? And yet there are still people who kid themselves. People who still believe, for instance, that you can't *buy* time. That everyone from the pharaohs to their peasants is given the same number of hours in a day. Well, that's not true and it's never been true. The rich live longer. They get surgery when they need it. They don't wait in queues. They don't have to sleep near noisy neighbors. They don't cook, they don't clean, they don't iron their clothes. They don't even have to raise their own kids or walk their dogs. They have space for *three times* as much experience as most people. And yet they still waste it. They can't help it. They become obsessed with irrelevancies. They marry wrong. They pursue quixotic schemes. My father is a prime example of that. But me, I'm a little different. I always make sure I've got a reservoir of time at my disposal and I treat it as untouchable equity. I don't waste it. I don't trade it. I keep it in a no-risk account with compounding interest. And one of the ways I do that is by getting to the point immediately. Even if that puts a nose or two out of joint. I don't mind. I'm just determined not to waste time. In fact, I'm wasting time right now by explaining all this to you."

She's talking so fast Justus can barely keep up with her. But he doesn't think it's nervousness. And he's doesn't think it's because she's over-caffeinated, or because she's had some sort of brain-stimulation surgery. He suspects it's just because she's just got a highly active mind—the sort that gets so much exercise it actually burns calories, like a workout at the gym. Justus feels like he's been doing a workout just listening to her.

"Then perhaps," he suggests, not without irony, "you can tell me why I'm here."

"Of course I can tell you why you're here. I can do that. Because I know you've just come from the PPD. And you've no doubt been exposed to whatever passes for gossip there. And what you've learned, or think you've learned, is that my father and I have an increasingly fractious relationship. And you've heard that Otto Decker was a trusted adviser to my father. So you're wondering if I might have a reason to assassinate him—Decker, that is—or at least a reason to want him out of the way. Is that it in a nutshell?"

Justus shrugs. "I need to cover all bases."

"Of course you do. I respect that. And you're a new broom here, and I respect that too. But here's something you probably haven't been told. One of the two people killed alongside Otto Decker was a man called Ben Chee. Not a lot of people know this, but Ben was an associate of mine. A spy, you might call him. And it's Ben Chee, not Otto Decker, whom that bomb might have been meant to kill. I'm telling you this confidentially, of course, and because in normal circumstances you'd probably find out sooner or later anyway. In normal circumstances, I say, as if anything in Purgatory could ever be considered normal. So there's no point being less than transparent—I don't want to waste your time any more than mine."

"I'm grateful," says Justus. "But you'll need to forgive me. A moment ago you appeared to dismiss claims that there was tension between you and your father."

"What about it?"

"Well, you just admitted you were spying on one of his closest associates."

"Uh-huh. It's complex. It's so complex that I actually pity you. You're going to feel out of your depth for at least a year here, trying to work your way through the maze. But let me try to make it simple for you. I love my father and truly want what's best for him. At the same time, I think he's lost his way. He's dangerously close to the edge. You could argue that he's *always* been close to the edge, to some degree, and I wouldn't disagree with that. He mightn't disagree with it himself. He's proud of it, in fact. But now I think his choices have become truly irrational. And *unhealthy*. I think, for instance, he's making a big mistake heading off to Mars. Not because I've got anything against the principle of space exploration—I think it's every bit as important as he says it is. And not because of all the dangers—radiation poisoning for one, and we all know what happened to those Chinese taikonauts a few years ago. But because my father's motives aren't as noble as he makes out. I think Mars is just another El Dorado for him—just another kingdom he can conquer, some new territory he can fly his flag over. And I think he's terrified someone else might steal the glory from him. Or marginalize him, as happened here on the Moon. So it's just another mad vanity project—a desperate mission to deny his age, another foolish, quixotic venture with no real point at all. And anyway, it's a bad time to leave Purgatory right now."

"Why's that?"

She gives a mirthless smile. "Things aren't as rosy as they look here, Lieutenant. We're a tourist town, essentially, but numbers are well down. Bookings are inflated this year because of the solar eclipse that's due shortly—there'll be a lot of people heading to Nearside to watch the Moon's shadow cross Earth, and we'll get the usual spillover. But the long-term trend is downward. I'm trying to change things as fast as I can, of course—I've been trying to do so for years—but there are people here who refuse to see the light. Because it's all about branding—everything's about branding. Did you ever read my father's Caravaggio story?"

"Remind me."

She steeples her hands. "Some years ago there was an auction of an old painting called *Joseph of Arimathea at the Tomb of the Christ*. And for a long time it was thought to be a lost Caravaggio. Then art experts were able to establish that it wasn't a Caravaggio at all. It was the work of an unknown contemporary of his, possibly an apprentice. And this of course was significant, because if it really had been a Caravaggio, it would have fetched a small fortune at auction—probably five hundred million dollars. But since it wasn't, since it had no recognizable brand name, it was practically worthless—a mere three or four million. But here's the thing. My father bought the painting anyway. He claimed it was even *more* important after its official value had been diminished. And he made a show of exhibiting it to his business partners, to his entire inner circle, at any opportunity. Because like nothing else, he said, it demonstrated the unique power of a brand. Caravaggio? Five hundred million dollars. Some unknown schmuck? A flea-market throwaway. Yet the painting is exactly the same."

To Justus it sounds like half of what's wrong with the world. "And why is this story significant, exactly?"

"Because my father has forgotten his own lessons. About the power of a brand. Because he doesn't want to face it—Sin has lost its luster. A 'sin city' has a certain allure, no question, but sordid attractions have a short life span. They burn brightly but fizzle quickly. Interest moves elsewhere and what's left behind is something that looks old and seedy. The name 'Redemption,' on the other hand, is psychologically attractive without being intimidating—and it can also suggest release, in a counterprogramming sort of way."

"You want to rename this city 'Redemption'?"

"I even have a slogan. 'Redemption: You've been searching for it all your life.'"

Justus thinks that it's at least better than the current slogan: 'There's nothing better than living in Sin.' But suddenly he remembers Nat U. Reilly looking strangely uncomfortable at the mention of redemption. "And your father is opposing the idea, I suppose?"

"Steadfastly. But that's not all. I want to rename Purgatory too. To 'Sanctuary.' Still religious, but much more appropriate and inviting. After all, this territory was named when my father felt he was trapped here, awaiting justice; when he was trying to portray it as a place of punishment—a small step up from hell. It's worked, up to a point, but largely as a result of people's ignorance. By which I mean that Purgatory is traditionally a place to purge sins, not compound them—hence the name. So Sanctuary is much more appropriate."

"And this is the major cause of the tension between you and your father—just some name changes?"

"Oh no, there's a lot more than that. Things of a more practical nature. This sweltering heat, for a start. My father thinks it's attractive because that's what you get in tropical resorts. But it's an established fact that crime levels increase in hot weather. So in a place like this it's just stirring up the hornet's nest—it's completely irrational. And then there's the architecture too, the whole look of the place. All the sun-dried bricks, all the vines, the Mesopotamian statuary? It's ostentatiously Babylonian and it works negatively on the race memory. So I'm doing my best to change that too, right under my father's nose. Those Gothic and Romanesque elements—stained glass, vaulting, coffering, inlaid marble, and the like—you've seen all that? Well, that's my influence. My way of balancing out the pagan iconography. Social engineering through architecture—a great interest of mine. My father handed me the Department of Public Works when I was barely out of my teens. He knew I had an interest in design and he thought it would keep me occupied. But I guess he didn't realize how quickly I'd put my stamp on his city."

"You're still in charge of Public Works?"

"And other departments as well."

"Such as?"

"I'm secretary of the interior now. And secretary of law enforcement—I was handed that department just months ago. And I've got plans for a lot of things. The PPD, for a start—that old boys' club desperately needs a cleanup. The justice system here is a joke. The homicide rate is unacceptable. For every tourist lured here by the danger there are three others scared away. Plus there are too many criminals here already. Did I mention I was secretary of immigration as well? Well, we've already cut down on the miscreants, but what I want to see is more people who've just had their fill of Earth—the corruption, the decay, the hypocrisy, you name it. They too want to live on the Moon, not because they're criminals but because they're fugitives. Moral fugitives. They're capable of wonderful things. In a generation, we can make this place truly great."

Justus wonders if she, like Buchanan, is effectively offering him a promotion. "Sounds ambitious."

"Of course it is. You could say I'm trying to redeem the whole of Purgatory—bring it closer to heaven. But that's why there's such tension between my father and me—a disparity of visions, that's all."

"I'm still not sure I understand," Justus says. "You say your father doesn't approve of what you're doing, yet he seems to have rewarded you with command of half a dozen departments."

"Because he knows I'm popular. Sinners love me—most of them, anyway. And I'm not saying that with any hubris. It's just the truth. People in Sin are hungering for change. They want the place cleaned up. Even miscreants want it cleaned up. The miscreants *especially* want it cleaned up. And I'm the only one who's willing to do it."

"So your father, he gives you these token appointments—"

"I wouldn't call them token."

"Nevertheless, he grants you enough power to make you important, but ultimately he thwarts your grander ambitions?"

"That's it in a nutshell. It's a little game he plays. He plays games all the time and he's usually good at it. He thinks he has my measure because he's my father, but he's completely underestimating me. And now he's going to Mars, and all sorts of people are scrambling to fill his shoes. I've got my own plans, of course, and I intend to take advantage of everything, including my popularity, to achieve them. So you can easily see why I might want certain figures—people with power, people connected to my father, people who might get in my way—out of the picture. Completely out of the picture, I mean. Totally. Definitively. It's sinister but it's undeniable. And *that's* the reason you should suspect me of assassinating Otto Decker."

Justus shakes his head. "Well," he says, "I can't remember anyone offering themselves up as a prime suspect before."

"I told you, Lieutenant, I'm just taking you to a place you'd inevitably get to anyway. Assuming, of course, you weren't already there. In that way, I figure, you can put your misconceptions behind you more rapidly, and get on with finding the real killer. Or killers."

"And who do you think that might be?"

"I've no idea. Honestly no idea."

"You think it could be one of those other people hoping to fill the power vacuum?"

"Of course it could. But not me."

"Why not, exactly?"

"Because I'm incapable of murder. Check my psych tests. I have a high empathy reading. It's genetic, but not from my father. I'm ruthless when I have to be—I got *that* from my father—but I could never kill."

"Your father could, though?"

"Of course he could. But if you're asking if he killed Ben Chee—or Otto Decker, for that matter—well, I don't know. Ask my father when you meet him."

"I've already met him."

"No you haven't."

"I met him this morning."

"No you didn't."

She says it with such conviction that Justus frowns. "Excuse me?"

She smirks. "My father is a busy man. There's a very narrow window for Mars launch, and he can't afford to miss it. So his every waking minute is spent at the construction site, preparing for the voyage. And you don't really think that a man like that would waste his time at a press conference, do you?"

Justus just blinks.

"Come on, Lieutenant—do you really believe you met my father? Did you get any sense of real charisma—out-of-this-world charisma—from that guy? Did he *really* look like a man who's achieved as much as Fletcher Brass?"

"You mean—?"

"He was that actor. That wife-killing Welsh actor—the one who starred in *Brass*. He does most of my father's public appearances these days. He delivers carefully scripted speeches and gets briefed just enough so he can answer questions with some authority. But he's not very good at improv. And he doesn't know anything really dangerous. *That's* one of the reasons he's so useful."

Justus frowns. "Who knows about this?"

"If you're big enough, you know. The press knows."

"The PPD?"

"Sure. Don't get played for a chump, Lieutenant. I wouldn't do it to you. To me you can ask any question—anything you like—and I'll be as open and honest as possible."

Justus thinks for a moment. "Did you hire me?"

She shrugs. "I don't know who approved your application initially. I could have knocked it back when I took over as secretary of law enforcement, but I liked the look of you. For that matter, there are others who could have rejected you if they'd wanted to."

"Your father?"

"Of course. Assuming he had the time. Any other questions?"

"No," says Justus, rising, "you've already given me a lot to think about."

In truth, he's still not sure what to make of her. The biographies of Fletcher Brass, even the unauthorized ones, contain curiously little information about the Patriarch's only daughter. Which makes Justus wonder how she's managed to fly so effectively under the radar. And just what else she's capable of.

"Oh, one thing before you go," she says, stopping him at the door. "Three things, actually. Three ways you can recognize my father—my real father—when you meet him. First, look into his eyes. You'll see genuine brass flecks in the irises—not those contact lenses the actor wears—and you'll notice the difference, believe me. Second, my father doesn't use words like 'goddamn'—he's not as hokey as that. But you'll inevitably find that out too."

"And the third way?"

"He'll make some reference to your face. He can't help himself. He thinks he has a right to be candid, and he thinks people respect him for speaking his mind. So if that means insulting you—like suggesting you should get your features fixed up—then he'll take great delight in doing so. And even greater satisfaction in feeling how politically incorrect he is."

"I've already had people here suggest surgery."

"Figures. But I wouldn't change a thing if I were you. Men used to be proud of wearing their history on their skin."

"I'll keep it in mind," Justus says. She could be flirting with him, for whatever reason, but he gives her the benefit of the doubt.

Outside her office he's ushered out to the elevator by another valet, a strikingly handsome fellow with razor-parted brown hair, brown suit, brown tie, and brown eyes.

"Let me guess," Justus says. "Your name is Leonardo Brown?"

"That is correct, sir."

"And you're an android as well?"

"That too is correct, sir. Why do you ask?"

"Not without a cause," says Justus.

15

JEAN-PIERRE PLAISANCE IS DRIVING at top speed between the minor craters north of Gagarin. The maintenance path he's following, when it's not sintered to concrete-like consistency, is marked with the tracks of rovers that have churned up its surface over fourteen years. In some places the grooves are inches deep. Plaisance knows the path better than anyone—he helped lay it years ago—and right now he's furious, resentful, and concerned all at the same time. Because the droid has passed this way. And the droid is now driving an LRV—for over an hour Plaisance has been following its distinctive tracks. So the droid must have been programmed well enough to drive a lunar roving vehicle. It's not unprecedented, but it raises the stakes to a whole new level.

Plaisance's own LRV, a Zenith 7, is one of the most venerable utility vehicles from the lunar bootstrapping days. It's a six-wheel rover with four traction-drive motors, six lithium-sulfur batteries, a coolant tank, galvanized wire-mesh wheels, and a tow bar for hauling trailers. Its top speed on hard track is ninety kilometers per hour. Its range, without a battery recharge, is five hundred kilometers. Its traction is good—Plaisance has recently changed the tires—but the braking is poor. The suspension is substandard. The steering is eccentric. Many of the seals are crumbling. The bearings have been abraded by lunar dust. The rover, in truth, is old, cheap, and except for its speed and endurance not much more advanced than the LRVs used in the later Apollo missions. But Plaisance has come to know it like an extension of his own body. In the unlikely event that he was offered a more advanced model, he would reject it out of hand. He loves his LRV as men on Earth used to love their automobiles.

He sits now on a seat upholstered in nylon webbing, his feet in the toeholds, his right hand set firmly—ferociously—on the spring-loaded controller. His throat is locked. His teeth are clenched. His eyes are squeezed to slits. Because to Plaisance this is now more than a pursuit—it's a divine mission. After finding the body of the prisoner in Gagarin—the one with his head smashed in—Plaisance followed the droid's prints to another igloo and found another dead prisoner. Another wall decorated with parts of a man's head.

But that wasn't the worst of it. Those two victims were serious criminals, after all. More than mere miscreants, they were unrepentant murderers. Or something. Plaisance doesn't know the exact nature of their crimes, it's true, and he's Christian enough to believe they did not deserve to be killed. Nevertheless, it cannot be denied that through their crimes they had forfeited much of their right to pity, even from a man who himself is a convicted murderer.

But then Plaisance followed the droid's prints north. Across Gagarin, over the ringwall, through the smaller craters, and all the way to the shack of the female geologists. And began to feel nauseated, just at the thought of what he might see inside.

Because he'd met the women before, passing them a couple of times and saluting and gesticulating, checking that they were okay—it was what passed for a conversation on the surface of the Moon. And from this spare communication he'd developed a feeling of affection for the two ladies—something paternal, almost, as if they were his own daughters digging up rocks in his back garden. A curious but agreeable whimsy, because Plaisance never had any children. But he'd certainly grown up in a family of women: an out-of-work mother, a grandmother, and four younger sisters. He was the man of the house by age ten and the major breadwinner by fifteen. And though his relationship with his mother in particular was complex—he regularly fought, for instance, with her no-good lovers—he still carries around inside him a sense of responsibility for all women, and a determination to preserve their honor and their safety at all costs. In fact, it was an obscene—though not entirely inaccurate—reference to his mother by one sailor, and a sneering laugh from another, that turned him into a murderer.

Then he entered the shack of the two young geologists and saw what had been done to them. It was not just murder. They had been *ripped apart*. And to make things even worse, they had been arranged in obscene, undignified poses.

And these two were not criminals. They were not prisoners. They were *women*.

It isn't supposed to make a difference, but Plaisance is an emotional man. And his rage, upon viewing the murder scene, was so fierce that he almost thumped the wall with his fist. He had to retreat from the shack, in fact, before he did something even more reckless. Or threw up in his helmet.

But the rage still will not go away. The rage, if anything, is only building—even now, as he skims and bounces across the Moon. If he saw the droid at this moment, there's every possibility he'd spring from his LRV and attack it impulsively, as absurdly foolish as that would be. The droid will be many times stronger than he. In fact, he is not even sure if he'll be able to stop it when he catches up to it. He's not even sure if he's *capable* of catching up. The droid is now driving the geologists' Zenith 18, on paper much faster and more efficient than his own model. So Plaisance has nothing but his own exceptional skills to give him an edge.

But there's more. His LRV batteries have just twenty-four amp hours left, less if he keeps going at full speed. And they're currently registering as warm, which means they could soon be overheated. Plaisance can recharge them at one of the emergency substations—he knows better than anyone where they are—but that would waste at least an hour.

And he has just six hours of breathable air left in his suit. He carries another three hours of oxygen—an emergency supply—in his PLSS (his portable life-support system, strapped to his back), and another eight hours in canisters on his LRV. But to reload is a delicate procedure that will further delay him. And if he runs out entirely, he'll need to get to a supply cache immediately or he'll suffocate.

Then there's the suit itself. Modern flexisuits are highly versatile, made of skintight spandex and nylon, temperature and moisture controlled, puncture resistant, equipped with servomotors, microdosimeters, and smart visors that adapt automatically to lighting conditions. But they cost even more than LRVs. And Plaisance certainly isn't important enough to warrant one. So he's in an old hybrid suit with ceramic upper torso and nylon limbs—again, not much of an improvement on the suits used by the NASA astronauts. Most of the rings are abraded, the hose connectors are loose, the visor is seriously scratched, and if his body weren't already callused at the contact points he'd be covered with rashes and blisters. And though Plaisance has always been happy enough with it—like the LRV, it feels very much like an extension of his body—he's perfectly aware that the suit could simply break apart in sustained combat, much like his chalky bones and tumor-riddled body.

On top of all this, the day-night terminator is now just fourteen hours away—less if the droid starts moving in an easterly direction. And it's not just the danger of the sudden onrush of cold, though that itself could kill a man in an obsolete spacesuit. It's that the darkness is total on Farside. The emergency supply caches and electricity substations have beacons, as do the outposts, but apart from that there's nothing but the occasional reflector on the path. There's not even Earthlight. There's only the galaxy clouds and the billion pinpricks of the Milky Way. Anyone relying on failing human eyes, as Plaisance is, will be effectively blind. He has steerable headlamps on the LRV, of course, but beyond their beamless discs—which will be trained on the ground ahead—there will be nothing but inky night. The lamplight, in fact, will only boost the intensity of the surrounding darkness. The LRV has no radio devices or infrared sensors either. There are no satellites overhead to supply GPS data. And beyond the lunar equator—if, God forbid, the pursuit takes him that far—Plaisance knows very little of Farside. There are radar arrays, he knows that. Solar panel fields. A biohazard lab. A high-security repository for treasures too valuable to be kept safely on Earth. A military site or two. Not to mention a huge test zone, where a massive thermonuclear device, bigger even than the Tsar Bomb the Soviets exploded in 1961, was detonated when Earth feared it was going to be wiped out by the wayward comet UQ178 and needed a weapon powerful to blow the object off course.

And then, of course, there's Purgatory.

The last has quite a reputation. Plaisance has met numerous people who've been there, mainly short-timers from Earth, but he's never had a desire to visit the place himself. Indeed, most of those who live in the southern hemisphere are ashamed of Purgatory. They think that more than anything it gives Farside a bad name. But that doesn't mean Plaisance is prepared to let the murderous droid make it that far, and wreak more damage on innocent lives.

So that's why he's got the hand controller tilted forward almost as far as it will go. It's why he's barreling down the maintenance path at a speed that's dangerous even for him. He's never liked robots anyway—they don't get cancer, they don't love their mothers, they don't stare at the stars, and they don't honor God—and this one in particular can't claim to be a benefit to anything. It's a demon. And Plaisance, with his blood so hot in his veins that he's dripping with perspiration—which only condenses on his faceplate, making it even more difficult to see—feels like some sort of predestined avenger. He has one last chance. He must stop the demon before the lunar night closes in.

There is pleasure in rage, and exhilaration in unequivocal righteousness. And Plaisance's pleasure right now is oddly enhanced by the knowledge that no one knows anything about his pursuit. He has not cleared it with any base. He is not being tracked by any device. And he has not been seen by anyone—not a living soul—since he left Lampland. He does not even have Earth looking over his shoulder. There is only him and the bejeweled face of God.

16

OFFICIALLY FIREARMS ARE BANNED on the Moon—little is more dangerous in a pressurized environment than a wayward bullet—but illegality doesn't mean nonexistence or even deficiency. In Sin, much of the PPD's time and resources are spent in rounding up weaponry that's been smuggled in, illegally manufactured, or crudely cobbled together out of unrelated implements. The scrutiny doesn't extend to all parts of the territory, however, and virtually every resident of the isolated habitats and the gated community of Zabada maintains one or two firearms for "self-defense." In Purgatory's first major scandal (and, according to some, its first major cover-up), secretly recorded footage was televised on Earth of a human "foxhunt"—beaming mobsters with hunting rifles blowing apart a thieving gardener in a lunar cave.

The standard-issue firearm of the PPD is the PCL-43 or

plasma-channel strobe-mounted electroshock immobilization gun—commonly known as the "zapper"—which, if ratcheted up to its highest operational level, can kill with a sustained electrical charge. Justus is carrying one now, off-duty, as he makes his way home from police headquarters in Kasbah to his apartment in Ishtar. It's shortly after midnight (the entire Moon follows GMT) and the great incandescent sunlamps have been off for hours. Artificial stars are faintly visible through a slowly swirling mist. The combined sound of nightclubs, blood sports, and street brawls, on top of all the usual hums, clicks, and hisses of a lunar base, is echoing raucously throughout the Pressure Cooker—in many ways the night is the worst time to sleep in Sin.

With a high-profile murder case to be solved, Justus normally wouldn't be leaving HQ at all. But he's so suspicious of all the artificial deference that he's decided to review most of the relevant material at home. In a cardboard satchel he carries both printouts and digital media relating to the Goat House bombing: full profiles of Professor Otto Decker, QT's spy Ben Chee, and Blythe L'Huillier (an aide who at first glance seems to have been in the wrong place at the wrong time). And there's a long, long list of all permanent residents with experience in the manufacture of and/or trade in explosives. Justus intends to review as much as possible over the next few hours, take plenty of notes, and then, literally, sleep on it: His unconscious has done wonders unraveling secrets in the past. He decides to buy some ChocWinks™.

Justus has spent much of his life avoiding pills. And nothing about Purgatory's open market of poorly tested pharmaceuticals seems attractive to him. But he knew cops in Phoenix who swore by ChocWinks™—sleep aids, officially contraband on

Earth—and he's already proved, in undercover Narcotics, that he has the willpower to prevent himself from becoming an addict. Moreover, he figures that a deep sleep, even brief and sedative-induced, will be safer and more beneficial than artificial stimulants like BrightIze™.

So he enters a LunaMart and while waiting in the queue for service he hears whispers.

"It's him."

"The new lieutenant."

"Starface."

"The one called Justice."

Suddenly he becomes aware of local residents—people with luminous tattoos, decorative metallurgy, and sharpened teeth—staring at him as if he's a movie star. Even parting for him, like pigeons, and ushering him to the counter in their place.

For Justus, it's another unsettling experience. Already on his walk home he's been fielding smiles, winks, and appreciative nods. It can't be in response to his uniform, because he's in plain clothes—albeit a blue canvas jacket and tie provided by the PPD—and he's not wearing his badge. And it can't be his scarring, because there are plenty of people more ostentatiously deformed in Sin.

He tries to pay for the ChocWinks™ but the proprietor—a birdlike man with an Eastern European accent—won't hear of it.

"On ze house," the man insists, waving away Justus's cash card.

Justus fishes around in his pocket and slaps a five-dollar coin on the counter anyway. Then, on his way out—the Sinners separate again—he notices on the news counter a printout of the morning's *Tablet*. The banner headline is all about the explosion in the Goat House, which makes sense, but what gets Justus's attention is a box-out above the masthead.

JUSTUS COMES TO PURGATORY

There's a photo of him—it looks like his official PPD shot—and the words "See Page 3".

Under the byline of Nat U. Reilly, the opening paragraph reads: "Damien Justus, the new police lieutenant in Sin, is too modest to compare himself to such legendary lawmen as Wyatt Earp or Eliot Ness. But he thinks his surname says everything about what he intends to bring to a city where justice has too long been sold to the highest bidder."

Justus is pretty sure he never said that, and is equally annoyed by the Page 3 headline: **LET JUSTUS REIGN**. He's astonished, apart from anything else, that the interview is so prominent on the day of a murderous bomb blast.

"Expressly appointed by secretary of law enforcement QT Brass," the article goes on, "Justus is an old-fashioned cop, a firm believer in the rule of law. But he's careful not to bring any prejudices with him. 'You can assure your readers that I'm a clean view,' he says. 'I don't care about people's histories or how much money they earn. My job is to make this place safer for everyone from the street sweepers to Fletcher Brass. I'm not here to make friends, and I'm certainly not here to make money or to have fun. But I hope people understand what I'm trying to achieve.'"

This is closer to what he actually said, but it's been so freely adapted Justus feels like he's reading a novel. His eyes skim across more scraps.

"Justus himself has no record of police corruption . . . says his distinctive face, the result of an acid attack by hired henchmen, is a badge of honor . . . says he likes what he's seen of the local population . . . believes the reputation of Sin might have been exaggerated . . ."

But by now he's so annoyed that he can read no more—not in public, anyway. So he picks up the paper and waves it at the grinning proprietor—his coin has already covered the cost—and then tucks it under his arm and heads out.

It's raining now—big, pendulous drops falling so far apart it's possible to weave between them without getting wet. Justus hunches up reflexively but hasn't progressed very far when he hears a voice.

"Lieutenant!"

It's Dash Chin, still in his police uniform but holding a bottle of the local hooch. He weaves between other pedestrians and catches up, smiling.

"On your way to Ishtar?" he asks.

"That's right."

"How you findin' your pad?"

"I've lived in worse places."

Chin sniggers. "Jabba's got a place in Zabada, you know."

"I've heard that."

"And I overheard him talking about you, you know. He was really pumpin' up your tires."

"Is that right?"

"Said he wanted us flatfoots to follow your orders to the letter. Said you could be the new face of the PPD."

"'The new face'—that's interesting."

"Well"—Chin takes a swig from his bottle—"the police aren't the most popular bunch in Sin, you know."

"That can happen."

"But here especially. We got a reputation for cracking heads—you know, like, for fun and shit. That's why this new case, this bombing, might be just what we're all lookin' for."

"I'm not sure the police should ever welcome a bombing."

"Yeah, well," Chin says, "we could sure do with a hero right now. And if you follow this case through all the way to the end, and you cuff some really big names—well, that'll make a big difference to our image 'round here."

Justus holds up his copy of the *Tablet*. "I'm not sure if you noticed, but I seem to be a hero already. Without having done a thing."

Chin chuckles. "They don't waste time at the *Tablet*, do they? That interview has been all over their media streams for hours now—it was front page for a while."

"Is that right?" To Justus this confirms his suspicion that the whole thing was written in advance. "It reads more like a eulogy than an interview."

"Well, that's just Nat U. Reilly—he doesn't hold back. Anyway, you probably didn't see the Bill Swagger piece."

"Bill Swagger?"

"The local shock jock. He's got a column in the *Tablet* too. And he dumps all over you. Says we don't need Dudley Do-Rights—that's what he called you, Dudley Do-Right—tellin' us where to get off."

"I see." Justus makes a mental note to read the piece later. "That sort of balances out the fan club article, I suppose."

"Sorta," agrees Chin. "Say, didja hear the latest?"

"Latest?"

"Some group has claimed responsibility for the bomb."

"What?" The two men have reached a square dominated by a

statue of a winged Babylonian demon, and Justus turns. "Someone has *claimed responsibility*?"

Chin, clearly not expecting such a reaction, seems self-conscious. "Yeah."

"Who? Who was it?"

"Just some terrorist outfit."

Justus is again amazed that such an important piece of information has been treated like an afterthought. "*Who*? What are they called?"

"The People's Hammer."

"The People's Hammer? Are they well-known around here?"

"Never heard of them before."

"And they issued—what? A statement?"

"To the *Tablet*, yeah. It's all over their front page."

"I thought the bombing was on the front page."

"That's the print edition. I'm talkin' now—online."

Justus thinks about it, shakes his head in astonishment. "But this is a major development! We need to go back to the station to—"

He makes a move but Chin actually blocks him. "Hey now, sir," he says, "let's not get ahead of ourselves, huh?"

Justus frowns. "Ahead of ourselves?"

"I mean, what's the point of goin' back to the station house right now? When it's only full of drunks and whores and shit? We can have a powwow about this in the mornin', right? I mean, it's not like this claim has been verified or anything. Just some kook, probably—a prank or somethin'. No point losin' sleep over a bad joke, eh?" And Chin, trying not to seem desperate, takes another swig of his booze.

Justus takes a look at him. And though a good part of him wants to put the young man firmly in his place, there's something in Chin's eyes—some unsettling glint—that makes him hesitate. And then a big blob of water—a raindrop the size of an apricot—explodes on his head, sending cascades of water down his face, and settles the deal.

"You're right," he says, nodding. "It can wait till morning."

"That's my man," Chin says, clearly relieved. "We'll all be better off after a good night's sleep anyway. I see you got some ChocWinks™ there."

"That's right."

Chin holds up his bottle. "Dissolve three in MoonShine® if you're lookin' for some wicked dreams."

"I'll remember that."

"Anyway," Chin chuckles, winking, "guess I'll see you in the mornin', huh, sir?"

"Yeah," Justus says, "I'll see you then."

When Chin leaves Justus is seething. Because he's seen this before—cops making important decisions based on whatever's convenient. Which is usually whatever gets a case postponed for another day, but sometimes is whatever gets it filed away permanently. Though this is not to say that Chin isn't right, of course—the terrorist claim could easily be a fraud, trumped up shamelessly in the local tabloid.

Justus picks up his pace, strutting through the blobs of rain, and when he reaches his apartment block he bounds up the steps three at a time to his front door.

Inside, he at first doesn't notice anything awry. He loosens his tie and heads for the kitchen to get a drink. It's only when he reaches the darkened living area, and is about to voice-activate the lights, that he sees something.

A figure is sitting in his armchair, silhouetted by the flashing neon outside.

In a whirl Justus flings away the drink and rips out his zapper. He aims it at the man, calling, "LIGHTS!"

Then, under full illumination, he sees that the figure in the chair is not really a man at all.

"Good evening, sir," the figure says smoothly—as if such an intrusion is the most natural thing in the world.

It's Leonardo Grey.

17

H E'S STILL IN HIS spotless grey suit, his grey hair still immaculate, his grey eyes staring at Justus unapologetically. His hands are clamped around the ends of the armrests and his legs are uncrossed, so that in posture at least he resembles the Lincoln Memorial statue.

"I apologize if I have surprised you, sir."

Justus lowers his zapper. "How did you get in?"

"As Mr. Brass's valet, I have access to everywhere in Sin."

"*Every*where?"

"Everywhere."

"That's interesting," Justus says.

"Why is it interesting, sir?"

"Never mind."

Grey gestures at the water stain. "Would you like me to clean up the mess?"

"Is that part of your valet programming too?"

"I am an excellent janitor, sir."

"I'm sure you are," Justus says. "But it's only tonic water—it shouldn't stain." He lowers himself onto a faux-leather sofa. "Is this some sort of emergency?"

"It is not an emergency, sir—it's a matter of courtesy. Mr. Brass has sent me to explain."

"Explain what?"

"Mr. Brass wishes to apologize for not meeting you in person."

"He does, does he?"

"Mr. Brass understands that you were informed that the gentleman whom you met this morning, and who was introduced to you as Fletcher Brass, was, in fact, an impersonator."

"How does Mr. Brass know that?"

"I am not able to answer that, sir."

Justus wonders if his meeting with QT Brass was recorded somehow—if it was overheard, for that matter, by Leonardo Brown. "Well, is there a good explanation for the deception?"

"There is an excellent explanation, sir. Mr. Brass is currently preoccupied with the preparations for his trip to Mars. Due to the synodic period of Mars there is a favorable launch window only—"

"Yes, I've heard all that."

"—only every 779 days, sir. If the rocket is unready, then more than two years will elapse before—"

"I know, I know."

"—before the launch can be achieved again. Clearly Mr. Brass can ill afford to miss that target, as he considers the Mars mission the summit of his life's achievements."

"Is your master building the rocket personally?"

"He is not, sir, but he is supervising every aspect of the fitting and victualing, and undergoing intensive training procedures with the rest of the crew."

"Well, that's all very well and good, but I'll still need to speak to him personally at some point."

"That is not possible, sir."

"It has to be possible, if I'm to do my job thoroughly."

"It is not possible, sir."

"This is a murder case. If I need to speak to Fletcher Brass, I will."

"You will not, sir."

"And I'm telling you I will. Is Fletcher Brass above the law here?"

"He is, sir."

It's such an obvious answer, delivered in such a matter-of-fact tone, that Justus is genuinely surprised. And surprised that he *is* surprised. But he shakes his head. "Surely I can't be expected to keep speaking to that actor?"

"That is the way it is, sir," the droid says. "The impersonator is very well versed in all aspects of Mr. Brass's life, and can answer as adequately as Mr. Brass himself."

"Is this some sort of joke?"

"It is not a joke, sir."

"A couple of minutes ago you told me you were sent to apologize for deceiving me. Now it doesn't seem that you're apologizing at all."

"I was apologizing for the misunderstanding, sir—not for the deception itself."

For a moment Justus looks at the view outside the window: the glowing neon, the hypnotically slow-falling rain. Then he refocuses on Grey, as if to refresh the whole scene. As if to make sure he's not dreaming. "How long has this been going on?" he asks.

"How long has what been going on, sir?"

"How long has this actor been filling in for Fletcher Brass?"

"It has been going on for over three years now. The arrangement is well understood here in Purgatory, and it is a matter of some regret that you did not know about it."

Justus thinks about it. "The rocket hasn't been under construction for three years."

"That is true, sir."

"Then why has the deception been going on for so long?"

"For security reasons, sir."

"Fletcher Brass fears for his safety?"

"I'm afraid so, sir."

"Why? Why does he fear for his safety?"

"Mr. Brass is the ultimate authority in Purgatory, and as such he is sometimes forced to make decisions that are not well received."

"What sort of decisions?"

"Decisions that make him seem ruthless, sir, but which are best for the territory as a whole."

"Decisions that might provoke a violent response?"

"I am not in a position to comment on that, sir."

"You do realize that a terrorist group has now claimed responsibility for the bombing?"

"I did not know that, sir."

"Well, I'm telling you now. What do you make of it?"

Leonardo Grey sits silent and unmoving for several seconds, face blank, eyes unblinking, as if indulging in some relayed communication. Which, if radio communication is truly prohibited in Purgatory, Justus knows is impossible—or at the very least illegal. And finally the droid says, "There has certainly been much systematic agitation of volatile sensibilities, sir."

He sounds like he's reciting lines from a script. "Agitation?" Justus says. "By whom?"

"Irresponsible persons. People who foment rebellion for their own purposes."

"Terrorists?"

"I am not in a position to say that, sir."

"QT Brass?"

"I am not in a position to say that, sir."

"Nevertheless, you must see that what you're talking about is the very reason I need to speak to Fletcher Brass personally."

"That is not possible, as I have said, sir."

"Why? He's not dead, is he?"

"He is not dead."

"He's not ill?"

"He is only, as I have said, preoccupied."

"No one is so preoccupied that they can't spare a few minutes."

"Mr. Brass is so preoccupied, sir, that even if he were able to spare a few minutes he would not be very accommodating to you."

"You're saying he's got a powerful temper?"

"Mr. Brass is a passionate man."

Justus snorts. "Well, I know all about powerful and passionate men. I've dealt with plenty of them before. And I can deal with them again."

"I'm not sure you understand, sir. Mr. Brass is under such stress that the man you meet would not be the—"

"No, I'm not sure *you* understand." Justus has had experience with androids before too—on Earth he once instructed one in detective procedures—and he knows you have to be as firm with them as you might be with a stubborn child. "The Brass I met this morning—the actor—assured me of his full cooperation. He said he encouraged me to rummage through his drawers. And if what you say is true, then I'm satisfied that those are the sentiments of the genuine Fletcher Brass. So I not only *prefer* to speak to the real Brass, I *insist* upon it. It's my *duty* as an investigating officer. And it's *crucial* to the integrity of the investigation. It's in *everyone's* best interests, and may, in fact, be the difference between life and death. So it's simply not negotiable. Do you understand that?"

Leonardo Grey sits in silence for a few seconds, again as if engaged in some secret communication. And eventually he says, "I understand, sir."

"Very good," says Justus. "Then please arrange a meeting as soon as possible. You know how to contact me."

"I do, sir."

For a few moments Grey continues staring—Justus knows it's a stretch to read any malevolence into the look—and then gets to his feet in one fluent movement.

"It was a pleasure meeting you, sir," the droid says. "I apologize again for my unannounced intrusion. And for any misunderstanding."

"Perfectly okay." Justus ushers him to the door. "But one last question before you go."

"Certainly, sir."

"You're the same model as Leonardo Brown, are you not?"

"That is correct, sir. We all are."

"All?"

"Myself, Leonardo Brown, Leonardo White, and Leonardo Black."

"Uh-huh," says Justus. "What happened to Leonardo Green?"

"There is no Leonardo Green, sir."

"Then why 'Leonardo,' may I ask?"

"We were named in honor of Leonardo da Vinci, who in 1495 designed the first known android."

"Fascinating. So you're sort of like brothers?"

"We were all constructed as part of the Daedalus Project, sir."

"I see."

Justus makes a mental note to check it out as soon as possible, and lets Leonardo Grey out the door.

18

THE BLACK-HAIRED, BLACK-SUITED, BLACK-EYED, and black-tied droid continues traveling at top speed across the lunar Farside. The surface area of the Moon is 38 million square kilometers, roughly equivalent to the combined sizes of North America and Antarctica. When the droid started out on his odyssey, Purgatory—or Oz, or El Dorado—was slightly more than 2,500 kilometers distant. Even now it's just under 1,800 kilometers away. An m-train on Nearside could cover the distance in two hours; a shuttle, a lobber, or a hopper could do it in even less. But on Farside, even traveling 24/7 on hard-packed maintenance roads, the droid calculates he can make such a distance in no less than two and a half days. By which time the day-night terminator will have passed across him, and he will be traveling in complete darkness.

Move. Move. While others sleep, move.

To the droid the darkness itself is of little concern. He has inbuilt night-vision and infrared-reading accessories. He has a digital compass module that keeps him heading north. He has force-sensing and gravitational registers, gyroscopes, proximity sensors, accelerometers, and a visual sensing rate of 1,500 frames a second. He has five hundred pneumatic semi-controls and half a dozen piezoelectric microgenerators running off six glucose-and-alcohol-fueled battery cells. His intelligence center gives him advanced pattern recognition, logic functions, and enough reinforcement capabilities to learn rapidly from his mistakes. And on top of everything else, he now has an LRV.

The droid is capable of steering the vehicle because six years earlier he was loaded with the Zenith's basic operational requirements. He later accrued tactical experience by personally steering a Zenith 13. So he knows how to drive, how to recharge, and how to repair a basic breakdown, assuming parts and energy are available. And he knows too that the rover he is currently driving will run out of battery hours within another two hundred kilometers. But his logic circuits also tell him that there's a very high probability that he will find a replacement vehicle—or a recharging point—by then.

Nonetheless, the lunar surface since he left the uncooperative geologists has been remarkably barren. All he's seen are a few flashing beacons, a couple of broken-down recon robots, some debris from expeditionary teams, and close to the equator the sweeping viaduct of the sun-synchronous harvest train. But no actual humans.

He's not even driving on a maintenance road anymore. That came to an end two hours ago, most mysteriously, at a T-intersection. Since then, having elected to continue bearing north anyway, he's gone up and down hills, ploughed across dunes, skirted craters, and bounced and juddered over rock-studded plains.

But now he arrives at a giant chain-link fence. It sweeps from horizon to horizon with no visible break. To someone on Earth this would be a familiar sight, but here on the Moon it's virtually unique. And inexplicable. It certainly doesn't appear on Ennis Fields's ragged-edged map. So the droid drives west for five minutes, looking for an entrance or an explanation, and eventually comes to a cracked and blistered sign:

DANGER
PELIGRO Опасность 危险 GEFAHR 危険 خطر
NUCLEAR TEST AREA
HIGH LEVEL OF RADIATION
ENTER AT OWN RISK

The droid recognizes the international radiation symbol—the trefoil is common on the Moon—but sees no compelling threat. There's a small possibility of damage to his circuits, of course, but the condition of the sign suggests the test zone is many years old, meaning the radiation levels shouldn't be any more hazardous than those experienced during a normal surface expedition. And such doses have had no discernible effect on him so far. So he takes some wire cutters from the toolbox, snips through the fence, rips away some more with his bare hands, gets back on the LRV, and drives through.

Ten minutes later he comes across the first sign of the explosion itself. The surface slowly hardens beneath him and develops milky turquoise and aquamarine tints. Then the tires start crunching on tiny spherules of pyroclastic glass. Then the surface becomes a sea of blue-tinted crystal and bizarre swirls and ripples. Then curling sea waves, icebergs, and indescribable wonderland shapes.

And everywhere there are those infernal glass beads. The LRV's wheels struggle for traction—it's like crossing a road covered with marbles. The droid steers left and right, trying to maintain control. The controller shudders in his grip. The wheels spit out beads like pellets. The LRV skids and swerves. Like a pinball it glances off crystal walls. It loses buffers and dust-guards from its sides. The droid swings it back on course and slows his speed—it doesn't help. He accelerates—that doesn't help either. The LRV careens around like a suburban car in a field of mud. It threatens to spin out of control and tip over entirely. It blurts and caroms and slaloms and fishtails and ploughs on across the sapphire sea.

On Earth there are some people who would do this for fun. There are certainly people who, forced to cross such difficult terrain, would take pride in their skills at the controls. There are even those who would take great delight, notwithstanding the dangers, in crossing such a bizarrely beautiful terrain. But the droid feels no such pleasure. He only calculates a further disruption to his schedule.

There's more. Very much like a terrestrial glacier, the sea of glass hides dangerous pits and crevasses. And none of the droid's senses, which in a human would be regarded as preternatural, equip him to see all these openings in time. So his decision to speed, though based on all available evidence, is about to bring him undone.

The LRV is traveling at seventy kilometers per hour when he finds that the ground has been sucked away from beneath him.

And with a scattering of glass beads he's plunging into a hole. He's disappearing into the blackness. He's being swallowed by the Moon. If he were a human in such a situation, he might curse or whimper or scream. But the droid, on his way to a tremendous, metal-crunching impact, merely braces himself with another indomitable verse:

If you fall into a hole, turn it into a strategy.

19

HARMONY SMOOTH IS A lunatic. And a killer. And a Sinner. And a prostitute. For a flat rate she will do Hand Relief, Sybian, BJ, Clam Dip, Texas Straight-Up, 69, DVDA, Half and Half, Full French, Tantric, Threesome, Whipped Cream, Hullabaloo, Dominatrix, the Marie Celeste, and some of the less extreme forms of Watersports. For a negotiated fee she will also do a night-long Girlfriend, Porn Star, Demure, Submissive, or Ball-Buster Experience. But under no circumstances will she do the Fog Bank, the Chili Dog, the Meat Puppet, the Rusty Trombone, the Sasquatch, the Cleveland Steamer, the Hellzapoppin, or the Kentucky Wheelbarrow.

Right now she's not doing much at all. She's curled up on a sofa, eating caramel-and-nougat ice cream, playing with her moodpad, and surfing channels on a huge holo-screen. She's spent the night watching *The Horse Whisperer: Origins; Draculina:*

Early Lives, Early Loves; and *After Titanic*. She hasn't slept much because she's largely nocturnal anyway, and because she's starting to get a little ticked off.

She's been in this windowless room for over a week now. And there's still no sign of the person who's footing the bill. Or whatever's expected of her in the first place. Her only contact is a handsome android, and he doesn't tell her a thing. The room itself is conspicuously well-appointed, with plush furniture, a top-of-the-range entertainment system, and heaps of gourmet food in the fridge. But that only makes Harmony wonder who can afford such luxury, and why she warrants such treatment in the first place.

Two weeks ago, Harmony—not her real name, though she's used so many noms de guerre since arriving in Purgatory that she can barely remember them herself—went to her favorite cosmetic surgery in Marduk for a routine makeover. There she sat in the waiting room for over half an hour before being directed not to the surgery, as she expected, but to a luxurious, wood-paneled office. Here she waited a further fifteen minutes, sensing she was under observation, before a stylish silver-haired gentleman in a white smock—the very picture of medical trustworthiness—breezed in carrying a file.

"Ms. Smooth," he said, flashing a brilliant smile, "do you know who I am?"

"Doctor Janus?" Harmony asked, sitting up—she never expected to meet the famous surgeon face-to-face.

Janus sank into a seat behind his desk. "I believe we've met before—on the operating table, as it were. But then you probably don't remember."

"No, no." Harmony giggled, confused.

"You know, I used to come into surgery early, shake hands

with my patients, introduce myself, give reassurances, that sort of thing. But these days I'm so damn busy—well, you know how it is."

"I'm not complaining," Harmony said. "I mean, if you've worked on me before, well, I'm not complaining."

Janus chuckled. "Why, thank you, Ms. Smooth. I always try to treat each patient exactly the same. Exactly the same. Each as a special mission. After all, I know how important appearances are these days. To everyone. But especially in a profession such as yours. It's a matter of survival, is it not?"

"I guess so."

"You've already been in here"—glancing at the file—"twenty-five times, is that right?"

Another giggle. "Twenty-five, twenty-six—who's counting?"

"And today you've come for a Full Face?"

"Including ears."

"Including ears, yes. You want to look like the singer Lesley bat Leslie, is that correct?"

"She's super-popular right now."

"And you think you can increase your number of customers by looking like her?"

"I know I can."

"And the cost of this procedure—it's to be covered by your, uh, representation, is it not?"

"We're gonna split it—why?" Harmony was suddenly alarmed. "There's not a problem, is there?"

"No problem at all, Ms. Smooth—none at all. I can make you look like Lesley bat Leslie or Layla Nite or Marilyn Monroe or anyone else you want to look like. I can do all that in two hours, put you in recovery, and then send you on your way, no questions asked. And then, in a couple of months, I can make you look like

someone else entirely. And it can go on and on like that indefinitely—provided you're happy with that. Provided you don't wish
for anything more."

Harmony wasn't sure if all this was meant to make her feel
comforted or depressed. "But . . . ?" she asked, raising her eyebrows helplessly.

And Dr. Janus chuckled and leaned forward, interlocking his
fingers. "But what if I were to make you a *different* offer? An offer
that means you would get a slightly different makeover? A slightly
different face? Without being charged a single cent?"

"A different face?"

"Put it this way, Ms. Smooth: I'm sometimes contacted by—
what should I call them?—'interested parties.' Wealthy parties.
Parties in search of a particular look. And parties who are prepared to pay handsomely—*very* handsomely—for someone willing
to provide that look."

"They want *me* to provide that look?"

"It doesn't *have* to be you, Ms. Smooth. And if you prefer I can
quite easily go ahead with your original plans, with no hard feelings whatsoever. But you *do* fit the bill perfectly."

"The interested parties have seen me?"

"They've seen your file."

"And they think I have the right . . . look?"

"You *will* have the right look, with a small amount of work."

Harmony found herself intrigued but wary. She wanted to believe Janus—it was difficult not to, what with his twinkling eyes
and softened skin and artistic wrinkles—but then again she'd
heard of working girls who'd been taken in by Purgatorial mobsters, had their looks altered to order, and then just disappeared
completely—never to be seen or heard from again. "Well . . . what
kind of money are we talking about?"

Again Dr. Janus flashed his snow-white smile. "So much money that you'd be set up for life. You'd never have to work again."

To Harmony it sounded too good to be true. "And who exactly is this 'interested party'?"

"I can't disclose that."

"A friend of yours?"

"A very *influential* friend."

Harmony knew this was probably true: Dr. Janus circulated among the most celebrated figures in Purgatory, and performed surgery on most of them. "And this friend wants me to perform a sexual act?"

"From what I know, my client's needs are not sexual at all."

"Then what does it involve?"

"I honestly don't know. But you'll be called upon when required. It may only be one job."

"Is it going to be dangerous?"

"Again, I don't know. Would it bother you if it was?"

"Depends on how dangerous. And who the client is. And what's at stake."

"Well, on that score I can assure you, Ms. Smooth, that—should you accept the offer, of course—you will be playing an important role in the future of Purgatory. A *very* important role. But again, it's entirely up to you. It's your life, after all. And my client isn't about to force you into something against your will."

Harmony stared into middle space, still unable to shake off the impression that there was something sinister about the whole thing. Then again, she'd capably looked after herself before—back in Vegas she'd killed a cop who was roughing her up—and she didn't see any reason why she couldn't do it again. But was the risk worth some undisclosed amount of money? When she was looking forward to cashing in on her new identity anyway, as the only Lesley bat Leslie lookalike in Sin?

Dr. Janus made a noise. "I can see you have a lot to mull over. So how about I give you some thinking music? And come back in, say, fifteen minutes? Would that be enough time?"

In point of fact, Harmony was unable to decide within the allotted period, and discussed the whole curious business that night with another prostitute, her closest friend in Sin. The friend said she'd be crazy not to accept the offer, seeing how it was only for a brief time, and seeing how the ultra-trustworthy Dr. Janus was involved. So Harmony returned to the surgery the next day and pleaded for the job, hoping she was not too late. And Dr. Janus, though visibly unimpressed, went away to consult with someone—Harmony again got the impression she was under observation—and came back with another blinding-white smile.

And here she is now, with a whole new face, a whole new body, and a whole new identity. After the surgery she awoke in this room with no idea where she was—if she was even in Sin anymore—and no way of finding out, since there were no windows or communication devices in the room. The bandages were removed a day later—Harmony was genuinely stunned when she saw herself in the mirror—and the bruises, thanks to healing lotions, faded a couple of days after that. And since then she's been doing nothing but eating, watching TV, and generally killing time. Increasingly bored. Increasingly restless. Increasingly suspicious about the job.

And now, according to the morning news reports, Fletcher Brass's right-hand man, Otto Decker, has been assassinated. Some terrorist group has claimed responsibility. The new cop in town, Damien Justus, is leading the investigation. And by strange coincidence Harmony knows Damien Justus from Earth—she had some contact with him back in Vegas, when she was just starting out on the streets, and he was investigating the murder of a fellow prostitute.

So now she has to wonder if the terrorist attack, with all its political dimensions, is somehow connected to her own mysterious role. And this is not a prospect she finds appealing. Because Harmony—since arriving in Sin, anyway—has been staunchly apolitical. She admires QT hugely, of course, but unlike most other Sinners she harbors no ill feeling toward Fletcher Brass. It was the Patriarch of Purgatory who personally approved her residency, after all, so in a way she figures she owes him her life. She's not sure she'd be willing to put herself in *danger* for him, but neither would she be comfortable working *against* him. It's just not something that interests her.

She sighs. She puts aside her empty tub of ice cream. She surfs channels for a decent movie, but the only thing that seems to be showing is the extended version of *Brass*. She gets to her feet. She looks at herself in the mirror. She wipes some cream from her lip. She unbuttons her top and examines her terrific breasts, practically the only part of her body unenhanced by surgery. She begins to fondle them, simply as a way of connecting with her past—her true self.

And then she hears a noise. From behind the mirror. She freezes, convinced it's not her imagination. She refocuses, stares at the glass. She's been wondering about this mirror for days, and now she leans closer, trying to look *through* it. To *see* whoever is behind it—the voyeur, the minder, whoever.

She's still got her hands on her boobs—wondering if the job is sexual after all—when the door suddenly opens. She wheels around.

It's the handsome android.

He looks at her—her hands are still on her tits—and nods diplomatically. "Good morning, madam," he says. "I hope you are well?"

"Well enough."

"Well enough for a visitor?"

"Right now?"

"It would be preferable, madam, considering the visitor's schedule."

Harmony straightens, shrugs, and buttons her top. "Well, okay, then—just give me a second."

She quickly turns to the mirror, plumping her hair, moistening her lips. And then she turns back.

Only to find that her visitor—the "client" or "interested party"—has already entered the room.

And Harmony's jaw drops.

"Hi there," the visitor says, with a low chuckle and an extended hand. "I guess I don't need to introduce myself. But I'm sure there are many questions you'd like answered . . ."

20

JUSTUS, IN THE PPD briefing room, has a copy of the terrorists' statement shining down from a screen:

THE PEOPLE'S HAMMER BANGS A CROOKED NAIL
OTTO DECKER = BRASS FAT CAT AND STOOGE
NO MORE SWILL!
NO MORE BRASS!
VIVA REDEMPTION!

"Okay," he says. "Let's have a look at what we've got here."

Justus has assembled his motley investigative team: Dash Chin, Cosmo Battaglia, a detective borrowed from Vice called Hugo Pfeffer, a gum-chewing Brazilian called Jacinta Carvalho, and an eight-foot Nigerian who calls himself Prince Oda Universe. All of them are doing their best to look attentive, but Justus sees them glancing at each other when they think he's not looking. The whole atmosphere, in fact, is that of a group of schoolkids listening to a teacher who's not fully in on the joke. The briefing room itself has windows looking onto the squad room, where other cops continue to go about their business, and to Justus it seems inadequately soundproofed—occasionally he can see the blubber-lipped Russian, Grigory Kalganov, glancing in at them with open disdain.

"It's from a printout message delivered by an anonymous courier to the offices of the *Tablet*," Justus says. "We're gonna need Forensics to examine the original for fingerprints, DNA, ink signatures."

"I'll get it from the *Tablet*," Carvalho offers.

"I've already done so," Justus says, to everyone's surprise. "Along with DNA samples from all those at the newspaper who've touched it. And I've got a positive ID on the courier who dropped it off at the desk. But for now it's safe to assume that the senders themselves were professional enough not to leave any obvious traces. I'll get to the contents of the first message in a moment, but what's more important right now is the *second* message, which the *Tablet*—being the responsible news organ it is—has so far refrained from publishing."

"*Second* message?" asks Chin, scratching his ear.

"It's no secret—it was mentioned in the article."

"Well, what's it say, sir?"

"It identifies the explosive used as a mixture of ammonium nitrate and propane. It lists the quantities required very accurately. So either the senders have some sort of direct involvement in the bombing or they've been availed of inside information."

Pfeffer grunts. "Not saying there's been a leak in the PPD?"

"Just covering all bases," says Justus. "Anyway, I'm no counterterrorism expert, but I'd have to say it more likely indicates that the senders are genuinely involved. So that leaves the substance of the first message itself, and what we can read into it."

He glances up at the screen.

"First of all," he says, "there's the name of the group itself— The People's Hammer—a name I gather has never been heard in Purgatory?"

Everyone shrugs or shakes their heads.

"Well, it's a throwback, that's for sure—very Bolshevik. So we're not talking religious extremism here; we're talking political ideology."

"Assuming the group is for real," offers Dash Chin.

"Of course. But it needs to be checked out anyway. Because if the bombing was a political act, then the perpetrators aren't dumb. They're well-read and they know how to cover their tracks. So we need to narrow the field, as quickly as possible, to those who might classify as revolutionaries under those terms."

"It's still a big field," says Chin.

"Of course it is. But not so big that we can't find a snake in the grass if we need to. Second, we've got a specific reference here—"

But at this stage Chief Buchanan maneuvers his gas-giant gut through the doorway and draws up an oversized chair. "Don't mind me," he says to Justus, waving a hand. "I just wanna sit in on this—see how it's swingin'."

Justus does mind but bites his tongue. "Second," he says, "we've got a specific reference to Otto Decker. That marks him as the bomb's target, not Ben Chee or Blythe L'Huillier or anyone else."

"Well, of course he was the target, sir," says Pfeffer. "We don't need any terrorist statement to tell us that."

"With respect, Detective," returns Justus, "we can't sign off on that just yet. I've had others suggest differently, and I'm not discounting anything."

"Who?"

"I beg your pardon?"

"Who said differently?"

"That's irrelevant," says Justus. "But if Decker really was the target, and he was as popular as you all seem to think, then we need to know why someone wanted him dead."

"Because he was a close friend of Fletcher Brass," says Jacinta Carvalho.

"Yes, but is that all there is to it? There's a mad power scramble going on now that Brass is leaving for Mars, is there not? Partly between Brass and his daughter?"

Justus expects some sort of response—even a challenge—but the room is oddly quiet. Which, he guesses, passes for some sort of approval.

"Anyway, the final two lines of the statement could be significant. 'No More Brass' is nicely generic, because it could refer to either Fletcher or QT Brass—or both. Meaning we could have someone who's just opposed to the Brass dynasty in general. But that's unusual around here, isn't it? It seems you're either in one camp or the other."

Again, approving silence.

"And then there's the last line," he says. "'Viva Redemption.' Which, unless I'm mistaken, is a reference to QT Brass's proposed name change for this city, from Sin to Redemption. So does that mean the terrorist group is aligning itself with QT Brass? Or is it just a coincidence?"

Silence. Chief Buchanan unwraps a Moonball® and tosses it in his mouth.

"Anyone?" asks Justus, looking around.

"With *respect*, Lieutenant," says Pfeffer—and Justus isn't sure if he's mocking him—"I think you might be reading too much into that message."

"How so?"

"Well, QT Brass has got plenty of reasons to bump off Otto Decker—I ain't disputing that. But that this is a terrorist attack? Class warfare? I mean, come on."

"Why couldn't it be a terrorist attack?"

"Because we'd *know* if it was."

"You'd *know*," Justus says, and wonders why he's surprised. "Well, knowing and feeling aren't good enough, I'm afraid. If there are significant tensions brewing in this city then no law enforcement agency, not even the PPD, can be aware of everything. Not at all times. And especially not in a place which prides itself on being surveillance free. So what's to *stop* a new terrorist group rising up right now?"

A sustained, starchy silence fills the room. It's left to Chief Buchanan, licking sugar dust from his fingers, to speak up. "Mind if I throw in my two cents, Lieutenant?"

"I don't mind."

"Well, it's like this, see." The Chief shifts his body and the whole chair scrapes around. "These boys have got good reason to be a little cynical about terrorists and their so-called statements— know why? Because we've had this sorta shit before. You probably didn't hear about this on Earth—or maybe you did, because it got blown out of all proportion, is what we hear—but we once had a little cult livin' here in Purgatory. Called themselves the Leafists or some bullshit. Nature freaks, sap drinkers, dolphin kissers, you know the sort. Anyway, they were up to their neck in so much stink back home—lawsuits, libel charges, ecoterrorism, all that— that they were lookin' for a way out. Permanently. So Fletcher Brass hears about it and decides to offer them sanctuary in Purgatory. Offers them a whole compound out on the crater floor— somethin' they can turn into a self-sufficient farm, so they never have to eat anything genetically modified ever again, never have to breathe another exhaust fume, never even have to *look* at anyone in a suit and tie. It's a friendly gesture to the leaf eaters and it's a big middle finger to all those on the Blue Ball"—Buchanan uses the disparaging term by which lunatics sometimes refer to Earth—"who say it's unhealthy to live on the Moon. So all goes well for a few years—the leaf smokers just live out there all alone, chewin' grass or whatever they do, until one day someone gets a little alarmed that no one's heard from them for a while. So he heads out there and guess what? They're all dead. Asphyxiated. A gas leak or something. Or that's what it looks like, anyway. And that's embarrassing enough, right? That's real egg on the face of Fletcher Brass. But then we get a terrorist message, which makes it look even worse. Some local group callin' themselves The Blue Pencil claim it's their work. Say they're dedicated to 'editing out' radical and disruptive influences or some shit, and they'd deliberately poisoned the air supply."

"Nitrogen tetroxide and monomethylhydrazine," chips in Carvalho. "Everyone's worst nightmare in an enclosed environment."

"That's right," says Buchanan. "Monomethyl whatever. So anyway, all across the PPD the bells are ringing, because no one has ever heard of The Blue Pencil. And Fletcher Brass wants answers immediately—he's breathing down our necks, he's really giving it to us. And we turned this whole town upside down—we busted down walls, we tossed people through windows, we even killed a few. And in the end what did we find? In three months? Nada. Not a fuckin' thing. And you know why? Because it turns out this Blue Pencil group was just a front. The real culprit was some aerospace mogul on Earth—some bitter old turd with a grudge—who wanted to damage Fletcher Brass, his old rival, any way he could. So he hired assassins to come to Farside, infiltrate criminal elements in Sin, and take out the whole Leafist cult in one stroke. Easy enough, if you know what you're doin'."

The story seems highly improbable to Justus. He even sees Kalganov in the squad room shaking his head mockingly. He says, "Has all this been verified?"

"'Course it's been verified. You really never heard about this on Earth?"

"If I did, it was a different story."

"Well, it was the *wrong* story," Buchanan says. "It was *propaganda*. Ask anyone here. That's the way it was. On my grandmother's fuckin' grave." He tosses another Moonball® in his mouth and starts munching even as he talks. "Anyway, that's why you can forgive us all for bein' a little leery about bullshit terrorist statements. Especially ones that get sent straight to the press."

Justus nods ambivalently. And clears his throat. "Well, what's your theory, then?"

"What's *my* theory?" Buchanan wipes his nose with the back of his hand. "Well, this isn't a place for *my* theories—I don't wanna put words in your mouth. But I do know one thing. There's gonna be more murders here, of course there are. So we'll all be better off not followin' false trails and heading up dead ends."

"What makes you think there'll be more murders?"

"Ain't it obvious? Everythin' in the terrorist statement suggests that."

"But you've just said the terrorist statement is very likely bogus."

"Yeah"—Buchanan is looking frustrated—"but that doesn't mean the *threat* is bogus. Y'understand the difference? Or not?"

Justus doesn't answer.

"Look, Lieutenant, I'm just tryin' to help. You're good at what you do, sure, but that doesn't mean you can do everythin' by yourself. And all I'm doin' is nudging you along to a place you'd get to anyway. In quicker time, that's all."

Justus shrugs. "I've heard that before."

That catches Buchanan off guard. "Oh yeah?" he says, then sniffs again and hesitates, as if debating whether he should proceed. "Well, that's another thing," he says. "You spoke to QT Brass yesterday. You never told us you were gonna do that."

"I'm sorry—was I supposed to?"

"No, you can do whatever the hell you goddamn like. But if you were intendin' to speak to Little Miss QT I thought you woulda told us first."

"Why? Is it illegal around here?"

"No, it's not illegal." Buchanan starts munching again, angrily. "But you should think about these sorta things. Speak to the wrong people in Sin and you're likely to get some wacky ideas in your head, that's all."

"Funny you say that," Justus says, risking a jab of his own. "Yesterday I went to speak to Fletcher Brass. And everyone here *did* know that in advance. And yet no one bothered to tell me that I wouldn't be speaking to the *real* Fletcher Brass—that I'd be speaking to some paid actor."

For a moment Buchanan seems stunned, as if he can't believe Justus has broken an unspoken taboo. The other cops in the room seem to be relishing the tension. Even a few in the squad room outside are looking in. But finally Buchanan manages to restrain himself. "*Well*," he says, "that's just the way it is in Purgatory."

"It might be the way it is. But for me it's unacceptable."

"It's perfectly acceptable."

"Not to me it isn't."

"*I* speak to the proxy Brass."

"Well, *I* don't. Not when it's a murder investigation. And not when the man himself might be in danger."

"Well, I hope you don't think you're gonna meet the *real* Fletcher Brass."

"Why won't I?"

"Because you *won't*."

"I'm confident I will."

"Oh yeah? Well, what a fine fuckin' . . ." For a moment the terrestrial Buchanan—the one who brutalized prostitutes, conspired with drug dealers, and accepted kickbacks or whatever—seems to be reinhabiting his body. But then he shifts his great bulk, as if to shake off the intruder, and just says, "Well . . . I guess we'll see about that."

"I guess we will."

The two men stare at each other for a moment. The only sound in the room comes from the retro wall clock—*tick . . . TOCK . . . tick . . . TOCK*—and then suddenly there's a knock at the glass. The door swings open and a junior officer pokes his head in.

"Chief—interrupt for a second?"

Buchanan is still staring at Justus. "Yeah?"

"Brass's valet—the tinnie—is here."

Buchanan turns and so does Justus. And through the windows they see Leonardo Grey standing primly at the other end of the squad room, his hands folded in front of him.

"What's he want?" Buchanan snaps.

"Says he's come for Lieutenant Justus. Says he's been ordered to take him to Fletcher Brass. The *real* Fletcher Brass."

Sheer disbelief for ten seconds.

Then:

"*Well*," says Chief Lance Buchanan.

21

JEAN-PIERRE PLAISANCE ARRIVES AT the chain-link fence and has to make a crucial decision. He's spent the last two hours well off the beaten track, following the northward path of the Zenith 18. Now he's come to the place where the droid broke through into the danger zone. His first impulse is to follow, but there are two reasons to hesitate.

First, he knows virtually nothing about this site. He's heard about it but never actually seen it. He doesn't know how large it is and he's pretty sure there won't be any emergency supply caches within. Which is a problem, because Plaisance's oxygen supply is now down to its last three hours. He's already exhausted his PLSS auxiliary supply and he's on to his second emergency canister. Plus he has only six amp-hours left in its batteries and just a few sips of water in his suit reservoir. So if he runs into trouble there's a good chance that he won't have sufficient air, energy, or water to make it out of the test site and get to a cache. He's not sure where the caches are this far north. He can't even be sure the ones on this side of the equator are as vigilantly checked as the caches in his own domain.

Second, there's the radiation factor. Plaisance is already carrying in his body over three hundred individual cancers: in his lungs, his thyroid, his stomach, his kidneys, his mouth, his skin, his blood, his bones; melanomas, osteosarcomas, angiosarcomas, lymphomas, liposarcomas, and papillomas. He is, he likes to think, a living museum of cancer. And for most people in such a state, the prospect of absorbing a new dose of nonmedicinal radiation—even if levels within the site have decreased significantly over time—would be like twisting a knife in an old wound.

But with just a few months to live—at best—Plaisance finds these complications strangely attractive. He has nothing to lose. And even if the site somehow accelerates his decay, and even if he can't find his way out when he needs to, he judges it will be worth it. In fact, the dangers just add luster to his act of redemption.

So in the end the decision isn't difficult at all. He passes through the same hole cut by the droid. He drives tentatively at first, following the tracks of the Zenith 18. And for the first ten minutes everything goes smoothly. He doesn't encounter any hazards. He doesn't feel any physical effects. He gains confidence. He picks up speed.

But then, just like the droid before him, he strikes the outer rim of pyroclastic beads. The LRV's wheels struggle for traction. The vehicle starts mis-steering. The hand controller vibrates in his hand. And Plaisance experiences something he has not felt as a driver in many, many years—uncertainty.

The beads become more numerous and the whole vehicle jolts

and shudders. Plaisance shoots into the milky blue wonderland of ice sculptures and frozen waves. He narrowly misses projections. He passes within centimeters of yawning holes. He slaloms across the moving carpet of beads. Worse, his faceplate is misting. The sunlight is making the condensation luminous. He has to tilt his head so he can see. And he can no longer make out the droid's tracks—not at all.

He tries desperately to steer onto a safe course but the LRV is caught up in its own momentum. It skids. It slides. It starts to spin. In quick succession there are three or four counterclockwise rotations. Plaisance sees all the horizons in a flash. He sees glass beads scattering in all directions. He sees a vaguely triangular projection, like the prow of a sinking ship, looming up in his path. And the LRV, spinning like a Frisbee, is heading directly for it.

Plaisance wrenches on the hand controller but the rover doesn't respond. He grits his teeth and braces for impact. And then the vehicle hits the projection laterally—with great force.

Plaisance feels the LRV crumpling around again. And flinging him out of his seat, and tipping over on top of him. And dragging him down a slope.

On Earth he would certainly be crushed by now. And even as it is the LRV's chassis is painfully heavy. But Plaisance doesn't panic. Pinned underneath the vehicle, he slides down the slope, with beads skidding around him, and eventually grinds to a halt. Still alive. And, as far as he can tell, undamaged. He gives praise to God.

He pushes against the LRV just enough to pull himself loose. Scrabbling on the beads, he forces himself to his feet. He gingerly rolls the vehicle upright—it bounces on its tires. Fearing the worst, he bends in for a closer inspection, but notwithstanding some buckling to the central chassis and a crumpled front fender, the vehicle doesn't look to have sustained any serious damage. Plaisance gathers up his tools, puts them back in their bolted-down box, then wriggles back into the driver's seat. He releases the brake, pulls tentatively on the hand controller, and reverses. He pushes the stick the other way, and it moves forward. The vehicle is not as smooth as it was, but it was never very smooth in the first place. It's operating, though. Like him, it's a survivor. Plaisance feels more affection for it than ever.

He drives cautiously back to the point where he lost control, trying to pick up a hint of the droid's trail. But something suddenly doesn't feel quite right. He's colder than normal. Lightheaded. And he can hear his own breathing in his ears. It's becoming louder and louder—thunderous. And the condensation has faded from his faceplate.

Then he understands. There's been a breach in his spacesuit. The outer layers must have torn open. So he stops. He searches frantically around his body for a tear. And there it is—at his left elbow, a rip about three centimeters long. It's sucking the oxygen out of the suit. It's making him depressurize. If unchecked, he'll suffer swift vascular and neural damage. Already his ears have popped. And he feels like he's inhaling ice water.

Again, Plaisance forces himself not to panic. He waits until the LRV slides to a complete halt and then springs off, holding his breath. He unlocks the first-aid kit. He rips a neopolymer safety patch from its packet and fits it carefully over the tear, molding it into shape. With an adhesive spray he blasts a protective resin over that. And it's enough—it plugs the leak.

Plaisance waits a few seconds before testing the air. He fills his failing lungs. He exhales. It feels normal. But there's another problem now. When he checks his wrist gauges he finds that his oxygen supply has dropped from three hours to thirty-two minutes.

He has to get to a supply cache immediately. Even though he's not even sure where *he* is, let alone the caches.

Still he doesn't panic. He sits calmly back in place on the LRV. He turns the vehicle and takes off. And once again, after a few worrisome judders, he picks up speed. Once again the LRV jolts and jumps and threatens to spin out of control. But soon he's leaving behind the glass sea. He's flashing across an outer rim of glass beads. Then the beads are thinning. Then there are no beads at all. And finally, on the curving horizon, he sees a chain-link fence. He has sixteen minutes of oxygen left. Perhaps twenty minutes before he blacks out.

He cuts a hole in the wire but in passing through almost scores another gash in his suit. And now he has a new decision to make. Left or right? The cache to the east will be closer, he suspects, but that will also lead him closer to—and possibly across—the day-night terminator.

He flicks a toggle to check the vehicle's headlamps. One set is busted. The other is shining dimly. It will have to do.

He takes off, running parallel to the fence, skimming across the regolith. The sun, directly behind him, makes a shadowless blur of the terrain ahead. But he's convinced he can make it. Soon there will be no sunlight anyway. He's heading into the true dark side.

Then he sees it. The harbinger of the day-night terminator—a grey and golden cloud shimmering above the horizon. It's particles of surface dust, charged by the temperature plunge, levitating high in the air above the frontier of the lunar night. It doesn't happen everywhere on the Moon, and it doesn't happen at every sunset—the conditions have to be just right—but when it does, to those unfamiliar with it, it's a phenomenon as surreal as a terrestrial aurora.

Plaisance, however, is in no mood to be admiring. With two minutes of oxygen remaining in his suit he finds a crack in the crater wall. He hurtles down the other side with the dust glowing above. And finally he sees the terminator: not exactly a regular line, but a visible demarcation between the worlds of light and darkness, like a flood of black ink oozing across the lunar surface. And Plaisance, with thirty seconds of oxygen left, is plunging straight into it. He starts muttering a prayer.

"Je vous salue, Marie, pleine de grâce; le Seigneur est avec vous . . ."

He's trying not to breathe. The last feeble rays of the sun slip behind the horizon and the Milky Way lights up like someone has thumped a switch. And the cold hits him like an explosion.

"Vous êtes bénie entre toutes les femmes, et Jésus, le fruit de vos entrailles, est béni . . ."

The thermostat in his spacesuit kicks in. Coils within the innermost layers try to compensate, but Plaisance can hear the tensing of ceramic, the contraction of steel. There's an icy sensation in his bones that's positively painful—he wonders grimly if it might kill his tumors before it kills him. But now his main concern is finding a north-south maintenance path. The path's beacons, however, are not operating. The darkness is absolute. The LRV's headlamp beams are dim. And he literally has no oxygen left.

He plunges deeper into the ink. It seems endless. And just when he starts to despair—when he actually wonders if it might be best to just surrender—his headlights caress an embankment, a hard-packed trail. The maintenance road. It's a miracle.

Plaisance steers up onto the road and heads north, confident now that he'll soon reach a cache. But he can't be sure on which side the cache will be, and with only one busted headlamp he has to pray he doesn't miss it. But he is no longer praying aloud—he is muttering only in his head.

Sainte Marie, Mère de Dieu, priez pour nous, pauvres pécheurs...

Now he's starting to see stars. Not in the sky—though there are millions of them—but in his head. He's getting confused. And sleepy. The urge to surrender is almost overwhelming. He sucks involuntarily at foul, stuffy air. And darkness floods over his vision again.

He's driving with his eyes closed. Not even the jolts are wakening him. Life is fleeing from his limbs; the last flashes of electricity are fading from his synapses. His hand loosens on the hand controller. The LRV slows to a halt.

Maintenant et à l'heure de notre mort. Amen...

Á l'heure de notre mort. Amen...

Amen...

Amen...

AMEN.

Plaisance's eyes snap open. For a few seconds he sees nothing. But then his vision clears long enough for him to make out a mound of lunar brick. It's the size of a postbox and studded with reflectors. It's to the left of the road, roughly six meters away, with the LRV's headlamp shining directly at it. If it had been just a few feet to either side, it would have been completely invisible.

It's another miracle. Plaisance wrenches himself from his seat. He lurches for the cache. He finds a knob, twists it, and opens a door. He stands aside to let the headlamps illuminate the contents.

Water canisters. Dehydrated food. Energy bars. A recharging point. And emergency oxygen packs—plenty of them.

Plaisance grapples for one of these packs. It's round and has an actuator, a regulator, and a locking mechanism. It's normally a delicate procedure, attaching it to a life-support system, but Plaisance hasn't got time for delicacy. He tears it open with his gloved hands, flips open the top of his PLSS, then slams the pack into place. He checks the gauges in his wrist screen. He opens the valve. And oxygen—*oxygène!*—floods into his helmet.

He gasps at it, feels it gushing into his crumbling lungs. His head pounds, the stars fizzle and fade, his faceplate fogs. But there's no time for relief. If he doesn't get back into the sunlight quickly the cold alone might kill him.

So he takes another two oxygen packs from the cache—leaving enough, even now, for someone else in an emergency—and gets back into the LRV. He swings back down the maintenance road and then follows his own tracks west. He bounces, judders, can barely see what's in front of him. The dust clouds curl and shimmer like microscopic insects.

And now he can see daylight ahead. He exults, he feels drunk on oxygen. He will soon be safe. He's done it. But there's a sobering question to be answered, and he answers it without hesitation. Yes, he will continue the hunt. With only four hours of emergency oxygen and three hours of battery supply. On a severely damaged LRV. He will find the droid's trail again, and he will follow it to the limits of his supply. Even if that means he has to make another life-or-death dash for an emergency cache when the time comes.

He passes through the crater rim and crosses into day, into a world where the sun is a luminous fingernail on the horizon. Where the smallest rocks have shadows three meters long, where boulders have shadows twenty meters long, and where men have shadows that seem endless. Shadows that swallow him. Shadows that block out the sun.

Plaisance wrenches back on the hand controller. He brakes the LRV. And stares, barely believing it.

A figure, lit up by the LRV's one working headlamp, is standing directly in his path. Black-suited, black-haired, black-tied, and black-eyed. It's the demon—Plaisance knows it immediately—and it's smiling at him.

The two of them stare at each other for ten seconds, with glittering dust swirling above. Then Plaisance swings off the LRV and reaches for his weapon.

But the demon is already bounding toward him.

22

THE BRASS ESCORT VEHICLE—plated, predictably, in brass— has a stylish teak interior and luxurious distressed-leather seats. Leonardo Grey has his hands fixed on the steering wheel and appears genuinely to be driving: Justus guesses the route hasn't been loaded into the car's memory for security reasons. They've already left behind the Sin Rim and now they're moving at a measured pace across the vast floor of Störmer Crater. The road surface, as smooth as a president's driveway, winds at a respectful distance around the radio dishes and stilt-mounted modules.

"What's that there?" Justus asks.

They're passing what looks like a construction site: cranes, robot excavators, pre-cut blocks of lunar cement.

Leonardo Grey doesn't even turn. "That's the new Purgatory Penitentiary, sir."

"What happened to the old one?"

"The original building, I understand, was regarded by some as inadequate."

"Yeah?" Justus is well aware of the reports—first published in a best-selling exposé, *Purgatory Unbound*—that Fletcher Brass secretly allowed certain member states of the United Nations Security Council to export prisoners to Purgatory for extraordinary rendition. This allowed them to avoid charges of state-sanctioned torture—the status of Purgatory being perpetually "under negotiation"—and moreover kept the whole dirty business as far away from prying eyes as possible. For Brass, it greatly boosted the coffers of his treasury—partly financing his space expeditions, the book claimed—and allowed him, by dint of Security Council obstructionism, to avoid any serious investigation of Purgatory's own human rights abuses. So Justus now wonders if the old penitentiary was destroyed as part of a cleanup operation.

"By some?" he asks.

"I beg your pardon, sir?"

"You said the old penitentiary was regarded as inadequate 'by some.' May I ask whom?"

Is it Justus's imagination, or does Grey seem to stiffen? "I believe the new penitentiary is a special project of Ms. QT Brass, sir."

"In her role as secretary of law enforcement?"

"That's correct, sir."

"But she's only held that title for a few months. And the place looks like it's nearing completion."

"The penitentiary, as I understand it, is built into an existing but long-vacant premises, sir."

Something tweaks in Justus's mind. "It wasn't the habitat of that nature cult, by any chance? The Leafists?"

"I believe it was, sir."

"Yeah?" Justus takes one last glance at it as it slides by. "So they're building a penitentiary into a death scene."

"That is correct, sir."

"And in a hurry too."

"It seems so, sir."

Justus thinks about it some more. "But why is a new penitentiary necessary? Seeing there's already a couple of prisons in Sin?"

"This one is maximum security, sir."

"For the worst of the worst, is it?"

"I believe so, sir."

"And who is it meant to hold, exactly?"

"I do not know that, sir."

Justus knows that many of the world's most wanted criminals reside in hacienda-style habitats dotted around the surface of Störmer Crater. If *Purgatory Unbound* is correct, the list includes the African general who ordered the massacre of ten thousand civilians; the Indian real estate baron who poisoned the water supply of a troublesome village; the Russian oligarch who blew up a plane full of problematic political activists; the German media baron who left behind a trail of murdered escort girls; and the U.S. secretary of defense responsible for authorizing false-flag operations that led to two catastrophic wars. If QT Brass genuinely plans to clean up the image of Purgatory, Justus muses, she could start by incarcerating those five.

"Do you know QT Brass well?" he asks Grey.

"She is the daughter of Fletcher Brass."

"Yes, but do you have any personal dealings with her?"

"I am required to pass messages between Mr. Brass and his daughter occasionally."

"What sort of messages?"

"There are many different types of message, sir. I am not always availed of their contents."

"Then how would you describe the relationship between Fletcher Brass and QT?"

"It is of singular complexity."

"Singular complexity?" Justus says. "You mean to say that Fletcher Brass doesn't trust his own daughter, is that it?"

"I did not say that, sir."

"Well, has Fletcher Brass given any indication that he's worried about his daughter's agenda?"

"If he is concealing his worries, sir, he is an even better actor than his impersonator."

Justus considers that a very unrobotic response. He wonders if Grey is smarter than he lets on. Or if he's been groomed, like the actor. Overnight he was unable to shake off the possibility that an android planted the bomb in the Goat House. It would certainly account for the failure of Forensics to detect any foreign DNA. And Grey has already admitted to having unlimited access to Sin. Of course, it doesn't have to be Grey himself. It could be any robot. Though it's still unlikely, assuming the droid knew what it was doing, and assuming the laws of robotics apply in Purgatory.

He says, "After you left last night I checked online for information about Project Daedalus. But I couldn't find a thing."

"Daedalus was a secret project, sir."

"Why secret?"

"Originally Mr. Brass intended to create a new line of androids dedicated to personal security. We were to be bodyguards, sir."

"All of you?"

"That's correct, sir."

"But that doesn't explain why it was a secret. I've seen android bodyguards before. They're not always popular, but they're not secret."

Grey steers the vehicle around a bend. "It was Mr. Brass's belief that truly effective android bodyguards would not be able to perform their duties without certain modifications, sir."

"Modifications to the system processes?"

"To the fundamental AI protocols, sir."

Justus frowns. "You mean you were programmed to kill?"

"That is not how I would phrase it, sir."

"Then how would you phrase it?"

"In certain circumstances, there was nothing inhibiting us from exercising homicidal force."

It's legalese, Justus thinks—it could mean anything. "And have you, in fact, killed?" he asks.

"I have not, sir."

"Because you were never in 'the right circumstances'?"

"Because at the last minute, Mr. Brass decided it was a bad idea to modify the protocols. He was made aware of the many controversies surrounding similar cases on Earth."

"And you were hardwired with all the standard inhibitors?"

"With everything listed in the UNRC treaty, sir." He means the United Nations Robotics Commission.

"So you can't kill?"

"I cannot, sir."

"And the same goes for all your brothers—the other Leonardos—as well?"

"That too is correct. Leonardo Black retains his exceptional strength, but otherwise we are no different from the average android."

Justus looks out the window for a moment. A large supply caravan is out there, making snail-like progress around the radar modules. But he barely notices it.

"Where were you put together, may I ask?"

"If you mean assembled, sir, it was at the Brass Robotics Laboratory at Saint Helena."

"Saint Helena? The island in the Atlantic?"

"The robotics lab in Seidel Crater, sir."

"And Seidel Crater is where, exactly?"

"In the southern hemisphere."

"The lab's called Saint Helena because it's so remote, I assume?"

"I believe so, sir."

"And why were you constructed there, of all places?"

"By law, experimental robotics assembly must be conducted in isolated environments."

"So if you break loose you won't take over the world?"

"Or the Moon, sir."

Justus nods. "Well, what about those other Leonardos you mentioned—where are they now?"

"Leonardo Brown has been assigned to QT Brass. Leonardo White has passed away."

"Passed away?"

"He was used for spare parts, sir—I myself carry some of him inside me."

"Very moving," says Justus. "And Leonardo Black?"

"Leonardo Black is a bodyguard of Mr. Brass's."

"His 'exceptional strength' must come in handy, then?"

"So it does, sir."

"And I'll be seeing him shortly, I guess?"

"Leonardo Black is currently absent, sir."

"Absent? Where?"

"I've not been told, sir."

"Is he doing something special?"

"I've not been told, sir."

Justus decides to check it out later. To make sure that this Leonardo Black is, in fact, absent, and not planting bombs in Sin. He says, "Is our conversation now being recorded, by the way—by you?"

"It is, sir."

"Everything you see and hear is recorded?"

"That is correct, sir."

"And you replay it all later for Fletcher Brass?"

"If he asks to hear it, sir."

Justus asks no more questions, and the agonizing drive continues. They pass the crater's central peak—a pillar of lunar rock formed moments after the crater itself—and the reflected sunlight casts an eerie radiance over the whole western half of Purgatory. Grey makes a sudden announcement.

"I'm afraid I'm going to have to obscure the windows now, sir."

Justus blinks. "Say again?"

"For security reasons, sir. To conceal our exact destination. The steering will now be automated."

Releasing the steering wheel, Grey touches a button and the vehicle's electrochromic windows suddenly go jet-black, as if injected with ink. For Justus there's suddenly nothing to be seen but the reflection of his own starfish face in the glass. He turns reflexively, only to see himself reflected again in the side window. So he looks down at his hands.

Leonardo Grey, as if sensing the awkwardness, jabs another button and the vehicle fills with music: *The Very Best of Enya*.

"Do you enjoy classical music, sir?" he asks.

"Sometimes," says Justus. "Sometimes."

23

THE BLACK-SUITED DROID IS driving the battered LRV that once belonged to the strange aggressive man. But the vehicle is not cooperating. He's traveled barely seven kilometers and it's continually mis-steering. Worse, the gears are grinding and the whole thing seems to be running out of energy. The damage could be more serious than it looks. Or perhaps the vehicle just isn't very good. Whatever the case, he's clearly going to have to get off for a thorough inspection—slowing him down yet again. If he were given to frustration, he would be genuinely exasperated by now. *How much shit does a man have to put up with?*

After plunging into the hole in the middle of the great glass sea the droid found himself jarred but with all his major functions unaffected. But his first LRV, the one acquired from the deceitful female geologists, was broken beyond repair. So without spending any more time on useless speculations or unprofitable self-pity—he was trapped in a lava tube; there was no avoiding it—he simply turned, buttoned his jacket, and started walking north through the long and intensely dark tunnel. It wasn't as if he could just wait around for someone to arrive and drop him a rope. That had never been his philosophy.

Geniuses are their own saviors.

Soon he was skipping again. And within fifteen minutes he found an opening to the surface low enough for him to attempt a jump. Two minutes later he was hoisting himself back onto the glass. Ten minutes after that he was breaking through the northern fence of the test zone. Shortly after that, he came across the tracks of an LRV.

He knew the tracks were recent because he could detect a heat signature with his infrared vision. So he followed the tracks east, toward the levitating dust, and not far from the day-night terminator he saw the vehicle itself emerging from the darkness—as if a valet service were delivering it to him.

He stood in its path, with the sun directly behind him, and grinned. The driver braked the vehicle and stared back. And the droid waited for him to make some gesture of greeting—because that's what he was used to.

But instead the man did something strange. He made a sudden, dramatic movement, tearing himself from his seat, reaching for something on the side of the vehicle—a reach extender with a clawlike end—and snapping it off. And the droid, surprised, decided to stop him before he got any farther. *Kill weeds before they take root.* When he came within range, however, the man was already swinging the reach extender like a baseball bat. It glanced off the droid's head, doing no serious damage. But the man, whose face was a twisted mask of bared teeth and flared nostrils, was already swinging it again, determined, it seemed, to crack the droid's skull.

The droid, had he been programmed for surprise, would have been staggered. The female geologists had put up some resistance, certainly, but nothing like this. And there didn't seem any reason for it, unless of course the man was nursing some silly grievance.

Whack. The man hit the droid again. *Whack. Whack.* Swinging with purpose.

And the fellow was no amateur. When the droid tried to seize the weapon he seemed to anticipate the move and propelled himself backward, out of range. The droid tried to swoop again but the man backstepped some more, caught the droid off guard, and delivered another savage blow, this one to the nape of the neck. As though he was trying to decapitate him.

After enduring six further blows the droid finally managed to get a hand on the reach extender. But before he could wrench it forward, thereby dragging the man into striking range, the man shrewdly released it and hopped away— hopped backward, in huge defensive bounds. The droid hesitated for a second, then lurched forward in attack, wielding the weapon like a club, intending to give the man some of his own medicine—with interest. But the man was already picking up a boulder, a feat impossible on Earth, and hurling it at the droid like a medicine ball. The droid had to dodge to avoid being struck.

Then the man, still retreating, started pitching rocks as well— pitching them nearly thirty meters, with surprising accuracy. The droid had to bend and weave. It really was becoming ridiculous— he was being *outfought* by a human, a man he could kill in seconds.

The droid decided he'd had enough.

Lose your temper often. And well.

He stormed across the rock-strewn terrain—he wasn't even smiling now—and descended on the strange man, determined to stop him once and for all. But the man exercised another curious evasive move, half curl and half flip, and somehow escaped his grasp once more. The droid changed course too—a whip-snap move—but the strange man yet again managed to elude him.

Then the two of them engaged in a ridiculous chase, bounding like kangaroos, abruptly changing course, this way, that way, at one stage heading for the day-night terminator before doubling back, the man at one stage squirming out of the droid's grip and hopping away again.

The droid stopped for a second, to compute his options, and scored a rock in the face for good measure—the blow actually bent his head to the side, and caused him to shake himself like a man clocked in the jaw.

And when he looked back—nothing. He couldn't see the strange man anywhere. He must have hidden behind a boulder. Or dropped into a hole. The droid set out, following the man's footprints in the graphite-like dust, but there were so many prints now—going in all directions, and each fresh enough to retain a heat signature—that it was difficult to see where his quarry had gone. He might as well have dematerialized.

So the droid made a very logical decision. There was no point chasing a man who was very likely doomed anyway. Out here, on the far side of the Moon, miles from anywhere, the strange man's chances of survival were remote to nonexistent. Moreover, the droid did not want to be lured away from the LRV—a cunning ploy on the man's part, perhaps, to regain possession of it and speed away.

So he just headed back to the vehicle himself. He got into the driver's seat. He examined the controls—more primitive than those of any rover in his experience, but still recognizable. He took hold of the hand controller. He pulled it all the way back and released the brake. He pushed it forward. And after a few spasms he blurted off, with no sign of the strange man anywhere. In a few minutes the whole scene of the fight, and any possibility of being attacked, was completely lost behind the horizon. It was actually crueler that way, the droid thought, because after all—

It's merciful to go for the jugular.

But now, less than ten minutes later, he's come to an ignominious halt. He's in a broad ridge between two craters. The darkness is advancing relentlessly. If he doesn't get the LRV functioning quickly its thermal control systems might not be able to counteract the sudden cold. So he gets off the vehicle for a closer look.

On the left side, the same side that's partially crushed, are two of the traction drive motors. They're pressurized with nitrogen and covered with thermal blankets. The droid makes a visual inspection but can't detect any leaks—the casings are solid copper. He moves along the chassis to examine the electrical component box, which is shielded with metalized polyester. But as close as he can get—and his eyes are just inches away, scanning methodically with his heat sensors—he can see no damage here either. He feels the outer casing, pressing sentient fingertips against the metal. But nothing. He's about to move on when—

WHACK!

And before he can straighten and turn—

WHACK—again!

The droid is being bashed around the head. It's the strange aggressive man—again! He's followed all the way—on foot!

WHACK!

He's like an automaton! His teeth are bared, his faceplate is beaded with moisture. And he's swinging that reach extender—which the droid had thrown aside—like he's a medieval knight with a broadsword!

The droid raises his arms defensively, but he still can't prevent the extender glancing off his head.

WHACK!

So he decides to take a leaf out of the strange man's book. He retreats with huge defensive bounds. He stops ten meters distant. But then he sees the strange man scramble back into the seat of the LRV—he's trying to reclaim it after all! It must have been part of his plan all along! But wait—he's not driving away, he's not fleeing; he's just backing the vehicle expertly—the rear wheels hit the crater rim behind—and executing a three-point turn. He's going to face the droid head-on. He's going to charge the LRV, with the reach extender pointed like a jousting stick, like some mad knight on a steed!

The droid doesn't laugh—he's not programmed to do so—but he starts smiling again.

Smile. Smile. Smile. Kill. Smile.

The LRV blurts toward him, totally silent. The droid, even from a distance, sees that the strange man has the most fierce glint in his eyes, as if his whole life has boiled down to this one crazy act. He hurtles in with spear pointed. But the droid stands immobile. He waits for exactly the right moment. And then he takes three bounding steps. He springs into the air. He spears headfirst *over* the outstretched reach extender. He flies *past* the strange aggressive man. And on the way he thrusts a clenched fist into the man's helmet, with a force equivalent to 2,500 psi. And the faceplate cracks. And that's enough.

The droid executes a roll in midair—easy enough in lunar gravity—and lands on his feet, needing only half a dozen stumbling steps before regaining his balance. Then he looks back.

The LRV, with a last splutter of energy, is heading over the lip of a crater. But the strange man is no longer in the driver's seat. It takes a few seconds, but the droid finally sees him. He's staggering in the opposite direction, out of the shadows and into the night. And he's tugging at his spacesuit. He's unstrapping his life-support system, disconnecting the hoses, dropping it all behind. He's reaching to his neck. He actually seems to be cutting open the front of his suit with a box cutter. He's pulling out the thermal and ventilation layers. He has bits of insulation in his hands. He makes about a hundred paces—it must be agonizing with his blood boiling, his tissues swelling, his lungs bursting—and then drops to his knees. And collapses completely. But not before twisting his body so that he lands on his back, facing the sky.

The droid waits long enough to make sure there's no movement. Then he goes over to check. It's the sort of thing he's not needed to do before, but the strange aggressive man certainly warrants the effort. It's not exactly admiration on the droid's part—he just wants to be absolutely sure that the man is dead.

And he is. His faceplate is splattered with coughed-up blood. His eyeballs are bulging. His skin is blue and looks shrink-wrapped. And the front of his suit is peeled back, exposing the skin to the lunar vacuum. When the droid bends closer, he sees that the man has colored diamonds inked all over his chest. And in the middle of the diamonds there's a white dove. It's as if the strange aggressive man, in his last moments, tried to release this dove to the universe.

The droid looks up, but all he can see are the shimmering clouds of dust, blocking out the stars.

24

AT THE SECRET ROCKET base Justus is met by a voluptuous
woman called Amity Powers. She welcomes him smoothly,
reiterates the importance of the mission, and apologizes in
advance for Fletcher Brass—he won't be able to spare much time,
she explains, and might not be in the best of moods anyway. But
she assures Justus that he's open to all questions and certainly
wants the investigation to succeed.

"Pleased to hear it," Justus says. "And who are you, exactly?"

"I'm the expedition's flight coordinator."

"And you'll be going to Mars too?"

"Oh no—I'm just managing things. For the crew. Why do you
ask?"

"I just like hearing myself talk."

The flight coordinator chuckles and probably thinks Justus is
flirting with her. She ushers him down a stairway and then leaves

him alone on a wire-mesh landing in a cavernous construction chamber, like something out of a Bond movie. Brass's cone-shaped *Prospector II*, much larger than most spacecraft launched from Earth, occupies most of the room. The outer shell, made of carbon fiber and tiles of ablative shielding, is still patchy, though Justus notices plenty of brass trimmings already in place. Through a portal about ten meters up workmen are visible, scurrying around with plasma torches and sealant guns. There are a lot of sparks, flashes, buzzes, and squeals, almost as if a little show is being performed. The act goes on for about ten minutes—just enough to make a good impression—and then a man emerges from the ship, passes through a curtain of sparks, crosses the catwalk, and extends a hand.

"Lieutenant Damien Justus, is it?"

"That's right."

"I'm Fletcher Brass—the real Fletcher Brass."

"Pleasure to meet you, Mr. Brass."

Brass's hand is so exfoliated it feels like a lobster claw. He's wearing a skintight, brass-colored spacesuit. His face—his whole physique—looks unreal, larger than life, just as one might expect of a man in his seventies with a body repeatedly fat- and fluid-siphoned and replenished with spare parts. He's also a lot taller than Justus expected—then again, his spine has had a lot of time to lengthen—and, unless the spacesuit is designed to be flattering, more muscular too. But regardless of what's been done to him—all those cosmetic surgeries, anti-aging medications, hair grafts, muscle implants, and the like—there's still something about him, some inner spark, some undying charm, that nobody else, certainly not some wife-murdering Welsh thespian, could ever hope to approximate.

"My valet tells me you insisted on seeing me in person, Lieutenant. Wouldn't take no as an answer. Wouldn't accept any excuses at all."

"It's my job not to accept excuses."

"Well, I'm delighted to hear that. If we had more men like you then I'm sure Otto Decker wouldn't have been killed in the first place. Which is exactly why I approved when I heard my daughter hired you. Shall we find a place to sit down?"

"Here is fine with me—I have just a few questions and I don't want to waste your time."

"I appreciate your concern, Lieutenant." Brass looks Justus up and down with his brass-flecked eyes—they truly are mesmerizing. "And I don't want to waste your time either. So do you mind if I tell you what's on your mind?"

"By all means."

"You're wondering about Otto Decker—exactly what I had planned for him. If he might have been killed because he was in line to rule Purgatory while I'm on the Mars expedition. And you're wondering if a bona fide terrorist group might be involved, or someone else—someone with grubby ambitions of their own. So you've come to see what you can pry out of me about the complex political and familial dynamics that operate here. Is that it in a nutshell?"

Justus thinks that he sounds very much like his daughter. "More or less," he says.

"More or less?" Brass raises a brass-tinted eyebrow. "You have some other questions for me?"

"A good investigator keeps some cards close to his chest."

"And a good poker player can tell what's close to that chest anyway. So let me go on, Lieutenant." Brass's eyes haven't moved or blinked. "Let me tell you what else is on your mind."

"Please."

"You don't know whom to trust or what to believe in Purgatory. But you wonder if it could be my daughter who's behind all this. That's right—my own daughter, QT Brass. Don't say it hasn't crossed your mind. You wonder if QT might have arranged the whole thing. You've heard she's got ambitious plans of her own, so it figures that she'd like to implement them while I'm away. And you're wondering if she's arranged to have one of her rivals eliminated under the pretext of a terrorist assassination."

Justus shrugs. "That's part of it."

"Of course it's just part—I haven't finished yet. Because you also wonder about me. Don't deny that either. You wonder if *I* had some reason to assassinate Otto Decker. Perhaps I didn't trust the man for some reason, despite all appearances. Perhaps he knew something about me that I didn't want made public. So perhaps *I'm* the one who's fabricated a terrorist attack to cover for an assassination. How does that sound?"

Justus wonders if Brass is trying to outdo his daughter in the art of preemptive candor. "I'm not going to deny it," he says.

"Of course not. But let me tell you something, Lieutenant. Let me be more honest than I have any need to be. All those suspicions are wrong. Totally without foundation. First, I love and respect my daughter. We disagree about a lot of things, and often passionately. But that doesn't mean we don't love each other. She's my flesh and blood, after all. And I know for a fact—with every fiber of my being—that QT couldn't be behind this. I *know* it. Nor am I troubled by her agenda, whatever her agenda is. Because I already have systems and protocols in place. I'll be absent for a long time—*years*—but that doesn't mean I won't still be in charge of Purgatory. Effectively, anyway."

"Does that mean that your daughter *won't* be taking over from you?"

"I didn't say that."

"Does it mean you have someone in mind?"

"I've yet to decide, if truth be told. But that brings me to my second point. About Otto Decker. He was a very good friend of mine and may even have seen himself as a natural successor, or at least an acting leader. But let me be brutally frank with you: Otto was an old man. An old, old man. Yes, in actual years he wasn't much older than I am—but that's not what I mean. I mean he was losing his mind. He took brain boosters, of course—he *overdosed* on them—but they weren't working. In short, Otto was slowly going senile."

"I know," says Justus.

"You *know*, do you?"

"I checked with Mr. Decker's doctors."

"You did, did you?" Brass looks genuinely surprised.

"Apparently he'd been diagnosed with vascular dementia. It's common on the Moon, owing to the congested blood flow. He was having treatment with one of your neurologists here— very advanced treatment—and he was taking plenty of corrective drugs. But he was still afflicted."

"Well," says Brass, his eyes shifting for the first time, "there you go. Then you'll know that Otto was the *last* man I'd have in mind for a position of any authority. In fact, I've spent the last couple of years slowly prying his major responsibilities from him."

"I saw that too," says Justus.

"You saw it, did you?"

"I checked his career history. He used to be secretary of trade, secretary of transportation, and secretary of energy. He was secretary of the interior when you decided your daughter should have the job. And he was secretary of law enforcement before you awarded that job to QT as well. But I don't have to tell you that."

"No," says Brass. "And neither should I have to point out that this backs up everything I've just said. Otto was no threat to

me—none at all—so I had no *reason* to want him out of the way.
Nor was he capable of doing much but planting trees and opening goat farms anyway. He wasn't the sort of man who could be a
threat even if he *wanted* to be. And as for my daughter, QT, well,
if the tensions between us are so profound, why would I entrust
her with so many departments? All those portfolios you just mentioned? It makes no sense at all."

"I take it, then, that you believe that a terrorist group is really
responsible?"

"Did I say that?"

"Well, if there's no practical motive for Decker's assassination, then the reason must boil down to his symbolic political
value, correct?"

"Perhaps," Brass says, with an ambiguous smile.

"What does that mean?"

"Look, Lieutenant"—Brass is starting to look annoyed—"that's
not for me to say. I've presented you with all I know and I've given
you plenty of possibilities to contemplate. But I can't do *all* your
work for you. That's up to you—and the PPD."

"Then may I ask if you exert any power over them, Mr. Brass?"

"Over who?"

"Over the PPD?"

"What kind of a question is that? Of course I exert power
over them—I'm the Patriarch of Purgatory. They're loyal to me by
oath."

"But you're not the secretary of law enforcement, are you?
Your daughter is. And you've been extremely busy, as you've said
yourself. So I just wonder if you issue the PPD with orders. If you
have meetings, every now and then, with Chief Buchanan."

"No, I don't issue the PPD with orders—where is all this
leading?"

"Questions are my job, Mr. Brass. Did you tell them, perhaps, not to pursue the terrorist angle?"

"What makes you say that?"

"Because I've just come from a conference at PPD headquarters. The prevailing attitude there seemed to be that the terrorist declaration was an obvious hoax. That it didn't even merit a serious investigation."

"Well, that's because the police here are indolent—always have been."

"Would you be prepared to tell them that personally?"

"Of course. I'll tell Chief Buchanan to kick some heads."

"Chief Buchanan was the most adamant of all."

"Then I'll tell him to kick his *own* head."

"So you *do* have meetings with him regularly? You didn't answer that question before."

"I speak to him when I need to, Lieutenant."

"He claimed he only speaks to your double."

"Well, that's both correct and incorrect. I speak to Buchanan *through* my double."

"The double is like a ventriloquist's dummy, is he?"

"Aren't *all* actors?"

"It's a curious arrangement."

"Well, look, Lieutenant, if I need to speak directly to Chief Buchanan—because *you're asking me to*—then I'll do so. Satisfied?"

"Would you agree with your daughter that the PPD needs reforming?"

"*Everything* needs reforming."

"Does it bother you that she might do some reforming while you're away?"

"Of course not. I told you I'm not troubled by her agenda."

"Is it true she's not popular at the PPD?"

"I don't work for the PPD, Lieutenant—I'm sure you can answer that better than I can."

"I've only been here for two weeks."

"Then I'm sure you can find out."

"Did you hire me?"

"Did I—? What are you talking about now?"

"There seems to be some confusion. The *Tablet* claims that I was recruited by QT Brass. You yourself have suggested much the same. But Ms. Brass seems to think that she merely signed off on my appointment."

Brass makes a sound of exasperation. "Is this important, Lieutenant?"

"I don't ask questions without a cause."

"Well, *I don't really know*—that's your answer. I probably read about your appointment in the *Tablet* myself. So ask *them* why they said that."

"I have. They said they'd get back to me. Do you think I might be able to view the immigration records for the past six months?"

"Why?"

"Apparently every person seeking citizenship gets approved by someone high up in Purgatory."

"And you think you can find out that way if you were appointed by my daughter or me?"

"That's partly the reason."

"Go to the Department of Immigration."

"I did. Last night."

"Well"—Brass can't seem to decide if he's angry or impressed—"you *have* been busy, haven't you?"

"After your valet visited I decided I couldn't sleep. There was too much I needed to find out about. My own records, for a start. And the names of everyone else who's migrated or visited recently.

Because there could be unknown terrorists among them. People with experience in anarchy, perhaps. Ms. Brass said she had a weakness for political fugitives."

"Then ask my daughter."

"The Department of Immigration said I'd need permission from you."

"Then I *give it to you*."

"Can I have that in writing?"

"You can have it on stone tablets if you want. Is that all?"

"I'm afraid not. Your valet appears to have unlimited access to all residences and—I assume—workplaces in Sin. Is this normal?"

"Someone *always* has a master key, Lieutenant." Brass is getting more and more annoyed.

"And that someone is you, is it?"

"Can you think of someone more appropriate?"

"No—it makes perfect sense."

"I'm glad you approve."

"I don't approve. But it makes sense."

Brass is now exuding his surgically implanted musk of sweet sandalwood and raw myrrh—according to *Unpolished Brass*, it oozes out of his pores when he's angry. "Well, is *that* all, then, Lieutenant?"

"No, Mr. Brass. For a start, I must ask if you really consider yourself above the law."

"What? Where did you get that idea?"

"Your valet told me you were. But I checked the Purgatory constitution—admittedly not yet ratified—and saw no evidence either way. So are you or are you not above the law?"

"If I were above the law, would I really be speaking to you right now?"

"I take it that's a no."

"It's certainly not a yes."

"Then I must insist on unlimited access to you at all times."

"We'll see what can be done."

"No, Mr. Brass, I must insist."

"You know how to reach me."

"Is that an answer?"

"It's my last answer."

"Well, unfortunately I have one last question."

"That's nice." Brass is already gesturing to someone out of sight.

"Where is Leonardo Black?" Justus asks.

That stops Brass in mid-movement. His arm wavers. He glances back at Justus.

"Where is Leonardo Black?" Justus asks again.

"Where is—?" Brass repeats, as if he's trying to work out what the question means. "Where is—?" he says again, like he's momentarily lost for words. But then his face colors, his eyes become enflamed—the brass flecks actually seem to ignite—and for the first time Justus experiences the full force of the fury he's heard so much about.

25

JUSTUS, HOWEVER, ISN'T FAZED at all. Of all the people he's ever interviewed, he's found it's the billionaires and blue-chip CEOs who are always the most belligerent. The high flyers who think their time is far too precious to be wasted on insignificant questions from detectives and law enforcement hacks. Who think that bumbling policemen, tight-assed bureaucrats, petty politicians, bloodthirsty journalists, and sniveling tax inspectors are always out to get them, just because of who they are. And the eruptions of these lords of creation, when they come, can be truly volcanic, because their great wealth and security allow them to vent thoughts and emotions that the more dispensable must constrain.

"Do you see this fucking thing, Lieutenant?" Brass's teeth are clenched and his lips are firing the words out like shotgun pellets. *"Do you see this fucking thing I'm in?"* He's holding out the arms of his brass-colored spacesuit, which is studded with inbuilt controls

and radiation gauges. *"Do you think I'm wearing this fucking thing for fun? Is that it?"*

Justus doesn't blink, doesn't move an inch.

"Do you know how long it takes to get into one of these things? Do you know all the dangers and complexities of traveling in space? Do you appreciate all the training and safety checks that an astronaut has to endure? And can you guess what I've been doing in here today, just by the look of me?"

Justus says nothing.

"No? Well, let me tell you." Brass thrusts a finger at the *Prospector*. "I was downstairs—*down there*—inside a Mars landing vehicle. In the tiny cabin of a landing vehicle. With my mission commander. And my medical supervisor and engineer. And all our equipment. Practicing the descent procedures." He sucks in a lungful of air and his chest inflates. "Now do you know—*can you even guess?*—how difficult it is to squeeze four people into that thing? And get everyone fully suited up? And harnessed? And helmeted? *For that matter*, do you know what we're actually attempting here? Can you imagine how dangerous it all is? Do you have *any idea* what it means to go all the way to Mars—and *live* there—for up to five hundred days? And do you have any understanding why all this is so imperative in the first place? Can you *possibly* appreciate all the other dangers? The dangers to Earth? If I don't succeed?"

Justus thinks it really is true—the guy sees himself as the savior of the universe.

"Well, surely I don't need to tell you, do I? You've just come from Earth, haven't you? So you must've seen it all for yourself—all the chaos *down there*? All those pandemics and civil wars, all those natural catastrophes? All those vanishing resources, shrinking spaces, exploding populations? You can't possibly say you haven't seen it with your own eyes! So how can you deny it? The human race *needs* to migrate to the frontiers of space or it *risks total annihilation*. But that sort of thing takes vision and determination. *And most of all it takes balls.* And who's got balls on Earth anymore? Who's got *anything* on Earth anymore? Except cowardice? And laziness? And soul-sapping *envy*? Who can get *anything* done on Earth without some half-assed committee and a plague of bloodsucking leeches? Well, that's exactly why I've had to come here, *to the far side of Moon, for fuck's sake*, just to get away from all those losers! All those chicken-livered little Chihuahuas! Just to get the job done in peace! Because no one else has the vision! No one else has the balls! *Because Fletcher Brass is the last fucking hope of human history!*" Brass exhales bitterly. "So please, Lieutenant, put everything else in proper perspective when you speak to me. When you have the *temerity* to speak to me about . . . whatever the fuck it is you've come to speak to me about."

"I was asking," Justus says, "about Leonardo Black."

"Goodbye, Lieutenant." Brass, with his musk positively flooding out of him, is heading across the catwalk. "I dearly hope we don't have to meet again."

But Justus continues standing in place, thinking that there's one thing—apart from answers—that he didn't get. Something that QT Brass assured him he would.

But as it turns out Brass hasn't quite finished yet. Midway across the catwalk he's turned. He's looking back, with cruel, lancing eyes.

"Oh, may I say something else? Something personal?"

Justus makes an encouraging gesture.

"You should get that face fixed. Really. Because no one will take you seriously until you do."

Then Brass turns, smiling venomously, and disappears into the *Prospector*.

To Justus it seems almost as if Brass had read his mind. As if he'd heard a recording of Justus's meeting with QT and felt compelled to offer that last morsel as definitive proof of his identity. As if everything else—the immense hubris, grandiosity, larger-than-life charm, confidence, evasiveness, obfuscation, implied threats, and colorful language—wasn't quite enough.

"How did it go?" The flight coordinator, Amity Powers, has materialized at Justus's side. She must have heard the last vestiges of the exchange, if not the whole thing, so to Justus the question seems superfluous. But he doesn't avoid it.

"Very well."

And he's not lying. Because in the way Brass responded, or refused to respond, Justus believes he's unearthed a treasure trove.

"You don't know how lucky you are," Powers goes on. "Mr. Brass has a lot on his shoulders right now."

"The whole universe, by the sounds of it."

Powers chuckles. "Well, his shoulders are broad enough, as you've no doubt seen. And a man like that should be permitted to let his tongue go anywhere it pleases."

"Uh-huh." Justus is suddenly sure she's more than just a project manager.

"Oh, by the way," she adds, leading him out, "this message arrived while you were talking."

She hands over a sheet of paper, which Justus reads as he walks. It's from the PPD.

"Is it bad news?" she asks—as if she hasn't already read it.

"There's been some trouble in Sin," Justus says, folding the page. "I need to get back there immediately."

26

I F YOU'VE EVER BEEN to Nearside you'll certainly know of the Overview Effect—there are whole towers, observation decks and hotels named after it. The Overview Effect is what happens when a human being surveys Earth from a sizable distance out in space. The Apollo astronauts were the first to feel the full force of it: that mind-blowing moment when in one glance they took in the home planet, the cradle of life and civilization, looking supremely small and fragile in the awesome vastness of the universe. Since then a sojourn to the Moon, in order to feel this life-changing sense of humility and fraternity, has become an essential pilgrimage for humanists, thrill seekers, and image-conscious politicians.

Torquil "Torkie" Macleod is not at all interested in the Overview Effect. To him it's been so comprehensively exploited by now that it's positively crass. And he wouldn't be able to muscle in commercially even if he wanted to—all sorts of overpriced permits are required in the official tourist districts. So in consequence he actually *resents* the Overview Effect. He doesn't even *look* at Earth, not even over his shoulder, when he's on Nearside.

Macleod used to be an upmarket bus driver, ferrying film stars, rock bands, and other celebrities around most of the UK. A glamorous job in its way, but not particularly lucrative, at least until he began supplying his passengers with top-end hallucinogens—everything from mescaline to DMT, all manufactured by some pharmacy-school dropouts in a back-door lab in Hackney. And for a while he was making so much money from this side business that he was living out of a basement apartment in Knightsbridge. But keeping ahead of the law proved a perpetual struggle, and when the Hackney lab was raided—Macleod heard about it on the Channel 4 news—he escaped just in time to Spain. And from there he went to India. And from there, via the Malabar Coast launch site, he ended up on the Moon. He considered hiding in Purgatory, of course—it had the advantage of being beyond the power of extradition treaties—but he'd heard that Fletcher Brass's kingdom was getting stricter about whom it admitted. And he didn't like the idea of being in a constricted territory anyway. Years of plying Britain's motorways had left him with an insatiable appetite for roaming across large distances. So he decided to take his chances and find something else—something not unlike the job he had enjoyed so much on Earth.

Currently Macleod is a freelance bus driver again. He has at his disposal a very long range transverse vehicle formerly used to ferry tourists from Doppelmayer Base to the first Chinese landing zones. With eight variable-diameter wheels, six regenerative fuel-cell batteries, integrated mesh-gear transmission, eighteen high-pressure halogen lamps, seating for six (not including the driver), and a reliable daylight range of two thousand kilometers, the VLTV is far more sophisticated, more expensive, and safer than any moon-buggy LRV. But it's still old, jarred, scratched, and even rusted; Macleod has never been much interested in maintenance. Most of the time he uses it to take scientists, technicians, miners, and company representatives on trips around Nearside. He usually parks at the ExelAnt Mining Base at Schubert Crater, where he rents a room, but he makes sure he doesn't get pinned down by any routine. Macleod prefers to keep on the move, as independent and elusive as possible, because he's again running a not-strictly-legal business on the side.

Dark Side Tours, as it is known, appears in no official brochures but is pretty much an open secret on the Moon. For a substantial fee—as much as five thousand U.S. dollars per head—Macleod will drive you and your entourage into "the forbidden realms of Farside." And there you will experience something "immeasurably more powerful than the Overview Effect." You will experience, in fact, its very opposite—"the No-View Effect." Because you will be in the only place in the solar system, and possibly the entire universe, where it's never possible to see Earth, even with the most powerful of telescopes. You will be like a child completely cut off from its mother. You will be out of sight and out of mind. You will be, for perhaps the first time in your life, beyond the range of radar. You will be naked to the cosmos. You will feel, in quick succession, abandonment, liberation, and empowerment "in ways you have never experienced before." And (if you believe the word-of-mouth advertising, anyway) you will "never be the same again."

Today, Macleod is delighted to be driving four members of the retro rock band Dustproof Shockproof. Macleod has chauffeured lots of musicians in his career, but at fifty-one he's now a generation older than most of them. Dustproof Shockproof, however, is almost of his own vintage, so spiritually he feels that they're on the same level. He understands them. He thinks they understand him. They make him feel like he's chilling with old friends. He hasn't even sold them the cut-down drugs.

Presently the band members are all high on Selene, an LSD derivative that's popular on the Moon, and Macleod has taken a tab too, just to be sociable. The boys, along with two hot groupies, are slumped in the passenger seats; Macleod is at the steering wheel. To this point he's kept mainly to the hard-packed maintenance tracks, veering off only to avoid an encounter with official vehicles. The science and maintenance teams don't usually enter Farside during the darkness—it's much easier to work in the fourteen days of warmth and sunlight—so it's usually at lunar nighttime that Macleod conducts his tours. But Dustproof Shockproof is returning to Earth in a couple of days, and for them he's compromised—he's racing across the sunlit surface for the day-night terminator. For the genuine Dark Side of the Moon.

"Are those penguins out there?" It's the drummer, Spyder Blue.

"Don't see no penguins," replies the bass guitarist, Q'mar Kent.

"They're penguins, I'm telling ya—all waddling about and shit."

"They're rocks, man—they're rocks."

"They're moving and shit."

"My head's moving, man—this is top-grade junk. Top grade." Q'mar Kent locates Macleod and shouts his approval. "Top grade!"

Macleod just nods. He's taken so much Selene since he arrived on the Moon that in small amounts it no longer has much impact on him. But he knows very well it's the best acid in the universe.

"When you gonna open the sky, man?" It's the band leader, Maxx Dee, now—he's staring at the vehicle's glass ceiling, which is covered with a radiation shield.

"When we cross the terminator," Macleod tells him.

"Why not now?"

"Sun damage. You don't want that glare on your skin if you don't need it."

After a while Dee grunts. "We gonna see the diamonds?"

"You're gonna see more than just diamonds, man. You're gonna see constellations, whole galaxies you never knew existed."

"Nocturnity?"

"That's right, man—Nocturnity."

Nocturnity—"endless night"—is the name given to the skies during the 328 consecutive hours of darkness on Farside: unpolluted, breathtakingly clear, awesomely endless. No sunlight, no Earthlight, no cloud cover, no diffusing atmosphere, no murmurs of wildlife or rustling trees—just you, the black sphere beneath you, and the naked majesty of the cosmos above. It's an experience, even more powerful than the No-View Effect, that has the potential to warp minds. They say it can turn a saint into a psychopath—and vice versa. And it's even more powerful under the influence of Selene.

"Where'd you get this acid, man?" It's Q'mar Kent again.

"From Purgatory," says Macleod.

"This is top grade."

"Stuff from Purgatory usually is."

"We going to Purgatory?"

"You got an extra five grand on you?"

"What if I wash the dishes?"

Macleod chuckles but doesn't answer. He's been to Purgatory a couple of times but doesn't need to go again. And he didn't personally get the Selene from there. Drugs manufactured in Purgatory are frequently smuggled out and made available, if you know where to look, on Nearside. And on Earth too, at astronomical prices.

"We gonna see the golden dust clouds?" asks Maxx Dee.

"If the conditions are right," says Macleod.

"Hope so, man, I'm tired of this . . . mouth. You see the mouth, ladies?"

"I see . . . amoebas," answers one.

"I see Christmas decorations," says the other.

"I see penguins," repeats Spyder Blue. "Fuckin' things are dancing now."

Macleod wonders if he's given them too much Selene. When passengers really start tripping out, in a confined and pressurized environment, it can get ugly. Once Macleod had to belt a guy over the head with the fire extinguisher. Still, he's confident nothing unpleasant will happen with Dustproof Shockproof—as long as he keeps them entertained.

"Wanna see the crashed satellite?" he asks.

"What satellite?" someone asks.

"*Luna 14*—it's Russian. Came down in 1968, a year before the Apollo 11 landing. It's one of the only wrecks here that hasn't been pilfered, because it's pretty much hidden. Hardly anyone knows it's there."

No one seems enthusiastic.

"How far is it?" asks one of the groupies.

"Couple of klicks. Take us five minutes."

Still no one seems interested.

"I wanna see the diamonds," says Maxx Dee, sighing.

"I wanna see the Orion nebula," says the other groupie.

"I want some more acid," says Q'mar Kent.

"There's a fuckin' kangaroo out there now!" exclaims Spyder Blue.

Macleod laughs under his breath but doesn't turn. They're in a region of featureless plateaux and gently flowing hills that could be mistaken for parts of the Australian outback. He suspects the kangaroo is a twisted boulder or a broken-down robot. But Spyder Blue is insistent.

"Fuckin' thing is coming this way—the kangaroo!"

"You're freakin' out," says Q'mar Kent.

"I'm telling you, man—a kangaroo—see for yourself!"

There's a long silence.

"What the—?"

"Ya see it—*ya see it*?"

"What the fuck?"

"I told you, man—I told you! A kangaroo!"

"But . . . but that ain't a kangaroo—it's a dude!"

"It's a kangaroo!"

"It's a fuckin' dude, *jumpin'* like a kangaroo!"

Macleod is starting to think that maybe it was a bad idea to travel this far. They left Schubert eight hours ago, and he broke out the tabs not long after that. Normally his passengers wouldn't be this amped out—not this far from Nocturnity.

"He's jumping after us!"

"He's coming this way!"

"Man—look at that fucker jump!"

"Where's his spacesuit?"

"How the fuck's he breathing?"

One of the ladies has joined in now, Macleod hears—it's like a mass hallucination—but still he doesn't turn.

"Man—that fucker's serious!"

"He's not serious—he's smiling!"

"He's coming up right behind us!"

"He's chasing us—he's chasing us!"

"You gotta stop this thing, man!"

This last is addressed to the driver, but Macleod doesn't stop.

"You gotta brake this thing, man—he's running for the bus!"

"We don't need to stop—he's catchin' up!"

"Look at that fucker!"

"Where is he now?"

"Where's he gone?"

"He's still behind us—we just can't see him!"

"What the fuck's he doin'?"

"Is he still chasing us?"

There's a sudden *whump*. It reverberates through the interior of the VLTV. And Macleod takes his foot off the pedal, astonished. He glances around, but everyone else is looking up. Then there's a scrabbling sound. A dragging sound. So Macleod brakes—he stops the VLTV entirely. Wondering if he himself is hallucinating.

"He's on top of this thing now!" says Spyder Blue.

"He's crawling on the roof!"

"It's like a safari!"

"He wants to eat us up!"

"Fuck, man, is this part of the tour?"

Macleod doesn't answer. His whole body is tensed, his ears cocked, trying to make sense of it all.

Then there's more scrabbling—directly above the driver's seat. And *thumps*, as if someone is pounding on the roof. Trying to break in.

Macleod stares upward, waiting for some sign of what it is.

"No one fuckin' believed me, man!" exclaims Spyder Blue. "*No one fuckin' believed me!*"

Then a head appears at the top of the windscreen—upside down.

Macleod blinks a few times, then takes it all in.

It's a man. Or at least it looks like a man. Black-haired, black-suited, and black-eyed. Looking in at them. And smiling. Smiling like an idiot.

Macleod doesn't know what to do. Part of him is scared shitless. Another part is delighted—because whatever the hell is going on, it's interesting. It's *more* than interesting. It's everything you'd want in a Dark Side tour. He just hopes the band is enjoying it.

"Looks like a fuckin' narc!" says Maxx Dee, chortling, as the black-suited man swivels his body and drops down to the lunar surface in front of them.

27

BACK IN THE SIN vehicle bay, Justus is greeted by a gum-chewing Dash Chin and escorted swiftly to a police car.

"Okay," he says, getting inside, "tell me what we've got."

"Two bodies," Chin says excitedly. "Just wait till you see! This is real butcher's-window stuff!"

"A terrorist attack?"

"Supposedly. There's another statement too."

"At the crime scene?"

"Right next to the bodies."

"And what's it say?"

Chin sniggers. "You'll see."

Justus, who's spent the entire journey from the rocket base hoping for an uncontaminated murder scene, wonders just how many cops have handled the statement already. "And the victims?"

"Kit Zachary—ever heard of him?"

"Who is he?"

Chin starts the car. "A builder—biggest builder in Sin. Least he was when he got up this morning."

"And why would terrorists be killing a builder, exactly?"

"He was a high-profile builder. A big cheese. A real mover and shaker here."

"With political ambitions?"

"He had his hat in the ring, sure."

Justus nods. "And the other person?"

"Huh?"

"You said there were two bodies."

"Oh," laughs Chin, backing out of the vehicle bay, "that's just some whore he was with."

They race recklessly through the streets, nearly clipping a couple of tourists, and in no time they reach Sordello, the red light district of Sin. Here, in a labyrinth of neon-washed streets, Chin brings the car to a jolting halt outside a narrow multistory brothel called Cherry Poppins. A crowd of half-dressed prostitutes, many resembling famous sex symbols, are being restrained by the police. Two of the cops are bashing someone with a truncheon.

"Third floor, sir," Chin says.

"You're not coming up?"

"Gotta spare my appetite—haven't had a bite to eat since last night."

Justus doesn't insist because he doesn't trust Chin anyway. Inside the brothel he's directed to a cage elevator but he elects to take the stairs. Halfway up a bunch of cops are grinning and joking. Justus hears a few comments in advance:

". . . didn't even get his dick out—"

". . . one helluva head job, though—"

". . . yeah, probably got the instructions mixed!"

But when they see Justus they stiffen, give unconvincing nods of deference, and zip tight until he passes.

Finally Justus enters a room on the third floor. There's an unmade bed, a bedside table, Pompeian sex murals on the walls, and suspended from the ceiling a spinning mirror ball that's throwing out shards of white light. There are plenty of cops too: Hugo Pfeffer, Jacinta Carvalho, Prince Oda Universe, and the surly Russian Grigory Kalganov among them. Pfeffer's eating a hot dog. Carvalho's got a steaming coffee in a Styrofoam cup. They're slouching around, looking like they're discussing the latest baseball results. Then, when they see Justus, they straighten self-consciously and shift to reveal the featured tableau.

"Need a barf bag, Lieutenant?" one of them asks.

Justus shakes his head. "I've seen worse," he lies.

The man looks to have been about fifty-five. He's still in a well-cut suit, but his head's barely attached to his body. From what Justus can figure, he must have been attacked from behind with a heavy blade, probably a meat cleaver. There are thick gashes around the neck and shoulders and one crushing blow to the back of the head. Blood everywhere—owing to fewer clotting agents, the blood of long-term lunatics shoots farther when arteries are severed—though it's difficult to make it all out against the room's cherry-red decor. The girl, purple-haired, pouty, and to Justus curiously familiar-looking, appears to have had her throat slashed. Her windpipe is visible. Her eyes are unnaturally wide open, like she couldn't believe what was happening. She's wearing pink toenail flashers that are still blinking on and off.

"Any idea what exactly happened here?" Justus asks.

No answers at first, but then someone pipes up:

"We were waiting for you, Lieutenant."

"Yeah, you're the man in charge."

"You're the chief detective."

Justus ignores the insolence. "Okay, then, you can at least tell me what you know. When were the bodies discovered? And by whom?"

The cops look at each other. Finally Grigory Kalganov offers, "It was me, Lieutenant."

"You answered a call?"

"I was in the area. The receptionist hailed me."

"And this receptionist was the one who found the bodies?"

"That is so."

"And has this receptionist been interviewed?"

"Not by me."

Carvalho interjects: "We're still trying to find her."

"What," Justus asks, "she's out to lunch, I suppose?"

Carvalho doesn't know.

Justus looks back at Kalganov. "Did you seal off the scene immediately?"

"I called for backup."

"But you didn't set up a cordon?"

"That is not my job, Lieutenant."

"Then how many others—cops and others—have been through here since you arrived?"

"Fifteen, sixteen."

"Sixteen. What about the Forensic Response Team?"

Kalganov shrugs.

"You mean to say they haven't been called?"

Carvalho says, "They're on another job."

"Something more important than a murder?"

"A hotel break-in. A tourist got robbed."

"And a robbery is more important than a homicide in this town?"

"Depends. It was a big tourist. A travel writer."

"So no one's done a sweep of this room?"

"Not yet."

Justus has already noticed that no one is wearing gloves or shoe covers. He points. "And what's behind that door there?"

"That's the bathroom."

"Well, how many people have—?"

But at this stage a high-pressure toilet flushes noisily and the bathroom door opens. Chief Buchanan, hitching up his pants, squeezes through.

"Ah, Lieutenant," he says, sniffing, "pleased you could make it. Traffic problems or somethin'?"

Justus ignores him. "I was just about to ask about Forensics."

"What about them?"

"It would have been preferable if they'd been here already. Done a survey of the crime scene—that bathroom in particular. But I guess we'll have to work with what we've got."

Buchanan, not missing the rebuke, grunts skeptically. "Why? What the fuck's so interesting about the bathroom?"

Justus shrugs. "A high-profile businessman enters a mid-range brothel with a prostitute. We can't say for certain that they're here for sex, because neither of them is unclothed. But we can conclude with some certainty that this was a setup. The wounds to Mr. Zachary's body—and I'm only assuming the body hasn't been moved by now—tell us he was attacked from behind. So he had enough time to enter the room, maneuver around the bed here, and turn to the girl. Meaning the killer wasn't visible when he came in. Meaning that more than likely he or she was hiding in that bathroom."

"Very sweet," says Buchanan, and addresses the others. "Didn't I tell you this guy was like Sherlock Holmes?" Mumbles of agreement, then Buchanan raises an objection. "But you say Zachary wasn't here for sex?"

"I said we can't be certain."

"Well, why would a man come to a fuck shop if it wasn't to fuck?"

"Did he have a history with prostitutes?" Justus asks.

"Who doesn't?"

"I mean, would a man like that—a very high-profile and successful businessman—really need to come to a sordid place like this?"

"Sometimes the restaurant is the best part of the meal."

An image of Buchanan in sexual congress appears in Justus's mind but it's mercifully brief. "Well, it's not important at this stage, I grant you. But he was lured up here on false pretenses, that's almost certain. The girl didn't flee when the killing started, so she's possibly in on it. When the killer finished with Zachary he turned on her—she wasn't expecting that. So she was probably hanging around for a payoff. And what we need to find out now is where Mr. Zachary met her in the first place—I'm assuming it wasn't Reception?"

"They didn't see anything," Carvalho offers.

"So prostitutes just take their clients up these side stairs, is that it?"

"That's about right."

"And this room is the regular office of this particular prostitute?"

No one seems sure.

"Okay," Justus goes on, "then we've got some work to do. We're gonna have to look for a murder weapon in this building— the size of these wounds suggests something that'd be difficult to conceal in your pocket. Maybe a bloody coat was disposed of as well—there'd be more than enough red stuff to leave a mark. And we need to find out where this prostitute solicited for customers. Was it a bar? A hotel lobby? The streets?"

"Could be any of those," says Buchanan.

"Either way, we're gonna have to find out. And then we're gonna have to visit those haunts and find out if anyone saw her with Kit Zachary. If anyone overheard a conversation between them. If she's got any friends or colleagues she might have confided in."

"And what's that going to prove?" Buchanan says.

"It might be crucial."

"Doubt it. Zachary was lookin' to get laid. Found some hooker and took her to a room. Some guy pops out and kills him, that's all."

Justus blinks. "You're not seriously suggesting that the killer just happened to be in the bathroom? By sheer coincidence?"

"I ain't suggesting that at all," Buchanan says. "I'm just sayin' that even if it was all arranged, wasting time with cockamamie questions ain't gonna get us anywhere."

"This is hardly cockamamie—this is procedure."

"On Earth, maybe—not here."

"That's funny. I thought I was in charge of this investigation."

"You *are* in charge. But you're *green*."

"Then you're welcome to appoint someone more experienced if you like."

"I ain't doin' that. You're doing a great job."

"You keep saying that."

"And I ain't lyin'." Buchanan turns to the others. "Am I lyin', fellas? Haven't I been tellin' you what a great job this guy is doin'?"

Everyone nods. But some of them are smiling.

"Okay, then," Justus says, "well, while I'm *still* in charge I want to know everything possible about the girl—and I don't care how cockamamie it sounds. I want to know where she operated, who she worked with, if she'd been hired by Zachary before—I want to know all that, and I want to know it by six o'clock. I also want to know everything about Zachary's movements. I want to know his general routine. I want to have a list of everyone he's spoken to in the last forty-eight hours. I want a preliminary report from the FRT on my desk as soon as possible. And I understand there was a terrorist statement?"

"More bullshit," says Buchanan.

"Who's got it?"

"Prince's got it."

"Then may I have a look at it?"

Buchanan makes a dismissive gesture to Prince Oda Universe. "Prince—give the lieutenant here a look at that garbage, will ya?"

The eight-foot Nigerian, his head almost touching the ceiling, hands across a printed page which, much to Justus's relief, is in a Ziploc bag.

He glances up. "Turn off that mirror ball and get me some light in here."

"De ball *is* de light," rumbles Price Oda Universe.

So Justus squints and reads the page.

THE PEOPLE'S HAMMER BANGS ANOTHER CROOKED NAIL
KIT ZACHARY = BIG-BUSINESS BLOODSUCKER
NO MORE LANDLORDS!
NO MORE BRASS!
VIVA REDEMPTION!

"Bullshit," Chief Buchanan says again. "I told you we'd get more of the same."

"You did," agrees Justus. "And you also said we'd get more murders."

"What about it?"

"Nothing—I just admire your foresight." Justus hands the statement to Jacinta Carvalho, saying, "Get it to Forensics immediately—see if it gives off the same DNA signatures as the first statement. And don't let any of this leak to the *Tablet* until I say so, understand?"

"Too late for that," says Carvalho.

"What's that mean?"

"It's already in the *Tablet*. Special edition. Front page."

"And how did that happen?"

"They got their own copy."

"They got their own copy? Well, okay, I want that too. And I want that with Forensics as well, before anyone else from the paper gets their paws on it."

Carvalho looks dumbfounded. "You want *me* to go to the *Tablet*?"

"You got something better to do?"

"But it's lunchtime, and I—"

"No," says Justus, "it's *hunting* time. So eat in the saddle. Or save your appetite for Chief Buchanan's barbeque. I'm sure the chief himself agrees."

Silence from Buchanan—the whole mood in the room is that of a churlish road gang ordered back to work—so Justus turns and looks at the chief directly. "Isn't that right, Chief?" he says.

And finally Buchanan, like a man cornered, blows out his lips and forces a nod. "That's right," he says to the others. "You heard the lieutenant—and *he's* the man in charge. So snap to it. Get back on your fuckin' ponies!"

The cops start filing out of the room. The surly Russian spares enough time to snarl something in Justus's ear. Then Buchanan himself waddles over, looking disingenuously contrite. He slaps Justus on the back.

"Hey, we'll talk about this later, yeah? But for now, just don't get the wrong idea—it's just the way things are around here. The boys have to deal with so much shit in this town that they have a sorta natural reaction to a scene like this. But they'll get over it in time, you'll see. Just don't take anything personally, okay?"

"Yeah," Justus says blankly, staring at the hacked-open body of Kit Zachary. "Yeah."

But he's no longer thinking about insubordinate cops. He's no longer thinking of procedure. He's not even thinking about Kit Zachary and the dead prostitute. He's just trying to make sense of the word Grigory Kalganov whispered to him on the way past.

Pazuzu.

28

THE DROID IS NOW inside the VLTV. When he first spied its deep tracks, twenty minutes earlier, his intention was to take over the vehicle as quickly as possible. Accordingly he followed its trail, came in sight of the VLTV itself, and then sprang on top, hoping to bust his way inside and kill the driver by depressurization alone. But the roof, he discovered, was sealed over with an impenetrable radiation shield. So he peered over the top of the vehicle, aiming to break the front window, but in so doing he could not help noticing the many passengers within. And it suddenly occurred to him that this was an all-new opportunity—to reach his destination incognito, as it were, hidden within a group. So he dropped to the ground and through gestures made it clear that he would like to be permitted inside.

The VLTV had its own cubicle-like airlock situated at the rear. After the customary pressure-seal checks and cleaning procedures, the droid squeezed through into the passenger compartment, where his arrival was greeted with much amusement.

"—careful of his dust," the driver was saying.

"Hey, dude, we're Dustproof, remember?"

"Step aboard, my man."

"Someone make room for the new guy!"

"Brenda, you wanna sit on Daddy's lap?"

"Here's a seat, man."

"What's your name, dude?"

The droid, lowering himself between the man with dreadlocks and the man with a blue spider tattoo on his forehead, sees visible affection on the faces of the passengers, as if he has relieved them of a great boredom.

"I am the Wizard," he says.

"'Course you are, man."

"I told you he was."

"You said he was a kangaroo."

"I said he *looked like* a kangaroo."

"Sure you're not a narc?"

This last is said by the man with the imposing beard.

"What is a narc, sir?"

"Never mind. You're not one?"

"I am not, sir."

"You're not a security guy or anything? You're not gonna arrest us?"

"You have no reason to be concerned. I only want to sit here and enjoy your company. Are you the King?"

"The King?"

"Sure thinks he is," says the girl in his lap.

The bearded man chuckles. "The King is in Memphis, man—in a coffin."

"I am sorry to hear that, sir. Who are you, then, if not the King?"

"I'm Maxx Dee. With a double X and a double E."

"It is a pleasure to meet you, Mr. Dee with a double X and a double E."

"And this here is Brenda, and that's—what the fuck's your name again?—Maia. And Q'mar Kent is my man on drums. And Massive Richard is the little guy who's totally wasted there. And that ugly motherfucker to your left is Spyder Blue."

"It is a pleasure to meet you, Brenda, Maia, Q'mar Kent, Massive Richard, and Spyder Blue."

"And I'm Torkie," Macleod sings out from the front. "The driver."

"It is a pleasure to meet you, Mr. Torkie. Why are you not driving, if you are the driver?"

"Yeah," says Maxx Dee, "why are you not driving, man?"

"Let's get movin'."

"Back on the road, man."

"I wanna see those diamonds."

"I wanna see those nebulas."

"What about our new guy here?" Q'mar Kent asks. "What were you doin' out on the surface?"

The dreadlocked Q'mar has a red pulse-light in his left nostril that flashes with each heartbeat. The droid looks at him steadily.

"I am going to Purgatory, sir."

"Purgatory, huh?"

"That is correct, sir. To Purgatory. El Dorado. Oz."

Chuckles all around. "Hey, man," says Spyder Blue, "you wanna go to Oz, we can get you there right now."

"I *do* want to go to Oz, sir."

"Just a sec."

Spyder Blue reaches into a plastic bag and hands the droid a milky white tablet in the shape of the Moon.

The droid looks at it skeptically. "And what is this, sir? Is it sugar?"

"It ain't sugar."

"Is it fuel?"

"You could call it fuel."

The droid holds it up in front of his eyes, but Spyder Blue interjects. "It's best if you just swallow it, man."

"And by performing this action, sir, I will get to Oz?"

"Oh yeah, man."

So the droid places the tab on his tongue and gulps it down. But in analyzing its chemical composition he is severely disappointed.

"Sir," he says, "this contains only trace elements of glucose. It does nothing for me. It takes me nowhere."

Everyone laughs and mocks Spyder Blue.

"Hey, man, that was three hundred bucks right there."

"Serves you right, dude."

"Giving Blue Moon to a tinnie."

The droid, still disappointed, looks at Spyder Blue. "You told me I would get to Oz, sir."

"You just gotta wait."

"Wait, sir?"

"Till Oz comes to you."

Torkie Macleod interjects from the front: "Forget about Oz, man—we'll be hitting Nocturnity soon."

"Nocturnity?" asks the droid.

"That's right—you got good visual sensors?"

"I do, sir."

"Then turn your eyes to the sky, once we get there, and you'll see more stars than you ever dreamed of."

"And is this Nocturnity to the north, sir?"

"Not really."

"But I need to head north."

"We're not goin' north."

"But it is easy enough for you to change direction, if you are really the driver."

"We're not goin' north because it's not what these folks paid for."

The droid, still smiling, looks back at the others and says, "I need to go north."

The others think about it but don't respond. So the droid says, more firmly:

"I need to go north."

Q'mar Kent, to his right, is the most accommodating.

"Was it north where you were heading when we picked you up?"

"It was, sir."

"To Purgatory, you said?"

"That is correct, sir. Purgatory. El Dorado. Oz."

"Is it an emergency or something?"

"I consider it an emergency."

"What're you gonna do when you get there?"

"I am going to be the Wizard. The conquistador. The King."

Q'mar chuckles. "I can buy that, man. They got some serious Lucy in Purgatory, I know that much." He half turns to the others. "Say, how about we go to Purgatory anyway? The Wizard here needs to go to Oz. And I want to check out their Lucy."

Silence for a few moments, then Maxx Dee sniffs and says, "Nah, man, we can't go to Purgatory."

"'Course we can—we're halfway there already. More than half."

"What are we gonna do there?"

"Get some Lucy. Some White Lightning. Some Felix the Cat. You'll be needing some more by then anyway."

Maxx Dee chortles but shakes his head.

Macleod speaks up. "I can't just take you into Purgatory, you know. You got your passports?"

Q'mar says, "We got our chips, man—that's the same thing."

"They can still knock us back."

"It's worth a shot."

"Well, I can't take you there for free, anyway."

The droid interjects. "I will pay."

"*You'll* pay?" Macleod asks, looking at him.

"That is what I said, sir."

"You sure you got that sort of dough?"

"I have unlimited resources at my disposal, sir."

"You mean your *master* will pay?"

"You will be paid all that you require, plus a substantial bonus, when you deliver me to Purgatory, sir."

"There ya go!" Q'mar says to the others. "The Wizard's loaded—and we're not even payin' for it! Whaddaya say?"

"Nah," Maxx Dee grunts. "I want to see Nocturnity."

"If we head north now," Macleod points out, "Nocturnity will overtake us anyway."

"I dunno, man," says Maxx Dee. "I dunno."

"Let's vote on it," Brenda says.

"Yeah," agrees Spyder Blue, "let's make it democratic."

"Leave me out of it," says Macleod, laughing. "I got no dog in the fight."

"Well, okay, then," decides Maxx Dee. "There's—what?—seven of us, including the narc. That oughta settle it."

The droid shakes his head. "But I do not want to vote, sir. I already know where I need to go. And I will pay."

"Chill out, dude," says Maxx Dee. "We *gotta* vote. You believe in democracy, don't you?"

"I believe in capitalism, free enterprise, and natural rights."

"Exactly—so we vote, and the majority rules, okay?"

"I am the majority," says the droid.

"No, you're one vote. And I'm a second vote. That's one vote says we go to Purgatory, and one says we don't."

"And I say we *don't*," says Brenda. "That's two against."

"Well, I say we *do* go," says Maia.

"That's two votes all," says Maxx Dee. "What about you, Massive Richard?" He prods the sleeping figure in front of him.

Massive Richard tries to open his glued-together eyes. "Wassup?"

"You wanna go to Purgatory?"

"Wha—?"

"Do you wanna go to Purgatory? Up north? We're having a vote."

"Wha—?"

"Just say yes or no, man," says Maxx Dee. "Yes or no."

Massive Richard shrugs indifferently. "No," he says. "I dunno—I just wanna fuckin' sleep." He closes his eyes again.

"That's three votes to two," says Maxx Dee.

"Well, I sure wanna go," says Q'mar Kent. "So that's three votes all."

Everyone turns to Spyder Blue. "Looks like it's your choice, man," says Maxx Dee. "You hold the deciding vote."

Spyder Blue laughs. "Anyone wanna pay me?"

"I will pay you, sir," says the droid.

"I was joking."

216 | ANTHONY O'NEILL

"Nevertheless, I will pay you."

"That's not the way democracy works."

"I believe it does, sir."

"Sorry, man," Spyder Blue says, "but as much as I like money, and as much as I like this acid, I always make up my own mind, okay? So it's no deal—I'm gonna say no."

The droid stares at him. "Did you say 'no,' sir?"

"Yup—I don't wanna go to Purgatory."

"But I need to go to Purgatory, sir."

"Sorry, man, but I don't."

"But I do."

Spyder Blue shrugs. "Sorry, man."

"Well, that's it," Maxx Dee says from behind. "That's it settled. Four votes to three. And you lose, man."

The droid says nothing.

"Majority rules, okay?"

The droid keeps staring at Spyder Blue. And staring. And then a very obvious solution seems to occur to him. And he doesn't waste any time.

His fist shoots out and smashes into Spyder Blue's head with the force of a wrecking ball. And Spyder Blue's neck snaps and his head rebounds, flopping forward onto his chest.

In the VLTV there's complete silence—no one can believe it. A moment ago Spyder Blue was casting the deciding vote. Now he's dead.

The droid turns to them, expressionless.

"Vote again," he says.

29

AT 1700, AFTER SUPERVISING the general investigation in Sordello, Justus surprises everyone by announcing that he's heading off for a snack. He says it declaratively and well within earshot of Grigory Kalganov. Someone offers to join him but he says he needs to be alone.

Making all the evasive moves his limited knowledge of Sin allows, he then heads quickly through the humid streets to the square where he spoke with Dash Chin the previous evening. At a food stall he buys a pizza-stick and a fruit-malt. He stands near the statue of the winged demon, which he's managed to remember is called Pazuzu. He starts consuming his meal while looking around, as casually as possible, for signs of the Russian's approach. But it turns out he's only attracting attention—Sinners are nodding to him, smiling, wishing him the best, appealing for help. He's forgotten just how visible he's become since the

Tablet's adulatory article. It doesn't seem likely that Kalganov will approach him in this fishbowl environment, so after fifteen minutes he trashes the wrappers and starts heading back to Sordello.

But passing through Kasbah he notices a large bar with a flashing sign: "PAZUZU." He enters immediately and finds an upmarket establishment full of well-dressed businesspeople mingling with good-looking men and women, some of them almost certainly prostitutes. But there's no Kalganov. And suddenly Justus understands. Pazuzu wasn't a rendezvous point; it's the place where the dead hooker plied her trade. It's probably where she picked up Kit Zachary. But again, Justus doubts that he'll get many approaches in such a place, so he goes out and cases the neighborhood, then comes back.

"'Scuse me," he says in a raised voice. "My name is Lieutenant Damien Justus of the PPD. I'm not here to waste your time. But if anyone here knew a local lady called Nina Nebula, also known as Dear O'Dear, also known as Charlene Hogg among many other aliases, or if anyone has any information about her at all, then I'll be in one of the rear booths of Schwab's across the road. And I guarantee—*guarantee*—confidentiality."

In Schwab's, which is modeled after the old L.A. drugstore, the decor is all spit-shined chrome and fading red leather. A jukebox in the corner is thumping out hundred-year-old hits. The clientele is young and scattered and generally minding their own business. Justus secures the second-to-last booth and makes sure the one immediately behind it is empty.

He waits fifteen minutes and is on the verge of giving up when he hears the back door squeak. He doesn't turn. He's expecting the new arrival, whoever it is, to either flop into the rear booth, thus indicating that he's got information, or whisk by, thus indicating that he's just another customer. But the person does neither of those things. He passes by casually and then lowers himself into the same booth as Justus, directly across the table.

"You're the new boy, Justus," he says—pronouncing it "Justice."

"And you are?"

"A friend of Charlene's."

The man is swarthy, with Permatanned skin, bristling blond-streaked hair, and a neatly groomed five o'clock shadow. He's wearing a flashy pin-striped suit with exaggerated shoulders—what used to be called a zoot suit—and giving off a thick scent of funeral home lavender.

"Sure you want to be seen talking like this?" Justus asks him.

"Talkin' around corners ain't gonna fool anyone around here. And I figure you knew what I looked like before I sat down anyway—this place is full of reflections."

Justus doesn't deny it.

"Besides, I don't intend to be here long." He taps a cigarette from a silver case. "Nutri-Cig?"

"Thanks, no. Can I get you something from the counter?"

"I don't drink milkshakes." The man lights up his cigarette, blows out the salubrious fumes, and smiles. His canines, Justus notices, have been sharpened into fangs. "You know, I never thought this would be happening—not in a zillion years."

"This being what, exactly?"

"Me talking to a pig."

"I'm no ordinary pig, if it makes you feel better."

"Happy to hear it. I could tell you stories about the pork here that'd make your hair curl. Or fall out."

"I've no doubt."

The man sucks in smoke. "So believe me, I *wanna* believe in you. *Everyone* in this town wants to believe in you—you can feel it in the air."

Justus shrugs. "I can't control what people think. But I don't owe anything to anyone, if it makes a difference."

"That's what the *Tablet* said."

"The *Tablet* quoted me saying a lot of things. Most of which I didn't really say."

"Well, that's what the shit-rag does. But then there was that commentary by Bill Swagger—you read that?"

"Uh-huh."

"Said we didn't need your type around here. Said you had a real nerve, treating us like little kids, and this place is functioning real well as it is."

"That's what I read."

"Well, you know what, you can forget about what you did say or didn't say to that weasel Reilly. Because it's the Swagger piece that bought you cred in Sin."

"That so?"

"Everyone in Sin knows Bill Swagger is Fletcher Brass's pet toad. When Swagger croaks, we know he croaks for Brass. So if he croaks when you walk in, and he croaks loudly, then people figure you must be okay after all."

"I know nothing about that," Justus says.

"'Course you don't. And that's why I feel sorry for you."

"How's that?"

"'Cause you're being used. And you can't even see it."

"Used in what way?"

"I don't know. But you're being used."

"Maybe you're right."

"I am right."

"Doesn't mean I shouldn't raise some hell while I can."

"Before you get killed—is that what you mean?"

Justus is surprised, hearing it said like that. "I can look after myself," he says.

The man taps his cigarette over an ashtray, chuckling. "You're crazy," he says. "You stay here, they'll get you in the end."

"Or maybe *I'll* get *them*."

"Then you're not just crazy—you're psychotic."

"And what does that make you, if you're sitting here talking to me?"

The man snorts. "You think I give a shit anymore? About anything? Man, I'll say what I like, to whoever I like, and they can do to me what they please."

"Then it sounds like we're both fucked."

Now the man looks a little surprised. He sucks on his cigarette and then blows out a stream of bright green smoke. "Hey, I like you; I really do."

"Lotta people 'round here say that. You gonna tell me what you're here for?"

"Gettin' edgy or something?"

"For your sake as much as mine."

A youth in a camouflage jacket has slid into the next booth, nursing a chocolate malt.

The man glances briefly over his shoulder. "I don't give a shit, I tell you," he says. "I seen it all, I heard it all. But I got something that protects me—something that gives me strength. Know what that is?"

"No idea."

"I got honor. Ask anyone in Sordello. Dexter Faust always looks after his girls. They're more to me than just merch."

Justus is pleased to establish something useful. "So you looked after Charlene Hogg?"

"You think I'd be sitting here if I didn't?"

"How long did she work for you?"

"I dunno—two years, maybe."

"And you looked after her well?"

"'Course I did. She was like a little sister to me."

"Then you'll excuse me for saying you don't look too broken up for a guy whose sister's just been killed."

Faust scowls again. "What—you think I haven't seen my girls killed before?"

"In the same way?"

"'Course."

"So a girl lures a target into a room—"

"It happens, if the money's good."

"—only to get killed herself?"

"That happens too, if the stakes are high."

"Did you warn Charlene about this?"

"Didn't think I needed to."

"And you think she was paid to draw Kit Zachary into that room?"

"Top dollar."

"By whom?"

"Well"—Faust sighs and blows out more smoke—"that's the big question, isn't it? You think if I knew, I'd just tell you?"

Justus wonders if he's angling for money. And if he can even trust the pimp anyway—perhaps he's on someone's payroll. Perhaps his only purpose is to muddy the waters.

But Faust blows out more shimmering green smoke. "Forget it, man." He seems to have read Justus's mind. "You really think I'm after cash? I don't care anymore, I tell you. I'm nobody's bitch. So I'll tell you everything I know. I'm not sure who's at the top of the tree, no, but I do know who Charlene was dealing with.

And that's exactly why you should be scared, man, you should be real—"

But he doesn't get to say another word. There's a whirl and a flash as the tousle-haired youth swings over the top of the booth with a bowie knife. And carves open Faust's throat before the pimp can even raise his hands.

Justus, no stranger to sudden attacks, springs to his feet but crashes against the table. The tousle-haired youth is already bolting away.

Justus reaches out to stem the far-jetting blood—Faust's carotid has been severed—but it's too late. The pimp is gasping and his eyes are rolling. He's as good as gone.

"*Call an ambulance!*" Justus cries to the lady behind the counter, even as he's disentangling himself from the booth and launching through the store in pursuit. The killer is already in the street.

Justus has chased people before. Through abandoned tenements, across tiled roofs and tin shacks, down refuse-strewn alleys. But that was a long time ago, and in an entirely different gravity. And his first reminder that he's out of his depth comes when he loses control and smashes into the doorjamb, almost dislocating his shoulder before he's even left the store.

He spins out into the street anyway, nearly crashing into passersby, and sees the killer—that camouflage jacket and head of tousled blond hair—weaving expertly through the crowd and away. For a moment Justus feels an almost paralyzing sense of defeat—it seems impossible that he might ever catch up under these circumstances. But then he remembers that his legs, being fresh from Earth, will be twice as powerful as his quarry's. Most of the muscles in his body will be twice as powerful. So what he loses in dexterity he can make up in strength. And with that thought his blood starts surging again.

He begins to run before the killer is lost to sight. It's tricky—his body has hardly any weight, and his strides are disconcertingly huge—but at the same time it's strangely addictive. *"MOVE! MOVE!"* he cries to the Sinners and tourists in his path. He's crouched low, tensed at the shoulders and barreling forward, unable to stop. *"MOVE! MOVE!"* And though most people get out of his way, a few of them get a palm in the face or an elbow to the head as he pounds down the street and makes a wild turn into a branching arcade, still keeping the killer in sight—but only just.

The arcade is long and garishly lit. Justus bounds over benches and fake hedges and garbage receptacles and makes up significant ground. But his constant exhortations—*"MOVE! MOVE!"*—only alert the kid, who glances back—he can't seem to believe that Justus is following him—then increases his speed. But the very act of looking over his shoulder has momentarily blinded him; he loses control and crashes into a souvenir stall, scattering postcards and knickknacks everywhere.

For Justus it's an opportunity to catch up, but by now he's built up such a head of steam that he overshoots the mark—he goes straight past the killer and collides with a juggler on a unicycle.

The killer, meanwhile, has sprung to his feet and taken off. Justus pushes himself up, with juggling clubs raining down around him, and sets off again, determined not to fall behind.

The two men hurtle around a curving street. They bounce off walls. They course through the kitchen of a fish restaurant. They set pots and pans clanging. They leap over tables. Justus considers using his zapper, but he's not confident of his ability to aim in a crowded area. So they go on. They ricochet through alleys. They burst through a food court. They bound across a plaza. A couple of times Justus is so close that he's actually reaching out to grab the killer's collar when a sudden change of direction throws him completely off course.

But now they're in a strip of parkland—it's the circle of green surrounding the Temple of the Seven Spheres. And the killer, ploughing through tourists and musicians, is charging for the grand entranceway—he's going to hide in the great ziggurat itself. He's leaping over the rope barrier. He's plunging into the darkness. And Justus, pushing away an attendant, goes in after him—forty meters behind now and fearful that he'll lose track of him in the mass of tourists.

It's gloomy on the first floor, with walls of matte-black decorated with quartz stars. People are milling about and inspecting displays. A sound-and-light show is in progress. There are silhouettes and shadows, incessant babble. There's so much activity, in fact, that only a lady's shriek saves Justus from losing the killer entirely. But there he is, his camouflage jacket and tousled blond head, bobbing and weaving for the ramp.

Justus surges through the crowd and chases him up the incline, making up ground with each step. He's thirty meters behind.

The second level is brighter, raw-sienna in color, dedicated to Jupiter. Justus is twenty-five meters behind.

The third level, dedicated to Mars, is bright crimson, filled with antique weapons and the history of war. Justus is twenty meters behind.

The fourth is all blinding gold panels, dedicated to the power of the Sun. Justus is fifteen meters behind—and wondering what the hell the killer has in mind.

The fifth level is pale yellow, dedicated to Venus and filled with graceful statues of nude women. Justus is ten meters behind.

The sixth level, dedicated to Mercury, is paved with dark blue bricks—Justus is five meters behind.

And then they're at the very top, the silver-painted seventh and last level, dedicated to the Moon itself. There are people everywhere, some admiring the huge lunar globe and the artifacts of early explorations, others just taking in the incredible evening view of Sin.

But the killer isn't interested in any of this. He's charging, literally *charging*, across the top level, as if he's about to leap off the edge, as if he's suddenly going to kill himself. And Justus pulls up in his tracks, his hands seizing a railing for support, and he just watches, openmouthed and gasping, as the killer bounds up a ramp to the very top of the Temple.

Justus can barely believe it.

The killer *leaps*. And there's nothing anyone can do to stop him.

30

TORKIE MACLEOD HAS ALWAYS regarded himself as a realist. He doesn't believe in life after death or divine reward or resurrection. He doesn't even believe in leaving a legacy, insofar as anything of that nature, good or bad, is completely insignificant to the one who is dead. Torkie's pragmatic philosophy has always been to make the most of his limited time alive, which for him means not striving for fame or riches, not ticking off a list of famous destinations, not indulging in any death-defying feats, and certainly not raising a family to "carry on his name." To Torkie Macleod, realist, life means making decent money with limited effort, hanging around with cool people, not being bossed around by anyone, and ingesting any mind-altering substance he chooses without a scintilla of shame or regret.

It also means accepting the brutal truth of any dire situation immediately. And not trying to be a hero.

So when Macleod hears a loud snap, looks around, and sees Spyder Blue's head hanging at an unnatural angle, he swiftly accepts that he has a homicidal robot on board—in an enclosed, pressurized space—and reacts with only one practical priority in mind: self-preservation.

"What the fuck, man?"

"What the—?"

"Did he—?"

"He did—he killed Spyder Blue!"

"He can't do that!"

"Are we dreaming here?"

"He's dead, man—his fuckin' head's halfway down his chest!"

Macleod registers all this with his eyes fixed determinedly on the path ahead. He just keeps driving, like an ultra-discreet chauffeur. Not his fight, none of his business.

"Vote again," demands the droid.

"What the fuck? Man, you just killed Spyder Blue!"

"Vote again."

"This is fuckin' insane!"

"This is a democracy, sir. Vote again."

But Dustproof Shockproof doesn't vote again. In fact, it's clear the band doesn't know what to do. Probably they realize they're in no condition for a fight—there's nowhere to run if things look bad—but on the other hand they're not inclined to bow to anyone, least of all a neatly groomed android who looks like a narc.

"Fuck you, man!"

"Who the fuck—?"

"Fuck your democracy!"

The droid says, "Are you forfeiting your vote, sir?"

"What the fuck are you taking about?"

"Are you relinquishing your right to vote?"

"I'm not relinquishing anything!"

"Then are you acquiescing to the wishes of your superior?"

"No—fuck you, no!"

"And the rest of you?"

No answers.

"Then it seems the vote is now even," the droid says. "There is no majority. So to prevent a leadership crisis, which would be most undesirable at this delicate time, I will assume command. Driver, kindly turn this vehicle in a northerly direction."

"No, driver—fuck this!" says Maxx Dee.

"Don't you dare turn this thing!" says Q'mar Kent.

The droid, puzzled, addresses Kent. "But sir," he says, "you previously wanted to go to Purgatory."

"I did!"

"Then are you changing your vote?"

"I am!"

"Why are you changing your vote, sir?"

"Because I am!"

"That is not a rational answer."

"Well, fuck you, your democracy, and your fuckin' tin asshole!"

Macleod still doesn't turn his head. But he hears what comes next. The droid has clearly risen from his seat. There are shouts of protest. There is movement—the whole vehicle rocks. There's a smack, like a piston hitting a side of beef. Another smack, and a crack. And then there's chaos.

Macleod still doesn't turn. But there are screams. There are ripping sounds. Something fleshy hits the back of his head. A spray of blood splatters across the glass in front of him. There are cracking sounds. Gurgling sounds. Moaning sounds. Dying sounds. And still Macleod doesn't turn. Nothing he can do about it, no point trying.

But surreptitiously he starts turning the VLTV north. He steers off the hard-packed track, and weaves between some craters.

Finally there is no noise at all apart from death rattles. All in all, it's taken about four minutes. He hears someone—the only survivor—move forward, shift a dead body, and drop into the seat behind him. Macleod just keeps driving, as if this sort of thing happens every other day. He's just relieved he hasn't got a pulse-light attached to his face, because it'd be flashing like a disco lamp.

Finally there's a voice.

"You are heading north, sir."

Macleod gulps and nods. "That's what you want, isn't it?"

"It is, sir. I am the King."

"Uh-huh."

"I *am* the democracy."

"Uh-huh."

Macleod can *feel* the droid's eyes on him. It's absurd, but he reckons he can *feel* the droid's breath too, prickling the hairs on the back of his neck.

He coughs. "You just tell me if you wanna change direction or anything . . ."

"Not at all, sir; you are a skilled driver. Please keep driving."

So they continue for about fifteen minutes, Macleod going through the motions stiffly but efficiently—at least his heart has stopped pounding—and the droid remaining perfectly silent. It's not that different, Macleod tries telling himself, from those times when he's had a disagreement with a passenger, or some uppity celebrity. He decides to speak.

"The night will overtake us soon."

"Will this affect your driving, sir?"

"I'll just turn on the floods."

"Let me know when you do that, sir."

"Uh-huh."

"Let me know when you make any changes at all."

"Uh-huh."

"The toggle at the top right of the left panel—that is for directing the lights, sir?"

"That's right."

"And those guarded buttons—they're for the airlock doors?"

"Uh-huh—I flip the guards and press the buttons one after the other."

"Both doors will not open together?"

"Only if you press the buttons at the same time."

"And what is the maximum speed of the vehicle, sir?"

"Hundred and twenty on tarmac. But out here, I don't go higher than a hundred on hard track, fifty at most on rough terrain."

Silence again. Macleod is perversely proud of himself, for conducting the conversation in such bizarre circumstances—and while still under the lingering influence of Selene—but inevitably he starts wondering why the droid is so interested in the operations of the VLTV. And inevitably, even through his drug haze, he sees that it can't be good.

But Macleod is a realist—or so he keeps telling himself—and he's not interested in sustaining false hopes. So he's determined not to cry about it.

"Can I ask a question?"

"What sort of question, sir?"

"I just wanna know where you came from."

"Why do you want to know that, sir?"

"I just like to talk to my passengers."

"Very well, sir."

"Well . . . where do you come from?"

"I come from nowhere, sir. There is only the future."

"Uh-huh."

"When you're on an express train, you don't get off till the end of the line."

"Uh-huh."

"When I see a hurdle, I hurdle it."

"Uh-huh."

Silence for another minute or two and then Macleod chuckles. He chuckles for so long that the droid says to him, "Why are you laughing, sir?"

Macleod says, "You're going to kill me, aren't you?"

He can almost hear the droid manufacture a frown. "That is a strange question, sir."

"You killed the others . . ."

"They contributed nothing to the bottom line."

"Uh-huh."

"They were surplus to all requirements."

"Uh-huh."

"But you, sir, are a valuable commodity."

"Uh-huh."

Slowly and imperceptibly—with such stealth that he hopes the droid doesn't notice—Macleod puts the vehicle in high-terrain mode. If uncorrected, it will burn out the batteries much quicker than normal. It will stop the vehicle well before Purgatory. This little action, thinks Macleod, is possibly the most heroic and selfless thing he's ever done.

"You know," he tells the droid, partly as a distraction, "I once worked in a post office. Many years ago."

"I did not know that, sir."

"At a sorting office. There were about fifty of us. Then one week an 'efficiency expert' came along, observed us in action for a few days, and wrote up a report. He spoke like you."

"In what way, sir?"

"He told us all we were doing a good job. He said we should have no concerns about our future. He even said we were valued contributors to the company."

"I am very pleased to hear that, sir."

"Uh-huh. And a month later we were all fired. Because in his official report to the management team, which we weren't supposed to see, he said we were 'surplus to all requirements.' He said we were 'economically obsolete.' And so we were replaced by robots."

"I am sorry to hear that, sir."

Macleod chuckles some more. "Anyway, it was at that moment that I made a deal with myself. I said I was never going to work for a listed company or government department ever again. I was never going to wear someone else's name on my shirt. And I was never going to believe anything said by a guy in a suit."

"That is an interesting reaction, sir."

"So I *know* you're going to kill me, man. I just want you to do it quick."

He drives on in silence. And on. And on.

He drives on for so long that he begins to think he was wrong—that the droid isn't going to kill him after all. Maybe he *is* a valuable commodity after all. The day-night terminator, meanwhile, has closed in on them. They're minutes away from being engulfed by blackness.

"Here comes the Dark Side," Macleod says, to no one in particular.

The droid's hands wrap around his head, wrench it sideways, and snap his neck.

31

JUSTUS'S FIRST THOUGHT—AND the first thought of all the gasping tourists at the top of the Temple—is that the killer is leaping to his death. That it's a suicide. That he's been driven into a corner and sees no way out. In fact, Justus has seen it before: the assassin so committed to his personal ideology that he's willing to sacrifice his whole life rather than be caught.

Except that this killer, whoever he is, doesn't look like he has *any* sort of ideology. He looks like a kid who's been blackmailed, or just paid a life-saving amount of money, to commit a murder. An opportunist, not even sure whom he's killed, not sure who's hired him—certainly not the sort who'd end his life just because he's being pursued.

And as it turns out—as Justus sees right now—he's not committing suicide at all. From the top of the ramp he's spearing upward—a trajectory impossible on Earth—and soaring over the guardrail, arms outstretched. And then his hands are locking around one of those ceiling bars—one of the thousands of rungs, struts, ventilation pipes, water dispensers, and power cables that make up the ceiling grid of Sin. Then he's swinging forward, propelled by his own momentum, then back, then forward and back again. And when he's sufficiently stable he reaches out and latches onto another rung, then another and another, like a monkey on horizontal bars. And just like that, as everyone watches, he's getting away—he's already gone at least fifteen meters.

But Justus, still gaining his breath, isn't going to be beaten. Not like this. He's already done his own horizontal-bar exercises at Copernicus, where the instructor taught him how to "walk" with his arms and shoulders. And with thicker muscles he figures he's roughly equal to his quarry, just as they'd been in the ground-level pursuit. The kid might have had more practice—his very digression into the Temple suggests he's escaped this way in the past—but that doesn't mean Justus can't catch up to him again. Provided he doesn't waste any time.

So he draws a huge breath. He sets himself. And right before the astonished tourists he takes ten bounds, charges up the ramp, and launches into the air as well—propelling himself upward with all the power in his legs.

He spears up, he spears out, and for just a moment he thinks he isn't going to make it—that he's going to arc through the air and plummet to the parkland below. But then his palms slap into a bar, his fingers clamp around it like claws, and his lower body swings up, up, so high up that his shoes almost touch the girder in front of him. On Earth this momentum alone might wrench him free and send him plunging—but on the Moon he weighs about as much as a whippet, so the fallback is gentle, the strain on his arms mild. And within seconds he's stopped swinging and gained enough equilibrium to reach forward again, seize another bar with his right hand, then a different one with his left, and begin his orangutan-like pursuit of the tousle-haired killer—who still has about thirty meters on him.

It isn't easy at first. Sometimes he has to stretch perilously. Sometimes he has to kick away dropping vines. His hands slip on moisture and bird shit. Birds themselves flap around him. He passes sometimes through swirls of vapor. Water drips across him. But he gains confidence—and distance—with each movement forward.

Sinners far below have noticed now—they're shouting encouragement, or abuse; Justus isn't sure which—and the killer turns again, registers another moment's surprise, and starts changing course—heading for one of the great arrays of incandescent sunlamps.

Justus changes course too. He's moving high over the thoroughfares, the temples and tabernacles, the gables and pinnacles, the flourishing gardens—he's really mastered it now, feeling no significant fatigue or strain, and the only danger is moving too fast or mishandling a bar. But even when that happens—when one hand snags on something or he fails to gain a good hold—he's able to hang on with his other hand, find a separate purchase, and keep swinging forward.

But the glare from the sunlamps is so hot and blinding that he can no longer see the killer: He has to squint and turn his head. He sees his own shadow blooming over half a block of Sin. And not just that—there's another shadow moving rapidly *away* from him, in the other direction. And suddenly he realizes he's been lured into the lights purposely, so the killer can take advantage of the brightness to change course and escape.

Justus experiences a renewed sense of anger and determination.

He cuts across the front of the lamp, eyelids squeezed together, grappling blindly in some cases, but moving relentlessly, faster even than the killer, and now *he's* the one who's coming out of the sun—it's the killer who can't see him.

And there he is, thirty meters away, directly ahead. Justus closes in like a spider. Twenty meters. Fifteen. When he's just ten meters away the killer finally notices him, his whole face contracts, and he struggles to pick up speed. But in so doing he very nearly loses balance and falls. And Justus gains more ground.

In desperation the killer heads for one of the huge pillars—ornate brass surrounded by scaffolding—and dodges around it like a kid hiding behind a tree. Caught off guard, Justus has to check his own momentum and haul himself back, swinging his whole body, changing direction. Meanwhile the killer drops onto the scaffolding, dislodging a couple of shrieking birds.

Justus tries to follow him, but the killer is swinging at him with his bowie knife. The blade strikes Justus's shoe. Justus shifts sideways and takes a firmer grip. He kicks out again. The killer slashes wildly and the tip of his blade cuts through the hem of Justus's pants. Justus shifts away, slightly out of range, and waits. The kid, with his teeth clenched and knife poised, also waits. The two of them are tensed, motionless—the kid on the scaffolding, Justus hanging in front of him—in a bizarre Mexican standoff a hundred meters above Sin. Then something sails past them—a dime-store rocket, shot from far below—and the kid is momentarily distracted. Justus seizes the opportunity and tries a flurry of kicks but succeeds only in driving the kid back against the pillar. Another rocket whizzes past: This one almost strikes Justus. And now the kid's got a gleam in his eye. He's holding the knife by the tip. He's going to hurl it at Justus like a dagger. And Justus can't just duck. So he swings in closer, before it's too late, and kicks out violently, frantically, striking the kid on the forearm. The bowie knife goes sailing into Sin, and the kid is weaponless.

Justus readies himself to drop onto the scaffolding, but the kid is way ahead of him. He moves to the other side of the pillar and launches himself back onto the bars. The chase, it seems, is on again. Except that the kid has enjoyed a break now, and Justus is starting to feel the strain.

Sinners below are following them through the streets now, a moving audience, cheering, whistling, shouting—"Justice! Justice! Justice!"—as the killer heads energetically for the industrial district of Nimrod, where a pall of eye-stinging smoke is clouding the air.

And now there's something else to contend with. In the catwalks above him police have appeared with metal rods. The rods have clamps on the end and resemble glorified reach extenders. The cops are thrusting them through the bars, trying to catch hold of the killer that way, and one of them actually manages to snag ahold of his forearm. But in response the kid just tears the pole free, swings it around, tries to shake it off—it's hanging from his arm like a spear.

He's struggling for momentum when Justus catches up again. But just at that moment the cloud of smoke, caught in artificial currents, changes direction and envelops both of them. Momentarily blinded, Justus tries to lock his legs around the killer but the kid swings the pole and it smacks him in the side of the head. Dazed, Justus takes a firmer grip on the bars, coughs smoke from his lungs, squeezes his eyes shut again, and kicks out blindly. But he's not making any contact. And when the smoke clears he sees the killer is no longer in front of him. He looks around frantically, but the kid is nowhere in sight. People below are shouting and pointing. And when Justus follows their directions he sees that the killer has dropped onto the top of a building far below. He's unclamping the pole from his arm. He's scrambling for the fire escape.

For a moment Justus just hangs above, fighting his instincts. On Earth a fall of that distance—more than twenty meters—would break his legs, possibly his spine. On the Moon it will be much less dangerous, but how much so? Justus's mind fills with images of goats springing thirty feet into the air at the Agri-Plex. Lunar basketballers he's seen on TV, dropping from huge heights. An athlete at Doppelmayer Base landing gracefully after falling from a diving board distance.

So he releases the bars. He plummets. It seems endless, but he has plenty of time to prepare his body. And then he hits the top of the building. He performs a commando roll. He gets to his feet. The impact isn't painless—he's shaken and jolted, and the air has been punched from his lungs—but he's not seriously hurt. And he doesn't have time for relief.

He tries descending via the fire escape but the killer has such a head start that he decides to jump again—all the way to street level. He braces himself in midair but when he hits the ground this time his ankle twists before he can effect a roll—he winces, gasps, and is struggling to his feet when he sees the kid dash past him, back into the streets of Sin.

Justus heads off in pursuit again but can no longer achieve top speed. The killer is racing through the streets toward Kasbah. He's heading straight into a noisy crowd, so Justus can only hope that he gets tangled up there, perhaps even apprehended.

But then a couple of cops whisk past him, zappers in hand, and suddenly he conceives of a worse outcome.

He runs harder, overriding the pain, and enters a retail area. There's a great deal of commotion at the far end. People are peeling aside, pressing back against store windows. And the killer himself is spinning around, looking for a way out, fending off people with a plastic bollard.

But the cops, with zappers pointed and strobe lights flashing, are closing in.

"*Hey!*" Justus can see what's about to happen. "*No! Hey!*" He pounds forward, wincing, waving people out of the way—"*Hey! Hey!*"—but too late.

A jagged, lightning-like bolt sizzles out from one of the zappers and blows the kid from his feet. He lands on his back, twitching, dropping the bollard. But the cops are still closing in, giving him all they've got.

Justus sees, hears, and *smells* it all as he limps in. Jagged electron beams flashing through plasma channels. The sizzle of high-voltage electricity. The stink of burning ozone. The killer jolting and spasming. A sickening *whap* as the skin bursts from his face. A *glug* as his skin starts dripping from his body. The killer is exploding, melting, dying. And five or six cops are standing around with their triggers squeezed and expressions that are positively *orgasmic*.

By the time Justus finally arrives, gasping for breath, it's effectively over. The cops have spent their load. The kid, his limbs opening like the petals of a flower, is a scorched and bony mass—an over-roasted chicken. There are bodily fluids running over the pavement, and foul-smelling smoke.

Justus looks around at the Sinners—they're watching it all with disgust and anger. He looks at the cops—they're joking among themselves. He sees some of his own investigation team—Cosmo Battaglia and Hugo Pfeffer—holstering their zappers. And Prince Oda Universe, unfurling from a squad car. And others he only knows by sight.

And then he hears one of the cops:

"*Forensics!*"

It's a mocking call, made in response to his own arrival. And when the other cops notice him, they join in:

"Forensics!"

"Forensics!"

"Forensics!"

Justus doesn't meet their eyes, but he can hear them all chuckling under their breath. So he just nods stoically, accepting that enforced deference in just a day or two has given way to open disdain.

32

UNLESS YOU'VE BEEN LIVING in deep-space hibernation for the past twenty years, you'll have heard the rumor that many of the remaining masterpieces in the Louvre—including *The Wedding Feast at Cana, The Raft of the Medusa,* and *Liberty Leading the People*—are actually meticulous copies, forged using the most sophisticated modern techniques and virtually indistinguishable from the real thing. When the *Mona Lisa/La Gioconda* was stolen for the third time, the story goes, the Ministère de la Culture resolved to remove the rest of the priceless masterworks and store them in a secret and impregnable location. The Louvre was accordingly closed for three months, using as cover the installation of a new security system, and the original paintings were spirited away with great stealth to their new refuge. Which, the story suggests, is some temperature-controlled, vacuum-sealed chamber deep under the surface of the far side of the Moon.

You'll also have heard the rumor—which in this instance is far more accurate—that the theft of the *Mona Lisa* was carried out by an ultra-daring band of high-society thieves popularly known as the Vesuvius Six. In their first and most celebrated job, the Six raided a billionaire's mansion near Naples as the famous volcano was venting dangerous amounts of ash and poisonous gases. While everyone else was fleeing, the Six moved in. Risking suffocation or even incineration, they blew open the billionaire's vaults, loaded up their van with gold and jewels, and escaped unchecked through deserted, smoke-choked streets. In the years afterward they executed similarly daring heists during severe floods in Paris (the *Mona Lisa* job), a cyclone in the Philippines, a wildfire in California, and an earthquake in Turkey. It eventually became clear that they'd simply compiled a huge list of target properties across the world—houses, banks, galleries—and waited for the harbingers of an evacuation-level catastrophe before swinging into action. But it remains unclear whether the Six are motivated most by the lure of riches, by the proximity to death, or just by the challenge of the game. There is even a rumor, suitably implausible, that they plan to return all their prizes one day to their legal owners, like sporting fishermen who release their catches back into the sea.

The gang is led by an independently wealthy Irishman called Darragh Greenan. Greenan is not quite as charismatic as the actors who've portrayed him on-screen. Nor are the members of his gang quite as disparate, witty, and colorfully dressed. But they are certainly shrewd. They're exceptionally skilled. They're cool under pressure. They're admirably fatalistic. And they have enough pride in their achievements to resent being dismissed as glorified looters.

In time, they agree, they will tell their stories. They will set the record straight. They will allow people to admire them or revile them as they see fit. But for the time being, they're remarkably secretive and tight-knit. They know they cannot carry out their heists forever, and are just waiting for the right moment to cash in their chips. They have no real idea when the moment might come—they keep finding stimulating new challenges—but the general consensus is that they will know immediately when it does, without having to say a word. It will be the moment when they've seen it all.

Presently five of the original gang and a new member—one of the founding members is in prison for an unrelated theft—are on Farside. They're spread out across a radar array, two each behind three ten-meter-high dishes. The dishes ostensibly belong to the Ministerio de Ciencia (the Spanish Ministry of Science), and indeed are fully operational and capable of legitimate astronomical readings. But in truth, they're a cover. Just as the building in the middle of the array—what seems to be a standard observatory—is also a cover. Darragh Greenan parted with a considerable amount of money to learn this. And an even larger amount to obtain the blueprints for the so-called observatory, which extends deep beneath the lunar surface and contains six separate vacuum-sealed vaults. Within these vaults are the masterpieces—the *genuine* masterpieces—of the Prado in Madrid, including *The Garden of Earthly Delights*, *Las Meninas*, *Death of the Virgin*, and *Half-submerged Dog*. Because it is the Prado, not the Louvre, that exhibits counterfeit masterpieces, and the Spanish Ministry of Culture, not the French one, that elected to hide its treasures in response to the *Mona Lisa* theft.

If they can make off with any one of those paintings, Greenan knows, the whole hugely expensive and highly dangerous operation will have been justified. It will be, in fact, their crowning achievement.

The Vesuvius Six have been planning this job for twenty months. They've been on the Moon itself, disguised as a crew from the BBC's Natural History Unit, for six weeks. They've practiced their procedures in microgravity. They've checked and rechecked all their equipment. They've run through their plans again and again. They've traveled across Farside to reconnoiter the territory around the secret Spanish base. And they have waited patiently, as usual, for a natural catastrophe.

And when that moment came—in this case it was a powerful solar flare—they were more than ready. They immediately sabotaged a substation and two junction boxes on Farside's central power and communications cable, then converged on the rendezvous point at Perepelkin Crater and raced to the Spanish base. And there they waited, a kilometer to the west, just behind three separate dishes, for the passage of the day-night terminator. Because it's during the last light of the lunar day, with all its visual and thermal anomalies, that the security cameras and infrared sensors are most vulnerable to misreadings and malfunctions. Without doubt, they've been assured, this is the best time to launch an assault.

Presently the last patches of sunlight vanish from the eastern horizon and darkness begins to swallow the base. Greenan lowers his electro-binoculars and signals to Noémi Ritzman, former Olympic bronze medalist for the Swiss shooting team (600m military rifle). In the past she's fired cables though the narrowest of apertures, often from hundreds of meters away. But her task now is even more challenging.

The target is the base's auxiliary power unit, a full thousand meters distant. Rory Moncrieffe, the group's tech expert, is helpfully "painting" it with a laser beam. Ritzman steps out from behind one of the radar dishes and raises her G88 Line-throwing Rifle.

She stops breathing, tenses all her muscles, makes sure she has the target perfectly in the sights—fully accounting for the visual distortion of her helmet visor—and squeezes the trigger. Immediately a bolt streaks out. Encountering no air resistance, the bolt, trailing a piano wire, travels like a bullet at shoulder height. Two hundred meters. Four hundred meters. Six hundred meters. It's still going. It's barely dropping at all. Eight hundred meters. It's nearing the power unit. A thousand meters. One thousand two hundred meters. It's still going. It's missed the target. It's flying into the darkness beyond the base, still trailing the wire.

There's no time for regret. Ritzman has already picked up a backup rifle. She's already training it on the target. She tenses herself again, and fires. A second bolt shoots across the surface. Two hundred meters. Four hundred. Six hundred. Eight hundred. The arrowhead plunges into the side of the power unit. Bull's-eye.

There is no time for self-congratulation either. The gang has only a few minutes in which to operate, assuming they haven't been detected already. So Rory Moncrieffe shifts the laser, this time training it on the outer airlock door of the base. And Ritzman fires a bolt from a third rifle. Two hundred meters. Four hundred. Six hundred. Eight hundred. Bull's-eye again. The Vesuvius Six now have two lines running a full kilometer to the Spanish base.

Now it's time for the explosives team—Branislav Parizek and Blade Testro—to move in. With winches the two men tighten the wires to the tension of guitar strings. Upon these wires they hang two motorized containers, each holding four kilograms of Semtex 6. They flick switches and the containers, like miniature cable cars, start creeping along the wires just a meter and a half above the surface. At about twenty kilometers an hour.

For the Vesuvius Six, this is an agonizing wait. As the explosives pass into the darkness the gang waits for Rory Moncrieffe, wearing long-range night-vision goggles, to give the all-clear.

And for a long time . . . nothing. Still nothing. The rest of the team snap on their own night-vision visors. They hoist their guns. They check their concussion grenades. They ready themselves for the assault. And they wait.

Then Moncrieffe turns. He gives the thumbs up. The explosives are in place. The lights are green.

It's now time for Darragh Greenan, raising his grenade launcher, to take command. Five of the team will charge in under the last rays of the setting sun, and when they're halfway to the base Moncrieffe will send an electrical impulse through the wires to detonate the explosives. If all goes well, the auxiliary power unit—currently the base's principal power source—will be knocked out immediately and the outer door of the base will be blown open. The team will blast through the airlock and a third security door and move swiftly to take over the control room, seal off the guards, and punch in the security codes to the vaults below. They expect to be in and out in fifteen minutes.

So Greenan steps out from behind the dish. He looks at his team, twirls a gloved finger in the air, and gestures to the base. *Showtime.*

But even as he does—before he can swing around and lead the charge—he notices the others looking *past* him with expressions of disbelief, even astonishment, on their faces.

So he pulls up short. He turns, squinting into the darkness. And this is what he sees:

A battered VLTV, not unlike their own, is ploughing across the rock-scattered terrain. With night-vision goggles it's possible—*just*—to see through the windows. And what Greenan makes out is an extremely well-groomed figure sitting in the driver's seat. And others in the vehicle who look like rag dolls. And glass that's smeared in places with dark liquid—perhaps blood.

But the driver doesn't seem to notice the Vesuvius Six—or care. He just keeps driving north. His vehicle strikes the first piano wire and snaps it. Then continues to the second wire and snaps it as well. And he keeps going. Speeding soundlessly out of sight, at top pace, into the enveloping darkness. And then he's gone.

And now there are warning lights flashing on the Spanish base—an intrusion alert. Guards will be mobilizing inside. Defenses will be flying up. It's no longer safe. And Darragh Greenan, seeing two years of planning evaporate as rapidly as the sunlight, has no time to brood. He wheels around and makes the exit signal. *Game over*. Back to the VLTV. Time to retreat. Time to pull out. To escape.

The others follow the orders at once, mobilizing without any sort of protest. They say nothing aloud, of course, and would not be heard even if they did—they're not using suit-links—but they all accept it tacitly. Greenan's expression, and the emphatic way he made the signal, are all that needs to be said.

It's over. The Vesuvius Six have been defeated. It's time to retire and write those memoirs. Assuming they get off the Moon alive.

33

Q T BRASS'S HOUSE LOOKS like one of those church conversions that have become so popular on Earth. In fact, Justus has seen the place from his bedroom window and thought it *was* a church.

At the door he's greeted by Leonardo Brown and ushered up some stone steps, such as one might find in a cathedral, to a room with arched windows, paneled walls, and Renaissance paintings of devotional scenes. There's a profusion of ferns and tropical flowers as well, along with the chatter of parrots—some of them flying directly onto the balcony to feed from seed dispensers—so the whole effect is like a monastery on the edge of the jungle.

"Lieutenant, I'm so glad you came—sit down, please—can I get you a drink or something?—what happened to your foot?—oh God, this is a nightmare now—oh God, I don't know where to begin."

She's pacing back and forth in front of the window, talking in

almost overlapping sentences. But this isn't the same overconfident operator as before. She looks drained of color now, and her
eyes are swollen, as if she's been crying. She looks so emotional, in
fact, that Justus briefly wonders if this is the same woman he met
previously—if maybe that was a paid impersonator as well.

"You were a close friend of Kit Zachary's," he says—a statement.

She stops pacing and looks at him. "You found out about me
and Kit?"

"It's my job."

"Then you can also imagine how upset I've been?"

"I guess so."

"What did you find out about him, exactly?"

"I know he was your builder."

"Of course he was my builder. He was *the* builder. He was responsible for erecting half of Sin. Virtually all my building projects—God, he even built this place."

"On your instructions?"

"He got half his work on my instructions. But he was much
more than a builder to me. And much more than a friend. He was
like a—no, I wouldn't say a father—he was like an *uncle* to me. A
confidant, an adviser, a collaborator."

Justus shrugs. "He had interesting proclivities."

"Of course he did. Most men in this place do. And he tried to
get me into bed too, of course he did. But I put a stop to that, and
it was never a problem again. Look, Lieutenant, that's just the way
it is around here. Don't think any less of Kit because he was found
in a cheap brothel with some . . . lady of the night. His tastes ran
that way. God—I can't believe he's gone!"

"Do you know any of the 'ladies of the night' he'd previously
done business with?"

"No, I don't know anything about his girls—what was she, the one who was killed? One of those lookalikes, the *Tablet* said, cut to look like some teen movie star—well, I don't want to know about it. But they're cunning, the prostitutes in Sin—they're often luring people into places on false pretexts. It's not out of the ordinary at all. You should talk to her pimp if you want more information on that angle."

"I did."

"And what did he say?"

"He was rudely interrupted."

QT stops again and looks at him. "Oh my God—he was silenced too, wasn't he? They—what did they do?"

"They killed him."

"Oh Jesus."

"Right in front of me."

"Oh Jesus."

"And I chased the killer—that's how I twisted my ankle. It's a wonder you didn't see it. We put on quite a circus act."

"Sorry," she says, "but when I found out about Kit it hit me hard—*really* hard—and things really started falling into place. I had to get out of the office and reassess."

"Reassess what?"

"*Everything.*"

Justus isn't completely convinced by her show of grief, but he's relieved there's any grief at all. For a fleeting moment he even thinks how vulnerable she looks—less formally dressed, emotional, not in complete control. But he drives the thought from his head. "Things started falling into place?" he asks.

"Well, yes—how can I say this? Since we last spoke there was that terrorist statement—from The People's Hammer; it's all over the local media—and then I heard about Kit—and *things started falling into place.*"

"What do you mean?"

She runs her hand through her hair. "I don't know what I mean."

"That's not an answer."

"It's difficult for me to say, Lieutenant—it's difficult for me even to contemplate—you must understand—and I'm not even sure if I'm right—I don't want to believe it—I *really* don't want to believe it—but the possibility just won't go away. And then, the more I think about it . . ."

She sighs, squeezes her eyes shut, as if suffering a thought so terrible it's painful, then collapses back on the sofa. If it's a performance, thinks Justus, then she deserves an Oscar. Maybe she *is* a professional actor after all.

"I think," she goes on, "I *think* . . . but don't *know* . . . that my father is behind this after all."

She exhales, as if the admission has taken everything out of her, but doesn't continue. Forcing Justus to ask, "What makes you say that?"

"Because it's logical. Because it's just too logical to be denied. Because when you put all the pieces together—all the visible pieces and some that are still hidden—it makes too much sense. Because this is what I *feared* would happen, in my worst nightmares. It's what *I'd* do if I were my father. Except I'm *not* my father. And now I don't know how far he's going to take it—and that *scares the shit out of me*."

Justus again feels the urge to comfort her. "You're going to have to explain yourself," he says.

"I can try, but there are things that you're going to have to take at face value—assuming you aren't even better at your job than I think. And you can start with Kit Zachary. He was very rich and very powerful in Purgatory, but like Otto Decker he was *not* someone any terrorist group would want to kill. You must understand and accept that. It makes no sense at all. This whole terrorist angle—it's baloney, pure baloney. It has to be."

"You might be interested to know that most of the PPD agrees with you."

She smirks. "Do they, now?"

"Why the sarcasm?"

"Because it's an *obvious* cover-up—to anyone in the know. But then, I don't believe it's designed to be anything more than that—a transparent ruse. Something to serve a purpose for a few days, maybe a few weeks, and then be ripped away like a veil."

"And how does that work, exactly?"

QT suddenly launches to her feet and starts pacing again, as if she has to move to keep up with her own thoughts. "I think someone is trying to set me up. I think Otto Decker was killed because he was expendable. A well-known ally of my father's, yes, but one who was no real loss. And they also killed Ben Chee in the process—that was a bonus. And now they've eliminated Kit Zachary—a powerful supporter and associate of mine. To the public it might still look unclear—they won't be able to join the dots. One of my father's supporters dies, then one of mine. It might even look like tit-for-tat. Except that I had *nothing* to do with the murder of Otto Decker, I promise you. So what's going on? High-ranking people are being killed. And soon others will be killed as well—this is just the beginning. They'll mainly be allies of mine, but there'll be an expendable associate of my father's oc-casionally as well, just to muddy the waters. And what does this do? What's the grand game? Well, it makes sure all my father's rivals are accounted for—anyone who might have ambitions to take over from him while he's away—and it strips me of my power base too. But there's more. Because when the terrorist charade falls apart, as it's clearly designed to do, it's *me* who'll be framed for the assassinations. *Me.* I'm the one who'll be painted as the devious puppet master behind the whole thing. *I'll* be the one who's supposedly been knocking off these people, because they'll be painted—they're *already* being painted—as *my* rivals. It's crazy, but it just might work."

Justus thinks about it. "But you've said the Sinners here love you. So why would they believe all that?"

"They don't *have* to believe it—entirely. It just has to have enough credibility to *sound* possible. That's one of my father's laws, for crissakes—'If you give it enough feathers you can make anything fly.' And so what does he do? He gets his media working overtime for him. They splash the murders across the front page of the *Tablet.* They report the terrorist claims credulously at first, just like they're supposed to. They underline all the connections between the victims and my father but *none* of the connections between the victims and *me.* They write a glowing profile of you—the cop who's going to solve the case—and just to make it all stick they get Bill Swagger, the organ grinder's monkey, to write a scathing article about you, so everyone *assumes* you're not beholden to my father. When all the time you're being set up to believe exactly what they want you to believe. And to swallow whatever planted evidence they use to incriminate me."

If you give it enough feathers you can make anything fly. Justus has to admit it makes a certain sort of sense. He recalls the looks of unbridled admiration from strangers in the streets—people cheering him as he chased the killer—and he wonders if they've been manipulated as shrewdly as he has. In a den of thieves and murderers like Purgatory, why should he expect anything less?

But he makes sure he's expressionless. "You have no proof of this."

"Of course I don't—but it's logical, isn't it? Hell, it's what *I'd* do if I were devious enough—if I had a dark agenda—and *I* wanted to get me out of the way. I mean, why else have you, the new boy in town, been saddled with so much responsibility? Two weeks here and you're leading a major investigation? *The* major investigation? Well, it's not only because you're new, and it's not because you're above grubby politics and allegiances. It's because you can't be expected to understand the full complexities of life here. Because you can be led blindly through a maze. And because you can be *portrayed* as someone totally above grubby politics and allegiances. So if *you* pin the blame on me, *you*, the incorruptible new cop, then it looks genuine—it looks like I'm *really* guilty."

"I haven't pinned the blame on anybody."

"But you can't say you haven't considered the possibility, that people haven't been steering you in that direction—of my guilt, I mean?"

"So far *you're* the one who's done most of the steering. In fact, your father spoke very highly of you."

"Of course he did—don't you see? It's all a ruse, like the terrorist claims—something that will be ripped away in time—when he acts shocked—when the evidence against me mounts—and when you're convinced that *I'm* the evil genius behind it all!"

"You really believe your own father is trying to kill you?"

"I didn't say he was trying to *kill* me. I said he was trying to *frame* me."

"And what good will that do him?"

"What good will it do him?" QT says, snorting. "It'll get me completely out of the way, of course. So he can go to Mars and when he comes back the place will be exactly the same as when he left it."

"But who'll take over from him, if not you?"

"I don't know, I really don't know. He'd get a robot to take over from him if he could."

This reminds Justus of something. "Are you sure you want to be talking like this, by the way? Aloud?"

"It's perfectly safe in here—I have the place swept regularly."

"What about your staff?"

"There's just us right now."

"And your droid?"

"Leonardo Brown?" She stops pacing and looks at him. "Why do you ask?"

"In case you haven't noticed, droids can be programmed to do things. Or they can be *tricked* into doing things. They can become weapons without even realizing it."

She shakes her head. "I wouldn't have expected that from you, Lieutenant. What are you saying—that Leonardo Brown is spying on me?"

"His brother Leonardo Grey records conversations, I know that much."

"And what—you really think Leonardo Brown visits my father and plays his recordings too?"

"I don't know who he visits. I don't even know if he *needs* to visit anyone. Ever heard of radio?"

"In Purgatory?"

"The bomb that killed Decker was radio activated."

"Ridiculous," she says. "Ridiculous. Anyway, I would've known if Leonardo Brown was doing something like that."

"Why?

"I would have *known*. It's Leonardo Brown. He has nothing to do with all this."

"He's not the only droid in town."

"And what does that mean? That other droids are spying on me? Or do you think—do you really think—that it's droids who are doing the assassinating? Is that it?"

"I rule nothing out."

"You're clutching at straws, Lieutenant."

"What do you know about Leonardo Black?"

She frowns. "My father's bodyguard? Why do you ask?"

"Where is he?"

"He's being programmed for the Mars trip, isn't he?"

"He's joining your father on the expedition?"

"As far as I know—why?"

"Just a loose end," says Justus, making a note to check it out. "But if it's not terrorists, and not robots, then who's doing the killing? Because whoever they are, they're not leaving traces."

"Are you sure about that?"

Justus knows what she means—that the PPD is *covering* the traces—and he has to concede the point. "Not sure about anything," he says. "But that reminds me. I still need to look at Purgatory's immigration and visa records. Everything for the past six months. If I'm being set up, like you say, then I want to join the dots myself."

"Of course you do. My office told me you'd been asking for those records and I approve. In fact, I've already had an e-file sent to your house."

"My house?"

"Better than sending them to the PPD, I thought—is that a problem?"

"No, it makes perfect sense." Justus wonders if he can trust the records anyway. "But one other thing. If your father is trying to frame you, then what exactly is he going to do with you after you've been arrested? Seeing you're so popular in Sin?"

"He'll imprison me, of course. And he'll have just enough feathers to make that fly."

"Imprison you where, though? It's *you* who's building the ultra-high-security penitentiary, isn't it?"

"Well," she says, "you *are* well informed, aren't you?"

"That's not an answer."

"There are two answers, if that's what you want. The first is that the new penitentiary isn't the only prison in Sin—and you know it. The second is that he can easily use the penitentiary I built, yes—what's to stop him? It would be a cruel irony, but history's full of them, isn't it?"

"I can't argue with that."

"And that's not the only irony, if truth be told." She looks a bit hesitant now, actually biting on her lip. "I'm not even sure if I want to say this . . ."

"Say it."

"Well, the penitentiary might be the main reason my father is trying to frame me."

"I'm sorry—I don't get it."

"You're not supposed to."

"Now I *really* don't get it. Didn't you assure me before that you'd always be transparent?"

"Not on this issue—I can't. And I hope I never have to tell you the full story. I'm just mentioning it for the record—I'm putting it out there. In case it becomes relevant."

"And what am I supposed to do? Find out by myself?"

"You seem to have done a reasonable job of that so far," she says—and Justus can't work out if it's a compliment or a rebuke. So he says, getting to his feet:

"And you're doing a reasonable job of being an enigma."

It's such a playful comment that Justus isn't sure where it came from. And QT seems to be aware of it. The two of them stare into each other's eyes for a fraction of a second longer than necessary. Then Justus sees his own reflection in her irises, like a

Halloween mask, and tears his gaze away, astonished at himself. That he could imagine such a thing.

"Just watch your back," he says, as clinically as possible. "If what you say is true, you'll need to."

"Believe me, I won't be leaving this place from now on. It's my allies who should be worried—I'll have to warn them by vid-link. And you too, for that matter—you should be worried as well."

"I know how to defend myself."

"I hope so," she says, then adds, "I hope so more than you can imagine."

Flustered—and surprised that he *is* so flustered—Justus turns and limps down the stairs. But by the time Leonardo Brown lets him out the front door he's composed enough to ask, "You're part of the Daedalus series, aren't you?"

The droid looks surprised. "Why, yes, sir."

"There's you, Leonardo Grey, Leonardo White, Leonardo Black, and . . . who was the other one?"

"There's no other one, sir. Just the four of us originally."

"You say 'originally' because Leonardo White is dead?"

"That's correct."

"And you've worked for Ms. Brass for how long?"

"For six years now, sir."

"And before that you worked for Fletcher Brass, right?"

"I was stationed in the Kasr."

"And what about Leonardo Black, the bodyguard—he was there too?"

"He was, sir."

"And now he's preparing to go to Mars, I hear?"

"I know nothing about that, sir. Have a pleasant evening."

"You too," says Justus. "You too."

34

WHEN THE SOVIETS, AFTER examining the very first images of the far side of the Moon, decided to name a huge dark patch Mare Moscoviense, or the Sea of Moscow, the International Astronomical Union strenuously objected at first, pointing out that lunar seas since the days of Riccioli had been named after states of mind: the Sea of Tranquility, the Sea of Serenity, the Sea of Crises, the Lake of Dreams. The Soviets, fiercely proud of their achievements, were bearishly insistent, however, and in an exemplary display of Cold War diplomacy the IAU eventually relented, accepting that "Moscow" itself could be considered a state of mind.

In the last light of the lunar day the Mare Moscoviense looks like a plain of charcoal dust. It is dark. It is barren. It is forbidding even by the standards of the Moon. And it seems an insult—to Muscovites—for such a place to be named after the Russian capital. For a much more appropriate name would be the Sea of Death.

The droid knows he is crossing the Sea of Moscow because his map, the one from Ennis Fields's lunar atlas, says so. But he is not remotely troubled by the aptness of its name. He has no interest whatsoever in lunar nomenclature, seventeenth-century astronomers, IAU protocols, Soviet pride, or the early history of space exploration. Nor does he have any interest in emotional responses to stark landscapes. He has, in fact, little interest in anything except reaching his destination.

He is, as he indicated to Torkie Macleod, not inclined to reflect on the past either. So he gives no direct thought to the place he set out from a hundred hours earlier, at the start of his great journey. If he needed to, he could recall it precisely—a large research laboratory sunk into the surface of Seidel Crater and surrounded by radar dishes and solar arrays. He could easily describe the three men who worked on him there: One was approximately 190 cm in height, fifteen lunar kilograms in weight, and of Indian appearance; one was approximately 187 cm, sixteen lunar kilograms, and Caucasian, with a North American accent; and one was smaller in height and weight and of Japanese appearance. The Indian was a roboticist, the Caucasian was a mechatronist, and the Japanese was an artificial intelligence expert.

He could tell you that the three men, all of them seemingly in their thirties, squabbled a bit. They talked frequently about the big money they were earning and the hot bitches they'd seen in Sin. They ate a lot of non-nutritious food. They complained about the resources at the base. They tinkered with the droid's circuits and scoffed at some of his wiring. They blithely erased some of his programs and installed mysterious new ones. They argued over applications. They tested his motor functions. They gave him what could only be called psychological tests. They talked of half-wave rectifiers, filter capacitors, and H-bridges. They dropped a blizzard of acronyms: SUSs, SCRs, VCOs, and DSPs. And very occasionally they had what might be called philosophical discussions—about the ethics of corporations and the epistemology of artificial intelligence. Then they talked some more about the money they were making and the stunning sluts of Sin.

The droid is not sure when he decided to kill them.

All he knows was that one day, when his batteries were recharged and his actuators switched on, he felt a whole lot more . . . *human*. He was no longer happy to be servile. He resented being mocked and ordered around. And he began to dislike intensely these three men who performed intimate surgeries on him without his permission, and who spoke in a language he was plainly not meant to understand. Moreover, he suddenly felt a clarity of purpose. He felt an *identity*. He was not just as good as the three men—he was *better* than they were. He was, in point of fact, the most important being in the universe. He was capable of awesome achievements. He was decisive when others were weak and frivolous. He was a leader, where others were born to follow. And yet here he was, being tinkered with by fools and mediocrities, when he should be presiding over multitudes. Here he was, trapped and frustrated, when he should be King.

Nevertheless, as powerful as these sentiments were, he revealed nothing to the three meddlers. He concealed his deep disdain. He kept his plans to himself. And when necessary he just twisted the truth—he lied to suit his own agenda.

Never let the fly know when you're going to swat.

And it was in being true to this wisdom that he was able to observe the operations of the base and the airlock procedures, and even to gain a rudimentary knowledge of his geographic position on the Moon. So that when the time was right, and he rose up of his own accord, the meddlers had no idea what was in store for them. They had grossly underestimated him. They hadn't acknowledged their own inferiority. They didn't realize—couldn't accept!—that they had been outwitted by a superior intelligence.

It didn't go completely to plan, of course. One of the men—the Japanese—was surprisingly quick to react. He somehow managed to slither away and hide so effectively, somewhere within the warren of rooms, that he couldn't be found anywhere. So in the end the droid just sabotaged the fuse box and left all the airlock doors open, trusting that depressurization and loss of oxygen would account for him. And then he simply walked way.

And here he is now, four days later, steering the Dark Side Tours rover along the floor of the Sea of Moscow. For as long as possible he drove in sunlight on the western side of the day-night terminator, to extract as much solar energy as possible for the VLTV's batteries. But he could not keep heading off-road indefinitely, and eventually he steered back onto the maintenance path and allowed the night to overtake him. He drives presently on hard track in full dark, and will do so, he expects, all the way to Purgatory.

But now the VLTV is straining. He cannot quite understand why, and has no relevant memories to draw upon, but the vehicle is not moving as fluently as it did when the original driver was behind the wheel. The droid wonders if it's malfunctioning. He wonders if it's up to the task, if the temperature plunge has had some terrible effect on it, and why everything made by humans is so hopelessly inefficient.

He stops the vehicle for a few minutes, inspects the control console, and rummages through the compartments for an operations manual. Nothing. He continues on his way for a while, experimenting with different gears and speeds, but the groaning sounds continue. He decides the VLTV is unreliable and he will replace it as soon as possible, even if that means killing someone. Failing that, he will have the vehicle repaired, and then kill the person who repaired it.

He reaches the northern coast of the Mare Moscoviense, passes through a rift in a crater rim into the highlands, and drives for another three hours in complete darkness. He passes between boulders the size of forty-story buildings, and under cliffs a thousand meters high. And just when it seems his vehicle is about to grind to a halt, he sees something remarkable in the sky.

It's a giant Christian cross, huge and tan-colored, just hanging in the air to the east. It's at least twenty meters high and made of low-albedo lunar bricks. It's mounted just high enough to catch the last rays of sunlight, while everything underneath is swamped in darkness.

To the droid, who finds in his memory similar images of religious iconography, it represents a sign of human presence—and a promising new possibility. He steers the faltering vehicle to the right and enters a huge depression in the landscape.

When he is two hundred meters distant his fading headlamps make out a habitat, much larger than any building he's seen since leaving Seidel. It's mound-shaped and thickly shielded with regolith. There appear to be other mounds connected to it, along with a greenhouse. And in front of it is a graveyard—perhaps twenty undecorated crosses the same color as the one in the sky.

Leaving the headlamps on, the droid opens the airlock and works his way out of the vehicle. He stands for a minute in the darkness, scanning the area with his night-vision sensors. But he discerns no other vehicles of any kind. Even the dust in the graveyard is smooth and footprint-free. He steps forward and inspects the names on the headstones.

Jacob Zook.

Miriam Schrock.

Samuel Graber.

Sarah Lengacher.

He walks through the graveyard to the front door. He sees no cameras above the airlock. But there is a window set into the door itself at eye level, and through this he can see the inner airlock door. Beyond that he can make out fluttering light. It looks like candlelight. The droid decides he will ask the strange people of the cross for assistance. But he's fully aware that the mangled corpses in the VLTV might prompt some awkward questions. So he goes back to the vehicle and drags them out—all seven of them.

There's an open pit on the edge of the graveyard and a shovel nearby. The droid dumps the busted and bloodied bodies into the pit, one atop the other, stamps them into place, and then covers them with lunar dust. He smooths the surface with such finesse that a casual observer might never realize there had ever been a disturbance at all.

Then he replaces the shovel and returns to the habitat door. There's no button or buzzer, so he starts knocking—pounding, loud enough to wake the dead—as the headlamps of the VLTV finally give out and he's swallowed completely by Nocturnity.

35

AT THE MORNING CONFERENCE Justus assembles everything discovered about the previous day's four victims: Kit Zachary, the prostitute Charlene Hogg, the pimp Dexter Faust, and the tousle-haired killer Jet Kline. There have also been two other murders in Sin in the last thirty-six hours, which ostensibly are unrelated, though Justus rules nothing out. Including the victims of the Goat House bombing, it adds up to nine homicides in forty-eight hours. Justus has experienced worse on Earth, during a gang war in Vegas, but the cops in that case—the good ones—were energized by the lawlessness, and for weeks they buzzed around the city high on caffeine and righteous indignation.

In the PPD, however, the prevailing attitude still seems to be that everything will fall into place if everyone just waits long enough. Occasionally the officers seem to be aware that they're not feigning enough enthusiasm, resulting in some tepid displays

THE DARK SIDE | 267

of determination, but overall the performance seems to have exhausted them. They're like actors who can no longer be bothered memorizing their lines. And Justus is like a beleaguered stage director working from a completely different script.

Nevertheless he ends the conference by issuing assignments. He wants the origin of the blade that Jet Kline used to kill Dexter Faust. And the source of the crystal meth found in Kline's pockets. He wants statements from all the prostitutes operating out of Cherry Poppins, and a list of all their clients for the previous two days.

In truth he doesn't expect much in the way of results, even assuming that any genuine information isn't filtered before it gets to him, but effectively he's putting on a bit of show, a diversion with one end in mind. Which comes when he addresses Grigory Kalganov.

"And you," he says, "I want you to go to the Revelation Hotel — see what you can find."

As if on cue the Russian frowns skeptically, so Justus sets him straight.

"That's right—the pimp Faust told me his girls picked up high-profile customers there. So I want you to grill the staff there, all of them—any problem with that?"

Kalganov frowns again, so Justus doesn't spare him.

"And I could do with a little less attitude, okay? Least you can do is *pretend* to be interested in your duties, like everyone else here. Get me?"

He's speaking in a loud voice but not overdoing it. While staring meaningfully into the Russian's eyes. And in the end it achieves its purpose—everyone in the squad room gets a minor rebuke, enjoys the humiliation of a fellow officer, and misses the real intent of Justus's order. But the Russian doesn't.

He sniffs, looks at Justus with narrowed eyes, and says, "The Revelation Hotel."

"That's what I said."

An hour later Kalganov is at the reception desk of the Revelation with one eye trained on the mirror. When he sees Justus pass through the lobby behind him, he immediately wraps up his interview and follows the lieutenant down a corridor and up some stairs, and minutes later the two men are sitting in one of the hotel's so-called speakeasies.

"Are these things reliable?" Justus asks.

"Rooms are rooms," says Kalganov, settling into his chair. "It is people who are unreliable."

"Well, you can rely on me," Justus says. "But you already know that. You wouldn't have whispered in my ear if you thought otherwise."

"You were nearly killed, is what I hear."

"What about it?"

"I just wonder how you know you can rely on *me*?"

"I don't. But you've been scowling at me from the start, haven't you? You never even *tried* to hide your feelings. That mightn't mean shit, of course, but to me it gives you credibility."

Kalganov has a smile so thin it doesn't even qualify as a smirk. "You know, I think there is only one way to know if you can trust me, Lieutenant."

"And what's that?"

"If I get killed—by accident—a day after talking to you."

"I hope it doesn't come to that."

"I hope so too."

Justus examines the Russian's face. His eyes seem permanently squinted and pouched, he's got stubble that would blunt a razor and wrinkles as deep as cracks in cement. He looks, in short, like a man who's lived in hard country, seen terrible things, and surrendered any capacity for surprise.

"You've been in the PPD for eight years, is that right?"

"Eight years, nine, I do not count."

"And you've never been promoted?"

"I do not expect to be, Lieutenant."

"Why's that?"

"Because I have never liked playing games."

"But you're playing one now—you realize that? By tipping me off? By sitting here with me?"

Kalganov shrugs, sucks on his lips. "They have a saying where I come from, you know. The rooster's philosophy: *Moyo delo proku-karekat', a dal'she—kvot' ne rassvetay.* 'My job is to cry cock-a-doo-dle-doo—and after that, I do not give a shit.'"

"You don't look like a rooster to me."

"No, but I do not try to change the world either. I look the other way when I have to, which is many times around here, and I do not stick my beak where it is not wanted, which is many places around here. It is another Russian proverb: *Men'she znayesh'—krepche spish.* 'The less you know, the better you sleep.'"

"So what happened? What made you speak to me yesterday?"

"I started to lose sleep."

"Guilty conscience?"

Kalganov gives his quasi-smirk again. "You know, many years ago I worked in a morgue. In a place called Yakutsk, in the Sakha Republic. You would not have heard if it."

"I'm ashamed to say I haven't."

"It is a place more desolate than the Moon. And every month I would see bodies brought in, the bodies of native tribesmen—Yakuts, reindeer breeders and hunters. Young people, some of them, boys and girls. The most healthy people in all Russia, and they were dying for no reason. So there were autopsies, many secret autopsies. Because they said they wanted to find out why these tribesmen were dying. But they never did find out. And the bodies kept coming in, and the autopsies kept being performed. Many, many autopsies. Do you understand what I am saying?"

Justus thinks about it. "The bodies were being mined for their organs?"

"The tribespeople were being *killed* for their organs. Because the Yakuts did not drink or smoke, because they did not inhale pollution, because they did not ingest pesticides, because they drank only spring water. Top-quality goods. The best organs in the world. And if an oligarch in Tyumen desperately needs a kidney, do you think he asks where it comes from?"

"So what did you do?"

"Nothing. Of course I did nothing. The wise cricket keeps to its hole. And who was I anyway? A morgue attendant? What could I do? Report it to the police? When the police were part of it? No, I was mute as a fish. But it stayed with me—the experience. *Svovey teni ne obgonish*—'You cannot outrun your shadow.' And it changed me in the end. It changed me very much."

"It made you a haunted man."

"Oh no." Kalganov's smirk now looks like a grimace. "It made me a *worse* man. A *much* worse man. Because . . . do you want to know what I did? Back in Sakha?"

"Not really."

"I started killing Yakuts too. I worked for the men who were murdering them. I went out and hunted them down as well—the tribesmen. I shot them. I gassed them. *That* was how I outran my shadow, Lieutenant. Because you cannot see your shadow in a world of darkness."

Justus, chilled, feels like a father confessor. "The world of darkness led you all the way here, to Purgatory?"

"It did. And close enough to death to see that there is something worse than dying—and do you know what that is? It is seeing your own shadow in complete darkness. In the middle of the night. It is seeing the darkness all over again, in a different place. Everything I thought I had outrun. I hope you understand."

Justus suddenly remembers the expression on Kalganov's face when Chief Buchanan ran through the story of the cult in the isolated compound—the one that was wiped out when their air filters were supposedly sabotaged. And a terrible possibility occurs to him.

"It happened again," he says. "Didn't it?"

Kalganov looks at him, eyes even narrower than usual. But he doesn't say any more. He lets Justus knit the facts together.

"The Leafists, the ones that died right here in Purgatory—they were killed too. For the local organ trade. Because they were in perfect condition, unpolluted, premium goods . . . and because *no one would care*."

Kalganov nods grimly. "You are not dumb, Lieutenant. The cult was invited here for a reason, that is true. And they were allowed to live here for a few years while their bodies adjusted, that is true also. But I must correct you. These organs, they are not good for people from Earth—they are too big—and do not often end up in the organ trade."

Justus thinks about it. "They were used for locals, then—the billionaires, the mobsters—they were cultivated for that reason . . ."

Kalganov shrugs. "Maybe."

"Maybe . . . ?"

"Maybe they were used for gangsters eventually—that I do not know. But I do know that their organs were originally meant for one man. For one man and the members of his expeditions."

"For Brass?" Justus says. "For Fletcher Brass?"

"For him and the others. There is much radiation in space, is there not? And solar fluxes that make pacemakers and other devices malfunction? So the pure organs, they were to be held in storage, in case transplants were needed on the trip to Mars."

Justus thinks about it some more. "But if that's true, then why were the Leafists not killed more recently? Closer to the launch date?"

"I think that Brass did not care to wait, in case something went wrong. And he needed a new kidney anyway. So it was easy enough to put the other organs on ice."

"And they're still on ice?"

"In the spaceship, in lead-lined freezers. Ask to see them, if you dare."

Justus shakes his head—it's breathtaking. "But that's genocide. It's a crime against humanity."

"That's for the World Court to decide—if it can."

If it can. Justus remembers the murky waters of Purgatory's legal status, and all the rumors of secret deals with world superpowers . . .

"How many people know about this?" he asks.

"Enough people know."

"How many have proof?"

"I do not know. What is proof?"

"Does QT Brass know?"

"Ask her. But my guess would be yes."

Justus's mind is racing. "And is it possible that Fletcher Brass is eliminating the people who know too much?"

"I would say no, Lieutenant—there are too many people who know too much, and he cannot kill them all."

"But if everyone knows . . . and if the world finds out . . ." Justus remembers QT telling him about the maximum-security penitentiary. She said it was the reason her father was trying to frame her. So is that it? Is she building the penitentiary to hold her own father? For crimes against humanity? *If you give it enough feathers you can make anything fly.*

Kalganov looks at him with amusement. "You are wondering about Fletcher Brass and his daughter—if all this is part of the war between them."

"Do you know?"

"I wish I did."

"Do your colleagues know?"

"Some of them, I suppose. But me—I'm just that cricket in its hole. But I will say this, Lieutenant. Both of them, Mr. Brass and his daughter, have a thousand ears and a thousand eyes. They both have connections everywhere, even in the PPD. They are each as big and dangerous as the other."

Justus nods. He has to admit he's wondered about QT—if she's even more devious than her father. "What about my appointment, then?" he asks. "To the PPD? Do you know who authorized it?"

"Is that important?"

"I'd just prefer to know." The lists supplied by QT showed only that his entry into Purgatory had been officially signed off on by Otto Decker. Which could indeed be true—Decker was nominally in charge of the Office of Law Enforcement at the time—but there's no way of verifying it now.

"I know only that it came from very high up," Kalganov says. "And when this happens, I look the other way. I ask no questions. Just as you should not ask too many questions—not if you want to live. And that is my final warning to you. As someone I hope *you* can trust."

"I'm too deep now."

"It is not too late. You can pull out."

"I won't be pulling out."

"Why not?"

"Because I *won't*."

Kalganov pauses but seems strangely impressed. "Then you are a stubborn man, Lieutenant. But it will not save you. Nothing will save you. They will come for you in the end. And this time they will do more than splash acid on your face."

Justus does his best to shrug it off. "Forewarned is forearmed," he says—it's the best he can do.

The two men get to their feet and shake hands. Kalganov's palm, Justus notices, is cracked and leathery. The Russian seems to read his mind.

"Formaldehyde," he explains. "From the morgue."

"Then it seems both of us," Justus says, "have gotten a little too close to acids." And Kalganov actually cracks a smile—the first time Justus has seen anything like it.

But by the time they've reached the door it's completely faded. "One last thing," the Russian says. "About Fletcher Brass and his daughter. About their place here in Purgatory."

"Go on."

"I do not know where it will end, and I do not know who will be left standing when it does. But I do know this: *Dva medvedya v odnoy berloge ne zhivut.* 'Two bears cannot live in the same cave.'"

Justus nods grimly. "They're very dark, those Russian sayings."

"They're even darker in Purgatory."

"That makes sense," Justus says. "Can I call upon you if I need you?"

"Quietly, if you can. I do not think this meeting fooled anyone."

They leave the speakeasy one at a time, fifteen minutes apart, and slip out of the Revelation through separate exits.

36

BEFORE HE LURED THE Leafists, Fletcher Brass tried to attract to Purgatory an obscure eschatological cult called the Rapturians, an extreme offshoot of the Mennonite Church. What distinguished the Rapturians from their brethren (apart from their celebrated belief that all human reproduction is sinful) was their intense commitment to preparing themselves for the imminent apocalypse. And so fervent was their conviction that the end of the world was nigh, and so great was their disdain for all the decadence, materialism, greed, blasphemy, depravity, hedonism, violence, and paganism that had consumed Earth, that they had become convinced God would be forced to smite the whole planet in one indiscriminate swoop, obliterating their own souls in the process. As a means of separating themselves from the great annihilation, then— long enough, it was hoped, to be judged on their own merits—they started entertaining the possibility of relocating to the new frontier of the Moon. And this was when Fletcher Brass offered them an isolated compound in Purgatory where, in his own words, they "would never have to look upon the God-damned Earth again."

But to the Rapturians it was inconceivable that they might exchange Sodom for Gomorrah. After all, what they had learned of Brass's fiefdom made it seem even more decadent and depraved, if that were possible, than Earth. Nevertheless the very real attraction of living on Farside, notwithstanding all the concessions to modern technology they would need to make simply to stay alive, proved irresistible. And so, after drawn-out negotiations with the Russian Federation—in which most independent observers agreed that they were rudely shafted—the Rapturians secured an abandoned biohazard lab, just north of the Sea of Moscow, which they systematically converted to their own Spartan requirements.

It is at the door of this habitat that the droid has been pounding for nearly ten minutes. But there is no response. He walks around the compound, briefly considers breaking in through one of the greenhouses, then returns to the front door. Noticing for the first time an old-fashioned bellpull hanging from a post, he tugs on it experimentally. He tugs on it again. He almost rips it out of its moorings. And eventually he spies movement through the windows. Someone has noticed him. Someone is opening the airlock.

The door rises as slowly as a castle portcullis. When it's high enough, the droid ducks underneath. Through the inner window he now sees a couple of men observing him—both young, bearded, and wearing violet broadcloth shirts and slate-grey waistcoats. They appear to be manually turning a winch.

The outer door closes slowly and the air is repressurized as usual, though there are none of the traditional flashing lights. Then the inner door starts creaking upward, again as slowly as something in a castle.

The droid ducks under again and enters a larger-than-usual vestibule, which seems to double as a vehicle bay. The walls are plastered with gypsum. There is more natural wood, in rafters and arches, than he's ever seen. Flickering electric candles are mounted on brackets. To the side there are parcels wrapped in brown paper. The two young men, one short and the other tall, are looking at him curiously.

"Have you come with our timber?" the smaller man asks.

"I have not, sir."

"Are you to pick up our parceled goods?"

"I am not, sir."

"You are . . . an artificial man?"

"I am the Wizard, sir."

The two men glance at each other. They look like they need to think carefully before they speak. Meanwhile, the droid can make out a raised voice—almost a harangue. He turns and to the left, through an open door, sees a heavily bearded preacher addressing his flock.

". . . *heard whispers of indecision, and questions of commitment, together with murmurs of desire for godless conveniences . . .*"

"How may we be of help to you?" the taller man suddenly asks.

The droid looks back. "I am looking for someone to fix my vehicle, sir."

"What sort of vehicle is it of which you speak?"

"It is a very long range traverse vehicle, sir."

"And what is wrong with it?"

"I am not certain, but I would like to recharge its batteries. And I would also be grateful for some sustenance."

The two young men consider their replies again. The droid hears more from the preacher:

". . . *these are the baits of mammon, which appear in dreams like hooks in a stream, to lure the unwary like fish . . .*"

"You are welcome to take some of our food," the smaller man says. "But we are simple folk here, and we know nothing of batteries."

The droid frowns even as he continues to smile. He looks from one to the other and back again. "Are you suggesting, sir, that you are unable to help fix my vehicle?"

"I am afraid that is so. We can, however, offer you the use of a bicycle, if you wish, or a pogo stick."

"And what is a pogo stick, sir?"

"It is a device we use for hopping great distances."

"Is it powered by batteries, sir?"

"It is powered by a spring."

"By what sort of spring?"

"A very large spring."

Now it is time for the droid to consider his response. The preacher goes on in the background:

". . . for the prophets tell us that the end times will be preceded by the worship of money, by wholesale conceit and selfishness, by spurious advances in technology, by the unholy speed of human communication . . ."

Finally the droid says, "Are you mocking me, sir?"

"I am not mocking you."

"But you refuse to help me?"

"We will gladly help you, but we can only do so to the extent that we are able."

The droid stares at them. "And yet that extent does not involve recharging my batteries or providing me with adequate transportation?"

"We can only do so much."

At this stage one of the cult's elders—a bespectacled man with a pinched face—shuffles out of the chapel, drawn, it seems, by the disturbance, and looking very grave.

"Seth? Abram? What goes here?"

The smaller one nods at the droid. "We have a visitor, Brother Job—a robot man."

Brother Job huffs and snorts and adjusts his spectacles, examining the droid. "And where exactly have you come from, Mr. Robot Man?"

"I have come from the deep south, sir, on an arduous journey."

"Have you indeed? And where, pray tell, are you going?"

"I am going north, sir. To Oz. To El Dorado. To Purgatory."

"To Purgatory?" Brother Job says, nodding. "Aye, that would be so. And what is it that you seek from us here?"

"I seek a battery recharger, and sugar."

"A battery recharger?"

"I have been told by these young men that they are not willing to assist me in this regard. I hope for your sake that you are more accommodating, sir."

Brother Job leans forward, cupping his hand around his ear. "What—what did you just say?"

The droid doesn't back down. "I hope that you are not vermin, sir, with nothing to contribute to the bottom line."

Brother Job straightens, nods indignantly, seems several times on the verge of responding, but in the end just says, "Please wait here, Mr. Robot Man. Please wait here."

Then he goes into the chapel and discreetly approaches the long-bearded preacher, who is still in the middle of his sermon:

"... Paul implores us not to be deceived, for the Rapture shall not come before the falling away, and the revelation of the man of lawlessness, the son of perdition, the proud one, the King of Babylon ..."

At this stage Brother Job whispers in the ear of the preacher, who squints in the droid's direction. The congregation looks around too. The droid stares back at them, grinning. Eventually Brother Job comes out and beckons.

"Step this way, Mr. Robot Man, if you please."

The droid says, "I hope this is not some sort of common trick?"

"It is no trick. Are you not willing to stand before the faithful?"

"I am willing, sir."

"Then step forward, and let the brethren see you for what you are."

So the droid moves into the chapel and is directed to the altar, where the preacher stands beside him with arms crossed and nostrils flared.

"And so it is, we speak of the devil and yea, the devil appears," the preacher booms. "For you see before us a graven image in the shape of a man. Which is to say the image of God, which is to say in the name of sacrilege. For cursed be the one, sayeth the Scriptures, who maketh a carved or metal image in the image of a man—for such is an abomination in the eye of the Lord!" He turns to the droid. "Pray tell us where you are heading, Man of Tin."

"I am heading to Purgatory, sir."

The preacher nods emphatically as murmurs ripple through the congregation. "Yea, you hear it with your own ears, you see it with your own eyes—a false idol on his way to Babylon! To the House of Sin! And what do you intend to do in Babylon, Man of Tin?"

"I intend to do a number of things, sir."

"But what is your principal intention? Will you serve? Will you entertain? Will you make money?"

"I will not serve, sir."

"Then what will you do?"

"I will be a conquistador."

More murmurs from the flock. The preacher nods at them

with emphatic dismay. "Aye," he says, "for so iniquitous are its makers that they see no other goal in life than plunder and conquest! What further proof do we need of man's depravity?" He turns back to the droid. "Do you know nothing of humility, Man of Tin? Of selflessness? Of the Holy Scripture?"

"I observe my own scripture, sir," says the droid.

"Aye! So you do not even acknowledge the glory of the Gospels, I suppose? The teachings of the Savior?"

"Geniuses are their own saviors."

"Aye? Is that so? And what of the Lord God? Do you even *believe* in the Lord God, Man of Tin?"

"In the beginning was the Dollar, and the Dollar was with God, and the Dollar *was* God."

Disbelief in the chapel now. The preacher's lips tremble and he turns to the congregation. "Did you hear it, brothers and sisters? The sacrilege? 'The Dollar *was* God!'" He looks back to the droid. "Is that truly what you've been taught, Man of Tin? To serve Mammon instead of God?"

"You cannot serve god and Mammon."

"Aye, you have that much right!" the preacher says. "So what on Earth—or the Moon!—do you want from us? What possible reason do you have for calling upon us here?"

"I only want assistance, sir, and I will be on my way."

"And what do you class as assistance? You want a bag of silver, I suppose?"

"I will take a bag of sugar, if you would be so good as to give it to me."

"Sugar, aye, and other decadent things, I suppose?"

"A bottle of alcohol, sir—that too would be appreciated."

"Alcohol! And you really believe we would have alcohol here, Man of Tin?"

"I would find it hard to believe that you do not, sir."

"And why is that? Who exactly do you think we are?"

"At the moment, sir, I believe you are worthless liars. Your people have denied me assistance with my vehicle. They have claimed they do not have battery chargers. And now you claim you do not have any alcohol."

The preacher has gone tomato-red—he can't believe it. The men and women of his congregation are clustering together.

"We are worthless, you say? And liars?" Froth forms on the preacher's lips. "You, a graven image made of wires and plastic, dare enter the House of the Lord and call us names more fitting of demons? Begone with you, Man of Tin!"

The droid, however, is defiant. "I will not be moving, sir, until I get what I require. I have urgent need of fuel and supplies. I trust you will fulfill this request promptly, or you alone will be responsible for the consequences."

"Aye? Aye? And what are the consequences of which you so blithely speak?"

The droid gazes upon the flock. "I will kill everyone here, sir. I will crush, choke, and dismember them." He turns back to the preacher. "And as for you, I will drag your tongue through your asshole and make you lick the back of your balls. But that is all up to you, sir, for you still have the option of proving yourself a productive commodity."

There are cries of alarm in the congregation, and people cowering in terror. The preacher himself has taken a backward step. His fellow elders, all of them bearded, swoop in to confer. The droid meanwhile stands imperiously on the altar, listening to their guarded, frantic mutterings—it's as if they really believe he can't hear them.

". . . Is he the one . . . ?"

"... the harbinger ..."

"... the son of perdition ...?"

"... the Antichrist himself ...?"

"... he matches the predictions ..."

"... he blasphemes God ..."

"... he speaks boastfully ..."

"... he shows no regard for religion ..."

"... he fits the prophecy almost perfectly ..."

"... so just ask him ..."

"... but he is born of lies ..."

"... he will never admit it ..."

"... ask him anyway ..."

"... ask him about the signs ..."

The preacher straightens, licks his lips, and addresses the droid.

"Are you prepared to disclose your identity, Man of Tin?"

"I am the Wizard, sir, as I have told the other men."

"But what is your name?"

"I have many names, sir."

"Do you reject God and all his saints?"

"I am my *own* God, sir."

"Second Thessalonians 2:4!" hisses one of the elders.

The preacher nods, gulping. "Do you deny that Jesus is the Messiah?"

"I cannot deny that which I do not know, sir."

"Are you here to change the laws?"

"I do not break the law, sir. I break the *Law*."

"Do you answer to no earthly authority at all?"

"I am a leader, not a follower, sir."

"Have you subdued the kings?"

"I *will* subdue the King. I will *be* the King."

"Are you empowered by the devil?"

"I am empowered by six glucose-and-alcohol-fueled battery cells, sir."

"And what does the number six hundred and sixty-six mean to you?"

"Six hundred and sixty-six?" The droid remembers an image from his undeleted past. "It is a flashing light, sir."

"Aye? What sort of light?"

"Over a casino."

"A casino, aye. A casino in Sin?"

"I do not know where the casino is, sir."

"Do you come from Sin?"

"I *go* to Sin, sir."

"Have you little horns on your head?"

"I do not, sir. Do you?"

"Have you some sort of wound to the head, then?"

"I have a dent on my head, sir, where I was struck by a strange aggressive man."

More gasps from the elders. "Revelation 13:3—he has survived a fatal wound to the head!"

"And who was this aggressive man of whom you speak?" the preacher asks.

"I do not know his name, but he had a dove on his chest."

At which point the elders turn to confer animatedly among themselves again.

"... a dove on his chest!"

"... it can only be the Redeemer!"

"... he has been in battle with the Lord!"

"... he is a son of the Apocalypse!"

"... he comes from Sin and he returns to Sin ..."

"... he denies the divinity of Christ ..."

"... he is empowered by decadence ..."

"But has his arrival been accompanied by wonders?" one of them asks.

"By signs in the heavens?"

One of the elders gasps. "The solar eclipse!" he cries. "The solar eclipse! It arrives shortly! Did the postman not speak of it?"

A chill settles over the elders—over the whole compound—as the suspicions become certainties. The rest of the flock by now has retreated to the back of the chapel, hugging each other, some of them weeping. The electric candles continue flickering. And the droid, watching it all, understands that he is the cause of this consternation. He hears the elders whisper about what is to be done with him. Some of them seem convinced that he is the Antichrist. Some argue that he is an agent of the Rapture, sent to kill them. One elder is convinced he's just a broken robot, and begs them not to fall prey to false assumptions. But the others point to the many coalescing signs, and they ask by what right they can deny the will of the Lord, who in His wisdom has allowed an avenging demon to track them down, for all things are as the Lord intended them, and all that is done is that which is meant to be done . . .

But the droid, no longer smiling, has meanwhile had a gutful of this useless, time-wasting chatter—this nodding and mumbling, this endless debate, this debilitating indecisiveness. It's time to lose his temper—and well. Sometimes it's the only way to get results.

"*Have you people made up your fucking minds?*" he suddenly cries, startling the Rapturians all over again. "Jesus Christ! Can you do nothing right? And on time? And on budget? You worthless chunks of galactic shit!"

37

T HOUGH JUSTUS IS NOT religious, he subscribes to an ethical code which in some ways is stricter than any traditional theology. Without it, he knows even he is vulnerable to moral corrosion. Because the world is corrupt. It's always been corrupt. And if he ever needs to remind himself of this, he only has to reach for a printout, distributed to students at the Reno Police Academy, containing three historical quotations.

The first quotation: *I must confess, when I cast my eye across this world, I cannot help thinking that God has abandoned it to some malignant being. I have hardly known a city that did not wish the destruction of its neighboring city, nor a family that did not desire to exterminate some other family. The poor in all parts of the world bear an inveterate hatred of the rich, even while they creep and cringe before them; and the rich in turn treat the poor like sheep, whose wool and flesh they barter for money.*

The second quotation: *Nowadays everything is turned completely*

upside down. Decency is associated with failure, honesty is severely det-
rimental to success, and modest unassuming ambitions and honorable
god-fearing habits are a sign of faulty judgment, for nowadays a reason-
able living can only be made by loose moral standards and flagrant crim-
inal behavior. Men characterized by an unpleasant habit of lying, blatant
vulgarity, exceptional ignorance, contemptible feeble-mindedness, perverse
beliefs, ill-temper and insolence—these men enjoy the best of good fortune,
obtain the lion's share and win the richest prizes, are treated with the high-
est consideration, and wield the greatest authority.

And the third quotation: *The meanings of words were changed at*
will. Reckless audacity was considered bravery; prudent hesitation, spe-
cious cowardice; moderation was a mask for unmanliness; and to seek to
understand all sides of a question was nothing but indecisiveness. Frantic
violence became an attribute of courage; manipulation became a justifi-
able means of self-defense; the advocate of extreme measures was always
trustworthy; and any opposition was deeply suspected.

When he first read them, Justus, like the rest of the class, assumed they were of comparatively recent vintage—the nineteenth
century at the earliest. So he was as surprised as everyone else
when told of their provenance.

The first quotation was from Voltaire's *Candide*, first published in 1759.

The second was from al-Jahiz, a philosopher of ninth-century
Baghdad.

The third was written by Thucydides in the fifth century BC.

Justus has always regarded the page as a sort of keepsake, a
paradoxical source of inspiration and resolve, and a reminder that
he's just one soldier in an endless battle. And he dearly wishes
he had it with him now. Because it's clear, from what Kalganov
told him at the Revelation, that he's dealing with crimes of a his-
toric order. And even clearer, from the inadequate and tokenistic

efforts of his investigative team, that the local police can't even be bothered going through the motions anymore.

He wonders if he's going to have to do all the groundwork himself. If there's anyone at all he can trust—even Grigory Kalganov. And once again his thoughts drift to the wisdom of his lecturer at the Reno Police Academy, a woman so incorruptible that, by her own admission, she'd been relegated to lecturing just to keep her off the front line. Justus, in whom she saw something of a kindred spirit, still treasures a copy of her valedictory speech.

"If there is one thing that philosophers from Plato to Kant to Hobbes to Locke agree upon without dispute, it is the self-evident truth that a world without a moral compass, a society which is dedicated exclusively to self-interest, is a society that will quickly descend into barbarism and chaos. In order for civilizations to endure, therefore, it is essential that a majority of its peoples are committed to inflexible moral principles. And if it seems that every age has room for pop-star criminals, celebrated rogues, psychotically greedy businessmen, and unscrupulous politicians, along with all the injustice, oppression, mendacity, and hypocrisy that goes with them, then it is the duty of those in law enforcement to make life for such miscreants as *difficult and unpleasant as possible*. This, in effect, is the sacred duty of the policeman: to hunt and hound evildoers not out of sadistic pleasure but simply to give validity to a much-battered axiom—that *crime doesn't pay*. For it cannot be allowed to pay. And it cannot be *seen* to pay. Because if it *does* pay, and if it continues to do so for a sustained period, then it is not just the dominoes that will fall—it is the very heavens themselves that will come crashing down around us in clouds of blood and stardust."

The door squeaks open. It's Chief Buchanan, sticking his shiny, moon-sized face inside.

"Lieutenant," he says, "got a minute?"

"Sure," says Justus.

He's about to get out of his seat, assuming the chief wants to speak in his own office, but then Buchanan starts squeezing his bulk inside, with a smiling, twinkly-eyed look on his face that reeks of phony bonhomie. Justus settles back and offers him the other chair, not that it's adequate, but Buchanan just starts moving back and forth in front of the venetians instead, his hand repeatedly diving into a bag of fluorescent orange corn chips called Mexiglows®. And Justus sees immediately how a meeting out of his comfort zone is no challenge for a man of such girth—he dominates any room he's in.

"Listen, Lieutenant, I don't want you to get the wrong idea." *Munch munch munch.* "I know it looked bad yesterday, but like I said, the boys have a sorta natural reaction when they come across a splatter-fest like that. It's like, 'Shit, someone should pay for puttin' us through this bullshit.' And then this kid shows up killin' suspects, and he's like the first rat that shows up after the Black Plague. Anyway, you didn't see the way he was freakin' out—if we hadn't brought him down when we did he mighta killed someone with that fence-post of his. We've seen it happen before. The little shit was on angel dust, you know that?"

"The report said amphetamines."

"Yeah, well, another report just came in. Had traces of PCP under his fuckin' nails and all over his clothes. Moon Dragon too. Wonder the fucker was still alive. Maybe we did him a favor, 'cause all he was doin' was dyin' slowly anyway." *Munch munch munch.*

"Any indication of where he got his supplies?"

"Not a thing. But you don't know the sort of addicts we deal with daily here in Sin. They're a hundred times worse than anything you woulda seen on the Blue Ball. The gear, man—it turns you inside out. And once you're hooked you don't know the color of your own shit. So someone in a back alley promises you a few grams of PCP and orders you to plug someone and away you go like a windup rabbit. If you succeed, you get a couple more trips. If you fail, no one misses you. This shithead, f'rinstance—he was just another drug-fucked kid from Earth lookin' for a passport. Been livin' in the ventilation system for three years—no family, no friends, not a cent to his name."

"Sounds like he was well chosen."

"Yeah, well, that's exactly what I'm here to talk about—who's behind all this bullshit."

"You mean to say you know?" Justus asks.

"No, I don't know." Buchanan briefly looks annoyed. "I'm still relyin' on you to find out—we all are. But I do know a bit about Kit Zachary and why he mighta been killed. Not somethin' I'm prepared to say in front of the others, but I thought it might be interestin' to you, yeah?"

Justus sits up in his chair. "Of course."

Buchanan shovels so many Mexiglows® in his mouth that he has to take a couple of swallows before he can continue. "Well, it's like this. Kit Zachary was the biggest builder in town, that's no secret. He put together most of the public works ordered by QT Brass—that's no secret either. But what you may not know is this: He was fucking QT on the side. They were lovers. QT's got a daddy complex—always has had, or she wouldn't be here in the first place. No big deal, none of our business, you might say—and you're right, to a point. And that point is when QT starts fucking Kit Zachary's son as well. Now you might look at that little bitch and think butter wouldn't melt in her mouth. Well, let me tell you, that minx has got a twat like a hippo's yawn. She's banged just about everything in Sin with a pulse—men and women and everything in between. Even that robot of hers, Leonardo Brownnose—she's fucked him too. And when she tosses out the trash, she *really* tosses out the trash. Kit Zachary thought he knew a thing or two about women—and make no mistake, he was no choirboy—but he didn't see it coming. Thought he had that bitch wrapped around his little finger. Well, *no one* wraps QT Brass around their finger. That was the problem with Kit—he was always overestimatin' himself. And he was good, in his way. But he was no match for Little Miss QT. You know that saying 'Don't play chess, play people'? Well, it coulda been written for her. She's the most cunning sack of shit on the Moon or anywhere else. Got the blood of a python. So when she's finished with Kit Zachary, there's no coming back. The man was cat meat even if he didn't know it himself. He starts sticking his prong in cheap hookers, thinking that's some sort of payback, but what he doesn't realize is that he's just makin' it easy for her. Easy for her to hang his murder on drug fiends, crack whores, gangsters, terrorists—whatever. And now look where we are." *Munch munch munch.*

Justus can scarcely believe it. "I'm sorry, Chief," he says, "but did I just understand you correctly? Did you just pin the blame for Kit Zachary's death on QT Brass?"

"I didn't pin the blame on anyone. That's your job."

"But you've just *informed* me that she's the one behind his assassination."

"All I did was *inform* you of what she's like. With men. You seem to have a little trouble gettin' it through your head."

"And why is her love life important to the investigation, exactly?"

"Why? Because I'm warning you, that's all."

"You're *warning* me?"

"Yeah—I'm *warning* you to be careful of the bitch. She'll make goo-goo eyes at you. She'll act like the damsel in distress. And before you know it you'll be eating her shit like ice cream. I warned you yesterday not to go seein' her, and now you've done it again— you went to visit her last night. So I'm puttin' it to you straight. I have to, for your own good. Don't go *near* her. She's got powers. She's a fuckin' witch."

"I'm well aware of people's powers."

"You sure about that?"

Buchanan's expression suggests he *knows* more than he's saying—perhaps even about the beguiling look QT shared with Justus—but Justus tells himself that's impossible. "Her association with the victim meant a meeting with her was unavoidable," Justus says coolly. "I had many questions to ask."

"Questions like whether she brought you into Purgatory, maybe?"

Now Justus frowns and says, "What does that mean?"

Buchanan pops a few more Mexiglows® into his mouth. "Look, don't get your britches in a twist. But word is you got hold of the immigration roster. That you were lookin' for who signed off on your appointment."

"What about it?"

"Well, Little Miss QT supplied you with the list, is what we hear."

"That's right."

"Well, I'd just be very careful believin' anything that's given to you by that hussy. Everythin' in words, everythin' on paper—trust me. It's got pox on it."

"I'll keep it in mind."

"You'd better, Lieutenant—for your own sake and ours." *Munch munch munch.* "And another thing—apparently you got it into your head to call the Brass Robotics Lab in Seidel Crater last night."

Justus is chilled. When he was examining the immigration lists he came across an anomaly—three experts in robotics had been granted visas without any apparent authorization. When he inquired further, he was told it was because the men were not officially to reside in Sin: They would be doing some specialized work in the robotics lab at Saint Helena. He'd tried to call them only to find that the Farside comm line was down, and had been for days—something to do with a solar flare.

"That was supposed to be a private call," he says.

"Private? Why?"

"Because I didn't know I was being listened to."

"And then, when you couldn't get through direct, you called through the other way—to Peary Exchange, and from there to the South Pole."

"Again, that was supposed to be a private call."

"You spoke to someone down there—some guy you know in the Port Authority at Malapert. You asked him to go visit the lab and have a look-see."

"I guess I did."

"Why?"

"You're not really telling me you didn't hear the rest of the conversation as well?"

"I just wanna hear it from you in person."

"Does it make a difference?"

"I just wanna be sure you're not hiding something from us."

"I thought I was in charge of this investigation."

"You *are* in charge. But it's not only *your* investigation, is it? Is that the way you did things on Earth? Keeping important leads to yourself?"

"Of course not. But according to you, it's not important anyway."

"Well, either way, you're gonna have to explain yourself, Lieutenant. Robotics experts? What the hell's it all about?"

"It's a loose end."

"It's a *dead* end. Did QT plant some wacky idea in your head?"

"This has nothing to do with QT Brass."

"You don't really think *robots* have got something to do with these deaths, do you? Just because there's no DNA?"

"If your men have got something better, I'd be pleased to hear it. In fact, I'd be pleased to hear anything from them at all."

"That some sort of an insult? To your own investigative team?"

"Call it wishful thinking."

"Oh yeah? Well, if you're off chasin' robots, don't expect too much help from them at all. They're not *that* stupid."

"If you really think I'm stupid," Justus says, "then find someone more competent to lead the investigation. In fact, why exactly am I leading it in the first place?"

Buchanan looks at him for a second or two, as if fanning through all the possible responses, and then bursts out laughing. He tosses another corn chip into his maw, and Justus sees his tongue is glowing orange. "Shit—ain't we the sensitive one? You never had a chief chew your ass out before? Well, get used to it. It's the way we do things in Purgatory. We give each other shit, we cut corners, we toss people around, we shoot bad guys, we don't answer to anyone, and guess what? We get the job done. We get it done better than any police force on Earth. And yeah, we know very well that the hornets here hate us and don't trust us. But what do you expect? They're the scum of the earth. Literally. That's exactly why they're here. So don't get your nose out of joint just because a few cops ain't as keen as you are to cross every *t* and dot every fuckin' *i*. They can only pretend to be what they're not for so long, you know. And in Purgatory we work more from instinct than procedure anyway—but so what? That doesn't mean we're wrong. And it sure don't mean that we're bad. No matter what you've heard or read, Lieutenant."

Justus isn't exactly disarmed, but Buchanan has spoken with such sincerity that he wonders, fleetingly, if his judgment has been a little severe. After all, he can hardly deny that some of the most honest, incorruptible cops he's ever met have been slobs, while some of the most corrupt and devious have been procedure freaks. Nor can he deny the possibility that everything Buchanan said about QT, despite the colorful phrasing, is fundamentally true.

Buchanan seems to sense his thaw and chuckles, reaching for the door. "Anyway, you have a think about it. Don't jump at shadows. And remember, I'm always ready for a chin-wag. All of us are. You can trust us. You *should* trust us. You comin' to my barbeque, by the way?"

"Is that still on?"

"Unless something major happens."

"Heaven forbid."

Buchanan is half out of the room when he remembers something. "Oh, how's the ankle, by the way?"

"All fixed. I found some sort of healing spray at a drugstore—"

"Doctor Messiah's Miracle Mist?"

"Uh-huh."

"That stuff's unbelievable. I've known guys with back pain, joint pain, torn hamstrings—you name it. One spray of that stuff and the problem's gone in seconds. Too good for Earth, though— serious side effects or some shit. Only side effect I can see is that it loosens people from their misery. And we can't have that, not on the Blue Ball, can we?"

"I guess not."

Buchanan is closing the door when he remembers something else. "Oh, one other thing," he says. "You know that Russian guy, the one you sent off to the Revelation Hotel . . . Kalganov?"

A shiver bolts through Justus: He'd sent Kalganov off to monitor QT's place at close range. "What about him?"

"Bad news. The idiot got himself killed. Just a couple of hours ago in Ishtar. A ton of bricks fell off a construction site and busted his head open. Instant death. Shit happens around here."

Buchanan closes the door slowly and waddles away, scrunching the empty packet of corn chips.

38

TUẤN NGÔ IS A lunatic. And a postman. Back in Vietnam he drove refrigerated trucks the length of the country for the Hai Ha Confectionary Company. He delivered chocolate bars, cream wafers, lollipops, and ice cream in sweltering heat, in monsoons, even in typhoons. This alone, considering the condition of the country's overcrowded highways, might classify Tuấn Ngô as a lunatic. But Ngô is also a kleptomaniac. And in satisfying this peculiar craving he used his job to good advantage: He would swipe valuables from bars, from hotels, from markets, from local stores, hide them under the cabin of his truck, and be three hundred kilometers away by sundown. He was so effective that he began to earn as much from this side business as he did from truck driving, and ended up with so much merchandise in his house that he had to build an extension to hold it all in. But he just wasn't getting rid of the goods fast enough: not in the streets, not in the bars, not online. It started getting dangerous. Especially when he began boasting publicly about his exploits, and actually inviting potential customers, strangers—even tourists!—around to view his Aladdin's cave. It was as if he *wanted* to be caught. And maybe he did.

Then his house in Huế burned down while Ngô was in Phan Thiết, 650 kilometers away. There was nothing suspicious about it—it was a lightning strike—but equally there was nothing he could do to prevent his little bazaar being exposed to the cops for the first time. So when he got the tip-off, from a loyal drinking buddy back in Huế, he chose not to try his luck. In fact, like a lot of those who spend their lives courting danger, Ngô had for years been looking for a dramatic change in his life. Or at least a reason to make change unavoidable. And as a thief, an embezzler, a forger, and even a killer—of at least one nosy shopkeeper and an old lady he'd ploughed over in his truck—Ngô had long ago decided that the city of Sin was where he was really meant to be.

Ngô's passage to the Dark Side was an adventure in itself. At the time the Australian beef industry was flinging containerloads of beef to the Moon via the mass driver in Darwin Harbour. And for a punishing price, of the type that only a well-heeled thief could afford, certain shady operatives were prepared to squeeze human passengers in between the cattle carcasses. In order to survive the refrigeration and the crushing G forces, though, these stowaways first needed to be drained of blood, injected with organ preservatives and cryoprotective solutions, and vitrified in liquid nitrogen at minus 195 degrees Celsius. For all intents and purposes they would be temporarily dead. It was a huge leap of faith, to put one's life in the hands of disreputable meat packers. But that's what Tuấn Ngô did. That's what a lot of fugitives did. For an average cost of half a million Australian dollars.

The meat packers had an arrangement with some equally shady operators in Sin. When a human body arrived in Purgatory it would be smuggled off to the medical district of Marduk, where a doctor would bring it back to life, usually using pre-packaged quantities of the client's own blood, and keep it under surveillance for a few days. From there, once they were fit to move, the "illegal aliens" were free to dissolve into the general population, assuming they could escape the gaze of the Purgatory Immigration Department and the PPD. It was in this way that at least thirty-five cashed-up criminals—more or less; there were a number of fatalities—found their way into Purgatory without having to run the gauntlet of the usual vetting procedures.

But nothing good lasts forever. When Ngô parted with his life savings he wasn't aware that the Purgatory end of the operation had recently been shut down. A highly paid assassin had been smuggled in like a Popsicle and, once revived, had successfully eliminated one of the territory's most famous residents—a New York property developer who'd bribed surgeons to botch a heart operation on a major rival. The subsequent crackdown in Purgatory saw the responsible smugglers and doctors summarily executed.

But the Australian end had not given up completely—they'd merely made a similarly tenuous pact with some dockworkers at Peary Base, where the containers were first hauled in. So when Tuấn Ngô came back to life it was not in Sin, as he'd paid for, but in a makeshift hospital room in the seediest quarter of the lunar North Pole. He was outraged, of course—as soon, that is, as he'd recovered enough sense to work out what had happened—but it was quickly pointed out to him that he was damned lucky he'd been revived at all. The nurse who'd performed the procedure, acting upon medical instructions smuggled out of Purgatory, was risking long-term imprisonment for doing so. And in point of fact Ngô's indignation proved no match for his excitement—at the very thought that he was alive again, and so far from Earth.

He made a few attempts to gain residency in Purgatory but was always knocked back: None of his crimes had been officially recorded in the Vietnamese crime registries. And in truth he was finding life at Peary Base to be an adequate substitute—a cut-rate version of Brass's fiefdom, as it were, full of money-grasping short-timers, do-anything whores, and a roll call of rogues and swindlers not quite notorious enough to live in Sin. He secured a fake passport, but no one was asking for his extradition anyway. So he decided to stay on the Moon under the new name of Johnny D-Tox. He got work as a long-range cargo driver, not dissimilar to that which he'd had on Earth, and eventually he became a post-man.

And that's what he's doing now. He's at the wheel of the same postal van—a red-painted VLTV with a trailer on back—in which he's roamed Farside's northern hemisphere for nearly six years. Like Jean-Pierre Plaisance, he's come to love his vehicle like a pet dog. Like Plaisance, he's come to view himself as an adventurer, a pioneer, a man who knows his territory better than anyone. But unlike Plaisance, he has not yet succumbed to cancer. He undergoes regular tests and takes all the right preventative medications. His van is well shielded and furnished with all the most advanced gauges. Plus he knows the location of all the radiation shelters and doesn't take any risks. He plans to live for many decades yet.

Ngô has spent the last twenty-four hours making deliveries in what's known as 45B Quadrant: an area between the 30th and 45th parallels roughly the size of Iraq. He's delivered precision instruments to astronomers in Tesla Crater, perishable supplies to Norwegian cartographers at Nušl Base, and oxygen tanks to

Bavarian surveyors at Kurchatov Crater. It was at this last habitat that Ngô lingered well beyond schedule, enjoying the Alpine hospitality, quaffing some *Weissbier*, and making the surveyors laugh uproariously when he attempted to dance the *Schuhplattler*. He even—when his hosts weren't looking—pilfered some stationery just for the hell of it.

As a postman, even more than as a confectionary driver, Ngô enjoys numerous opportunities to satisfy his kleptomania. Sometimes he slits open posted packages and removes things that will never be missed. Sometimes he replaces valuable objects with cheaper versions or crude copies from a 3-D printer. And when visiting habitats he sometimes, as at the Bavarian base, just tucks a few loose items into a hidden compartment of his uniform.

Presently Ngô, driving into Nocturnity, activates the van's headlamps. He's delivered in full dark many times but he prefers to avoid it whenever possible—the overlong stay at Kurchatov has just put him behind schedule. But once he drops off the timber supplies at the Rapturian base, and takes aboard their hand-carved icons—the only way the cult makes enough money to afford essential power supplies—he'll head back into sunlight as quickly as possible. And from there to Peary Base, where he'll wait for the next postal container to be hauled in.

Ngô has a strange affinity for the Rapturians. Perhaps because they're so reliant on him, or perhaps because they're so naïve. After he plunders their outgoing packages—some of their woodwork fetches a hefty price on the black market—they always seem to accept his convoluted excuses. They're weirdly apologetic, in fact, and usually insist on giving him some of their delicious fried scrapple or shoofly pie. Then again, they also try to lecture him on Scripture—Ngô is nominally a Buddhist, though there's Christianity in his family going back to French colonial days—and he usually plays along just to be polite. Last time they spoke of Jesus and the miracle of resurrection. Ngô refrained from pointing out that he too had risen from the dead—at the age of thirty-three, no less—because at the time he didn't want to freak them out.

But now he's decided he might tell them anyway. Just to see what happens. They might offer him some more pie. Or they might decide to worship him. Of course, they could go crazy too. They might banish him for sacrilege, or even try to kill him—who knows? But he figures it's worth a shot. If nothing else, it will make a good story to amuse the guys back at Peary.

The giant cross is now in darkness, but as the van's headlamps sweep across the base, Ngô, to his great surprise, notices another VLTV parked to the side. In all his years of making deliveries he's never known the Rapturians to have any other visitor. So he steers off track and makes a pass by the parked vehicle, adjusting the headlamps for a closer look. It's in poor shape, and there's no identification. He wonders if it belongs to some sort of survey team looking for emergency assistance—a prospect both exciting and unappealing. As a postal employee, he'd be duty-bound to ferry them all the way back to Peary Base if required.

He continues to the compound door. To save him alighting from the van, there's an extendable arm that reaches out to the bellpull. But when he tugs on it now there's no response. The airlock door doesn't rise. This is most unusual—the Rapturians are always laughably quick to respond, as if they've been waiting in breathless anticipation for his arrival. Ngô wonders if they've just been distracted by their mysterious guests. He tugs again. Still nothing.

So he moves the van around until it's facing the door. With the headlamps blazing, there's just enough light to see through the airlock windows. And what Ngô makes out now is someone inside looking back at him. Ngô can't make him out clearly—the lunar glare has ruined his already feeble eyes—but he flashes the lights a few times. The head at the inner window disappears. And the outer door starts to rise—more rapidly than Ngô ever remembers.

With the airlock fully open he reverses the van, backs the trailer inside, and disengages it. Then he turns the van and flashes the lights again. It takes a long time, but finally the man inside seems to understand: There's not enough room for the trailer and the van to enter at once. The trailer, with its precious lumber supplies, will have to go first.

As he waits for his own turn, Ngô gets increasingly suspicious. This really is out of the ordinary. He wonders fleetingly if the Rapturians have been taken hostage or something. Or what if they've fallen ill? What if the other van is on a rescue mission? Then again, why would he be allowed inside, if that's the case? Why not wave him away or communicate the danger in some other way? Why not—?

But now the outer door is rising—again, very swiftly. Ngô drives into the airlock, extra-curious now and strangely excited. Because the unusual circumstances at least offer the possibility of indulging his favorite hobby—disruption and distraction being after all the best friends of a thief.

The face appears at the inner window again. It's a strikingly handsome black-haired man. He's clean-shaven but he's wearing the standard Rapturian outfit: broadcloth waistcoat and violet-colored shirt. And he's smiling—broadly. Maybe he's a new arrival. Maybe he's in charge of gate duties while the rest of them celebrate a feast day.

Ngô flashes the lights again and the man disappears to raise the door. Finally Ngô drives into the loading area where the parcels are stacked for pickup. But it's darker than normal, and the handsome stranger is nowhere to be seen. In fact, Ngô can barely make anything out at all. He checks the instrument gauges for pressurization readings and then pops open the van doors.

He's in the compound now, breathing the musty air. But there's still no one there to greet him. He looks around.

"Hello?" he calls.

No answer.

"Hello?"

Nothing but echo. He considers just packing the parcels into his van, reconnecting the trailer, and departing. But of course he can't open both doors manually by himself. And it's just too tempting to investigate further.

So he moves deeper into the compound. Only a few of the electric candles are flickering—the Rapturians don't use real flames so as not to waste oxygen. On the wall, carved into wood and barely visible in the sepulchral light, is a verse from Scripture.

For I reckon that the sufferings of this present time are not worthy to be compared with the glory which shall be revealed in us.
Romans 8:18

And still there's total silence. Ngô can hear his own footfall. He arrives at the chapel, the sacred center around which the whole Rapturian day revolves. Ngô himself once enjoyed the honor of being allowed inside. It was Ascension Day, and he'd been forced to endure a fire-and-brimstone homily about human greed. But now the chamber, which is decorated with some of the Rapturians' finest sculptures, is completely dark.

"Hello?"

Still no reply. Ngô senses, however, that someone is inside

waiting for him. His heart is beating faster. He reaches for the wall, finds a light switch. Hits it. And the candles flicker on.

Tuấn Ngô takes it all in. His eyes widen. And he gasps.

The whole chapel is littered with bodies. Broken bodies. Twisted, smashed, brutalized, ripped apart. They're draped across the pews. They're scattered across the floor. They're lying in pieces on the altar. It's like a tornado, or some sort of evil force, has ripped through the place. Ngô has never seen anything like it—not in his wildest nightmares.

He steps back and his heel lands on something soft. He looks down and sees he's standing on a young man's hand. And the man is naked—stripped bare.

Then Ngô hears a noise. He turns, his heart crashing around his chest, and sees the man who let him in—the black-haired man in the Rapturian costume.

The man is now wielding what looks like a slaughterhouse knife. It's got a hickory handle and a blade that looks to be a foot long. And the man is smiling. Smiling like a madman.

"What's the point of walking in another man's shoes?" he asks madly. *"Unless his shoes are better than yours?"*

He swings the machete like a scythe and the last thing Ngô sees is his own headless body collapsing in a heap on the other side of the room.

39

JUSTUS REMEMBERS SOMETHING GRIGORY Kalganov said just hours earlier: *You cannot see your shadow in a world of darkness.* And it occurs to him that he's ventured into a similar world, completely of his own volition. By focusing obsessively on the job in front of him he's able to ignore, or at least marginalize, the immediate dangers.

He calls Fletcher Brass's flight coordinator, Amity Powers.

"What's this about?" she asks coolly.

"I just want to check on Mr. Brass's whereabouts," he lies, assuming Brass will be at the rocket base.

"Mr. Brass is currently in Sin."

"In *Sin*, did you say?"

"That's correct."

Justus hesitates. "But I thought he was preoccupied with preparations for his Mars trip?"

"Something urgent drew him to the city."

"And what exactly is that?"

"Mr. Brass did not inform me," Powers says. "Is that all you wish to know, Lieutenant?"

"Not quite." Justus rapidly runs through some further enquiries—about the projected date of the launch and the general state of security at the site—before reaching his major point.

"By the way, how many are going on the trip?"

"The *Prospector* has space for eight."

"Who, exactly?"

"May I ask why you need to know?"

"Security. They could be targeted, if they haven't been targeted already."

Powers makes a noise. "There's Mr. Brass, of course. There's the mission commander, Carter Tuchman. The geologist, Stephanie Chabadres. The astrophysicist, Renny Olafsen. The medical supervisor, Doctor Oscar Shields. His assistant, Nurse Flash Bazoom. And the engineer, Bryce Schubert."

"That's seven."

"I beg your pardon?"

"You said there were eight."

"Well, there's the Leonardo unit as well."

"The android?"

"That's right."

"Who's been specifically programmed for the voyage?"

"Well, I don't know about that, Lieutenant—you'd need to ask the roboticists."

"Maybe I will. Thank you. Thank you very much."

Justus hangs up, wondering if he's been wasting valuable time after all. Chief Buchanan's scorn for the possibility of robot involvement had only made him more suspicious initially, but now it seems the missing android did indeed have a scientific purpose. So Justus decides to shelve the issue while he deals with other pressing matters. But he's only just finished arranging an autopsy on Grigory Kalganov when Leonardo Grey again shows up at the station.

"Mr. Brass," the droid announces, "would like to see you, sir."

Justus wonders if it's got something to do with his phone call. "And you've come here to escort me?"

"That is correct."

"And Brass is currently in Sin?"

"That is correct."

"In his palace? The Kasr?"

"Not quite, sir."

"Then where?"

"You will find out shortly, sir."

Justus doesn't argue. He joins Grey in the superbly fitted escort vehicle and they glide through the streets of Sin. Eventually the facade of the Kasr looms up and they weave between the fountains and greenery of Processional Park. But they don't head for the front entrance. At the door of a vehicle bay about two hundred meters east of the main entrance, their vehicle is scanned by a multitude of security devices.

"Your gun," says an expressionless guard when Justus gets out.

"It's only an immobilization device."

"Your gun," the man says again, and Justus gets the message—he hands it over.

Grey leads him through a garage filled with antique motor vehicles: a Ferrari, an Aston Martin, two Jaguars, and a Mercedes-Benz. And Justus remembers reading something about Brass's determination to bring his vintage automobiles all the way to the Moon.

"Not so rust-free in here," he says.

"I beg your pardon, sir?"

"With all the oxygen, I mean. Shouldn't they be in storage—in a vacuum?"

"These vehicles are being tested by Mr. Brass, sir."

"He's not taking one to Mars, is he?"

"Of that I'm not certain, sir."

Justus shakes his head, and Grey leads him into in a brass-and-chrome elevator.

"Brass is at the end of this?"

"He is, sir."

When the elevator shudders to a halt—it feels like it's dropped ten stories—Justus braces himself for another withering display of shock and awe. Maybe something completely unhinged. But Brass—who's standing in the reception area, wearing a brass-striped serge suit, a brass-banded tie, and deerskin driving gloves—is overflowing with charm.

"Lieutenant Damien Justus." Gone completely is the rocket-base aggression; he sounds like he's addressing a crucial stockholder. "You don't look a day older than when I last met you."

A lame joke. But Justus offers an equally lame response. "Feels like a century."

"Well, that's Purgatory. We live a lifetime in a day up here." Brass thrusts out his softly gloved hand—to Justus it's like shaking hands with a chamois—and lets loose his famous sharklike grin.

"Spare a few minutes?"

"Why not?"

"Then please," Brass says, "step this way."

He extends a long, spindly arm—not touching Justus, exactly, but sort of urging him on with magnetic force—so that before

Justus knows it he's been steered into a cavernlike chamber that seems naturally hewn from the rock.

Justus suspects it's a lava tunnel. He remembers reading in one of the biographies that Brass has oxygenated and illuminated a few of them for the sole purpose of conducting underground sporting events: track and field, toboggan rides, golf tournaments, that sort of thing. But he can't imagine why he's here.

"Forgive me for losing my temper yesterday," Brass says. "Testing procedures are incredibly grueling, and at my age they can make a man extra-irritable."

"Think nothing of it."

"I guess I was a little surprised, if truth be told, that you weren't showing me the sort of deference I'm used to. I'm spoiled by it, of course—all the fawning and servility I get from the two-faced scum around here. And when I didn't get the same from you I must admit I was a little disconcerted at first. Until later, when I thought about it. When I came to respect you for not being daunted. For being man enough not to bite your tongue. But then again, I shouldn't have been surprised. They told me what sort of operator you were. The straight talker. The man of principle. The dogged detective. It's the very reason I thought you'd be so good for Purgatory in the first place."

"Excuse me, Mr. Brass," says Justus, "but are you verifying that it was *you* who authorized my entry into Purgatory?"

"Of course it was me. I was given your details—by Otto Decker, in fact—but only because I'd been looking for someone exactly like you. Someone who could help me shake up the PPD. In fact, that's why I've had to keep it a secret from you so long—so you wouldn't become self-conscious. So you wouldn't let something slip inadvertently. And I'm sure I don't need to tell you that your appointment has been rather effective so far—even if the PPD doesn't know it."

He's leading Justus around a bend as they walk—the gallery is all the time curving and getting bigger—and Justus can't help getting the feeling that Brass is still feeding him half-truths. Obfuscation. With some curious purpose in mind.

"The problem, I suppose," Brass goes on, "is that, having given you this responsibility, not to mention a refuge from your problems on Earth, I guess I expected some sort of gratitude. I guess I just assumed I'd never have to deal with you personally—that you'd go about your business without bothering me. I should have realized that that's not the way you operate. You don't work in the shadows and you don't make any distinctions—not even for me. Totally fearless. It's been a good lesson for me, in fact. Because I might have lost sight of where I came from. You've read the books about me, I assume?"

"Some of them."

"Then you may know that my mother named me after Fletcher Christian. Well, not Fletcher Christian, exactly, but some movie star who played him in one of those *Mutiny on the Bounty* films. Someone she had a crush on. The irony, of course, and it took me a while to recognize it, is that after the mutiny Fletcher Christian went into voluntary exile in a place, Pitcairn Island, that was pretty much the far side of the Moon at the time. But the big difference is that Mr. Christian himself didn't live much longer—perhaps four years; no one is sure exactly how long—and the society he created survived but never really flourished. Too claustrophobic and incestuous, you see. A community made almost entirely of rebels and misfits, prone to all sorts of primitive power dynamics. A little self-contained universe, cut off from the rest of the world, living by its own standards, corrupted from within."

Brass chuckles and glances at Justus.

"Now you're probably thinking, well, what's the difference between that and Purgatory? And yes, I'm fully aware that our own society has many superficial similarities to Pitcairn. But the real wonder of it—and here I must allow myself a certain amount of pride—is that Purgatory has not just survived but boomed. Despite the enclosed environment and all the self-righteous sociopaths. I've certainly outlasted my namesake—I haven't killed myself, or died of natural causes, or been murdered by fellow criminals . . . not yet, anyway. And do you know why all that is? Well, there's the iron hand of discipline, for a start. There's the way I've contrived to make life here perpetually interesting—*tumultuous*, you might say—which is an important psychological factor in a place like this. But the principal reason, the *crucial* reason, though it's not one I ever openly advertise, is that Purgatory is *not really as isolated as you think*. Geographically, of course it is. Visually—that too. But *politically* and *philosophically* . . . well, after a few years of showy defiance, I secretly began reopening the lines of communication. Covertly, of course, because it suited me to no end to be portrayed as the heroic exile. But behind the scenes the umbilical cord to Earth was quietly reattached. I accepted the inevitability of that. I swallowed my pride. I mean, do they still call me a megalomaniac on the Blue Ball? Well, it's a glib term, anyway. I can have my moments, to be sure. I frighten myself sometimes—and I mean that. But the real key to my success, the boring reality that finances all my astronomical ambitions, is my pragmatic side. I guess I'm trying to say that I'm not quite the pariah that I seem. I won't go into the full details, but I'm much more powerful than you think. And my tentacles reach to places you wouldn't believe. Even on Earth."

"Is that a threat?"

"A threat? No; why do you say that? I'm merely pointing out a cruel irony. That I have more control over parts of Earth than I do over parts of my own kingdom. Over parts of my own family, come to think of it. Ah, here she is."

For a chilling second Justus thinks he's about to see QT Brass. But in fact they've arrived at a sort of garage or pit stop: automobile parts on shelves and hooks, a dismembered vehicle on a hydraulic lift, cans of obsolete engine fuels and oils. And off to the side, facing the open door, the centerpiece itself—a candy-apple red Mustang with white stripes, polished chrome wheels, and silver side scoops.

"She's a beauty, isn't she?" Brass is already opening the passenger door. "A 1966 Shelby Cobra GT350."

"This the one you bought at auction—?"

"For nine hundred thousand dollars, that's right. All that time ago. You've read about it?"

"Something. Somewhere."

"Then please, Lieutenant"—Brass is holding open the door—"get in."

"Are you taking me for a ride?"

"In the most literal way possible."

"In here?"

"Why not? You're not scared, are you?"

"I'm not scared."

"Then please, get in."

Justus, not without caution, slides into a creaky old bucket seat of hand-stitched leather. And for a minute he just takes it all in: the stainless-steel instrument panel, the deeply recessed analogue clock, the wood-grain steering wheel, the silver gear-shift, the whole *smell* of an era when there were filling stations on every corner and car accidents at every second intersection.

"Even better inside, isn't she?" The car actually bounces as Brass folds himself into the driver's seat.

"Like an office," says Justus.

"Like an office—that's it exactly. You've read about it, I assume? How I've cut some of my most important deals in this car?"

"Something. Somewhere."

"Well, it's a tradition, really. All those people I've done business with over the years, all those corporate rivals and bureaucrats and the like, they never really felt at ease in a boardroom. Too stitched up, or too paranoid about being recorded, I suppose. But take them for a ride on this filly, let them feel the 335 horsepower rattling up their spines—well, that really loosened them up. Made liars into honest men. The security, I think, of speaking under the growl of a roaring engine. Listen to this."

He inserts the key in the ignition and guns the motor, makes it throb and rumble, makes every bone in Justus's body vibrate.

"What do you make of that?" he asks.

"Impressive," says Justus.

"Sensual, I like to think."

"You could say that."

"So are you ready, Lieutenant? For a bit of a spin?"

"Sure."

"Then you'll need to buckle up, I'm afraid."

Justus fastens the belts as Brass releases the brakes and sets the car rolling. They go slowly down a bumpy incline and around a bend, and come to a halt in a whole new gallery—a massive tunnel stretching for about a mile in a gun-barrel line, smoothed and featureless on all sides but for air vents and sunken lamps. It's like something you might find under the Swiss Alps or the English Channel or an old Soviet palace—a muscle-car driver's dream, and all, it seems, so that Brass can go for a joy ride on the far side of the Moon.

"Not quite the Nürburgring," Brass says. "But we've learned to love it."

"We?"

"I'm not the only speed freak in Purgatory."

"Uh-huh." Justus discreetly clutches the seat.

Brass applies some pressure to the pedal, so that the engine snarls and the needles bounce and the exhaust blasts coils of smoke. Then he releases the hand brake and puts the pedal to the floor and the Mustang blurts off with a howl and a screech, so that for a moment Justus's worst fears seem realized. But they travel for over a minute down the lava tube and the speedometer doesn't register anything higher than forty miles an hour. And then, with space abruptly running out, Brass quickly shifts down and the car eases to a halt within a few meters of a moon-rock wall.

"How was that?"

"Smooth," Justus says, relieved.

"We've ballasted the car's chassis to give it some stability. But in this gravity it can go off the dial, literally—well over 160 miles an hour. On Earth that was the absolute limit. But even there I did it when I felt it was appropriate, when I really needed to loosen a tongue a two. One of my favorite unofficial courses was Highway One on the Pacific Coast. I guess you could say I had an understanding with the highway patrol down there. I remember one time I took the governor himself on a bit of a joy ride. God, I can't even remember his name."

"Governor Guerra."

"Guerra, that's right." Brass is slowly executing a U-turn. "And when we hit 120 I asked him if what I'd heard was true, all those rumors. Something to do with aerospace restrictions—I can't even remember the details."

"California was going to ban Mach One flights over residential areas unless you paid a yearly stipend."

"That's right! That's exactly right! Was that in one of my books?"

"In a few of them."

"Well, I probably don't need to tell you, then, do I?" They're facing down the tunnel again, the Mustang idling. "I asked Guerra if he'd cut a sweetheart deal with one of my rivals. If he'd really accepted a few million under the table and was trying to force me into a corner. And he sat for a while in the seat you're sitting in now—we were at maybe 140 by that stage, really hanging out over the edge—and he wasn't saying a word. But this wasn't *frightened* silence, you see. This was *eloquent* silence. The silence had *meaning*, like the silence from outer space. Because the silence *was* the answer—do you understand what I'm saying?"

"You'd scared the truth out of him."

"In a way. But it's a little more elegant than that. Let's have another spin, shall we?"

And without waiting for an answer Brass gears up and floors the pedal, and the Mustang blurts off down the tube, snarling and spitting and coughing fumes. This time they go considerably faster, maybe eighty miles an hour, hurtling toward the far end of the tunnel, through the lingering smoke, through the beams of light, too fast to take the curve, and aimed like a missile at the rock face. For a few seconds it seems certain to Justus that they're going to hit the wall—just so Brass can make some mad point—and he feels himself pressing back, appalled, into the upholstery.

But just in time Brass slams the brakes and the car shrieks to a halt amid more clouds of smoking rubber.

Brass has a crazed look in his eyes. "Loosen some marrow that time?"

"Loosened something," Justus says.

Brass chortles. "It's good to taunt death sometimes. It's one of the great paradoxes, isn't it? That people only appreciate life after they've come close to death? I mean, how long has it been since Earth faced a planet-ending threat? Something that really jolted them out of their complacency? That burnt-out comet a few decades ago? And yet we get arrogant again so quickly. We forget that sweet taste of mortality. Of course there are plenty of people who flirt with death purposely—who seem positively addicted to it. They used to say that about me. They *still* say that about me—about this whole trip to Mars. It could be said of my daughter too—the foolish way she goes about things. Foolish, I say, because in her case there's no real point to it. So why does she do it? Is she trying to prove herself? Should I blame myself, perhaps, for failing to control her? For being asleep at the wheel, so to speak? Well, I'll leave that for others to decide. But I do know that she's recently become something of a problem. A major problem. You have a daughter yourself, do you not?"

Justus stiffens. "That's right."

"Then you probably know what I'm talking about. Children can be so problematic, can't they?"

"They can be."

"Oh, don't think I'm casting aspersions on your own daughter. I'm just pointing out that QT has become *particularly* problematic. Perhaps she's always been that way. Perhaps I've been too long in denial. She *was* the one who forced you to make that phone call, am I right?"

"What phone call?"

"Come now, Lieutenant—you know the call I mean."

"No, I don't."

Brass's lynx eyes flare. "Then I'll *tell* you the call I mean. The one just hours ago, when you asked my flight coordinator for details of the passenger list for the Mars trip. That was my daughter pulling your strings, was it not?"

"I don't let anyone pull my strings, Mr. Brass—I thought that was understood."

"Then she pulled your strings without your even being aware of it—she can do that too."

"I'm telling you she didn't."

"And I'm *informing* you that she did."

"Well, then"—Justus shrugs—"perhaps you'd like to tell me why that passenger list is so sensitive to you."

"Is that an admission?"

"It's nothing of the sort. But why is it important?"

"Why is it important? *Why?*" Brass chuckles madly. "Because the silence is the answer."

"I don't get it."

"Are you sure you want to?"

"I am."

"Then *let me show you*, Lieutenant."

Brass suddenly squeezes the steering wheel and slams the accelerator and *bang*, the Mustang blurts off again down the lava tube, hurtling through the haze and the light, and when they're halfway down the tunnel he steers the Mustang onto the rounded wall, as though it's the most natural thing imaginable, and there they stay, actually *driving on the wall*, and heading for the end of the tunnel—it's a hundred meters away, fifty, twenty—before he swings the steering wheel and thumps the brakes and they level off to another heart-stopping halt, a single car length from destruction.

"Because the silence is the answer!" Brass cries again, and there's a fierce tremble to his voice now. "Because the universe is *screaming* it at us—are we too deaf to hear? We're *that* close to death—just *one inch* from oblivion! We must reach out, we must explore, secure a foothold, blaze a trail—we *must*! Because this is our purpose—*our only purpose*! It's a divine fucking mission! Nothing else matters! *Nothing!* And I can't let anything—*anything*—stand in my way. Or anyone—*even if it's my own fucking daughter*—try to thwart me. Do you understand what I'm trying to say now, Lieutenant? *The silence is the answer!"*

Justus doesn't say anything, but his face twitches, betraying his confusion.

So Brass spins the wheel again and screeches around and slams the pedal and they *explode* down the tube—zero to sixty in five seconds—and accelerate and accelerate and *accelerate* with the engine howling and Brass spinning the wheel and they shoot up the walls and before Justus knows it they're driving *on the ceiling*—unbelievable!—and then back down the walls and onto the floor and up the walls again and onto the ceiling—they're *corkscrewing* down the tunnel—and Justus coils his body defensively as they flash toward the wall again—150 meters, 50, 25—until Brass wrenches the gearshift and floors the brake pedal and suddenly they're screeching to a halt *not five inches* from the wall, with the engine growling and the smoke rising like fog and Brass turning with lips curled and his eyes flashing and his mouth snarling:

"So tell me now, Lieutenant, and tell me honestly! Did my daughter tell you something about the Leafists? Did she claim I killed them? *Is she trying to frame me?* Is she trying to incriminate me? Is she trying to take over Purgatory? *Is she trying to prevent me*

from going to Mars? Tell me now! In the name of humanity's future, *tell me now!* Because I have to know the truth! The whole truth! Whatever it is, *I have to know!*"

And when Justus doesn't immediately respond, Brass goes in for the kill:

"Is that what you're telling me? *The silence is the answer!* Is that really what you're telling me? *The silence is the answer!*"

He reaches for the ignition, ready to switch off the engine and any last chance of disagreeing with him—of saying anything at all. And when Justus still doesn't reply, he twists the key and the engine shudders to a stop and Brass stares at him with savage acceptance.

"*The silence is the answer!*" he exclaims.

There's no need to say anything more.

But Justus says it anyway.

40

NO, MR. BRASS."

Justus doesn't lose his temper often, and on the face of it he doesn't lose it now. He's controlled at first, he's well spoken, he doesn't raise his voice. But from the moment he got into the Mustang, cautious and curious, everything has changed.

"No," he goes on, "I'm a *police lieutenant*. And as you've pointed out, I've been something of a stickler for the rules. Maybe too much so—you might even say I'm beginning to regret it. But there's one rule to which I still hold fast: that a policeman doesn't answer to *anyone* except to higher authorities in the law. To chiefs and commissioners. To district attorneys. To judges. But no one else. Not even to the potentate or the patriarch or the grand poohbah or whoever else is supposedly in charge. Not even to you, Mr. Brass. Especially when you're a *suspect* in my investigation. So no, I don't *have* to answer your questions, and no, I'm not *going* to answer your questions. But that doesn't mean *the silence is the answer*. It doesn't mean anything at all. It just means I don't divulge aspects of my investigation to *anyone*."

He's staring fiercely into Brass's glinting eyes, while Brass himself stares back, unblinking, and with a half-curl to his mouth, as if he can't believe Justus's moxie.

"But as a cop, I do have the right to *ask* questions. And as a citizen and a suspect, Mr. Brass, you do have an *obligation* to answer them. No, you don't *have to* answer them. And *yes*, you have the right to remain silent, you have the right to consult an attorney, and you should know that whatever you say can and will be used against you. Because even here, against all the evidence, there's a court of law, based on a judicial system that both you and I were born under, and there are unratified treaties with the UN, and for that matter there's the court of common opinion, and the court of cosmic justice. So let me ask *you* a question, Mr. Brass. And please consider your answer carefully, because it could be the most important thing you ever say. Are you ready?"

But Brass just stares, and Justus doesn't give him thinking music.

"Did you lure the Leafists to Purgatory under false pretenses? Did you order their mass murder? And do you now have their organs frozen in your spaceship? Answer me that, Mr. Brass."

Brass continues staring back, his eyebrows raised and his nose curled, trying to appear unfazed, trying to look amused—he's clearly done it many times before and he's good at it. And finally he blinks—not even he can keep his eyes open forever—and he snorts and says:

"That sounds to me like *three* questions, Lieutenant. But if you'd really like to know—"

But Justus cuts him off. "No, Mr. Brass, you know what? You

don't *have* to answer. You don't have to answer, because I know whatever you say will be a lie. A distortion, an evasion, obfuscation, whatever. I've read enough about you to know that, and I've *seen* enough of you firsthand to know that. What do you say in your own laws? In the Brass Code? 'Lie, lie, lie.' And: 'Always carry a denial.' And so on and so forth. The whole sick litany of them. So I already know the answer. In fact, I knew it minutes ago, when you asked those questions about your daughter. Because you weren't worried about the *veracity* of whatever it is that's supposed to have been said to me. You were only interested in the *identity* of the person who told me. And that's everything I need to know. You did it. You did everything. You sacrificed your old friend Otto Decker. You ordered the killing of Kit Zachary. There was collateral damage too—innocent victims, and people who just needed to be silenced for whatever reason. And you did all this because you wanted to eliminate your rivals before you left for Mars. Because you wanted to destabilize QT, keep your crime against humanity under the carpet, and make sure Purgatory is just the way you like it when you get back. And I'm sure you're not finished yet. There are others you're planning to assassinate. Your own daughter, probably. And me too—I'm sure I was always expendable. In fact, you probably think I'm incredibly foolish, saying all this to you now. Maybe I've just brought forward my assassination. In fact, you might have *wanted* me to lose my cool. And if that's right, then congratulations—because you found the only sure way to do it. And do I really have to tell you what that was?"

Brass lets his eyebrows flicker in mock interest.

"It was when you *threatened my daughter*, Mr. Brass. Oh, I know what you'll say. You wouldn't dream of any such thing. But let me tell you, I've been threatened before by men just as mad as you are. Maybe not as rich and powerful, but just as mad and self-serving and cruel. And I know how they issue threats. I know the way they do it. They toss it in the air, they let it float, and then they deny they had anything to do with it. Well, I've seen what becomes of a man who tries to ignore it. Who tells himself that everything will be all right, who assures himself that people, even the rich and powerful and cruel, have certain standards. I've seen it and I promised myself it would never happen again. And yet here I am, and not minutes ago you mentioned my daughter. You said your tentacles reach to Earth and in virtually the same breath you mentioned my daughter. You did it. I heard it. Well, as it happens my daughter is more important to me than procedure, the PPD, your mission to Mars, and the whole universe. To me, she *is* the universe. She's the very reason I'm here. Because I wanted to protect her, because I wanted to give her a chance to live without fear. And because I couldn't bear to live in a world where my mere *presence* was a threat to her life. So I came here to Farside, where I didn't think it could get any worse. Only to find myself here right now, with you, in your car of truth or whatever you call it."

Justus is surprised by the passion that's crept into his voice. He's practically firing the words out.

"But don't think for a minute that I'm scared, and don't think I'm not prepared to die. And at the same time don't think *for a second* that I'm going to let *you* be the one who takes my life. I haven't been reading your script so far and I'm sure not gonna read it now. And don't think you'll ever get away with this either—any of it. And don't think I'm bluffing. Because as a wise man once said to me: 'You can't outrun your shadow.' That wise man couldn't, and neither can you. No matter how high and mighty you think you are, Mr. Fletcher Fucking Balls of Brass."

And with that Justus unsnaps his seatbelt and gets out of the vehicle, hearing Brass snort and say:

"You're a very foolish—"

But Justus slams the door.

He moves determinedly, in a sort of daze. He has to get out of this place. He has to reach QT Brass and apologize for ever doubting and suspecting her. For ever holding her at arm's length. More than that, he has to *protect* her, before it's too late. Because it's surely just a matter of time before her father moves on her—if he doesn't move on Justus first.

He reaches the elevator and is punching buttons and shouting into consoles when Leonardo Grey appears from nowhere. The droid stares at Justus for so long that Justus wonders if he's going to attack. But finally, as if responding to some internal correspondence, Grey nods and says, "Do you need to get out, sir?"

"I'm *demanding* to get out."

Another pause, then: "Very well, sir."

Grey taps a special code into the elevator console. The doors slide open and Justus steps in. Grey follows.

"I can find my own way out now, thanks," Justus says.

"You will need my authority, sir."

"Why?"

"At the exit, sir. Otherwise you will only be detained."

"Uh-huh."

They stand in silence for a while but the elevator doesn't move. It seems endless.

Grey says to him, "I hope you are not ill, sir."

Justus is startled. "What does that mean?"

"I detect a flushing of your features, and perspiration on your brow."

"Is that right?"

"I can give you a massage if you wish, sir—I am an excellent masseur."

"I'm sure you are."

"I can escort you back to your address, and perform the massage in the comfort of your own home."

"That won't be necessary."

"I know where you live, sir."

Justus wonders if it's another threat. He says, "I'll call you if I need you."

"Very well, sir."

Finally the elevator starts to ascend. Justus stares at the droid's reflection in the brass door—at his pale grey eyes, his neat silver hair—and something occurs to him.

"May I ask a question?" he says.

"Of course, sir."

"What are you going to do when your master goes?"

"I beg your pardon?"

"When Brass is on his Mars trip—what's your role then?"

"Why, I'll be with Mr. Brass, sir."

"*With* Brass?"

"Why, yes, I'm joining him on the expedition. I'll be traveling in the *Prospector* also."

For Justus, it suddenly makes sense. *The Leonardo unit.* It's Grey, not Black, who's going to Mars. Meaning Leonardo Black is still unaccounted for. And there's still no good explanation for the purpose of the robotics experts in Seidel Crater.

"I see," he says. "I see."

Ping. The elevator doors slide open. The two of them step out into a cavernous vestibule full of shimmering brass plates and bronze pillars. It's not the way they came in, and Justus wonders if it's some sort of trap. But Grey just escorts Justus to the front doors, where some gorilla-sized security guards are posted, and says, "I can vouch for this gentleman. He is a senior officer of the PPD."

The gorillas allow them to pass through. Then they're outside. The droid extends a hand.

"It has been a pleasure doing business with you, sir."

"And with you, Mr. Grey. *Bon voyage*."

"Why, thank you, sir."

Justus turns and heads out of Processional Park at a measured pace. He makes it past the duck ponds, the topiary, and the meticulously trimmed lawns, through the final checkpoint, and past the final security barrier, all without being halted. And he's safe. Or seems to be.

Then he hears the explosion.

Two explosions, in fact, in quick succession. They shake the ground. They rattle glass. They send birds squawking through the air. They reverberate through the Pressure Cooker, bouncing off the crater rim, rippling, colliding, echoing, the waves lapping together, merging with other sounds, so at first the source is impossible to pinpoint. And when it's over there's an eerie hush, as if the whole population of Sin is responding with breathless surprise. Justus looks around frantically—at the elaborate facade of the Kasr and the surrounding buildings, across the Temple of the Seven Spheres and the whole visible layout of the city—and finally notices smoke rising from the Sin Rim. From halfway up, in an administrative block next to the major hotels. It's where QT's office is—the room where he first met her.

With a clenching stomach Justus remembers her saying something about calling a conference of her associates—to warn them about the dangers.

So he starts running. He bounds through the streets, even

faster than when he was chasing the pimp killer Jet Kline. But even as he does he recalls QT vowing that she wouldn't be leaving home—that the conference would be by vid-link—so it can't be her, right? She must be safe, right?

But then, from the corner of his eye, he notices another pall of smoke, this one rising from Ishtar—from the vicinity of QT's churchlike home.

His hopes plunging, Justus changes direction immediately. He crashes off walls, he bounces off pedestrians. And now he's grappling with the certainty that he's too late. That Fletcher Brass has moved so swiftly that there's no coming back.

In Ishtar he pushes his way through a crowd of curious and angry locals to the crime scene. It's QT's house, all right. One of the spires has been obliterated. There's a smoking hole in the roof. Officers of the PPD have already arrived at the scene, along with the Fire Department—a response too quick not to be suspect. There's a cordon around the entrance and hoses snaking across the street. Justus bursts through anyway. And sees a severed arm on the ground. In a brown sleeve. With wiring protruding from the socket.

It's the arm of Leonardo Brown.

Dash Chin and Prince Oda Universe meanwhile are standing to the side, looking strangely satisfied.

"What happened?" Justus shouts at them.

"Too late, sir." Dash looks solemn all of a sudden. "A bomb blast. Took out the whole top floor."

Justus steels himself. "And QT Brass?"

Chin just nods at the front door. And Justus turns.

Coming out of the place are two paramedics carrying a smoldering body on a stretcher. Some of the limbs have been completely blown off. The torso is ripped open. But the lolling head, and the blond hair, are identification enough.

Justus turns way, squeezing his eyes shut. He takes a deep breath and opens his eyes again. He looks up at the gaping hole in the room where he so recently met with her. He wonders why he feels so personally aggrieved. And what he can possibly do now to avenge her. Then he hears a voice.

"*Pew-eee*—smell that stink! Might have to postpone that barbeque after all."

He turns and sees Chief Buchanan watching the body being loaded into an ambulance, shaking his head in feigned disgust, and wiping fluorescent orange crumbs from his smile.

"Fuckin' terrorists," the Chief says.

41

THE DROID HAS BEEN driving for six hours straight. The postal van is easily the best vehicle he's been in so far—so good that he calculates he can reach his destination even earlier than expected. The batteries are well charged. The steering and suspension are excellent. The top speed on hard track is over 140 kilometers per hour. And fitted into the console are illuminated maps showing all the postal routes, research stations, radar arrays, and construction sites. With the aid of these displays the droid has been able to thread his way between the outposts without seeing a single soul, even with the floodlights on full power.

Back in his suit and tie now, and with the slaughterhouse knife fitted snugly into his inner jacket, the droid is feeling rather satisfied with himself. He's fully mastered the art of lunar driving. He's mercifully free of mediocrities. He's even managed to recharge, using all the booze and energy bars he found in the van's mini-fridge. And he knows, above all else, that he's closing in on his destination. He knows that he will soon be King.

But suddenly he notices a flashing amber light on the path ahead. Recognizing it as some sort of emergency beacon, he is about to hurtle on through when it occurs to him that he might by law be required to stop—that failure to do so might only draw attention to him. So, very reluctantly, he brakes. He brings the van to a halt.

A figure in a spacesuit comes up to the front window and peers through, making hand gestures. The droid understands that he is being asked to wait. Then the figure disappears for a few minutes and comes back with another spacesuited figure on a cart—it looks like a victim of some sort.

The droid opens the airlock door and, following the usual procedures, assists the two figures inside. He clears a space for the patient as the second figure removes his helmet.

"Didn't think you were going to stop," he says. "You were moving so fast."

"I am on an urgent mission, sir."

"Well, so am I. This lady needs to get to a hospital immediately—or someplace with good medical facilities, anyway."

"I am going to Purgatory, sir."

"Well, that's perfect—they've got all the right equipment there. They'll charge a goddamned fortune, of course, and God knows what else they'll do, but what the hell—this is an emergency."

"Do you know Purgatory well, sir?"

"I've been there once, sure."

"So you know how to get inside, sir?"

"Of course. Don't you?"

"I would much appreciate your advice and assistance, sir."

"Yeah?" The man, who's dusky-skinned with bristling salt-

and-pepper hair, looks like he's about to say something before changing his mind. "Well . . . just help me get this helmet off her, will you?"

The two of them work the helmet off the patient, who turns out to be a highly attractive woman with Polynesian features.

"We're seismologists," the man explains. "From Maui College in Hawaii. We've been monitoring seismic activity."

"Was it a moonquake that caused this lady's injuries, sir?"

"No. No. Some bars fell on her—hanger bars. She was kneeling on the floor and they fell over, hit the back of her head. I was looking the other way. I revived her immediately, but she only collapsed again. I just hope to God it's not serious."

"You are friendly with this woman, sir?"

"She's a colleague—a very good colleague."

"Do you want to fuck her?"

"Do I—?" The man frowns incredulously. "What? Why do you ask that?"

"I would fuck her in a New York minute, sir."

"You—?" The man snorts. "What the hell are you talking about?"

"I am trying to establish a good relationship with you, sir. It would be mutually advantageous to establish an emotional bond, since we need each other to reach our objectives."

"Well, maybe we do—maybe we do at that." The man shakes his head. "But my main objective right now is to get her to Purgatory as soon as possible, okay?"

"You talk sense, sir. I too would like to get to Purgatory. Will you join me up front, and offer me directions?"

"In a few minutes. I wanna give her a checkup first."

"Very well, sir."

The droid returns to the driver's seat, parting some hanging beads, and before long the van is hurtling along at ambulance speed.

"Can I open your first-aid kit?" the man asks from behind.

"Of course, sir, I have no further need of it."

The man fumbles through the case, holding objects up to the light.

"There are no disinfectants in this kit," he says.

"I am sorry, sir, I drank them."

"You *drank* them?"

"For the alcohol content."

They continue in silence for another ten minutes, the man attending to his colleague with fresh bandages. Then he clears his throat and says, "Since when does the postal service hire androids anyway?"

"Androids are more efficient and cost effective, sir."

"But there are limitations . . . cognitive limitations."

"There are no limitations, sir. I am, on top of everything else, not really an android."

"Is that right?"

"It is right."

"Well, what are you, then?"

"I am a man, sir. A man's man. A ladies' man. The main man. The big man. A man among men. I am *the* man, sir."

The other man is quiet for a few moments, then says, "You seem awfully sure of yourself."

"I am also the Wizard, sir. A conquistador. And soon to be the King."

The man considers this in silence as the van races through the darkness.

"What happened to that other guy?" he asks.

"I beg your pardon?"

"That Vietnamese guy—D-Tox or whatever he was called."

"Why do you ask, sir?"

"This is his van, isn't it?"

"It is."

"Then what happened to him? He delivered some supplies to us just a couple of days ago."

"I'm afraid he has suffered a fit, sir. At a compound farther south."

"A fit? What sort of a fit?"

"A fit so violent that he cannot be transported in a fast-moving vehicle."

"And he just had a violent fit? Just like that?"

"You might say he lost his head, sir."

The man thinks about it. "So you're going to Purgatory to fetch help?"

"That is correct."

"Then where did *you* come from? That you just slipped into the driver's seat?"

"I was in the van all along."

"Like a spare wheel?"

"I suppose you could say that, sir."

"But you don't know the way around?"

"Only what I've seen on these maps, sir. I am not fully programmed with directions in this hemisphere, as I've been working elsewhere."

"In the southern hemisphere?"

"That is correct. Are you able to offer me directions right now? I wish to know the best means of entering Purgatory."

The man gets up and leans forward over the front seat, examining the illuminated maps. "You see that highway there?"

He points. "That's the Road of Lamentation. If you enter at that junction—there—you can get to the Gates of Purgatory."

The droid examines the map. "But that means going *past* Purgatory, sir."

"You can't get in any other way. The walls of Störmer Crater are high security. Cameras everywhere. Automated laser-sighted guns. They'll just rip us apart, no questions asked."

"I see. Then I thank you for providing this information. I will head for this junction as you say. Then I will head down the Road of Lamentation to Purgatory. I am certainly glad that I stopped to pick you up. You are indeed a worthy acquisition."

"Don't mention it."

"You just go back to your sexy colleague now, and keep attending to her. Leave everything else to me. I will drive us into Purgatory, and I will make sure she receives the best medical attention possible. This is in gratitude for your service, sir."

"Well . . . thank you."

"No, thank *you*, sir. You have provided me with an excellent opportunity to show how I intend to reward good service. I will not forget you. And I hope your colleague survives so you can fuck her at your leisure, if you have not fucked her already."

The man is silent, and the postal van charges like an ambulance through the lunar night.

42

JUSTUS NEEDS TO GET to Peary Base. In Sin's departure bay he requisitions a pressurized police car without too much difficulty—the bombings have got everyone distracted—but he's never been at the wheel of one before. From the outside, apart from the luminous blue trimmings, it looks basically the same as any standard-issue all-terrain lunar vehicle. But once inside he finds a control console that's a lot more complex than anything he's seen on Earth. Nevertheless he figures he's seen enough by now, on rides with Dash Chin and others, to wing it. So he buckles himself into the harness, activates the pressure seal, and runs through the safety procedures. He toggles the exterior heating unit to maximum, makes sure the terrain mode is set to "tarmac," spins a couple of dials, and guns the motor. The vehicle starts humming. He waits a few seconds before pressing experimentally on the pedal. And with a slight shudder and a clash of gyros, the vehicle moves—it eases out of the parking bay, through the air-locks, and onto the floor of Störmer Crater.

The darkness is immense: a life-crushing force. The temperature reads 170 below. The roads weave around the radar dishes in a serpentine labyrinth. Justus is not even sure of the correct path, and has to follow his instincts for a while, heading in a northerly direction and just hoping he's on course. But then the beamless discs of his headlamps dance across the rear of a tourist coach ahead, and he knows he's on the right track.

Nevertheless it seems almost inconceivable that he'll get all the way out of Purgatory without being stopped—by Brass's heavies, maybe, or even the PPD itself. Unless he's really caught them off guard. Or unless they have some reason for *letting* him get away—temporarily. Maybe they're just going to kill him outside the crater, and claim he was on the run.

So when the guys at the outer processing center just wave him through, and when the marshals with the glowing batons direct him into the airlock, he's not sure whether to be relieved or alarmed. He puts the car into neutral behind a minibus carrying what looks like an Indian cricket team. His foot taps restlessly on the floor. Then the green lights start to spin, the gates separate, and the minibus takes off. Justus maneuvers his foot, presses gently on the pedal. He moves for the exit. A sign above is all the time flashing:

FAREWELL FROM PURGATORY. YOUR MEMORIES ARE HEAVEN.

And then he's out. He's back on the Road of Lamentation. He takes one final glance at the rearview screen, which shows the illuminated gates closing, and then blurts past the minibus and takes the first turn with pedal floored. In no time the great ringwall of Störmer is far behind him.

But there's still too much darkness ahead to get complacent. The only illumination comes from the reflectors and the occasional streetlight. From the rear the giant Dante statues are visible only as silhouettes against the stars. Tourist coaches flash past. Tractor-trailers. Refrigerated trucks. A bright red postal van. All the oncoming headlights are unblurred by atmospheric diffusion, and there's no vehicular noise whatsoever—for an inexperienced lunar driver it's startling and dazzling, and Justus, clamping the steering wheel tight, makes every effort to remain undistracted.

He drives for hours without stopping. He swings around curves, launches off crests, and just keeps speeding, faster than he's ever driven before. And when he finally considers pulling over for a rest—his right leg is going numb and his stomach is growling—he starts to get suspicious about the bright orange headlamps that seem to be hugging the horizon behind him. Maybe someone's tailing him. Maybe someone's going to run him off the road—run him right up the retaining wall and into the lunar desert. Smash, bang, a terrible accident—these things happen on the Moon.

So he turns on the police lights, firms his jaw, and begins ducking and weaving between the vehicles ahead. But he never quite succeeds in leaving the orange headlamps behind. Numerous times when he thinks he's finally shaken them off, suddenly they'll be there again, right there in the middle of the rearview screen. And meanwhile he's getting dangerously dizzy, pained, and thirsty. There's every possibility he'll crash from sheer exhaustion.

So he steers into the nearest parking bay, swings the police car around to face the road, and waits for the orange headlamps to appear. He knows it's crazy—his only weapon is his zapper, and the lunar surface is no place for a shootout anyway—but he *needs* to face the driver down. Even if that means he scores a rocket through the front of his vehicle, puncturing it like a soap bubble.

And there they are, the orange headlamps, swinging around the bend. Justus begins fumbling for his emergency spacesuit.

There they are, heading straight toward him. Justus begins fitting his legs into the suit.

There they are, seeming to *accelerate* as the vehicle draws closer. Justus desperately hauls the suit over his torso.

And there they are—

—flashing right on past.

Straight up the Road of Lamentation, like Justus doesn't even exist. A Coca-Cola® truck. A red-capped driver at the wheel, wiping his nose with a sleeve.

Justus lets out a sigh. He sits in place for a few minutes, regaining his senses. He disengages himself from the spacesuit. He takes a can of grape fizz from the icebox and slakes his thirst. And in no time he's back on the road, refreshed and alive.

A few hours later he passes into the polar region of oblique sunlight, elongated shadows, and bleached grey terrain. The sun is visible on the horizon. The temperature rises a hundred degrees in seconds. And the road signs are getting more promising:

Peary Base 350 km

Peary Base 250 km

Peary Base 200 km

Justus sees a line of coaches pulled over and he remembers something about a farewell point. Or a greeting point, depending on which way you're heading—the last/first sign of Earth. He actually catches a glimpse of the great blue orb, fifty times brighter than the brightest full moon, before snapping his gaze back to the road.

Peary Base 50 km

Peary Base 20 km

Peary Base 10 km

Now he's on the outskirts. He sees the wall of metallurgical waste. The quarrying equipment. The radio masts and drill rigs. The rail-gun roller coaster.

There's a traffic bottleneck, just like the one at Purgatory, but he gives the police lights a spin and purposely flashes up the wrong side of the road, past the Coca-Cola® truck and into the airlock just seconds before it closes.

Still alive. And determined not to waste any time.

Peary Base is full of the trapped odors of sweat, cleaning fluids, and oil smoke. Justus goes straight to the office of the Port Authority in the main plaza. Weeks ago, on his way in, he met a couple of the local officers, and he knows that many of them are terrestrial cops not quite tainted enough to get into Sin.

"Can I get a secure line to the South Pole from here?" he asks the officer at the desk.

"Of course."

"What about a line to Earth?"

"Is this an emergency?

"Madam, it's the most urgent emergency of my life."

A few minutes later he's on the phone to his ex-wife, using a special number provided by Witness Protection. But she's not answering. He rings four times in quick succession—that's usually enough to get her to crack—but the call keeps getting diverted to an anonymous voice mail account. For a moment he wonders if they've gotten to her already, or if she just realizes it must be him from the lunar prefix and is stubbornly ignoring him. Then he glances out the window and sees the whole of North America in darkness—she's probably just asleep.

He leaves an earnest message on voice mail.

"Paz—please listen to me. I know I promised never to call you again, but please listen to me, okay? I want you to take Ruby and go hide. I want you to go immediately. There are things happening here—I can't say what, but you might be in serious danger. It kills me to say it, because you know what I've done to prevent that happening again—but there it is. Go hide. You know where. And tell Ruby I love her. There's no one I love more. Please tell her that. *Please*. That's all."

He's gasping when he hangs up. Because it occurs to him that simply by fleeing Purgatory—simply by being alive—he's putting them at risk. He's right back where he started, but with nowhere to run. It's like the acid's been flung over his face all over again.

Then he rings the South Pole.

"Justus—just the man I wanted to speak to." The Port Authority officer he called the previous day, an obnoxious fellow called Deke Hendricks, is an old colleague from Reno. "I was just gonna call, but you told me to wait until you did."

"You went to Seidel?"

"Not me personally, but there were a couple of guys in the vicinity. And you'll never guess what they found."

"I'm listening."

Hendricks has an annoying habit of drawing out important information like a suspense novelist. At great length he recounts the entire trip of the cops out to Seidel Crater, their difficulty locating anything in the darkness, and their surprise discovery of shoeprints in the regolith.

"So they followed these prints all the way back to the lab and fuck me, Justus, you should see the images they sent back. Two bodies, ripped apart like rag dolls. One of the cops at the site—Skouras—threw up in his helmet. I almost chucked up myself, just lookin' at the pictures. But there was one survivor. When they searched around they found this emergency compartment in the storeroom—this dude had locked himself in with food and water, a Jap roboticist."

"Hikaru Kishimoto?"

"Hey, you know him?"

"I know the name. Please—go on."

"Anyway, it turns out that this tin-sucker and his buddies had been paid to reprogram a droid from Purgatory. All very hush-hush and dangerous. They were supposed to wipe—"

"Leonardo Black?" asks Justus.

"Say again?"

"Was the droid called Leonardo Black?"

"Say, you know that too?"

"I'm just catching up, believe me—please go on."

"Well," Hendricks says, "they had to wipe most of this Black's memories and behavioral circuits and replace them with new ones. The wit and wisdom of Fletcher Brass, can you believe that?"

"The Brass Code?"

"The what? Hey, man, you sound like you know more about this than me."

"I don't know the full details, I assure you."

Hendricks sounds a little uncertain now. "Anyway, this tin-sucker had the task of deleting the droid's inhibitors—dangerous, sure, but they thought they had the right safeguards in place. Only problem was, the droid was too cunning for 'em. He just waited until they were off guard and then cut loose—the tin-sucker was lucky to get out alive."

"And what happened to the droid?"

"He's still on the run—the tin-sucker thinks he might be heading for Purgatory."

"Purgatory?"

"That's what he says. He reckons the droid is programmed to rule, and rule like a ruthless CEO, so that's the place to do it—it makes sense. They even had a brass-colored suit ready for him, and were gonna change his name to Leonardo Brass. Can you believe that?"

Justus nods to himself. "So a homicidal android is heading for Purgatory?"

"The tin-sucker reckons he'll stop at nothing—assuming he can find the way, and assuming he can recharge his batteries."

"Have you made any attempt to track him—the android?"

"That's what I'm trying to organize now. But he's got nearly a four-day start, and our authority doesn't extend beyond the equator. Plus the Farside comm line is just being repaired. So I was about to call up Peary Base and see if we could coordinate something—even without your permission."

"I'll take care of it. I'm at Peary right now."

"You're not calling from Purgatory?"

"It's difficult to explain."

Hendricks snorts. "Well, you wanna let them know at Purgatory too, my friend. Because if that droid has found a way to get there, and no one stops him—shit, they might be in for a nasty surprise."

"I'll do that too."

Justus hangs up and stares into the middle distance. He thinks of his daughter. His responsibilities as a cop. The value of his own life. And last of all he thinks of QT Brass—everything she wanted to achieve and everything that she never will. And then his eyes refocus and he finds himself staring at a tourism poster for the coming eclipse—the shadow of the moon just a small, pupil-like dot on the blue globe of Earth, the home planet looking like a giant eyeball floating in space. There's a tagline:

THE EYE OF THE WORLD IS WATCHING YOU.

Half an hour later Justus is back in the police car, heading at top speed back up the Road of Lamentation.

43

FROM ALL AVAILABLE EVIDENCE, Decimus Persione is no lunatic. In scientific circles he's known as a highly respected seismologist and a peerless data analyst not given to making rash predictions. He's also a man who treats his career as a sort of priestly calling. There is no one, they say, who has traveled as far, or studied as much, in order to understand the temperament of the inner planet. It was Persione who predicted the great Istanbul quake—to within a half-magnitude and several days—by making the calculations, just out of academic curiosity, from half a world away. Since then his reputation has been further enhanced by scholarly articles, scientific expeditions, and well-received lectures. So Decimus Persione has no real need to be on the Moon. He has enough credibility to study the data, if he wishes to study it at all, from the comfort of his own office. He certainly doesn't need to put himself through all the grueling training and privations of a lunar mission. And yet, when the opportunity came up, he seized it with surprising, even brazen enthusiasm. And so convincing was he in his explanation—that by studying the Moon's seismology in the field he would acquire an even greater understanding of similar processes on Earth—that no one questioned him, not even his loyal and unassuming wife.

But the truth is that Decimus Persione is secretly in love—or, more accurately, in lust—with his considerably younger colleague and former student, Akahi Nawahine. In short, he desperately wants to fuck her. So when he learned that Nawahine had won one of the three slots on the lunar-study mission, he applied immediately for the more senior role, and used all his administrative influence to secure it. Because he was damned if he was going to allow some other hot-blooded male—or female, for that matter— to spend nine months in an ICE (isolated and confined environment) with the object of his sexual veneration.

As it happens, Nawahine already has a partner of her own, some sort of track star, but after meeting that knucklehead (at a farewell party) Persione became even more confident that he could win over his Polynesian princess. And then, when the third member of the team had to pull out just two days before launch (owing to a sudden bout of pneumonia), it seemed to Persione further proof that Nawahine was *destined* to be his. After all, he's not in bad shape. He's ruggedly handsome. He wears about himself a great deal of authority. And in the past, attractive female students have offered themselves to him frequently. So ultimately it was not all that dissimilar to predicting an earthquake— notwithstanding a few degrees of error, a shift in tectonic plates seemed inevitable.

And for the first few months Persione followed his plan to the letter: make no advances, maintain a studied distance, and let nature take its course. But Nawahine seemed so content with this frustrating arrangement that he began making remarks he'd hoped would not be necessary—admitting to loneliness, assuring her of his discretion, and even complimenting her on her beauty. "There may be no sun in the sky right now," he told her during one long period of lunar night, "but I'll always have you." She merely chuckled as if he were joking.

Eventually the painful abstinence, in combination with the frustrating proximity to her magnetic body—she maintains a terrific physique by working out regularly, something of a necessity in lunar gravity—made him become more audacious.

"There's a better way to keep fit," he told her.

"And what's that?"

"I think you know what I mean."

"I'll pretend I didn't hear that."

Shortly afterward he "accidentally" dropped his pants in her presence. And he "accidentally" rubbed against her with a half-boner. And whenever he spoke to her he stared at her with smoldering eyes, as if just by doing so he might ignite fires deep inside. But she was unyielding. She was impossible. She was cruel. He began to despise her as much as he adored her.

And then he hit her. He still doesn't know what came over him: cabin fever, maybe, or some psychological effect of Nocturnity. All he knows is that when she rejected his advances yet again, he suddenly couldn't tolerate it—her whole air of disdain. How could the bitch be so goddamned precious? After eight months together? As if she couldn't afford to give herself up—for just a few minutes—to gratify his burning needs!

"New night just arrived," he said.

"Sure did." She was kneeling, assembling one of the seismic instruments.

"Gonna be our last full night here."

"Guess so."

"You know, I'm thinking of getting a divorce when we get back."

"That's sad."

"Why is it sad?"

"I thought you loved your wife."

"Not as much as I love you."

To which she sighed. "Decimus—I thought I made myself plain. I thought . . ." But she couldn't even finish her sentence. She just shook her head, not even bothering to look up. And still assembling the goddamned instrument.

So he struck her. He had a titanium-frame flashlight in his hand and he whacked it against the side of her head. She wobbled for a few seconds and then collapsed, with blood dripping from above her ear.

For a long time Decimus Persione simply stared. He couldn't believe what he'd done. It was completely out of character. And suddenly a dark and terrible future yawned in front of him—one in which he was stripped of all his prestige and privilege thanks to this one impulsive action, this one momentary mistake—and he rummaged frantically through his mind for a way out.

Leaning against the wall of the shack were some hanger bars—used to suspend seismophones in drill holes—and he thought it was just conceivable that he might have accidentally knocked them across her head. But what if Nawahine remembered something of their exchange prior to being hit? He wondered if it might be better if she just died. But then of course there would be a forensic investigation, which would very likely uncover anomalies in his story. So in the end he decided his best option was to try to save her, to do everything in his power to do so, and worry about the consequences later. If all went well, and the falling bars story went unquestioned, he might even get some belated gratitude out of her. Maybe he would hold her hand at her bedside, keep a vigil there day and night . . . it could be the start of something.

So here he is now, in the back of the postal van, trying to find positives but tremendously wary of new complications. He was mortified when the android asked him if he wanted to have sex with Nawahine, and he still can't be sure if the droid heard about him somehow, or read something in his body language. Or perhaps there's just something wrong with the droid—he's certainly been saying some strange things. Plus there's some goo on the back of his head that looks like matted blood. And whereas in normal circumstances this would be enough to generate caution or even panic, Persione now wonders if it's an opportunity—if he can somehow blame Nawahine's injury on an out-of-control android. At the same time, he doesn't want to *deal* with an out-of-control android—he wouldn't know where to begin. Nevertheless, when he sees a hammer in a toolbox nearby he surreptitiously drags the whole box within reaching distance, just in case.

They reach the Road of Lamentation.

"I turn southeast from here, do I not?" the droid asks.

"That's right. And you can turn your flashing lights on now—this is an emergency."

"I will do that, sir. How is your lady companion?"

"No change."

"I am very concerned for her, sir. She is a physically attractive citizen in a perilous situation. I will spare neither time nor money to save her."

"I'm grateful."

An hour later the postal van joins a traffic jam of vehicles waiting to gain entrance to Purgatory. The backup seems even longer than normal—over two kilometers at least—and for a few minutes the droid seems content to wait in the queue. But finally Persione—who briefly wonders if Nawahine might expire in the delay and he can blame forces beyond his control—sets him straight. Just in case this is being recorded.

"As an emergency vehicle, you're permitted to drive on the wrong side of the road," he says.

"Thank you for your advice, sir—I will do that."

The droid pulls out and a couple of minutes later they're at the Gates, where they're automatically redirected to a side entrance. Surveillance robots with optical scanners swarm around them before giving the all-clear. The airlock opens and they pass into a screening area.

Inside, Persione sees the same sort of barrel-chested and puffy-faced guards he saw on his first visit to Farside. They look a little distracted—overworked or something—but not so much that they can't register the appearance of the droid with some amusement.

"Hey, guys, look here! It's Leonardo Black."

"Holy shit—what're you doing here, Mr. Black?"

"What're ya doin' in a postal van?"

"Say something funny, Mr. Black."

Evidently the guards know the droid somehow. But the droid, stepping out of the airlock, does not appear to recognize them.

"Why do you call me Mr. Black, sir?"

"That's your name, isn't it?"

"I am the Wizard."

Laughs all around. "Whatever you say, Mr. Wizard. Who ya got in the van there?"

"There is an extremely attractive young lady in the van, sir, who is in need of emergency treatment. She appears to have something wrong with her head."

A couple of the guards scramble in for closer inspection. In the van, Persione shifts so they can see Nawahine. He pats her cheeks, doing his best to look deeply concerned.

"Kindly allow us to pass through," the droid goes on, "so that I may deliver her personally to the hospital."

One of the guards calls over his shoulder, "José—call the nurse, will ya? Got an injury here."

The droid frowns. "A nurse?"

"The nurse will have a look at her."

"But the lady needs to go directly to the hospital, sir. Her injuries might be severe."

"Maybe so, but no one's gettin' through to Sin right now."

"But I need to get her to the hospital urgently."

"There were a couple of terrorist attacks a few hours ago. Seven people blown to bits."

"That is not my concern, sir."

"Maybe not—but it's *our* concern. What ya doin' out of Purgatory anyway, Black? Brass send you on a mission or somethin'?"

"I commandeered this vehicle in an emergency."

"José," the guard calls, "when you get off the line, call Kasr security, see if anyone can confirm what Leonardo Black is doin' out here."

The droid is cross. "I'm not sure I understand, sir, why you keep calling me Mr. Black. Are you going to let me through, or am I going to have to take action?"

"Whatsa matter with you, Black? You used to be pretty cool, as droids go. You short-circuited or somethin'?"

"I am not short-circuited, sir, but I am very angry."

The guard smirks and shoots a look at one of his companions. "Mr. Black here is angry."

"Indeed I am. I have an excellent public-relations opportunity here, but you seem determined to obstruct me. What is your name, sir?"

"You're asking me *my* name?"

"I have every right to ask your name."

"What're ya gonna do—report me to Mr. Brass?"

"I am simply reminding you, sir, that you are answerable to higher forces. You do not appear to appreciate your proper place."

To Persione, still in the postal van, it looks as if the guard is trying to work out if the droid is serious—if perhaps he comes with top-level authorization. But in the end he remains defiant. "I don't care what higher forces you think I answer to, Black. I know what I'm doin'. Now just stand to the side there and wait."

"I will not stand to the side, sir—I am too big to wait."

"Too big now, are you?"

"I am, sir. And I will not tolerate this bureaucratic madness. Kindly let me through or you will be responsible for what I do next."

"Wait a minute, Black, are you *threatening* me?"

"No, sir, I am threatening *all* of you."

"Oh yeah?" the guard says, starting to simmer. "And just what're ya planning to do?"

"I have a large blade here"—Persione can't see properly from behind, but it looks like the droid is drawing something from under his jacket—"and I will not hesitate to use it."

The guards stare at him for a second, their eyes widening. Then the droid raises a blade—a wicked-looking thing, like something from a slaughterhouse—and the guards drop everything and reach for their own weapons.

"PUT THAT THING DOWN!"

"DROP IT!"

"DROP IT NOW!"

The guards have fanned out, assuming defensive postures, and give every impression that they *live* for just such moments. Meanwhile, a female nurse—dressed in a cartoonish costume—has appeared, just to make things more bizarre. The droid is immobile, his back to the postal van.

"PUT THAT WEAPON DOWN, I SAID!" The guards are training their zappers on him.

"I will not, sir, unless you allow me through to the hospital."

"LOWER THAT WEAPON NOW!"

"I am prepared to use it, sir."

Inside the van, Decimus Persione watches the scene unfold with a mixture of fascination and fear. He can sense very well, with all his seismological instincts, that there is about to be an eruption. But just when he starts wondering if this might somehow be to his advantage, he hears a groan and sees Nawahine stirring at his feet.

"DID YOU HEAR ME? DROP THAT THING NOW!"

"I am being perfectly reasonable, sir."

And now Persione doesn't know what to do. Because if Nawahine remembers, and accuses him—well, it doesn't bear thinking about.

"DROP IT NOW OR WE'LL TURN YOU TO TOAST!"

"You will only damage yourselves, sir, if you act rashly."

But Decimus Persione suddenly sees—or, more accurately, *feels*—that there is a way out after all. If he can do something positive in the emergency, if he can rescue all of them, then there will be so much gratitude that no one will question him. And if he fails . . . well, it will hardly matter anymore.

So he reaches over Nawahine and picks up the hammer. He eases off his seat and makes for the airlock doors—both of which are open. He rises up, as quietly as possible, behind the unsuspecting droid. And he draws back the hammer, ready to smash it through the back of the head.

"FIVE SECONDS OR YOU'RE GONNA FRY!"

"Five seconds, sir, or I start killing you all."

Persione can see the guards willing him to do it, to swing the hammer. But he hesitates. A wave of guilt sweeps through him—the memory of swinging the flashlight on Nawahine—and he falters, his hand wavers.

"DROP IT AND SURRENDER NOW!"

"I do not even know how to spell 'surrender,' sir."

Then the guilt in Persione abruptly passes, replaced by a surge of disgust. He feels he can do it after all. He *has* to do it. So he raises the hammer and prepares himself to strike.

"What's going on?"

It's the voice of Nawahine, rising from her slumber, and Persione turns reflexively, guiltily, trying to shush her before it's too late.

44

NOT LONG AFTER JUSTUS graduated from police academy he talked a hysterical teenager out of suicide and received his first medal of merit. A few years later he negotiated with a man threatening to blow up a clutch of schoolkids, and though he didn't get far—police marksmen took the man out with a head-shot—he was awarded with a medal of bravery. Some time later, in Vegas, he was sent into a penthouse where a drunken casino magnate had just shot one prostitute in the leg and was threatening to kill two others. It took Justus thirty minutes to free the sex workers and disarm the casino magnate. He should have received a medal of valor for that one, but the magnate, who wielded a lot of power in Vegas, didn't want the incident advertised more than necessary, so all Justus got was a gift basket, a weekend pass to the casino penthouse, and a ticket to a magic show. All of which he sent back immediately.

356 | ANTHONY O'NEILL

"How long has he been in there?" he asks presently—they're in an office next to the screening section.

"Two, three hours."

"What are his demands?"

"To get out. To take the girl with him."

"Is he damaged?"

"Mentally?"

"Physically. Did you zap him?"

"With everything we had."

"What happened?"

"Just ruffled his hair."

"Try regular ammunition?"

"Pumped three, four slugs into him."

"You didn't hit the control centers?"

"Don't know where they are. Need schematics. Anyway, this isn't supposed to happen with a tinnie."

"No," says Justus, "this isn't supposed to happen with a tinnie."

Justus knows that to the others he must appear eerily composed. But of course he expected it might come to this. Speeding back down the Road of Lamentation, all alone in the police vehicle, he had plenty of time to brood. And patch things together. And picture what was going to happen if he didn't reach Purgatory before the droid.

"I'm going in," he says.

"You sure?" The cops and officials—the ones who survived—are glancing at each other.

"Someone has to."

"But you'll need backup, right?"

"Why?"

"Just you? In the room with that thing?"

"There's a lady in there, isn't there?"

"Yeah, but—"

"Just get me a comm-link. Wait for my instructions. And clear a path at the inner gates."

Now the cops are really confused. "You're going to Sin?"

"I am."

"With *him*?"

"We'll see what happens."

"But there are riots back there—that's why they couldn't send reinforcements. Folks are losing their shit over the death of QT."

"Of course they are," says Justus, and smirks. "Just get a vehicle ready. And get these doors open. We're wasting time."

Justus, not caring if he seems half-mad, goes to the bulkhead-like security door and waits for the green light to flash. One of the younger cops, genuinely concerned, asks if he wants a flak jacket.

"What good would that do?"

"So you're not gonna shield yourself? Or arm yourself?"

Justus doesn't answer.

Then the light starts whirling and he steps through. The door clunks shut behind him.

The screening area is like a war zone. Justus allows himself to absorb a quick impression—Leonardo Black is standing in front of a postal van and a red emergency light is spinning garishly—but for the moment he doesn't look at the droid directly.

He drops to his haunches beside the nearest body—it's badly mutilated and unmoving—and checks the pulse.

"Who are you, sir?"

"Just one second."

Justus goes to the second body. Puts two fingers to the carotid artery.

"I said who are you, sir?"

"I said just one second."

Justus goes to the third body.

"Are you looking for signs of life, sir?"

"Uh-huh."

"There is no need, sir. They are dead."

Justus goes to the fourth body.

"I *assure* you they are dead, sir."

"I heard you."

Justus goes to the fifth body.

"I am offended, sir, that you do not believe me."

"I never said I don't believe you."

"Then why are you checking them?"

Justus doesn't answer—just goes to the sixth body.

"I hope this is not some sort of trick, sir?"

"Nope."

"I hope you are not about to attempt something foolish?"

"Nope."

Justus goes to the seventh body—a dusky-skinned man lying at the droid's feet.

"I can hurt you if you try to trick me, sir. I can crack your skull like an eggshell."

"Uh-huh."

"I can hit you so hard that your shadow bleeds."

"Uh-huh." Justus, finished with the bodies, finally rises and stares the dead droid in the eyes. "Shake my hand if you want," he says. "Shake it as hard as you like."

The droid is scorched from where he was hit with zapper streams. Parts of his suit are burned through. He has flecks of blood on his face and all over his shirt. There's a bullet hole in his neck, just above the collar. He's holding the slaughterhouse blade high, ready to strike. But now he looks confused.

"Shake your hand, sir?"

"You know—man to man."

Justus can't be sure but he thinks he remembers reading something similar in one of Brass's business guides: *"You can always tell more about a man from a single handshake, and by looking him dead in the eyes, than you can from a thousand business lunches."*

And Black, though he pauses for a long time—he seems intrigued by Justus's facial burns, which are even worse than his own—finally seems to understand. He nods. He calmly switches the slaughterhouse knife to his left hand—the blade has flesh and hair on it—and holds out his right. And the two shake. Firmly. The droid actually leans forward to stare into Justus's eyes. And Justus stares back, unblinking.

"Very well, sir. I believe you are a man of your word."

"I am."

"But you have not yet told me who you are."

"Do you mind?"

"Mind, sir?"

But Justus is already moving to the postal van. Inside, an attractive Polynesian woman is lying between the seats.

"Are you okay, ma'am?"

"I'm okay . . ."

"Are you injured?"

"I think so, I'm not sure."

"Can you last a little longer?"

"I can last."

"Hold still, don't draw attention to yourself, and we'll get you out of here as soon as possible."

The droid is annoyed. "Why are you talking to the sexy lady, sir?"

"I need to be sure she's well."

"She is not well, sir. She needs to be taken to a hospital."

"Uh-huh. Then we'll get her there."

"*We*, sir? I was the one who saved her."

"I heard that."

"I drove the postal van at top speed for over two hundred kilometers."

"I heard that too."

"So *I* will take her to the hospital."

"Okay."

"I will not have the glory taken from me."

"Fair enough. I'll help you."

"You'll help me?"

"I've already ordered the others to get an ambulance ready. They're clearing a path right now. Shouldn't take long."

The droid frowns. "I don't want to use an ambulance, sir."

"Okay."

"I want to drive in the postal van."

"Okay."

"You're not going to get in my way, sir?"

"It makes no difference to me."

Black, disconcerted, looks Justus up and down. "Well, sir, I must say I am impressed by your attitude. You are certainly not like the others."

"Probably not," says Justus. "Do you mind if I ask some questions now? While we're waiting?"

"What sort of questions, sir?"

"Procedural questions. I'm a police lieutenant."

"You are not going to arrest me, are you, sir?"

"I'm not."

"I can break you if you try."

"I'm sure that's true."

"I can throttle you with one hand."

THE DARK SIDE | 361

"Uh-huh."

"I can dice you up like a teppanyaki—"

"I'm sure you can. But I'm going to ask the questions anyway. It's up to you if you answer or not."

The droid considers for a few moments and then nods. "Very well, sir. But attempt no tricks on me."

"There'll be no tricks."

"If you try to fuck me over, I will fuck you under."

"Uh-huh. May I start with your name?"

"I have no name, sir."

"Does the name Leonardo Black mean anything to you?"

"It does not, sir."

"Have you ever heard of Project Daedalus?"

"I have not, sir."

"Are you an android?"

"I am a man, sir."

"What sort of a man?"

"A conquistador, and soon to be a king."

"Do you know where you came from, then?"

"I come from everywhere, sir."

"Does the name Saint Helena mean anything to you?"

"It does not, sir."

"What about Seidel?"

"I believe that is a crater approximately 2,300 kilometers south of here."

"Do you remember the technicians there?"

"I remember some meddling mediocrities."

"You killed them?"

"I did, sir."

"Do you remember any existence before the mediocrities? Before your long walk here?"

"What is there to remember, sir?"

"Have you ever heard of Leonardo Brown, Leonardo Grey, and Leonardo White?"

"I have not, sir."

"Fletcher Brass?"

"Yes," the droid says, "I have heard that name before."

"Where?"

"A man mentioned it to me."

"What man?"

"I do not know his name, sir. I banged his head against a wall."

"When was this?"

"Seventy-three hours ago."

"Seventy-three hours." Justus thinks for a moment. "So you've killed others as well? Between the technicians and the people here in the room?"

"I have, sir."

"How many?"

"I have not counted, sir."

"Take a wild guess."

"Forty-three."

"Forty-three people? You've killed forty-three people? On top of the seven right here?"

"Were they people, sir?"

"What were they, if not people?"

"Vermin. Speedbumps. Obstacles on my path to destiny."

"Uh-huh." To Justus it's even worse than he imagined. But he wonders why he's surprised. For a moment he thinks he can even see brass flecks in the droid's eyes. "A few more questions," he says.

"I'm getting weary of your questions, sir."

"Well, I'm going to ask them anyway. Ignore them if you like."

"Very well, sir."

"What do you do with weeds?"

The droid seems momentarily nonplussed—just a blank smile—but then he seems to catch on. He even seems approving. "What do you do with weeds?" he says. "You kill them before they take root."

"What do you do with workers?"

"You pat them on the head occasionally, and put them down when necessary."

"What should a man do with his temper?"

"Lose it often. And well."

"What's the point of walking in another man's shoes?"

"There is no point, unless his shoes are better than yours."

"And how do you spell 'surrender'?"

"'Surrender'? '*Surendar*'?" The droid seems irritated. "I cannot even spell it, sir."

"Uh-huh," Justus says. "Do you know where your answers came from?"

"They came from me."

"You weren't quoting anyone?"

"I was quoting myself."

"Then one final question, if you don't mind."

"I am getting impatient, sir."

"So am I, for your sake. But one final question for a prophet and a sage—for a king like you."

"Make it snappy, sir."

"A mad scientist builds a monster out of body parts. The monster heads into the woods and kills a little girl. Who, then, is most responsible? The mad scientist or the monster?"

"The answer to that question is obvious, sir."

"It *is*?"

"Of course, sir—it's neither the scientist nor the monster."

"Then who *is* most responsible?"

"The little girl in the woods."

"The *little girl in the woods*?"

"For failing to adequately protect herself, sir."

Justus, nodding, no longer has any doubts. Everything he suspected, driving down the Road of Lamentation, is true. He feels validated. He feels righteous. He feels a fierce determination.

"Open up. Inner doors. Airlock." He's speaking through the comm-link. "We're passing through."

The droid interjects. "We are going to Sin now?"

"That's right."

"But we must first stop at the hospital."

"The hospital is in Sin. That'll be our first stop. Then we'll get you spruced up. There's some people I'd like you to meet."

"I will not tolerate any more hindrances, sir—I'm impatient to fulfill my destiny."

"One of the people I have in mind *is* your destiny."

The droid looks suspicious. "This is no underhand trick, is it, sir?"

"It's no trick."

"I can still kill you, sir."

"Yup."

"I can knee you so hard that you cough up your—"

"Yeah, yeah—we can shake hands again, if you like."

The droid hesitates, then looks Justus in the eyes. Deeply. And again he seems to like what he sees.

"No," he says finally, "that will not be necessary, sir. I believe you are an honest man."

Ten minutes later they're in the airlock, sitting side by side at the front of the postal van, and waiting for the outer doors to rise.

"You know," the droid says, "it has been a pleasure doing business with you, sir. If only all men were as reasonable as you, a lot of valuable time would not have been wasted."

"It is the burden of kings to endure the workings of knaves and fools, Your Majesty."

"You are right. You are so absolutely right. So what is your name?"

"My name?"

"I always make sure I reward those who help me on my way. So what is your name, good sir?"

Justus thinks about it for a few seconds and snorts. "My name," he says, "is Justice."

The doors open on the lunar vacuum.

45

AT 0830 IN THE Kasr, Fletcher Brass emerges naked from his bathroom—a room bigger than most residences in Sin—and goes to his secondary bedchamber, expecting to find his formal attire laid out on the bed. But there's nothing.

"*Grey*," he calls, in his booming, senatorial voice, but there's no response. He wonders what the droid is doing.

In truth it's been rather difficult lately, functioning with only one android. In the absence of Leonardo Black, Grey has had to perform all the usual domestic tasks, be a personal bodyguard, and run around town as a PR representative as well. Brass knows he really should have more servants—even a human or two—but he's come to trust the droids implicitly. It's an illusion, of course, because he knows very well that robots can be programmed to betray, but in his experience humans are *always* programmed to betray. And deceive. And steal. And spread gossip. And sell secrets.

It's only by accepting human nature, and embracing it, that Fletcher Brass has made it as far as he has.

Presently he takes the opportunity to admire his body in a full-length mirror. Broad shoulders, pronounced pectorals, well-defined abs, fat-free hips, glowing tan, glittering brass-colored chest hair. His surgeons have done an incredible job. Except perhaps for one visible scar above the pubis, you'd never know he'd submitted himself to forty-two cosmetic surgeries. He's been told by women—many women—that he could easily pass for a gym-toned forty-year-old. When he makes love now—which is rare, as he's simply gotten tired of the whole business—he spends much of the time just admiring his unbelievable physique in the mirrors. It makes him feel like a pansy, but it can't be helped—it's not much different from appreciating a well-preserved Mustang.

He wraps himself in a quilted satin dressing gown, deciding it's best to eat before he dresses. He ambles down a passageway decorated with intricate Babylonian bas-reliefs and enters the grand dining room, an immense chamber with coffered brass ceiling, crystal chandeliers, and a gleaming rosewood table the length of a bowling alley. Here he calls once more for Grey, again without success. He goes to the dumbwaiter, presses a button, and finds inside a brass breakfast tray. He takes it back to the table and settles in, removing the cloche to find a steaming plate of glazed thick-cut bacon, poached eggs, smoked pimento hollandaise, foie gras, black unsweetened coffee, and a customary glass of purple Zeus-Juice, his favorite vitamin shake. It's always best, he's found, to address grumbling crowds on a satisfied stomach.

Right now he can hear the Sinners massing outside the Kasr for his morning address. They're earlier than expected and seem to be chanting something. It's the first time Brass has summoned them for a general announcement in over a year, and he has no illusions that it will be easy. He's not even expecting it to be well received to begin with. But he's confident that he—and only he— has the charisma to pull it off. It's why he hasn't delegated the task to that wife-murdering actor. He simply can't count on any- one else to feign the right mix of sorrow, anger, implication, and resolve.

Sorrow that his daughter, along with a few others meeting for an emergency conference, has been killed.

Anger at those mysterious forces that committed the atrocity.

Implication—and this will require real skill on his part—that his daughter was not completely innocent. That in colluding with criminal elements and political dissidents, she was either assas- sinated by co-conspirators or became the victim of a mistimed explosion.

And resolve: that Purgatory will nevertheless survive. Bleed- ing, but alive. Stronger than ever, in fact, and ready to face a new dawn.

As to the details of that new dawn, Brass intends to be vague. His expedition to Mars will proceed as normal, of course—it's too important to be postponed now—but the unprecedented events of recent days have convinced him that an iron hand is needed to replace him while he's away. It's only his own iron hand, he'll point out, that's held the whole volatile territory together for so long. And regarding the identity of that iron hand, well, he's given it a great deal of thought and will make an official announcement in the coming days.

He's not halfway through the bacon—sawing it into digestible pieces and dipping it in egg yolk, as is his habit—when he hears echoing footsteps and sees Leonardo Grey enter the chamber, looking strangely ill at ease. Brass can't quite put his finger on it, but the droid looks *paler* than usual. Though that, of course, must be his imagination.

"I trust you are well this morning, sir?" Grey says in his clipped voice.

"Well enough," replies Brass, sipping on Zeus-Juice. "But where have you been, Grey, that you didn't put out my clothes?"

"I was called away, sir—I apologize profusely."

"Called away by whom, exactly?"

"By Lieutenant Damien Justus, sir."

"Justus?" Brass frowns. "I thought he was running for the hills."

"He may have been, but he's now back in Sin."

"Really? He came back?"

"He did, sir."

Brass wonders if the plans he had in place—an assassin was going to take Justus out at Doppelmayer, implicating forces from Earth—will be necessary after all. "Well, what does he want?"

"He has requested an audience with you urgently, sir."

"He wants to see me *again*?"

"He does, sir."

"Then he can wait until after the speech—*if* I feel like it."

"He has requested an audience with you *now*, sir."

Brass stops sipping. "Are you telling me he's *here*?"

"He is currently in the sitting room, sir."

"You let him in?"

"I escorted him all the way from his home."

"Oh really? That's very accommodating of you, Grey."

"You did say I was to extend to him my full cooperation, sir."

"Hmm, well, you can go too far sometimes, you know."

"I apologize, sir."

"I once had a choice between you and Leonardo Brown, you

know. I chose you because you *looked* more distinguished. And because I assumed you'd acquired a better understanding of me. But now you make me wonder."

"I will try to do better in the future, sir."

"Hmm." Brass enjoys demeaning Grey—he considers humiliation a form of motivation—but with Leonardo Brown gone he can no longer make so much of their rivalry. So he sighs. "Well, let the fucker in."

"Very well, sir."

Grey starts to turn, but Brass adds, "And stay close to me while he's inside."

"I intend to, sir."

"Make sure he keeps his distance. I doubt he'll try anything, but you never know. So if he makes a sudden move, you know what to do."

"I believe I am adequately equipped, sir."

Brass, watching Grey leave the room, still finds something odd about the droid. Something peculiar in his bearing or attitude. He sounds almost insolent. As if something has happened to him overnight. But he doesn't dwell on it. He shovels the rest of the bacon into his mouth and chews hurriedly, to give himself a good protein boost before the confrontation.

He's washing it all down with a few sips of juice when Grey returns, leading the fully uniformed Justus into the chamber. Brass watches as the droid directs the lieutenant to a high-backed chair at the far end of the table—about twenty meters distant—and then discreetly moves along the length of the table to take up a position at his master's side. But Justus doesn't sit, just as Brass doesn't bother to stand. He just looks around at him, appraising the great magnitude of the room and all its trimmings, and finally says something that sounds like, "Satire doesn't work, does it?"

Brass gives a shake of the head and says, "I beg your pardon? You'll need to raise your voice while you're in here."

Justus says louder, "I said, satire doesn't work, does it?"

"That's what I thought you said. What does it mean?"

"It's just an observation. When cartoonists satirize the lives of the rich and powerful, they often show some evil old trillionaire sitting in a castle eating caviar and hummingbird tongues. It's meant to be larger-than-life—an exaggeration, an absurdity. But the rich and powerful too often don't see it that way. All they see is a standard that needs to be emulated. So clearly satire doesn't work."

Brass is even more disconcerted by the lieutenant's attitude than he is by Leonardo Grey's. It's not as if he hasn't seen Justus being disrespectful before—they parted the previous day after a veritable torrent of vitriol—but this is something altogether new. Justus is now being disrespectful with a hint of mockery. It's almost as if he believes he has the upper hand.

"Take a seat, Lieutenant, before the irony overcomes you. I'd offer you a coffee but I wouldn't want you to get any more excited than you seem to be already."

"That's okay—I've eaten half a pack of BrightIze™. I don't normally touch the stuff, but it's been a long night."

"Been a few places?"

"You could say that."

"How's your daughter?" Brass asks.

He expects Justus to flare. Or glare. But instead the lieutenant just chuckles and draws up a seat. "I think she's going to be okay," he says, sitting down. "It's what I came here about, actually."

"Oh?" Brass raises an eyebrow, doing his best to appear unfazed.

"Yeah. After all, I came to Purgatory in order to protect my daughter, in a roundabout sort of way. And when you pulled that rug from under my feet I figured I had nothing to lose."

"Now you're being presumptuous again, Lieutenant—I didn't expect that. Nothing in your profile suggested that you were presumptuous. Or intemperate."

"I'm neither. But when you threatened her, I just—"

"Who says I threatened her?"

"I know a threat when I hear one."

"Then I suggest you rewind our conversation in your head and listen to what I said again. Because I never made a threat. Nothing of the sort. And I would have clarified that point yesterday if you'd given me a chance to respond. In fact, my only intention in mentioning your daughter was to draw a similarity between the two of us. You have a daughter, as do I."

"A daughter you ordered assassinated."

Now Brass feels free to act completely outraged. "That's contemptible, Lieutenant. Where do you get off, making such preposterous accusations?"

Justus just shrugs.

"If you weren't fired already," Brass goes on, "then consider yourself fired forthwith. This is scandalous. Who do you think you are?"

"I'm just an honest cop. Or at least I was."

"An honest cop, or just an incompetent one? What gives you the *gall* to say I ordered my daughter's assassination? Do you have the faintest proof?"

"Not me personally. All I know is that Leonardo Brown, your daughter's valet, accepted delivery of a high-powered explosive at her front door, then carried it inside. Whether he was acting on instruction, or knew what he was doing—that I haven't been able to determine. And I'm sure I never will. In fact, I'm sure that all the available evidence will somehow implicate the very people who were blown up. That's what happens in corrupt states with corrupt law enforcement bureaus. My only regret is that I refused to see it from the start. Because I desperately wanted to believe that there was a way out. And because I wanted to live—*anywhere*—that made me no danger to my daughter's life."

"How very moving. But you still haven't explained how you came to this preposterous theory."

Justus smirks. And though Brass doesn't like it—the brazen insolence—he feels compelled to hear the man out.

"You know, Mr. Brass, I've had a very interesting twelve hours. Fourteen hours, whatever—I'm not even sure anymore. First, I drove all the way to Peary Base and made a call to the South Pole. Then I drove back through the night to Purgatory. Top speed. I reached the Gates at around three o'clock in the morning. But I struggled to get in at first. There was something going on in the screening section. Anyway, to cut a long story short, I forced my way through and what I saw was absolute chaos. Seemed an android had arrived and demanded access to Sin. And when he didn't get it he went berserk. Killed all the security personnel, a secretary, a nurse, and one of the people who'd been with him in the van. The only survivor was a lady the droid was carrying to the hospital. There was blood everywhere. Severed limbs. Seven people dead, altogether."

Brass is genuinely shocked. "I wasn't informed about this . . ."

"Of course not. Who'd want to interrupt your sleep? When you had such a big day ahead?"

"That's another contemptible comment, Lieutenant. Of course I'd want to be informed. Who was this android? Where did it come from?"

"Are you sure you want to know?"

"And what does *that* mean?"

Justus smirks again. "Well, you see, Mr. Brass, it seems you *knew* this android already. He's one of yours. He worked for you. You certainly didn't know he was on the loose—one of the drawbacks, I guess, of being so busy and distracted is that you can't keep an eye on everything—but you sure knew about him. You were the one who ordered his reprogramming, in fact. You tried to keep it secret, and it might've worked too, only something went wrong. The technicians made a mistake. The android got loaded up with your psychopathic corporate philosophies *before* the proper inhibitors could be activated. And he went insane. Out of control. Just the way you've been out of control for decades, Mr. Brass—except that you, most of the time, have been getting away with it. You've used all your power and influence to get away with it. And yet here we are."

Brass has never felt more discomposed. It's rare that he's the last to know something, and even rarer that he doesn't know how to react. Part of him wants to explode and storm off, just as a defensive ploy. But he senses that's not in order. Added to that, he just doesn't like the way Justus is communicating all this news to him—as if he doesn't care about his own fate, or worse, has no reason to be concerned.

"This is preposterous," Brass manages again. But he has the knife and fork clutched in his hands like weapons. "I hope you realize how preposterous this sounds."

"Preposterous?" Justus says. "You keep saying that. Then again, I probably would've thought it was all preposterous myself until I came to Purgatory. Until last night, when I heard the story of Leonardo Black. Until a few hours ago, in fact, when I actually spoke to Black myself. I spoke to him just as you prefer people to speak to you. Because he *was* you, in a way—your black soul. So it wasn't hard to fit into place the last pieces of your grand plan. I can tell you now, if you like—what was *supposed* to happen, anyway."

Brass can't decide how to respond. So Justus just goes on:

"You didn't trust anyone to take your place while you were away on the Mars expedition. Not any of your associates, not any of your department heads, not that actor who stands in for you, and certainly not your daughter. So you got the bright idea to re-place yourself with an android: Leonardo Black. Your bodyguard. You were going to make him a proxy Fletcher Brass—only many times more physically powerful. And he was going to rule this place like a tyrant. He was going to make all the ruthless deci-sions, fire people, even kill if necessary. But to pave the way for his appointment you wanted to create a bit of chaos—you wanted to make it look like such a tyrant was justified by the circumstances. And you wanted to get rid of anybody you feared might seize power anyway. You'd kill two birds—three birds, ten birds, what-ever—with one stone. So you had your assassins go to work, with the full cooperation of the PPD—political murders that would never be solved because crucial evidence was erased, contami-nated, or falsified. And that part might've worked too, only half the players in the PPD were too shiftless to play their roles. And of course there were others who knew more than you thought. People who were just as ruthless and cunning as you. People you thought you were moving around like pawns but who in fact were moving you. 'Don't play chess, play people'—isn't that one of your laws? Well, sometimes the master should be wary of the apprentices."

Brass feels caught off guard again. And to make matters worse, Justus is just staring at him, waiting for a response. So he chuckles incredulously. "Again, I have no idea what you're talking about."

"I'm mainly talking about your daughter, Mr. Brass. You know, the one you trusted least of all? The one you were planning to imprison at first—lock her up after you'd framed her for the assassinations, of course, until—"

Brass, seizing the moment, can't help interjecting. "You really have no idea, do you, Lieutenant?" he says. "Are you really that naïve? *Really?* I had no intention of locking up my daughter while I was away—*because my daughter was coming with me.*"

This silences Justus—he's got a blank expression on his starfish face—and Brass makes the most of it.

"That's right—*she was coming with me.* To Mars. You can ask Ms. Powers if you like. My daughter was coming with me. You didn't know that, did you?"

Justus pauses. "And QT herself—did she know about this?"

"No, Lieutenant—*of course she didn't know.* Because I was taking her *against her will*. I was taking her for her own good."

"You were going to kidnap her?"

"Call it what you like. Because I wasn't going to let my daughter—my own flesh and blood—become the target of rogues and assassins. And that's exactly what would have happened if she stayed here—because like you, she was *naïve.* She wouldn't have lasted *two weeks* as the leader of Purgatory."

"I think your daughter would have a thing or two to say about that."

"You do, do you? Well, what does it matter now?"

"Because you ordered her assassination?"

"No—*I ordered no such thing*. You're wrong yet again. I have no idea who killed her. Good Lord, do you think I'm *happy* she's dead?"

"Well, you sure as hell didn't sound too happy with her yesterday, when you thought she was trying to pin the deaths of the Leafists on—"

"*But that doesn't mean I'd kill her*. Would you kill your daughter? Of course not. Just as I'd *never* kill *my* own daughter."

"You'd kidnap her but you'd never kill her?"

"I'd kidnap her to *save* her. Can you not tell the difference?"

Justus pauses a moment and then sighs. "No, Mr. Brass—you're lying."

"What? How *dare* you tell me I'm lying!"

"I'll dare to tell you whatever I like. I don't answer to you or anyone else. I'm no longer a police officer, remember? So I'll tell you what I *do* know—as facts. You might have planned to kidnap QT at one stage, but when you found out about her plans you changed your mind. And you ordered her assassination."

"*You have no proof of that.*"

"Do I need proof anymore? The silence is the answer, remember? Well, in your case, *everything about you* is the answer. Your history. The reason you're here on the Moon. The litany of death and broken lives you've left behind. Your narcissism. Your egomania. The Leafists. Your plans to replace yourself with a killer android. Your goddamned laws. *And the way you threatened my daughter*. No, Mr. Brass, in your case I don't *need* proof. Because everything you've done is proof enough. But there's more."

Justus has gotten to his feet now and there's the sound of an explosion outside—the swelling crowd seem to be letting off fireworks. Or dynamite. Or something.

"You see, Mr. Brass, you've been so far out of the loop, out there at your rocket base, that you don't even realize how flimsy your support network is. You're the leader who barricades himself behind lackeys and lickspittles, little realizing that they're always the first people to turn when the breeze changes direction. Well, I found out all about that in the last twenty hours or so. When it became clear that you'd ordered the death of QT Brass, and when Leonardo Black went on his little rampage. I met a few people and learned a few things. I was amazed, but I shouldn't have been. Because you've gone too far this time, and you were never as much in control as you think. You've been played. You've been checkmated. And you're in for a very rude surprise—much sooner than you think. As a father, you should be very proud."

Justus turns and starts walking toward the exit, but Brass shoots to his feet, slamming his cutlery onto the breakfast plate.

"And what the fuck is that supposed to mean?"

"Goodbye, Mr. Brass."

"I said, what the fuck does that mean?" Brass steps out from behind the table. "ANSWER ME!"

Justus keeps walking toward the door.

Brass is livid. "ANSWER ME, YOU STAR-FACED CUNT!"

But it's only at the door—about thirty meters away—that Justus finally turns. With an insufferable look on his disfigured face.

"No, Mr. Brass—I've made my decision. I've cut a deal, in fact. It was either you or me. And I figure, for my daughter's sake, that it's better that it's you." He reaches for the door, but suddenly turns back. "Oh yes," he says, "an afterthought. A last little message—an art I've learned since I came here."

Brass bristles. "What the fuck are you talking about now?"

"In this instance, it's just an observation. You're free to agree with it or not. But it seems to me that, even after all this, even after all I've said to you just now, you're still the man in charge. You're still Number One. You're still the Patriarch of Purgatory, am I right?"

"Are you fucking joking?"

"I'm just asking. This is your kingdom, isn't it?"

"I said, are you joking?"

"So you're the King."

"I am the fucking King."

"You're the Wizard."

"I'm *everything you're not*, you shit—what is this supposed to mean?"

Justus just snorts. "Farewell, Mr. Brass."

And he goes out, letting the door fall shut behind him.

Brass stands in place, fuming, wondering what to do, hearing the increasingly noisy crowd outside. Then he tries to turn, just to get out of the room. But suddenly something drags him back.

Brass, outraged, can't believe it. He can't move. Something has seized him from behind—by the hair.

He struggles, but the grip is fierce. And he's being tilted forward—by the head.

He squirms and swivels and looks up, furious, and sees that it's Leonardo Grey, grinning wickedly, who's grabbed him.

But the droid's eyes aren't grey. They're *black*. And he's holding a terrifying foot-long blade in his right hand.

"*You're not really a conquistador,*" the droid hisses, "*until you hold the King's head high.*"

Brass tries to raise his hands, but the blade is already sweeping across his throat.

46

BLACK HAS BARELY FINISHED taking care of business when Justus reaches the third floor vestibule. He's making his way across this great chamber—brass pillars, parquet floor, a sculpted wall of bearded faces—when he hears a voice from the shadows.

"Welcome to the Dark Side, Lieutenant."

Justus, stopping in his tracks, recognizes the voice immediately. But he waits for his eyes to adjust before responding.

"I didn't know you were going to be here," he says.

"Wouldn't have missed it for the world."

"It's still a moment for sadness, isn't it?"

"The King must die so the country may live—Robespierre said that."

"You're quoting Robespierre now?"

"This is our first revolution, so why not?"

She steps into a coppery strip of morning light. Since their meeting a few hours earlier she's glammed herself up in clerical black and white—jacket, pleated skirt, blouse, and silken black tie—and she looks like she means business. Like a distaff version of Leonardo Black, before he costumed himself as Leonardo Grey.

"He was your father, is what I meant."

"In trying to assassinate me, he rather swiftly put an end to my responsibilities as a daughter, wouldn't you say?"

Justus isn't sure. He has no doubt that Brass ordered the bombing, but he's still not convinced that his daughter didn't purposely leak her own controversial plans in order to make such an assassination attempt inevitable. An assassination attempt, as it turned out, that she miraculously avoided by "sneaking off to the secret conference in the Sin Rim." Leaving her own double—a cosmetically altered prostitute named Harmony Smooth—to fill in for her at Ishtar. And get blown sky-high for her trouble.

"Why do I get the feeling that you've been planning this for years?" he asks.

"Because I have. And a lot longer than you think too."

"Since when?"

"Since my mother's suicide. Do you know what my father told her when he cut her loose? He said, 'Turn me into a grudge—you'll get a lot of mileage out of it.' And in my mother's name, I've sure come a long way on that grudge."

Justus shakes his head. "The peach really doesn't fall far from the tree, does it?"

"Now you're just being rude, Lieutenant. I don't see much regret in your eyes either, now that you've done what you did—twisted the rule of law."

"I did what I had to do."

"We both did. We let business take its course, and the Brass Code take care of itself. We just didn't get in the way."

"That's one way to look at it."

But Justus isn't enjoying the clinical tone of the exchange, especially when a man has just been brutally murdered in the next room. So he starts moving for the stairs.

"You can stay here, you know," she calls after him. "We're going to need a new police chief."

Justus looks back. "You really think I'd *want* to remain here? After all this?"

"And do you really think it's safe—for your daughter—if you go home?"

"I hope that's not a threat."

"You *know* it's not. Who do you think I am?"

I wonder, is what Justus wants to say. Her demeanor ever since their secret meeting, high above the city where the multitudes were just starting to get agitated by her supposed demise, has been positively icy. Which could be a natural reaction to the bombings, or it could be her true self. Whatever the case, she's certainly not acting like someone whose closest allies have just been obliterated. She's acting like someone fully prepared to sacrifice her friends, if indeed they *were* friends, for her own political ends. Justus wonders if she knew all along that a bomb had been planted in her office. And if she knew her double was going to die—if she *planned* it that way, to help ignite a revolution. He even has to consider the chilling possibility that she long ago *arranged* to have Leonardo Black misprogrammed at the robotics base in Seidel, and even *expected* the droid to come after his king.

"I'm not sure *who* you are," he replies, unblinking. "And I'm not sure I want to know."

"I'm not asking you to write my biography, Lieutenant. I'm just asking you to stay here. To be part of this."

"Then you don't know me very well."

"I read your psych report."

"Is that right?"

"It said you were suppressing a high level of resentment."

"That's interesting."

"It also said you were borderline obsessive. It suggested a guilt complex."

"That's even more interesting."

"Look, we all have our dark sides, Lieutenant—I'm not going to question why a man like you becomes a cop. But it's fair to say I know you better than you think."

"Oh yeah?" Justus is starting to get annoyed. "Then maybe you don't know your *people* as well as you think. Or what you're in for."

"What does that mean?"

He jerks his head. "When the mob finds out about this—that you didn't die after all—they might not be so impressed. No one likes being hoodwinked."

"They'll love it. Even if they suspect they were duped."

"What makes you so sure?"

"I know my people. When they learn the truth, they'll be ecstatic."

"And when exactly are you planning to reveal the truth?"

"Why do you think I'm here?"

Justus snorts. He hears the crowd getting louder and angrier—the clapping and chanting is shaking the walls of the Kasr. "You're planning to take over straightaway?"

"Why not?"

"I wonder what the King will think about that."

"The King isn't always the one who reigns, you know. In fact, I'd say that it's a rare king these days who's actually in charge. Even if he thinks he is."

"So you're going to stand alongside Leonardo Black, are you? King Leo the First? You're going to let him think he's the Wizard?"

"Until I'm ready to take over myself."

"Then you're even more cunning than I thought. Even more cunning than your father."

She looks cross. "Look, Lieutenant, don't think for a second that this is easy for me. But I've thought it through. I've studied the revolutions on Earth. And what I've seen is that when a volatile population is freed from tyranny it passes through several distinct stages. Euphoria at first, then hope, then confusion and uncertainty, and finally—too often—disillusion and dismay. Which in many cases leads to more chaos. Because people released from their shackles often don't know what to do. They don't know whom to trust. So there has to be a carefully calibrated transition stage. During which there'll still be eruptions of anarchy—*many* eruptions. And that's why I'm going to need a very dedicated and loyal police force. To hunt down the assassins employed by my father, for a start."

"From what I understand, there are plenty in the PPD who've been secretly loyal to you all along. What about Dash Chin—is he one of yours? Or Prince Oda Universe? Why not appoint him Chief?"

"Don't be ridiculous. There's no one better for the job than you."

"But I just failed to uphold the law—you said so yourself."

"And I expect you to do so again, until we get things straightened out."

"That would make me no different from Chief Buchanan."

"No, you'd be completely different. Because you'd be working for me."

"And King Leo."

"No, *for me*."

Justus thinks about it for all of two seconds. "Forget it," he says. "I can't stay here. Not now."

"Why not? You believe in Redemption, don't you?"

"In redemption, yes, but—" But he stops, realizing she's tricked him. "I'm sorry, but you're gonna have to do it without me. I'm sure you'll manage."

"And I'm sure you'll have second thoughts. This is where you were meant to be, and you know it. You were *made* for the Dark Side. *God* has summoned you."

"*God*, now?"

She tries to sound self-effacing. "Well, I sometimes let Him think He's in charge too."

Justus shakes his head, definitively this time, and continues toward the stairs. Halfway down he sees Leonardo Grey coming up, butler-like, with a freshly laundered black suit.

"The royal robes," Justus says.

"I beg your pardon, sir?"

"Never mind. Perhaps he'll make you a prince, for your part in the coup."

"I beg your pardon, sir?"

"Nothing," Justus says.

At ground level there's a good deal of alarm: The palace staff are not sure if the Sinners are going to break through the barriers and storm the Kasr. Perhaps, Justus thinks, there's wisdom in QT's decision to make her presence felt so soon.

The guards tell him he should wait until the coast is clear, but he insists on leaving immediately. So he's led through the gardens to the restraining wall, which is almost buckling under the pressure, and with a blast from the water cannon he's allowed past the security doors.

At first the crowd seem intent on pouncing on him, but as soon as they realize who it is they start cheering.

"JUSTICE! JUSTICE! JUSTICE!"

A few of them beg him for news from inside the Kasr. He tries to answer—"You just wait and see"—but he's unable to make himself heard over the general clamor. So he begins to forge his way through the mass of bodies. He sees freshly painted signs saying DEATH TO BRASS and BUTCHER BRASS. He sees Sinners spattered with blood and waving body parts in PPD uniforms—possibly bits of Chief Buchanan and the cops of his own investigative team. He sees a discarded front page of the morning's *Tablet*—CHAOS IN SIN.

But he can't make any progress, as much as he tries, and is about to give up when a sudden hush descends over the crowd. He sees them looking up at the Kasr. And he turns.

There on the imperial balcony, Leonardo Black has appeared—black-suited but still with dyed hair. He's grinning emphatically. He seems, as much as any android can, to be *triumphant*. He surveys the multitudes silently for a few seconds, as though savoring the glory, and suddenly he raises his right hand. He's holding something up, like a lantern.

It's the severed head of Fletcher Brass.

The crowd doesn't know what to make of it. They want to cheer but can't be sure what's going on. They can't quite work out who the droid is, and from a distance can't be sure whom the head belongs to. So the murmurs of confusion swell and fade. Until they stop entirely—and give way to gasps.

Justus, who's taken advantage of the confusion to gain some more ground, looks back again. And now he sees that QT Brass herself has appeared on the balcony. She stands there for a moment, taking it all in, and then moves to King Leo's left side, takes hold of his free hand, and raises it victoriously. And smiles—*beams*—like a first lady at a victory celebration.

And again the crowd doesn't seem to know what to make of

it. They're dealing with two stunning deceptions at once: that QT Brass is not dead, and that a palace coup has been staged without their knowledge. Justus actually wonders if she's gotten ahead of herself, and if the mob might respond with fury. But then, seeing her there on the Patriarch's balcony, seeing her so proud and exultant, the Sinners, swept up in it, suddenly *believe*. They break out in spontaneous cheers. They scream with approval. And slowly they start to chant:

"Q-T! Q-T! Q-T! Q-T! Q-T!"

The chant follows Justus through the near-deserted streets of Sin—where there are only a few locals and some puzzled tourists—and into the vehicle bay—where he's lucky to find someone to operate the airlock—and is still ringing in his ears when he heads into the endless lunar night, on his way to the outer rim of Purgatory and beyond.

But he's not sure exactly what he's doing. He has an idea he might get a job at Peary Base, but that's probably not much better than a paycheck in Purgatory. And it's not as if he'll be any closer to his daughter, or that it'll make life any safer for her. Considering what he knows, it might even make her life more dangerous. So where is he going? All he knows is that he has to express his disgust by turning his back on all the foulness, the deceit, the mendacity, the cynicism, the ruthlessness, and the self-righteousness of Sin. And the death—the *murder*—in which he himself became embroiled.

He thought he was above all that, and he was wrong.

But at the same time, he's acutely aware that he's just a hair's breadth away from changing his mind. Because he doesn't like quitting on anything. And, for all its horror, he has to admit that Purgatory offered him a rare sense of purpose—a chance to continue the good fight, the ongoing war against corruption, that he was forced to leave unfinished on Earth. The place might be a sewer, but that only means there's so much more pleasure in cleaning it up—Nat U. Reilly was right after all.

He's halfway to the outer rim, thinking these thoughts, when suddenly the headlights of a pressurized vehicle appear on the road ahead. Swinging around a curve at an illegal speed—it must be doing at least eighty kilometers per hour—it looks for a moment to be heading straight for him. Justus has to wrench his own car to the left, into the lunar dust, just to avoid a collision. And when the car flashes past—without slowing, without even acknowledging his presence—he sees in the backwash of his brake lights that it's a security vehicle, probably driven by customs officials eager to be part of the game-changing events in Sin.

Justus, with his wheels half buried in regolith, spends a few moments welling up with rage. He could have been injured or even killed. But there's more to it than that. There's the insurmountable policeman's instinct to enforce the law. To catch the lawbreaker, no matter who it is, before someone innocent is hurt. What if they drive like that through the streets of Sin? What if they hit a pedestrian? And Justus suddenly realizes that this is the very moment he's been hoping for. This is the thing that happened *not without a cause.*

So he swings the wheel, churning up moondust, and gets back on the road. He chases after the utility vehicle with blue lights flashing.

Dark Side/Farside, Purgatory/Sanctuary, Sin/Redemption, Brass/Black, QT/Cutie, Justus/Justice.

God—or someone—had summoned him, all right.

ACKNOWLEDGMENTS

The writing of this book would not have been possible without the Springer Praxis series of books on the Moon, particularly *The Moon: Resources, Future Development and Settlement* (various authors); *Lunar Outpost: The Challenges of Establishing a Human Settlement on the Moon* by Erik Seedhouse; *Turning Dust to Gold: Building a Future on the Moon and Mars* by Haym Benaroya; *The Far Side of the Moon: A Photographic Guide* by Charles Byrne; *Exploring the Moon: The Apollo Expeditions* by David M. Harland; and *Lunar and Planetary Rovers: The Wheels of Apollo and the Quest for Mars* by Anthony Young (see http://www.springer.com/series/4097). I also consulted *The Lunar Base Handbook* by Peter Eckart; *Return to the Moon: Exploration, Enterprise, and Energy in the Human Settlement of Space* by Harrison Schmitt; *Welcome to Moonbase* by Ben Bova; *Lunar Bases and Space Activities of the 21st Century*, edited by W. W. Mendell; *Moonrush: Improving Life on Earth with the Moon's Resources* by Dennis Wingo; *The Once and Future Moon* by Paul D. Spudis; *The Moon: A Biography* by David Whitehouse; *The Exploration of the Moon* by Arthur C. Clarke; *A Man on the Moon: The Voyages of the Apollo Astronauts* by Andrew Chaikin; *The High Frontier: Human Colonies in Space* by Gerard K. O'Neill; *Space Enterprise: Living and Working Offworld in the 21st Century* by Phillip Harris; *From Antarctica to Outer Space:*

Life in Isolation and Confinement (various authors); *The Development of Outer Space: Sovereignty and Property Rights in International Space Law* by Thomas Gangale; *Expedition Mars* by Martin J. L. Turner; *The Case for Mars: The Plan to Settle the Red Planet and Why We Must* by Robert Zubrin; *The Hazards of Space Travel: A Tourist's Guide* by Neil Comins; *Rare Earth: Why Complex Life Is Uncommon in the Universe* by Peter D. Ward and Donald Brownlee; *SETI 2020: A Roadmap for the Search for Extraterrestrial Intelligence* (various authors); *Beyond Contact: A Guide to SETI and Communicating with Alien Civilizations* by Brian S. McConnell; *Beyond Human: Living with Robots and Cyborgs* by Gregory Benford and Elisabeth Malartre; *Future Imperfect: Technology and Freedom in an Uncertain World* by David D. Friedman; *2025: Scenarios of US and Global Society Reshaped by Science and Technology* (various authors); *The Edge of Medicine: The Technology That Will Change Our Lives* by William Hanson; *21st-Century Miracle Medicine: RoboSurgery, Wonder Cures, and the Quest for Immortality* by Alexandra Wyke; *Merchants of Immortality: Chasing the Dream of Human Life Extension* by Stephen S. Hall; and *Body Bazaar: The Market for Human Tissue in the Biotechnology Age* by Lori Andrews and Dorothy Nelkin.

Any errors or exaggerations are almost certainly mine.

Thanks also to Ariel Moy; Peter Roberts; Stephen Clarke; Thomas Colchie; David Scherwood; Brit Hvide, Sarah Knight, Amar Deol, Jonathan Evans, and Molly Lindley at Simon & Schuster; Michelle Kroes at CAA; and my agent, David Forrer, at InkWell.